CHAIN OF
WITNESSES

CHAIN OF WITNESSES:

The Cases of Miss Phipps

PHYLLIS BENTLEY

Edited by Marvin Lachman

Crippen & Landru Publishers
Norfolk, Virginia
2015

Crippen & Landru Publishers
P.O. Box 9315
Norfolk, VA 23505
USA

e-mail: crippenlandru@earthlink.net
web: www.crippenlandru.com

CONTENTS

INTRODUCTION

Phyllis Bentley was already established as one of England's leading regional novelists when relatively late in her career she became, at the urging of Frederic Dannay (as "Ellery Queen," the editor of *Ellery Queen's Mystery Magazine*), a writer of mystery short stories. She proved equally successful, gaining popularity with mystery fans in America and Japan, as well as in her native country. Two of her stories were selected for annual anthologies of the year's best crime fiction.

Bentley was born in Halifax in the West Riding district of Yorkshire on November 19, 1894. She went to high school in Halifax and then attended Cheltenham Ladies College and the University of London, receiving a B.A. from the latter in 1914. Few English women received college degrees at the time (Dorothy L. Sayers in 1915 was another exception), and Bentley was the first in her own circle of family and friends to do so. After unhappy experiences teaching school in London and Halifax, she worked as a clerk for the Ministry of Defense during World War I. In the World War II she was a volunteer ambulance driver in London during the "Blitz."

Bentley had long wanted to be a fiction writer, and she borrowed money from her brother to have a short story collection, *The World's Bane and Other Stories*, published in 1918. Her first novel, the partially-autobiographical *Environment*, followed in 1922. It was not until 1932 and *Inheritance*, generally considered her masterpiece, that she was established as a novelist.

Inheritance was the first book in a trilogy about the owners and workers in Yorkshire textile mills between 1812 and 1931. It was followed by *The Rise of Henry Morcar* (1946) and *A Man of His Time* (1966). In 1967 Britain's Granada Television began a ten-part serial based on the trilogy, with John Thaw, later to play Inspector Morse, in a leading role. A fourth novel about the same families, *Ring in the New*, was published in 1969.

1

Bentley was prolific, writing twenty novels, as well as enough short stories for seven collections. Yorkshire was the scene of her non-criminous fiction, except for *Freedom, Farewell,* her 1936 novel about Julius Caesar. She also wrote non-fiction, beginning with the humorous *Pedagomania; or, the Gentle Art of Teaching* (1918). In 1941 she published *The English Regional Novel,* a critical survey that especially appeals to me since I wrote *The American Regional Mystery* (2000). Her best known work of non-fiction was a biography *The Brontës* (1947), the first of six books she wrote or edited about the famous Yorkshire sisters. Bentley's own autobiography, *"O Dreams, O Destinations",* was published in 1962. She became Doctor Bentley when she was awarded a D.Litt, by the University of Leeds in 1949, and she was made a Member of the Order of the British Empire (O.B.E.) in 1970.

In its December 1952 issue, *Ellery Queen's Mystery Magazine* reprinted "Author in Search of a Character," a Bentley story that had first been published as "The Missing Character" in *Woman's Home Companion* for July 1937. It is the first story about her series detective, Miss Marian Phipps. In his lengthy introduction, Dannay says that Bentley is "considered by many British critics to be the 'greatest regional novelist of her day.' " Using the beginning of what would become a long-lasting correspondence with her, Dannay quoted Bentley on what she called her two overwhelming interests in life: "humanity and the enrichment of human life by culture" and that "the little unit of earth I call my native country shall be thus enriched."

As he did with other writers whose work he liked, Dannay encouraged Bentley to submit more stories to EQMM. Dannay was pleasantly surprised to find how little persuasion she needed. First, he published "The Way Round," a non-series story that captures the isolation of Yorkshire's Pennine slopes, in EQMM's August 1953 issue. Bentley then submitted "Chain of Witnesses," another Phipps story, and it won a Third Prize in the magazine's then-annual contest for 1954. She also informed Dannay that there were already five additional stories about Miss Phipps that had never been published in America; they were eventually published in EQMM.

Marian Phipps started as an armchair detective in "Author in Search of a Character." On the train to Edinburgh she meets Detective-Sergeant Tarrant of the "Southshire" Police. She is sitting opposite him, and their papers become mixed when the train speeds around a curve. She is suffering writer's block on the novel on which she is working, while he is reviewing his notes on a murder case he can't solve. Thinking like the novelist she is, she solves the case for Tarrant, pointing out that he has concentrated too much on physical clues, ignoring the "human element . . . characterization." At the same time, she resolves her own problems on the novel.

From her armchair at home, Miss Phipps solves other cases for Tarrant, who calls on her when he is baffled. By the second case on which they cooperate, he has been promoted to Detective-Inspector, largely due to the help she provided on the first case. A bond of affection grows with him and Tarrant's future wife, Mary, who first appears in "The Crooked Figures." Mary comes to call Miss Phipps "Aunt Marian." The Tarrants appear (or are mentioned) in 18 of the 24 stories Bentley wrote about Miss Phipps. In an anomaly reminiscent of Doyle's Doctor Watson, who was called both "John" and "James," Bentley seemed to have trouble keeping track of Tarrant's first name. It starts out as "John," becomes "Bob" in "A Telegram for Miss Phipps," returns to "John," but changes to Bill in "Miss Phipps and the Nest of Illusion," before reverting to "John."

Beginning with "Chain of Witnesses," Marian Phipps becomes anything but sedentary. In that story she is visiting her niece Ruth in a suburb of "Laire" in the equally fictional county of "Northshire." She proves that one single change of plan, caused by the inability of Ruth's hired help to come the night before, led to the murder of the local railroad stationmaster. As Phipps says, "In this complex modern world of ours . . . the lives of all of us are very subtly and intricately interwoven. Our every action, however simple, has far reaching consequence in the cosmic pattern." This is an idea that obviously appealed to Bentley because she also used it in her mainstream novel *Crescendo* (1958).

As the series progresses, it becomes increasingly clear that Bentley based the character of Marian Phipps on herself. Phipps is described as having "bushy white hair," a description that corresponds to a photograph of Phyllis Bentley. Neither married. In several stories Phipps solves cases while lecturing. Bentley went on five lecture tours to the United States in the 1930s and often gave talks in the United Kingdom. Bentley described the America she visited in the non-fiction book *Here Is America* (1941). Later, she wrote the story "Miss Phipps Discovers America."

Marian Phipps is an author from her earliest appearance, but what is not clear at first is the type of fiction she writes. As the series progresses, we learn that she is a detective novelist. Bentley, herself, only wrote one crime novel, *The House of Moreys*, a 1953 Gothic suspense story that was very successful, selling about a quarter of a million copies. Much of the fiction she wrote during her last two decades consisted of mystery short stories. In her next-to-last story, "Miss Phipps and the Siamese Cat" in 1973, Marian Phipps has just finished her latest book, one written for children. In the 1960s, Bentley wrote juvenile mysteries and received a Mystery Writers of America Edgar nomination in that category for *Forgery!* (1968; published in England that year as *Gold Pieces*.)

Phyllis Bentley died on June 27, 1977. In an essay in *Twentieth Century Crime and Mystery Writers* (1980), Nancy Ellen Talburt said of her work, "Stylistically, the stories are economically told and share a quiet humor and misleading simplicity of statement with the works of Christie . . . Bentley's contribution is small but not slight, her work informed and consistent with the classic traditions of the mystery."

Writing of her in a 1998 volume of *Dictionary of Literary Biography*, Hilda Hollis said, "The main importance of Bentley's work lies in her modernizing of the regional novel by focusing on the psychological motivations of her protagonists. Further, her feminist ideology is evident in her commitment to woman's rights in the labor force and her critique of patriarchal privilege in the home." To that assessment may be added recognition of the entertainment she provided with some of the best detective stories published in the second half of the 20th century, many of which you can read in this book.

MARVIN LACHMAN

AUTHOR IN SEARCH
OF A CHARACTER

I t was half-past two on a warm afternoon in autumn; the passengers in the northbound Pullman had lunched, wisely perhaps but certainly well, and were all ungracefully asleep in their corners, their open mouths and crimson faces cocked roofward at odd angles, like a bed of red dahlias turning to the sun. All, that is, except two persons who faced each other across a table at the far end of the coach. They were awake and indeed their eyes were particularly wide open, for each was staring glassily at a point just above the other's head. The table between them was strewn with writing materials, which, however, neither seemed inclined to use. That they were engaged in some mental travail seemed probable; with each mile the train rushed northward the woman's bushy white hair seemed to grow wilder, the young man's agreeable, plain face more haggard, the eyes of both more distraught.

Miss Marian Phipps, the novelist, was busy with a problem of characterization which had held up her work for the past three weeks. It concerned the heroine of her new novel, who was just about to emerge from her brain onto the written page. The girl had stuck on the threshold so long because Miss Phipps was utterly unable to decide her appearance. It was necessary for the plot that the hero should feel for her, at first sight, a love equally tenacious, respectful, and adoring; now Miss Phipps could not decide what kind of girl, if any, nowadays could command from a contemporary such a passion. She would probably be dark, Miss Phipps had decided; but was she richly rosy, full of life, with flashing eyes, or pale, mysterious, slender? As fast as Miss Phipps pronounced for one type, she revoked the decision in favor of another.

On this, the twenty-second day of the struggle, she had as a last hope booked a seat in the Edinburgh express. She did not in the least wish to go to Edinburgh, but found long train journeys stimulating to the creative faculties. But already a considerable number of miles had gone by, and she was no nearer her solution; she felt hot, tired, cross, and in urgent need of an excuse for ceasing work.

The train took a sudden curve without slowing; Miss Phipps and the large young man found their feet and their papers mixed in consequence. With mutual loathing in their hearts they murmured apologies and disentangled their property. For the first time Miss Phipps observed the young man's notebook; always avid for human detail, she tried to read it upside down. "S-u-l-l-e-n," she spelled; "aged thirty-five, sullen and vehement." At once her large mouth widened to a smile; her eyes beamed behind her old-fashioned pince-nez.

"You are a novelist too?" she exclaimed joyfully.

The young man gave her an unresponsive glare. He did not want to talk to Miss Phipps. He did not admire Miss Phipps. As an object of vision he found her definitely unpleasing. The round pink face, the untidy white hair, the too glowing smile, the bright blue jumper, the lopsided pince-nez moored by a chain to a kind of bollard on her substantial bosom — these clashed with his notions of female beauty; that she was a "lady novelist" as well was just, he thought, what might have been expected. "Only needs a Peke to be complete," he decided disgustedly.

"You are a novelist too?" repeated Miss Phipps, beaming.

"Certainly not," snapped the large young man.

"I beg your pardon," said Miss Phipps in an icy tone. "From a phrase in your notebook, which I confess I took a childish pleasure in deciphering from this angle, I surmised I might be addressing a fellow-craftsman."

The young man was rather startled. "More in the old girl than meets the eye," he thought. Coloring, he stammered apologies. "I was thinking of something else," he explained. "I'm a good deal worried just now by a serious problem."

Miss Phipps forgave him. "It's no crime not to be a novelist," she said. "Rather the reverse, perhaps, nowadays. And whoever we are, we all have our problems."

There was a hint of question in her last sentence and the young man was caught by it. "I'm a detective," he blurted. "Detective-Sergeant Tarrant, of the Southshire police headquarters."

"Really!" cried Miss Phipps, impressed. "A detective! On a murder case, perhaps? Do tell me all about it. My name is Marian Phipps."

The young man gave a heavy sigh. "I'm afraid I haven't read any of your novels," he said gloomily.

Miss Phipps had a stock rejoinder for this remark; she always replied: "No? You prefer the lighter fiction?" and found it not ineffective. But this time, hot on a murder trail, she would forego her mild revenge. With one plump little hand she waved her novels out of court. "Do tell me about your problem," she urged. "It will clear your thoughts to put them into words. Besides, I might be able to help. Psychology, you know. Characterization. Do tell me. I'm not a very discreet person, I'm afraid; but I don't live anywhere near Southshire."

Detective-Sergeant Tarrant rumpled his hair and sighed again, but more hopefully.

"Will you promise not to write up the story if I tell you?" he inquired.

Miss Phipps considered. "I will promise," she said, "that I will not use the story for five years, and that when I do, it will be unrecognizable."

Tarrant laughed. "Now that's the sort of promise you can believe," he said heartily. "Well, I'll tell you. I'd be glad enough of any help; I don't mind admitting I'm stuck with it myself."

He sat up, flicked the pages of his notebook, and began in a brisk official tone:

"On Wednesday last, September 13, I was summoned at 1:30 A.M. by the local police to a house on the front in the seaside resort of Brittle-sea; house called Lorel Manor, property of a financier named Ambrose Stacey. Large new house, standing in large grounds; newest architecture, modern luxury furnishings; marble swimming pool in rose garden. The call was received at the station at 1:20 A.M. from the butler, who stated that he had been awake in bed, reading, when he heard loud screams from Mrs. Stacey at approximately 1:15 A.M. He went down to investigate, found her in hysterics on the landing, and called the police."

"But who was dead?" demanded Miss Phipps impatiently.

"I went to Lorel Manor and found the whole household assembled on the upper landing," continued the detective with a repressive glance. "In their midst was lying Mr. Ambrose Stacey, dead. His neck was broken. It was plain that he had fallen down the short flight of stairs leading from his bedroom, a large octagonal apartment almost entirely surrounded by windows, to the main landing below."

"An accident!" exclaimed Miss Phipps, disappointed.

"On the contrary," said Tarrant grimly. "A piece of strong string was found dangling from the rail of the chromium balustrade at the very top of the stairs. The end was broken; a similar piece of string with a broken end was found attached to the opposite balustrade; on measuring and comparing —"

"You needn't labor the point," said Miss Phipps. "The string was put there to be fallen over and he fell over it. Go on."

"Mr. and Mrs. Stacey had entered the house by means of Mr. Stacey's latchkey," continued the detective, consulting his notebook, "shortly after one o'clock. They had been dining with a business friend of Mr. Stacey's. The butler heard them come in and go straight upstairs to their room. About 1:10 Mr. Stacey, desiring a whiskey and soda, found that the siphon was not in its usual place on the tray in his room; he went downstairs to find it, with fatal results."

"Ah," said Miss Phipps, "the siphon was not in its usual place."

"The problem is," said the detective: "who tied that string?"

"Who was in the house at the time?" demanded the novelist.

"Mrs. Eleanor Stacey, the second wife of the deceased; Rachel, his daughter by his first wife; Rachel's nursery governess, the butler, the cook, the housemaid, the parlormaid. Not, however, Mr. Stacey's secretary, Jack Thornhill."

"From your tone, Mr. Thornhill's absence seems to have a special significance?" queried Miss Phipps.

"His absence was perhaps rather fortunate for Mr. Thornhill," said the detective. "He has an alibi for the whole night, in Leeds; I'm

going now to investigate it. It's only fair to say, however, that it has
been investigated three times already. He was speaking at a birthday
dinner in Leeds at half-past nine; I don't see what you can do against
that. It's more than two hundred miles from Leeds to Brittlesea."

"Mr. Thornhill is young and handsome, I take it?" said Miss
Phipps, her voice warm with interest.

The detective nodded. "If you like that varnished type," he said.

"And Mrs. Stacey is also young and handsome?"

The detective nodded again emphatically.

"And Ambrose Stacey was neither young nor handsome?"

"He was fifty-nine," replied Tarrant consideringly, "but really
I'm not so sure about the handsome. A very big powerful fellow,
with penetrating blue eyes and thick graying hair which stands
up from his head, if you know what I mean."

"*En brosse*," suggested Miss Phipps.

"Very likely," said the detective. "Mrs. Stacey is prostrate
with grief; you'd certainly think she was devoted to him. She is
really very beautiful, you know; young and fair and gentle. Early
twenties."

"Poor before she married?" inquired Miss Phipps.

"Yes. Poor and county. Expensive tastes, I daresay. And she gets
a pretty fair amount of cash by the will," said Tarrant. "*And* young
Thornhill dotes on her. From appearances you'd judge she loved
her husband. But plainly she's the first to be suspected." He sighed.

Miss Phipps gave him a shrewd look. "Was the deceased financier what for the sake of brevity we call a gentleman?" she asked.

"Lord, no!" replied the detective more cheerfully. "No more a
gentleman than I am."

Miss Phipps surveyed him with approval. "Tell me more," she
said.

"Stacey was a thorough rascal, but a dashed interesting chap,"
went on Tarrant. "Ambrose Stacey wasn't his real name."

"I thought it sounded a little pseudo," said the novelist.

"Oh, you did?" said the detective, glancing at her respectfully.
"Well, he had one of those obscure middle-European names, you
know, which may mean anything. He'd been everywhere and

done everything, and collected a lot of cash in rather odd ways, and I expect also made a lot of enemies. It may be one of them who's bumped him off; that's the trouble, from my point of view. He married his first wife when he was poor, in the middle-European days, and she never quite fitted into his new setting. He was apt to find consolation elsewhere for that, if you understand me; but at any rate he must have been a decent father, for his daughter Rachel simply adores him. The first Mrs. Stacey died seven years ago, and he remained faithful to her memory, outwardly at least, till he married Eleanor. That was just the early spring of this year."

"And Rachel?" said Miss Phipps thoughtfully. "The daughter?"

"Well, of course I thought of her at once," said the detective. "She's twelve years old and the door of her room is just at the foot of the fatal stairs; and string tied to bannisters — it sounds like a child's practical joke."

"A curious set of circumstances, if so," commented Miss Phipps. "A child chances to seize the only possible five minutes when the joke could bring disaster. For in the morning Mr. and Mrs. Stacey would presumably be called by a maid with tea, going *up* the stairs."

"Don't let that worry you," said the detective grimly, "for it wasn't a practical joke. The small landing outside the Staceys' room is lighted by a wall lamp which turns on by a switch at the bedroom door. The bulb had been removed from it."

"Tchk!" exclaimed Miss Phipps. "How shocking!"

"The bulb was lying at the foot of the lamp, intact; therefore it had not fallen but been placed there. Nobody admits removing it," concluded the detective.

"Worse and worse," said Miss Phipps distressfully. "And the child? Rachel?"

"She's a pretty little thing, but delicate; thin and pale and as nervy as you make 'em," replied Tarrant. "Of course, I've only seen her in trouble, you may say; she was in despair about her father. But everyone tells me what a nervy delicate child she is; why, Mrs. Stacey had moved her to her present bedroom from a more distant one, so as to be able to hear her if she woke and cried in the night. At twelve years old, you know. Yes, poor kid; she's clever but nervy."

"Oh, dear!" sighed Miss Phipps, twitching her bushy eyebrows mournfully. "I'm very unhappy about this case, very."

"Why?" said the detective.

"Aren't you?" demanded Miss Phipps, looking at him shrewdly.

"Yes. But I don't see how she could have done it," said Tarrant. "Five past one, light there, no string; ten past one, string there, no light. How could she suddenly leave the bedroom and begin to fidget on her hands and knees just outside the door? What could she say if her husband looked out to see what she was doing? Why didn't she remove the string and replace the light before screaming to the butler?"

"Oh," said Miss Phipps, "you're thinking of Mrs. Stacey."

"Of course. Aren't you?"

"Never mind. Go on," said Miss Phipps firmly. "What steps did you take to solve the mystery?"

"I looked," said Tarrant, "first for the bulb and then for the siphon."

"Very proper," said Miss Phipps nodding. "A good point. You looked for the siphon. And where did you find it?"

"In young Thornhill's room," said Tarrant. "That's why I'm investigating his alibi for the third time. He says, however, that Stacey came into his room that morning as he was packing his case for his journey to Leeds, to have a last word with him; Stacey wanted a drink, pulled out his flask, and sent Thornhill for the nearest siphon, which of course was the one in his bedroom. A silly story, but in view of Stacey's habits it may be true. Thornhill says that as he returned, siphon in hand, he met Rachel going to her bedroom, and Rachel corroborates this, time and place."

"Oh, I'm delighted to hear it!" cried Miss Phipps with joy. "It's a very great relief to me indeed; I'm simply delighted to hear it."

"But why?" demanded Tarrant in some exasperation. "That doesn't clear young Thornhill of removing the siphon on his own, for a murderous motive."

"I never thought it did," said Miss Phipps. "But he has an alibi. Oh, I am so delighted to hear it, so delighted!"

"What do you see in this case that I don't, I wonder?" said the detective thoughtfully.

"My dear boy," said Miss Phipps firmly, "you said yourself that the method sounded childish. Rachel had the best opportunity of placing the string — better than anyone else in the house; her door is just at the foot of the stairs; you said so."

"But it wasn't a practical joke, because of the light," objected Tarrant.

"Exactly. The fall was quite premeditated," said Miss Phipps, "quite intended. But might it not," said Miss Phipps sadly, "might it not have been premeditated by Rachel?"

"You mean she meant to murder her father?" cried Tarrant. He paused to consider. "Good God!" He struck the table with his hand. "She knew about the siphon!"

"To my mind," observed Miss Phipps calmly, "that's just what clears her of the suspicion of murder and that's why I was so delighted to hear of it."

"Miss Marian Phipps," said the detective, "you're a very exasperating woman.

"My dear boy," observed Miss Phipps very earnestly, "I beg you not to take my criticism unkindly. But, if you will allow me to say so, you're making a great mistake. You're paying too much attention to the mechanics of your plot — bulbs and strings and siphons — and neglecting your human element, your characterization. Why should Rachel murder her father?"

"She had no reason on earth," said the detective. "She adored him."

"Exactly," said Miss Phipps. "Then dismiss that idea altogether from your mind and consider the facts you have laid before me. Don't you see what they all point to? The origin of the tragedy remains as yet obscure to me, because your sketch of the characters is so lamentably imperfect. But one fact emerges clearly. Don't you see that *the wrong person tripped over that string?*"

"What?" shouted Tarrant; his voice was so loud that several of the dahlias stirred and nodded. "How do you reach such a preposterous conclusion?"

"But you told me yourself," objected Miss Phipps mildly, "Mrs. Stacey moved Rachel's bedroom so that she could hear the child if she cried in the night. What do you do when you hear a child cry in the night? You hurry to soothe her. Who, then, often ran down those stairs in the night? Eleanor Stacey. Who knew that fact? Everyone in the household, including Rachel. So much is established fact. I then went one step further and said: What do highly-strung children often feel toward their stepmothers?"

"You mean Rachel meant to murder Mrs. Stacey out of jealousy? Good God! And she's such a nice little kid; I was so sorry for her. How horrible!"

"That's what I thought," said Miss Phipps sweetly. "But don't you see, the siphon clears her. She adored her father. She knew that he might come down to fetch the missing siphon. Would she, then, place the string there just that night? No; for to do so was to risk her father's life, and there were many other nights. Therefore Rachel did not place the string that night. But the string was placed that night. Therefore we must look elsewhere for the murderer — and how gladly," said Miss Phipps, beaming, "we do so."

"Rachel's only a child; she mightn't have worked all that out about the siphon; she might have forgotten all about the siphon," said Tarrant in a tone of gloom.

"In that case the siphon has no significance at all," snapped Miss Phipps. "For I refuse to believe that either young Thornhill or Eleanor would risk a method of killing Ambrose so dangerous to Eleanor; while if Eleanor was to be killed, the siphon had no part to play. We are just where we were before."

At this moment the train burst through a series of bridges with a lamentable clatter; the passengers, startled awake, tossed up and down as they took down hats and picked up handbags; evidently the train was approaching some station.

"We're much worse than we were before," shouted Tarrant above the din. "I had one clue, and at least the identity of the victim was clear, but now you've thrown away the siphon and confused even the object of the crime. If Eleanor Stacey was the intended victim, an entirely fresh set of motives must be found. I wish —"

"You wish I'd never spoken to you," said Miss Phipps regretfully. "That I can well understand. I really don't know," she added with a sigh, "how I came to commit such an impropriety —"

The detective colored and protested.

"— as to interrupt someone else's cerebration," concluded Miss Phipps firmly. "It was unpardonable and I offer you my sincerest apologies. How did I come to do such a thing? Good gracious!" she exclaimed. "I remember now! Mr. Tarrant! You've been deceiving me! You have omitted from your account of this tragedy one of the characters."

"I don't think so," said the detective, hesitating. "The servants had only been there since the marriage this spring. I don't think so."

"But I'm sure," insisted Miss Phipps. "Positive! Listen. Ambrose Stacey, aged fifty-nine. Eleanor his wife, fair and gentle, in her twenties. Rachel, child, aged twelve. Jack Thornhill, in his twenties. Then who was sullen and vehement and in the thirties?"

The detective stared.

"I read it in your notebook," cried Miss Phipps, pointing impatiently. "Who was aged thirty-five, sullen and vehement?"

Tarrant, startled, flipped the pages. "That was Rosa Dorlan, Rachel's nursery governess," he discovered.

"How long had she been with the Staceys?" cried Miss Phipps eagerly.

"Seven years," said Tarrant.

The station, an animated scene with porters, passengers, newsboys, and buffet attendants darting hither and thither like gnats above a flower bed, burst upon them.

"Then there you are!" cried Miss Phipps hastily in triumph. "Don't you see? Don't you see her? Rosa. Handsome. Dark. Ripe. Flushed cheeks. Vehement. Sullen. Involved with Stacey. Hopes to be his wife. The new wife comes. Finds child neurotic and unhappy. Dissatisfied with Rosa. Keeps child near her night and day. Often comes down in night to see her. Nurse knows this. String. Wife trips. End of wife. Nurse not lose job. Indispensable again to Stacey. Perhaps his wife. Siphon a chance, an accident. Wrong person killed. Great distress of Rosa. So great, she forgot to replace bulb and remove string. How's that?"

"So good," said Detective-Sergeant Tarrant, standing up and reaching for his hat, "that I shall get out at this station and go straight back to Brittlesea. It will make so much difference to — er, to all concerned, to have their innocence clearly established." He pulled out an official card and offered it to her respectfully. "If you have any ideas on any future murder problems, Miss Phipps," he said, "I wish you would drop me a line about them. Meanwhile, if there is anything I can do —"

"You've done it," sighed Miss Phipps happily, snatching her pencil and writing: "Fair, young, gentle."

THE CROOKED FIGURES

"It's a very serious responsibility to be a Detective-Inspector," said Tarrant gloomily.

"Who is the blonde this time?" inquired Miss Phipps flippantly.

"She's a brunette, and I'm going to marry her," Tarrant blurted out.

Astonishment so distorted the little novelist's features that her old-fashioned pince-nez slipped off her nose; they flew through the air on the end of their chain and came to rest with a click against the large black button on her bosom. Without her glasses Miss Phipps looked pinker, wilder, and more helpless than before; even her mop of white hair appeared to have become more disheveled.

Tarrant sighed as he looked at her; it seemed impossible that such a rabbit as Miss Marian Phipps appeared could be any help to him. That she had solved two of his most puzzling cases for him a few years before was surely a matter of chance, a pair of accidents; such an exterior as hers could not possibly hide a brain. Her eyes, however, now that he could see them without their enlarging lenses, were bright and kindly, and certainly he had found the solution of those earlier affairs in mere conversation with Miss Phipps. He had come to try it again and he *would* try it again; he cared so much about this particular affair that anything was worth trying.

"It's not a police case," he managed, holding his head down. "It's a matter of conscience."

Miss Phipps looked grave.

"Tell me all about it, my dear boy," she said. She drew the pince-nez firmly out to the end of their tether, and with an imperious gesture replaced them on her nose. "Who is the young lady? Have you known her long? Why is it suddenly so serious to be a Detective-Inspector?"

"Because she expects me to be able to solve this puzzle," Tarrant muttered, his head still down. "At least, she doesn't exactly expect it, but she hopes. And I hate to see her so troubled. She wants to know whether she ought to accept a legacy or not."

"A legacy!" said Miss Phipps, perplexed. "But what possible objection can there be to accepting a legacy?"

"It's twenty thousand pounds," said Tarrant.

"Oh!" said Miss Phipps.

"From a man she only saw for five minutes in the Strand," said Tarrant.

"Ah!" said Miss Phipps.

In spite of her efforts to conceal it, her discomfort was apparent in her voice. Tarrant looked up inquiringly.

"It isn't at all what you think," he said. "Mary isn't like that at all. She's incapable of telling a lie."

"Tell me about her," urged Miss Phipps kindly.

"I'll tell you about her meeting with the man first, if you don't mind," said Tarrant. "Mary is a nurse; she was trained in New York, but has come over here for a few years' English experience. She was in a hospital first, now she's in a nursing home."

"Is she American by birth?" inquired Miss Phipps.

"Yes. But her grandparents were north-country English before they emigrated," said Tarrant. "But I'll explain about all that later. Now, Mary was walking down the Strand in the rush hour one autumn evening — in point of fact," Tarrant broke off, coloring, "she had just seen me off to Brittlesea from Charing Cross. I'd been up to New Scotland Yard unexpectedly on business, and as I had a little time to spare before my train, I called at the nursing home. Mary hadn't much time before going on duty; I'm afraid she missed a meal to come out with me."

"How did you meet Miss — er — Mary?" asked Miss Phipps.

"Her name is Mary Fletcher Arneson," supplied Tarrant. "I met her when she was with a convalescent patient in Brittlesea. Luckily for me, a case took me to the hotel where they were staying."

"Was that patient the testator?" asked Miss Phipps hopefully.

"No, no! That patient was a young girl with a broken leg," said Tarrant impatiently. "She has nothing to do with this case at all."

"Go on," said Miss Phipps.

"Mary, as I said, was walking down the Strand in the rush hour. Just in front of her she noticed an old man with a middle-aged one.

The fiftyish one was just the ordinary stockbroking kind, but the old man was rather striking. He was tall, rather stooping, with curly gray hair sticking out beneath his hat, and a very strong, fierce old face. Like a hawk, Mary said. He was well dressed, she said, in a handsome coat of very fine cloth with an astrakhan collar. He had dark gray gloves and a new-looking dark gray felt hat, and a rather elegant silk scarf. Altogether an imposing old chap. He leaned quite heavily on his stick, an old-fashioned affair, Mary said, black with something white, carved, for a handle."

"What was the carving?" inquired Miss Phipps.

"Mary didn't see at the time," said Tarrant, "but later she found it represented a dog."

"What kind of dog?"

"An Airedale," said Tarrant with a touch of exasperation. "But really, Miss Phipps, such a detail is of no importance."

Miss Phipps snorted. "I don't agree," she said. "But how did Miss Arneson come to notice any of these details, as you call them, at all?"

"Because she was held up by the old man and his companion," explained Tarrant. "You know what the traffic is like in the Strand, both on and off the pavement. The old chap was tottering along slowly. Mary tried to pass him first on one side and then on the other, but he doddered about, and the crowd streamed by, and Mary couldn't pass without pushing him aside rather rudely."

"What is she like, your Mary?" asked Miss Phipps in a warmer tone.

"She's tall and dark and strong," said Tarrant, "but slender. Her hair has no waves in it, thank goodness; it's smooth and thick and done tight against her head, always very neat. She has dark eyes, large and bright; and thick eyebrows and thick eyelashes. She's been to Columbia University; she's very intelligent. And she's very candid, and very energetic, and always dressed just right; she always looks fresh and neat and easy on the eye, whether in uniform or in mufti," finished Tarrant hurriedly.

"She's better than you deserve, young man," said Miss Phipps with enthusiasm.

"I know that," mumbled Tarrant. "She has a warm, jolly sort of voice," he added, "and just enough American in her accent to make it — er — attractive."

"Very good," said Miss Phipps cheerfully. "All that is highly satisfactory. So she followed the old man down the Strand, and did not push him. Then what happened?"

"He stepped to the edge of the pavement," said Tarrant, "and held up his stick to wave for a taxi. The middle-aged fellow hung back, looking bored. Well, you know what taxis are, and you know what the traffic is, and you know old men; the taxis buzzed past, and the old man grew cross and waved his stick more frantically, and he took a step forward in his excitement —"

"Ah!" exclaimed Miss Phipps distressfully.

"Exactly," said Tarrant. "All in a moment a bus bore down on him, and the driver put his brakes on hard, and Mary snatched the old chap by the collar, and the next moment Mary and the old man and the middle-aged one and several other pedestrians were all lying in a heap on the pavement, with fragments of the black stick, and glass from the bus's broken lamp, flying about them."

Miss Phipps drew a deep breath. "He wasn't hurt?" she said.

"Not a mark on him anywhere," replied Tarrant cheerfully. "But of course it was a shock to him, being so old. Mary and the other man picked him up and carried him off into a chemist's shop nearby and gave him brandy and sal volatile and so on, and presently a constable came in and took their statements. But it was before that the old man looked at Mary so strangely."

"Ah!" said Miss Phipps. "He looked at her strangely, you say."

"Yes. It was like this," explained the detective. "At first he was so dazed, he seemed almost unconscious; he clung to her arm as old people do, not releasing her even when she got him seated in the chair at the chemist's. She had one arm round him supporting him; and when the brandy was brought, she offered it to him with her other hand. Well, as she brought the glass to his lips he gave a tremendous start. His whole body seemed to quiver, and he looked at her hand as if his eyes would fall out of his head. And then he moved his eyes to her cuff, and then slowly upwards till they rested on her face. It was a most extraordinary look he gave her, Mary said; she was very much struck by it, and somehow very sorry for him."

"But can't you define the look more clearly?" pressed Miss Phipps. "Was it fear, or hate, or horror, or love — or what?"

"A bit of all of them, Mary said," replied Tarrant.

"And what did he say to her?" asked Miss Phipps eagerly.

"Nothing," said Tarrant, "for the constable arrived just then. And as soon as she had given her account of the affair and explained that she thought the old man was not hurt, Mary had to hurry away. It was time for her to go on duty, and the old chap had the other man to take him home."

"Yes?" said Miss Phipps as the detective paused. "Go on."

"There isn't any more," said Tarrant confusedly. "That is the difficulty, you see."

Miss Phipps stared at him. "What do you mean?" she said.

"I mean," said Tarrant, "that the incident occurred in September. Mary heard no more of the matter — for the police did nothing, as no one was hurt and the bus driver was plainly exonerated — until October. And at the end of October, Mary received a letter from a firm of lawyers in Gray's Inn, saying that she was one of the legatees under the will of the late Sir John Kebroyd, and would she come to see them. She went, and found that Sir John Kebroyd had left her twenty thousand pounds. 'But who *is* Sir John Kebroyd?' asked Mary. Well, at that the lawyers hummed and ha'd, and said they ought to warn her that their client intended to contest the will. 'But who *is* your client?' asked Mary. 'If you would like to meet Mr. John William Kebroyd,' said the lawyers, 'we should be happy to arrange it; but we respectfully suggest that the meeting take place in the presence of your solicitor.' Well, of course Mary had no solicitor; but the way those lawyers looked down their noses at her got her back up — after all, she's an American, and American women are used to having their own way; so she consulted me, and I found her a good solicitor, and I went with her to the interview. And Mr. John William Kebroyd —"

"Was the fiftyish man who accompanied the old man in the Strand," concluded Miss Phipps.

"That's right," said Tarrant. "The old man's son."

"And on what grounds was the son about to contest the will?" inquired Miss Phipps sardonically. "He could hardly call it undue influence on Mary's part."

"No, though I daresay he'd like to," said Tarrant. "He's contesting on grounds of unsound mind. Old Sir John threw himself overboard in mid-Atlantic, from the *S.S. Atlantis*."

"Really! Poor old boy! That certainly was rather odd," said Miss Phipps distressfully. "Why did he do that, do you think?"

"I don't know, and seemingly nobody else knows either," said Tarrant. "The very day after that incident in the Strand, old Sir John Kebroyd made a new will, leaving twenty thousand pounds to Mary Fletcher Arneson. And the day after it was signed, he booked passage to New York on the *Atlantis*, and the day after that, he sailed on her. There was no reason why he should go to the States, and he didn't even tell his son he was going. There was certainly no reason for him to throw himself overboard — which, mark you, he was actually seen to do. But why did he do it? He was rich, and healthy for his age; his wife died many years ago, but he had his son John William, and some grandchildren, to care for. The son is contesting the will, as I say, on grounds of unsound mind, and Mary doesn't want to accept the legacy. But his throwing himself overboard," continued Tarrant, "doesn't really surprise me. A man who leaves half his estate to a girl he's never spoken to, and only seen for a couple of minutes, would do anything. It's true he may have thought she saved his life. And perhaps she did," commented Tarrant. "As Mary tells the story, she only helped John William to save it, but I expect she did most of it. But as Sir John threw his life away the very next week, that doesn't solve the mystery."

"Oh, come!" said Miss Phipps, smiling. "It's not really very mysterious, is it? A good deal of it is quite clear. Enough, at any rate, to show that your Mary is quite entitled to her legacy. *Half* the estate — that's so significant."

"Miss Phipps!" gasped Tarrant. "Upon my word! Really! No, it's intolerable! You say the story's clear to you? Perhaps you'll explain, then, first, how Sir John knew Mary's name and the name of her nursing home. They were both in the will, in full."

"My dear boy!" expostulated Miss Phipps. "That part is as clear as crystal. Didn't you say a policeman came and took down their statements? Mary gave her name and address to him. Americans usually (and very sensibly) give their names in full, and of course the old man heard her."

"Of course! How stupid of me," said Tarrant, blushing.

"They say," commented Miss Phipps, "that love is blind. Perhaps that explains it. But what *have* you done towards solving the mystery?"

"What would *you* have done?"

"I should have taken the first train to Yorkshire," snapped Miss Phipps.

Tarrant's mouth fell open. "Yorkshire? How did you know?" he spluttered.

"But it's so obvious," said Miss Phipps. "You said Mary's grandparents were north-country English."

"That's right. At least her grandmother was. She never knew her grandfather; he died on board ship when they emigrated," said Tarrant.

"Good heavens!" cried Miss Phipps, more impatiently than before. "You knew that, and yet you talk of a mystery!"

Tarrant gaped. "But what made you think of Yorkshire?" he said. "There are other places in northern England besides Yorkshire. Perhaps it was just a guess?"

"I never guess," replied the novelist sharply. "You told me yourself. Here is an old man with an Airedale dog carved on his stick and a very fine cloth coat and a name like Kebroyd. Airedale, my dear boy, is in Yorkshire; very fine cloth, my dear boy, is made in Yorkshire; the name Kebroyd, my dear boy —"

"But, Miss Phipps," interrupted Tarrant. "I was referring to Mary's people, who came from Yorkshire; I had no idea the Kebroyds did too. They live in London now."

.

"Listen," said Miss Phipps firmly. "The reason why Sir John Kebroyd left his money to Mary is very clear to me. Let us look, not at the problem as you presented it, but at all the data you have accumulated. Here we have a man and his wife, Mary's grandparents, leaving northern England — shall we say in the 1870s? — and emigrating to New York. Shall we say their name is Fletcher? A very Yorkshire name! You can check that with Mary, but from her own name it seems very probable."

"It's quite correct," said Tarrant, almost tonelessly.

"We don't know why the Fletchers left England," said Miss Phipps, "but presently we shall deduce something of the nature of the reason, and you shall find out the rest by routine inquiries. On the voyage Mr. Fletcher dies. His wife gives birth to a daughter, who presently marries in the States a Mr. Arneson (no doubt of Swedish descent), and has in her turn a daughter Mary. Mary grows up, becomes a nurse, visits England, and is seen by a Yorkshireman, John Kebroyd, who hears her name and at once makes her his legatee. John Kebroyd then promptly dies — he does not die the same death as Mary's Fletcher grandfather, it is true, but he is buried in the same place. The voyage to New York in the 1870s took longer than it does in the *Atlantis*, my dear boy, and Mr. Fletcher was no doubt buried at sea."

"He was," said Tarrant in a stifled tone.

"So much is fact. Now for deduction," Miss Phipps went on decisively. "It is clear there must be some connection between John Kebroyd and Mary's grandfather. Was his name William, by any chance?"

"It was," said Tarrant.

"Just so — Kebroyd called his son after him, you see," explained Miss Phipps. "They are both Yorkshiremen, and as soon as Kebroyd sees Mary he leaves her half his estate, takes steps to insure that she shall receive it soon, and goes off to — shall we say, to join his old friend William Fletcher? Or his cousin, perhaps; yes, I think Kebroyd and Fletcher might easily be cousins. Are we becoming far-fetched if we deduce some quarrel between Kebroyd and Fletcher, some remorse, some wrong? Yes, that is the way

I see it: Kebroyd wronged Fletcher in the 1870s, so profoundly that Fletcher left his native land. Sixty years later Kebroyd repaired the wrong."

"That's all very well, Miss Phipps," objected Tarrant, at last finding his tongue. "There's a great deal in what you say, and I even know further details which support it. But you must remember that it was *before* Kebroyd heard Mary's name that he gave her that strange glance."

"Yes, that's one of the most interesting features of the case," remarked Miss Phipps. "Now how shall I explain it to you? Do you know your Shakespeare?"

"No," said Tarrant bluntly.

"There's a bit in the prologue to *Henry V* which explains what I mean. "It runs like this:

> *. . . a crooked figure may*
> *Attest in little place a million.*

Do you remember that line?"

"No, I don't," said Tarrant. "And what's more, I don't understand it."

"It means this," said Miss Phipps. "A mere nought, provided it's put in the right place after a row of figures, can push the number up into the millions. That is to say, an object put in the right place, besides some other particular object, may magnify the significance of both enormously. Do you understand that?"

"Partly," said Tarrant.

"Look here, my dear boy," said Miss Phipps, somewhat exasperated. "Suppose you have lost a dish of chops from your pantry, and you see a dog sitting in your backyard, gnawing a juicy bone. Has that dog stolen your chops, or has he not?"

"Not enough evidence to say," said Tarrant stolidly. "But I should keep an eye on him."

"Exactly. But now, suppose when you approach the dog you see a broken piece of your own chop dish lying beside the animal. What do you do then?"

"Give the dog a good hiding," said Tarrant with emphasis. "I see what you mean," he added. "It's the underlying principle of all detection."

"Precisely," said Miss Phipps. "Now I believe," she continued, "that there were, about Mary's appearance that afternoon, some details which, when added to her name, convinced John Kebroyd that she was Fletcher's granddaughter. And perhaps, too, reminded him of that old wrong, of which he had so bitterly repented. He looked, you said, at Mary's hand, at her cuff, at her face. Her cuff . . . I rather gathered from your account that Mary was in uniform?"

"Yes," said Tarrant. "And I know what you're going to say next, and you're right; Mary's grandmother, Helen Fletcher, was a nurse both before and after her marriage."

"Mary's face might be vaguely like her grandparents', too," said Miss Phipps thoughtfully. "Arneson is a Swedish name, and Swedes are usually fair, so as Mary is dark she probably 'takes after' her mother's side of the family. But that's a little far-fetched, perhaps, and I won't press it. But John Kebroyd looked first at Mary's hand, and started. Now what was there about Mary's hand, do you think? Have you any idea?"

"Well, yes, as it happens I have," said Tarrant, looking shame-faced. "You see, Mary and I are engaged, and I had chosen an engagement ring for her —"

"That afternoon?" queried Miss Phipps sharply.

"No. I chose it myself in Brittlesea. I wanted to bring it to London that day, but the engraving wasn't finished," said Tarrant. "But the point is this: a week or so before that day, that last time I had seen her, Mary lent me a ring of hers so that I could give the jewelers the size of her finger. I brought that ring back to her that afternoon, and she slipped it on; she must have been wearing it when old Kebroyd saw her. It was an old ring of twisted gold strands, with —"

"A monogram," said Miss Phipps drily. "And it belonged to Mary's grandmother."

"No. It belonged to her grandfather's aunt," said Tarrant.

"Oh, my dear boy!" exclaimed Miss Phipps enthusiastically, her eyes gleaming. "But that's brilliant! That's really brilliant! It completes the whole story. Don't you see? Can't you imagine it? Some little Yorkshire town in the '70s, and the rich old maiden aunt lies dying, and Mary's grandmother is nursing her. And William Fletcher and John Kebroyd are cousins, and they each hope to inherit a share of their aunt's wealth, and they're each in love with Mary's grandmother. And somehow or other, by some mean little trick which we shall never know for certain, Kebroyd turns his aunt's affection away from Fletcher, and persuades her to leave all the money to him. She does so, and leaves only the ring to Fletcher. But the nurse, Mary's grandmother, knows the trick and despises Kebroyd, and marries Fletcher. Fletcher's so disgusted about the money — or perhaps it's a business, you know; yes, that's even better. There is now no place in the family business for Fletcher, so he emigrates to the States; while Kebroyd makes his aunt's legacy the foundation for a large fortune. And presently Kebroyd is sorry, and tries to trace Fletcher, and hears that he died on shipboard and was buried at sea, leaving a wife and daughter. But he can't trace the wife and daughter. And then one day, years later, suddenly he sees his aunt's old ring on a girl's finger, and the cuff above the hand is a nurse's cuff, and the face is almost the face of the grandmother — and add to that, the girl is American and part of her name is Fletcher. All those things are crooked figures in the right place, and they make a million; they make Mary his cousin's granddaughter. The stick, too, perhaps, with the carved dog — that may have been his aunt's; and now it is all broken. Symbolism, you know. As he sits there, dazed, in the chemist's chair, the whole drama of his life is set before him; and he knows what he must do. Yes, it's all as plain as a pikestaff, my dear boy; and your Mary can accept her legacy with a clear conscience. In fact, it's her duty to do so. You must confirm my hypothesis by inquiry at Kebroyd's birthplace, and then if John William cuts up rough, you can just throw his great-aunt in his teeth. Now, what would you like for a wedding present?"

Miss Phipps beamed at him.

"It seems to me," said Tarrant soberly, "that you've just given my wife twenty thousand pounds."

Miss Phipps giggled excitedly. "In that case, my dear boy," she said, "do you think your Mary would do me a favor?"

"If she wouldn't, she isn't my Mary," said Tarrant smiling.

"Then would you ask her to allow me — I would take very great care not to make it libelous — would you ask her to allow me," begged Miss Phipps, "to use the Kebroyd-Fletcher history in a story?"

Tarrant nodded emphatically.

THE SIGNIFICANT LETTER

"Miss Phipps," said Detective-Inspector Tarrant, "you mustn't blame your maid for my intrusion into your study this morning. She told me you were writing and forbade me to disturb you; but I pushed past her and came in. My need of you is so grave, so urgent, that I feel sure you will forgive me when you hear it."

The little novelist, surprised at her desk, had looked up at his entry with a bad-tempered frown on her round pink face. She hated to be disturbed at work, even by the large young man whom she had enjoyed assisting with advice in previous investigations. But his manner today was so unusually grave and formal, his agreeable face so pale and set, that she realized that the human importance of his errand exceeded that of the love scene she was writing, and threw aside her pen without hesitation. She smoothed down her mop of white hair, ruffled in the excitement of composition, looped back over one ear the chain which moored her old-fashioned pince-nez to the button on her substantial chest, and with the decks thus cleared, as it were, for action, turned to him with an encouraging smile.

"Sit down," she said, "and tell me all about it. I am entirely at your disposal for as long as you wish. There is nothing, I hope, the matter with your dear wife?"

"No, thank goodness. It's not Mary," said Tarrant. "It was she who urged me to come to you." Miss Phipps sighed her relief and gazed at him expectantly. The detective made an effort to control himself, and began in a stifled tone:

"The occurrence took place at Brittlesea."

It was Miss Phipps's habit to joke pleasantly with her friend about the excess of crime in his county of Southshire, and especially in the flourishing seaside resort of Brittlesea. This morning, however, she perceived that jokes were out of place, and merely nodded.

"The reason why I seek your help so urgently," went on Tarrant at once, grateful for her forbearance, "is that the man under suspicion for the crime — and the evidence undoubtedly justifies the suspicion — is my brother."

Miss Phipps leaned forward and laid her hand for a moment on Tarrant's knee, then withdrew it and sat back, without speaking.

"The crime in question," continued Tarrant hoarsely, "is assault and battery, and by this time it may have become murder, as it is feared the victim will not recover."

The look of distress on Miss Phipps's pink face deepened.

"Tell me frankly," she said in her kindest tone, "do you really fear your brother may have done it? Or is it just that circumstances are against him?"

Tarrant hesitated.

"Tom wouldn't hurt a fly," he said. "He's the gentlest, kindest fellow that ever lived — under normal conditions. But he went through the first World War and got a piece of shrapnel in his head —"

"He's older than you, then?" said Miss Phipps.

"Yes — that's one of the points which will tell against him," said Tarrant. "He's the eldest of the family and I'm the youngest; he's in his fifties. He was always my hero when I was a lad," he added.

"Why should his age tell against him?" inquired Miss Phipps.

"It was a crime of jealousy," said Tarrant, sombre.

Miss Phipps sighed. "A *crime passionnel*," she said. "I see. In that case, you had better give me full descriptions of the persons concerned."

"If you don't mind," said Tarrant, "I'll just tell you the actual occurrence first — to get it off my chest."

"As you wish," conceded Miss Phipps. "But don't tell me too much; don't let me approach the story with a preconceived notion of the characters which may be quite the wrong one. State the climax briefly."

"Richard Ellison, a motor salesman in the Brittlesea Royal Garage," said Tarrant, "was found half dead in the garage yesterday morning."

"Half dead," repeated Miss Phipps, dissatisfied. "I begged for brevity, but accuracy is even more essential. Please make your statement more precise. The man was injured? How?"

"He lay against one of the interior garage walls, unconscious, with his head crushed," continued Tarrant grimly. "His injuries were frightful; he must have been attacked with a huge weapon, wielded with tremendous strength. From evidence by his family and the garage employees, Ellison was last seen in the garage at eight o'clock the previous night. My brother is a man of great height and strength; he was seen going into the garage that night; his fingerprints have been found on the door; he had been heard to threaten Ellison. Since Ellison had been going about with Edna to a scandalous extent for some weeks there is a strong motive —"

"Stop, stop!" cried Miss Phipps. "This is, as I foresaw, quite the wrong approach to the problem. Action always springs from character, and may be deduced therefrom, but character cannot be deduced from a single action, still less from a partial account of it. Please begin at the right place, with a description of your brother and of Richard Ellison."

"My brother has farmed my father's land since his death," complied Tarrant. "He is six foot two in height, and correspondingly broad. He is dark in complexion; dark hair going gray, brown eyes. He went through a good deal between the wars, you know; economic worries; agriculture wasn't too easy at that time."

"Is he what you would call a handsome man?" asked Miss Phipps.

"No," replied Tarrant bluntly. "He's just a decent, honest, ordinary chap like myself. Very reliable, very kind. Fond of children. Good to animals but not soft about them. Decent to his laborers. Never let anybody down in his life. But perhaps," he added sadly, "a little dull to a woman. Women want something livelier, you know."

"That," said Miss Phipps sternly, "depends on the woman. Who is she in this case?"

"His wife," said Tarrant.

Miss Phipps exclaimed distressfully.

"You think he's just the sort of chap to resent that, though slow to mind anything else?" said Tarrant. "That's what I feel too, you see."

"Go on," urged Miss Phipps. "Go *on*. Who and what is she? Much younger than your brother, I gather from what you said."

"Yes. She's twenty-four," said Tarrant. "They were married three years ago."

"Was she of local parentage?"

"No, she was a Londoner, an attendant at one of those fruit and chocolate stalls on the railway station. In fact," he said bluntly, "we thought it a bit of a misalliance for Tom, and her family thought the same for her. A ramshackle, inconvenient house in the wilds of Southshire — such a dull county, too. That's what they thought of Starwick Farm, and Edna thinks it still."

"And they've been married three years. Any children?"

Tarrant shook his head.

"And are they sorry about that — or glad?" demanded Miss Phipps.

Tarrant colored. "How should I know?" he said.

"My dear boy," said Miss Phipps sternly, "this is no time for misplaced delicacy. You know perfectly well — please answer the question."

"Tom is sorry, but Edna is glad," said Tarrant gruffly.

"What is she like, this Edna?"

"Fair and pretty," said Tarrant promptly. "Blonde hair, beautifully waved. Large gray eyes. Small tip-tilted nose. Small mouth, very red. Very smart in her dress."

"Do you mean by that," inquired Miss Phipps with interest, "quiet colors and no jewelery; tweeds and big gloves in the morning?"

Tarrant hesitated. "Something rather livelier than that," he said. "She's a pretty little thing."

"Lipstick and plucked eyebrows, bright well-fitting jumpers, and lots of handbags to match?" suggested Miss Phipps.

"That's right," said Tarrant. "Very neat and bright and pretty."

"Were you ever," asked Miss Phipps hesitantly — "forgive me, but it's really very important — were you ever just a little in love with her yourself?"

Tarrant colored again. "Yes," he said gruffly. "Just a bit, at first. She was the first girl I had ever seen much of, not having sisters, you know. But when I realized how I was feeling, I cut out going to Starwick, for Tom's sake."

"Very proper," approved Miss Phipps.

"And then I met Mary," concluded Tarrant.

"Just so. I shall not ask you," said Miss Phipps kindly, "whether Edna encouraged your advances or not, because I don't believe you would know the answer to that question —"

"I never made any advances," put in Tarrant.

"— but I shall ask you," pursued Miss Phipps, "whether she seemed to resent your withdrawal. When you returned to the farm after some time, did she seem to resent your disappearance, or your reappearance, or both — or neither?"

"Neither," replied Tarrant. "She was just the same as usual. I'll be honest, and say that partly I rather resented her being so offhand when she hadn't seen me for six months, and partly I was relieved."

"Just so. She's not vicious, then, not a vixen, not a *femme fatale.*"

"I don't know what that means," objected Tarrant.

"Just an ordinary little suburban type, poor child," continued Miss Phipps compassionately. "Used to bustle and movement and quick Cockney talk and lights and shops. Married to a man twice her age, with a disability, and plunged into the country, miles from anywhere."

"There's Starwick village just down the lane," protested Tarrant. "And it's only five miles to Brittlesea, and there's a bus."

"Sheep. Cows. Turnips. Fields. Trees," observed Miss Phipps, shaking her head. "Her taste in clothes isn't appreciated, and if she fires one repartee at a man, the village thinks she's flirting, and purses its lips. Husband good, and she loves him as much as she's capable of loving; but she wants fun without responsibility, and that, my dear boy, is oddly enough, impossible. All the best fun comes from responsibilities joyously accepted. Therefore, the tedium suffered by the Ednas of this world is so dreadful as to excite pity."

"You're right, I daresay, but you're making it sound even worse for Tom," said Tarrant, turning pale.

"Truth, we must have truth," said Miss Phipps firmly. "If Tom is innocent it can't hurt him; if he is guilty it can't hurt him worse than he's hurt himself. We have elucidated Tom and Edna; now for Richard Ellison. Describe him."

"The worst of it is," said Tarrant gloomily, "that he's a very nice lad."

"No!" exclaimed Miss Phipps, startled. "You surprise me."

"Yes, he's a nice boy," said Tarrant. "I only hope I oughtn't to say, was. A tall, fair, lively fellow. Partner with his father in the Royal Garage. He's a salesman now, takes prospective clients out in cars and gives driving lessons and so on; but he used to be on the mechanical side — he's a skilled motor engineer. In fact, he's inventing something now, I forget what exactly."

"Something to do with synchromesh gears?" suggested Miss Phipps.

The detective looked startled.

"Didn't I tell you I was going to buy a little car?" said Miss Phipps in surprise. "I'm learning to drive it now."

"Well, Dick Ellison —" began Tarrant again.

"Don't tell me too much at once," said Miss Phipps. "You're apt to crowd your material. Pause a moment, and let me recreate the poor lad in my imagination."

Tarrant was respectfully silent.

"I should never have believed," exclaimed Miss Phipps suddenly, "that your brother would attack a nice boy like that."

"That's exactly right!" exclaimed Tarrant.

"Surely he would be fond of a boy like that! He might warn him about his wife, but never attack him, surely. And the injuries, you said, were very severe?"

"Terrible," said Tarrant. "The right side of his face and body were really — smashed. Surgeon says they are compatible with a heavy left-handed blow from a blunt instrument with one sharp edge."

"Left-handed," said Miss Phipps. "I see. Found the weapon?"

"It's suggested," said Tarrant, "that the weapon was a large coal-hammer, standing in the shed of Starwick Farm. The head of the hammer showed no trace of such a use, but a piece of bloodstained sacking was found stuffed away in a basket in the same shed."

"That," said Miss Phipps, "is very serious. And still, I can't believe it. If Dick Ellison had been one of these modern street-corner lads, a glib young man with waved hair and a distaste for manual labor — yes, I could understand it. But a tall, upstanding chap, and a skilled workman! No. There's something wrong somewhere. You've missed something," said Miss Phipps crossly. "Tell me the chronology of the crime as far as you know it."

"The police reconstruction is this," said Tarrant. "Last week Tom had a row with Ellison at the Royal Garage. Tom was heard to say: *Once and for all, I forbid you. It's got to stop, you understand, or I'll not be answerable for the consequences.* On the evening of the murder, Tom, who had been absent on business since lunch time, returned home, as witnesses from the village can testify, about 9:30 P.M. The theory is that he found Ellison with his wife; there was a row, and Tom attacked him. He then put Ellison, unconscious, in the car, and drove him back to Brittlesea."

"I didn't know he had a car. You said Edna could reach Brittlesea by bus."

"That's right," said Tarrant. "Because Edna can't drive. When they were first married she tried to learn, but she was very nervous and Tom wouldn't let her go on; the roads there are pretty busy, you know."

"I see," said Miss Phipps thoughtfully. "So Tom is supposed to have struck down Ellison at Starwick, and taken him back to the Royal Garage. How did Tom enter the garage?"

"With Ellison's key."

"Witnesses in the village saw him driving to Brittlesea? And back?"

"Well, no. But at that hour it's pretty quiet in Starwick — they go to bed early. Besides, it's dark at 10 o'clock, and he may have driven without lights. We may still find witnesses — the police," added Tarrant painfully, "are advertising. He was seen to go to the Royal Garage that evening, but it's true there's some discrepancy about the times."

"Who found Dick in the morning?"

"His father."

"Dear, dear!" said Miss Phipps sadly. "How terrible! There's no loophole at that end either."

"No. And you see," said Tarrant with an effort, "how it tells against Tom that he made no attempt to get a doctor or to take Ellison home."

"Did you see Ellison then?"

"No. Old Mr. Ellison got him off at once to the hospital. But I saw the place where he had lain. It was quite plainly marked," said Tarrant grimly. "The garage is a big place, with a huge central shed, strewn with cars at all angles and in all stages of repair. Ellison had his invention apparatus at the far end, and his body lay near there against the wall, partly concealed by his bench, which had been dragged in front of it."

"Why do the police believe the attack occurred at Starwick?" asked Miss Phipps. "I see no evidence for it."

"The hammer and the sacking are in the Starwick shed, remember. Also, if Ellison had been working late in the Royal — at his invention, as he often did — he'd have been wearing overalls. When last seen by the employees at the Royal he *was* wearing them; but in the morning the overalls were found hanging up behind the door. But wherever it happened, Tom was seen to go into the garage that night, and his fingerprints are on the door."

"What did your brother say when he was informed of the charge?"

"He seemed astounded, I'm told," replied Tarrant. "I was not present myself. Tom looked an innocent man, they say, until Edna gave it all away. She screamed out, 'Oh, I was afraid of this!' and fainted, and hasn't been fit to answer questions since. After that, Tom turned quiet and queer, and wouldn't answer questions."

"Well, well," murmured Miss Phipps gravely. Then she said, "I believe that clinches it."

"You do?" said Tarrant, his face white.

"Yes. It's a very painful and tragic affair," said Miss Phipps sadly. "That bright young life, perhaps thrown away, perhaps permanently damaged, just for mere vanity and silliness. Terrible. It will be a lesson to Edna that she'll never forget all her life, but of course that doesn't help Dick Ellison."

"Or Tom," said Tarrant.

Miss Phipps gave him a look of annoyance. "He *must* forgive her," she said firmly. "They must make a new life together, freer and finer than before."

"But, Miss Phipps!" protested Tarrant. "My brother —"

"Just a few final details to get everything clear," said Miss Phipps, unheeding. "Tell me what your brother had been doing on the day of the crime. He had, I imagine, taken a journey away from Brittlesea by train?"

"Yes," agreed Tarrant, surprised. "He'd been to London on the afternoon express, on some legal business."

"He drove in to Brittlesea in the early afternoon, left the car at the garage to be cleaned," said Miss Phipps, "and walked to the garage to pick it up, at night."

"That's what he says, certainly," said the perplexed Tarrant. "It seems Edna went with him to Brittlesea to do some shopping, and returned by bus."

"Clearer and clearer," said Miss Phipps. "Now you know, my dear boy, your observation in this case has been lacking in shrewdness — really it has. Your brother's car was examined for traces of Ellison's transport in it, no doubt. Was anything unusual found in it?"

"Nothing at all."

"Was there anything unusual lying on the floor of the Royal Garage?"

"Only Ellison," muttered Tarrant.

Miss Phipps was suddenly exasperated. "Have there, anywhere in this case, appeared two metal plates with a significant letter upon them?"

Tarrant gaped. "Whatever made you think of those?" he said. "There were two of those 'learner' plates, with the letter L on them, lying on the bench in front of Ellison."

"Exactly," snapped Miss Phipps. "And one of them was slightly damaged, wasn't it?"

"One was bent a little, yes. But —"

"Poor little Edna," interrupted Miss Phipps.

"You don't seem to realize, Miss Phipps," cried Tarrant, "that if Dick Ellison dies, my brother will swing for his murder!"

"Oh, no, he won't," said Miss Phipps kindly.

"If not Tom, then who?" asked Tarrant.

"Nobody," said Miss Phipps.

"Nobody! But why not?"

"Because, my dear," replied Miss Phipps, her eyes beaming behind her pince-nez, "no murder was committed. It's a deeply pathetic story, which may have a terrible ending, though we will hope not, but at least there's no malice about it."

"What do you mean?" gasped Tarrant.

"Dismiss from your mind altogether the murder-by-a-jealous-husband idea," explained Miss Phipps, "and let us see what we have left. A young married woman, bored, with very few duties, in a farm which seems to her remote; forbidden to use the car — that is, forbidden her easiest and best means of reaching the kind of life she loves. When she goes by bus, the villagers probably talk of her neglect of her household. In the Brittlesea Royal Garage we have a kindly, lively, agreeable fellow of her own age who, on your own telling, is accustomed to give lessons in driving. Local gossip maintains that Edna and Dick have been going about a great deal together, while Edna's husband is engrossed in his farm duties. Where have Dick and Edna gone together? Where have local gossips seen them? How have they gone together? In what? In Tom's car, obviously, when it was available — in one from the Royal Garage when Tom's car was not. The Starwick gossip of flirtation emerges, when examined, as the record of a mere series of driving lessons, given secretly. It was very naughty of Edna, and foolish of Dick, and they have both paid for it dearly. The quarrel between Ellison and Tom, overheard the previous week, surely related to this too. Tom has got wind of the driving lessons, and forbids them; he knows Edna, he knows she is unfit for the sudden emergencies of the crowded modern roads, and he won't be answerable for the consequences if she tries to drive. But Edna persists in the lessons, and Dick humors her; and the evening of that fatal day was to have been their triumphant climax. Tom and Edna go in to Brittlesea together, and Tom's car is left in the Royal Garage; Dick arranges to be there, as he often is, working late; Edna does her shopping, then calls at the Royal, and with Dick at her side — without his overalls, naturally — is to drive gaily to the station to meet Tom, who will thereby be convinced that his little wife, whom he thinks so silly, is really able to drive his car. But unhappily it didn't work out that way. Edna arrives, yes, and climbs into the car in the garage and proudly starts the engine, while Ellison begins to fasten on one of the 'learner' signs required by law — the one in front. They laugh and talk and are innocently happy together. And then Dick instructs her to reverse the car — towards the door."

"Yes?" gasped Tarrant.

"And she doesn't back up," said Miss Phipps sadly. "She's put the car into the wrong gear, and as soon as she releases the brake and lets out the clutch *the car moves forward!* Dick is there, right in front of it, just rising from attaching the L plate. Edna shrieks, loses her head, and jams her foot on the brake — she thinks. Really she has put her foot on the accelerator — hard. It's so easy to do, you know, when you're a muddle-headed learner. I'm not muddle-headed myself," said Miss Phipps calmly, "so I have never made the same mistake; but Edna is flustered and nervous. And there is poor Dick Ellison crushed against the wall before he knows what hit him."

"Good lord!" said Tarrant.

"Then Edna loses her head completely. She thinks he's dead. They're alone in the garage, nobody has seen them. She finally manages to reverse the car, then, mad with panic, snatches up some rough sacking and cleans the front of it, tears off the revealing 'learner' plates, pulls the bench forward to hide the body, stuffs the telltale sacking into her basket, and runs off."

"But Tom —"

"When your brother came, as he had arranged with Ellison, to fetch his car," said Miss Phipps soberly, "he calls out to Dick, but there is no answer. It's growing dark and Tom is late, so he drives off without waiting any longer. The next morning he's accused of a murderous assault on Dick, and his wife screams that she had feared it. Why did she fear it? — which means expect it, thinks poor Tom; has she given him cause to murder another man? Plainly she has, thinks he. Do you wonder then that Tom has been strange and quiet? But after all it was only an accident; Tom and Edna must forgive each other and start over again."

"But Edna —" began Tarrant. "Manslaughter —"

He was interrupted by a ring on the telephone which stood on Miss Phipps's desk. Miss Phipps took up the instrument, listened a moment, then handed it to the detective.

"The Brittlesea Infirmary."

Tarrant snatched at the receiver. "Detective-Inspector Tarrant speaking," he said in a cold formal tone. "Yes." He listened intently. "Yes? Yes. Yes!"

He replaced the receiver and turned to Miss Phipps.

"The doctor gives you hope there won't be a trial for manslaughter," said the little novelist promptly.

"How do you know that?" demanded Tarrant with a grin.

"My dear boy!" cried Miss Phipps, beaming. "Give me credit for an elementary knowledge of the human face and its primary expressions."

"I give you credit for a good deal more than that," said Tarrant gratefully.

THE INCONGRUOUS ACTION

Detective-Inspector Tarrant coughed, then wriggled uncomfortably on Miss Phipps's new divan.

"I should like your advice on a small but delicate matter which has arisen in my district," he began with a harassed air. "Delicate because of the position of the person concerned."

"I don't want to hear it," snapped the little novelist from her favorite armchair. "I have no sympathy with anything of that kind."

Tarrant stared, astonished by so much severity from one whom he had learned to regard as soft-hearted. Outwardly Miss Phipps was just the same: since the success of her novel *The Crystal Ring* (founded on one of the detective's own experiences) her dress was perhaps a little more expensive and a little less bright, but her white hair was as untidy as ever and her face as pink, and she still wore the old-fashioned pince-nez which perched so crookedly on her nose. It struck him, however, that the chain which attached these aids to vision to the button on her chest looked thicker than of yore, and the button itself had changed from black to gold. Surely success had not penetrated her ample bosom and turned her heart to stone!

Tarrant was disconcerted, and he showed it.

"That doesn't sound like you, Miss Phipps," he said reproachfully.

"Nonsense! It's profoundly like me," snapped Miss Phipps. "A belief in justice — in the equality of all citizens before the law, regardless of their social standing — is, I hope, the foundation of my character."

"But this is such a dear old chap," protested Tarrant. "To charge him with such a disagreeable offense, after a life spent in the honorable discharge of his duties —"

"Ah, now you are speaking of something entirely different," said Miss Phipps sharply. "An apparent incongruity between character and action. If it is on those grounds you wish to present the case, I am willing to hear it."

"I'll present it on any grounds you like," said Tarrant, drawing out his notebook, "provided you'll listen." He found the page he was seeking, cleared his throat, and began. "The gentleman concerned," he said, "is the Reverend Septimus Lancelot, vicar of the parish of Brittlewick. Brittlewick is a small, old-fashioned village in the country a few miles behind Brittlesea."

"That sink of littoral iniquity," muttered Miss Phipps, who had not yet recovered her temper.

"I beg your pardon? That flourishing seaside resort," countered Tarrant stolidly. "The Reverend Septimus has been vicar of Brittlewick for fifty years. He is now eighty. Throughout those fifty years he has had the respect and esteem not only of his parishioners but of all who know him."

"Why did he bury himself in a village at the age of thirty?" caviled Miss Phipps.

"He is a classical scholar," replied Tarrant, "who has devoted all his leisure to the preparation of a new edition of Lucretius. He has always supplemented his small income, until the last few years, by coaching young men, undergraduates or about to be undergraduates. These pupils sometimes resided in the Vicarage, sometimes in the White Doe, the Brittlewick inn. The Vicar has fulfilled his parish duties faithfully, and, as I say, won the respect and love of his flock."

"Love?" snorted Miss Phipps.

"Love," persisted Tarrant. "Brittlewick loves old Mr. Lancelot. It also loved his wife, until she died nearly twenty years ago, and it feels a personal pride in the achievements of his only son."

"Who is his son?" demanded Miss Phipps.

"Don't you know Philip Lancelot?" said Tarrant, astonished. "Lancelot of the *Daily Examiner?* He's said to be the most famous foreign correspondent in Europe — and what's more, the most honest."

"Oh, that man! He's just been writing some articles praising Sir Robert Nonsych's administration of some native population or other somewhere, hasn't he," said Miss Phipps, still in a disagreeable tone.

"That's Lancelot," agreed Tarrant. "But don't you know the story of his career? How he was reported missing, believed killed, after Dunkirk, and was really taken prisoner, and escaped through Holland into unoccupied France, joined the underground, and later —"

"My dear boy, of course I know," said Miss Phipps. "Everyone knows Philip Lancelot's career."

"But you said —"

"No, it was you who said," Miss Phipps contradicted him. "Do try to tell the story more straightforwardly, my dear boy, and leave our irrelevant matter. Have Philip Lancelot's war experiences anything to do with the present trouble?"

"Yes, they may have," said Tarrant. "Because, you see, the old Lancelots went through such a terrible time of strain when Philip was missing."

"A great many people went through times of strain in the War," observed Miss Phipps in a somber voice.

"But he was missing more than three years," contended Tarrant. "It killed his mother, you know. She believed to the last that Philip was alive; but as soon as she died the Vicar gave up hope. It's said he read the burial service for his son, and he certainly gave away all his personal possessions."

"That wasn't giving up hope, my dear boy," commented Miss Phipps gravely, leaning further back in her armchair. "That was to hide his hope from the gods, to cheat them, you know — the classical equivalent of not tempting Providence."

"I don't know about that," said Tarrant, stubbornly. "He encouraged the girl Philip had loved to marry someone else, anyway. Curiously enough, it was that Robert Nonsych you mentioned just now. Lady Tabitha married him in 1944."

"Really!" said Miss Phipps, sitting up. "Now that *is* interesting. Who was Lady Tabitha?"

"Her family," said Tarrant, "have lived at Brittle Manor for a couple of centuries. Lady Tabitha was the youngest daughter. She and young Philip Lancelot had a boy and girl affair before the War; they rode together, wrote each other notes, and so on.

Then later, while Lancelot was believed to be dead, the Manor became a nursing home and Captain Nonsych was sent there. She nursed him, and after some hesitation — on Lancelot's account, I suppose — married him. He had been a pupil at old Mr. Lancelot's in pre-war days. In fact, he was there, staying at the White Doe, at the outbreak of War — so old Ames the landlord told me — and he and Philip and old Ames's son all went off together to enlist."

"And what sort of people are Sir Robert Nonsych and his wife now?" inquired Miss Phipps.

"A bit stiff, but decent," replied Tarrant.

"Philip Lancelot's politics and Sir Robert's don't agree," mused Miss Phipps, "and Sir Robert took Philip's girl. I must read those articles again."

"Are you suggesting there's some hanky-panky about them?" demanded Tarrant indignantly.

"No, I am not," replied Miss Phipps with emphasis. "Firstly because England is England, secondly because the *Examiner* is the *Examiner*, and thirdly because Philip Lancelot is Philip Lancelot. I've read his articles for years, and I believe him to be a man of the most scrupulous integrity and fearless courage, whose work has international importance on account of his fastidious regard for truth and his ability to express it forcibly."

"In that case," said Tarrant with an air of triumph, "you'll be as sorry as I am if his father has either to be certified as dotty or charged with unlawful entering of premises."

Miss Phipps looked grave. "What exactly are the circumstances?" she asked.

"During the last fortnight," said Tarrant, "old Mr. Lancelot has been caught in more than a dozen houses where he had no business to be, examining their owners' property."

"Examining their property?" queried Miss Phipps.

"Turning over their books and papers, and so on," explained Tarrant. "In two other cases he called at a house and asked for a member of the household, who was out at the time; when told of this, he asked if he might come in and wait. Naturally, in view of his venerable appearance and his clerical dress, this was permitted, and he was shown into a room alone. In one house he was found, a few minutes later, wandering about in the back passage; in another, he opened the door of a room where other members of the family were sitting. They were naturally astonished, and talked a good deal about the incident after he had doddered off, for they had recognized him."

Tarrant paused for a moment, then went on. "All the places he visited were in Brittlesea, and he is pretty well known there by sight. He is a striking figure, very tall and thin, with silver hair and bushy eyebrows; nowadays he stoops a good deal, and is apt to be easily confused. But he's a great favorite everywhere; he reads the lessons as if he meant them, and preaches in a very kindly, simple way. He's really good, Miss Phipps, and I can't bear to think of charging him. But there's no end of gossip going about, and last Thursday came the climax."

"Yes?" Miss Phipps prodded.

"A grocer in a smallish way, who lives above his own premises, saw Mr. Lancelot slip through the shop and go upstairs. Now as bad luck would have it, the grocer had some money up there, waiting to be taken to the bank; and it also chances that he's not a church-goer and doesn't know Mr. Lancelot. So naturally he ran after the old man, hauled him downstairs, demanded an explanation pretty roughly, and there was a scene in the shop. Mr. Lancelot stumbled and stuttered, wouldn't give his name or explain his presence, and grew angry in a pathetic sort of way. The grocer, seeing him such a decent-looking old chap, was perplexed as to what to do, when luckily in came his son, a lad in the twenties who works in the Brittlesea Municipal Library. The moment this boy saw Mr. Lancelot, he addressed him by name. So the grocer let Mr. Lancelot go at once; indeed, he took him to the terminus of the bus for Brittlewick, and saw him safely to a seat. And then, naturally enough, he asked his son how he knew the old man, and the son replied that they had had trouble with Mr. Lancelot at the library. So then the grocer came to the police — to stop the old man from getting into any more scandal, the grocer being a great admirer of Mr. Philip Lancelot's articles. The moment the scene in the shop got to people's ears, half a dozen reports came in of similar occurrences. They're still coming in," added Tarrant gloomily, "though as far as we can judge, he's stopped his strange goings-on since last Friday."

"Before we take up the library trouble," said Miss Phipps, who was now listening with the keenest interest, "tell me this: could you discover any common factor linking the houses old Mr. Lancelot visited?"

"I could not," said Tarrant positively, "though, believe me, I tried. They are not in the same district of Brittlesea. The people concerned do not belong to the same profession, or business, or religion, or political party, or club. They haven't the same level of income — though on the whole they are not among Brittlesea's wealthier citizens."

"Do their names, arranged chronologically, fall into alphabetical order?" suggested Miss Phipps.

Tarrant frowned and consulted his notebook. "No," he said with regret.

Miss Phipps sighed. "If there is no common factor," she began.

"Then poor old Mr. Lancelot is falling into his second childhood," concluded Tarrant. "And his son should be informed."

Miss Phipps exclaimed distressfully. "Perhaps the library incident may shed some light," she said.

"The Brittlesea Municipal Library," continued Tarrant, "is a very fine institution and very well run. There is a librarian, an assistant librarian, and five in staff — three young women and two young men. The number of readers registered there per thousand of the population is a high one, and regarded with pride by the Brittlesea Town Council. The library occupies the whole of a handsome building just behind the promenade; on the ground floor are the reading rooms and children's library; on the first floor come the main lending library and staff rooms. It is the lending library with which we are concerned. At the entrance to this stands a wooden enclosure, with counters on two sides; behind these counters are the assistants on duty. They check the books and readers in and out by means of tickets, and boxes holding these tickets stand on one of the counters. Is that clear?"

"Clear, though not comprehensive," said Miss Phipps. "But is it relevant?"

"Very," said Tarrant dryly. "For the Reverend Mr. Lancelot temporarily appropriated some of those tickets during the past two weeks."

"What!" exclaimed Miss Phipps. "Now that really is interesting. How did it happen?"

"Mr. Lancelot was not a registered reader at the library," began Tarrant.

"Naturally. He's a scholar with a specialized library of his own. Go on," said Miss Phipps impatiently.

"A reader must either be a Brittlesea ratepayer or secure a ratepayer's signature as guarantor," Tarrant went on. "Mr. Lancelot was not a registered reader until a fortnight last Monday, when he suddenly walked in, the minute the doors opened in the morning, and expressed his desire to become one. He was given the necessary forms to fill in, withdrew, returned half an hour later with the Rector of Brittlesea's signature, and was formally enrolled as a reader. Directly he received his tickets he entered the library and betook himself to one of the nonfiction bays. The Librarian, who knew him, felt honored by his presence, went over to him, showed him round, and explained everything."

"How are the books arranged?" asked Miss Phipps.

"By subject," said Tarrant. "Under the headings of Science, Fine Arts, Literature, History, and so on. They have some sort of scheme by which certain numbers indicate certain subjects."

"Forgive me for interrupting, my dear boy," said Miss Phipps in a kinder tone, "but I must tell you that I believe you are overworking. Your appetite for detail is not what it was, and your detective skill will suffer in consequence."

"Mr. Lancelot spent the whole day wandering about the library," continued Tarrant, disregarding the interruption. "He was equipped with papers and writing materials, often consulted the catalogue, and made notes. The assistants received the impression that he was consulting every book included in a list which he had brought. The following day he spent in the same way. That night, the library was locked up, as usual, at eight o'clock, and the staff went home. The caretaker, leaving the building rather later — you can understand that it takes time to lock up the various departments — was horrified to see light streaming from a window above his head. Blaming himself for negligence, he went upstairs and found the Reverend Septimus Lancelot in the lending-library enclosure, bending over the ticket boxes. He said he had been inadvertently locked in. The caretaker didn't quite believe him, took his name, and gently but firmly showed him out. The old man hasn't been near the library since. Next morning, however, a number of the tickets were missing from their boxes. They continued to be missing for a week, while the Librarian tried to interview Mr. Lancelot and failed to catch him, wrote letters to him but received no reply. Then last Friday morning, as Dorothy Ames mounted the bus for Brittlesea, the Vicar came up and handed her an open gardening basket, and asked her to give it to the Brittlesea Librarian, with his compliments. It contained the missing tickets."

"But who," said Miss Phipps, "is Dorothy Ames?"

"She's the granddaughter of Ames the publican at the White Doe," replied Tarrant. "Rather a minx, but a clever girl. They thought she had some chance of a scholarship to London University last summer, but she just missed it; so now she works at the Brittlesea Library."

"Was she disappointed?" inquired Miss Phipps.

"I don't know, I'm sure," replied Tarrant irritably. "Mr. Lancelot was disappointed on her account, I'm told — he had coached her. Not for a fee — partly for the girl's own sake and partly for her father's; he was in the same company as Philip. But the point —"

"You know, my dear boy," interrupted Miss Phipps. "I'm very uneasy about this case; very uneasy indeed. There's a whiff about it of —"

"Kleptomania," supplied Tarrant mournfully.

"Blackmail," concluded Miss Phipps, shaking her head. "I do hope I'm not right about it, but I'm afraid I am. Mr. Lancelot and I couldn't both be wrong."

"Blackmail?" gaped Tarrant.

"My dear boy," said Miss Phipps impatiently, "don't tell me you don't see the significance of poor old Mr. Lancelot's actions. They were a little exaggerated, certainly, but purposeful; there was method in his madness."

"I haven't," stated Tarrant, "the faintest notion of Mr. Lancelot's purpose."

"No? And shall I tell you why?" said Miss Phipps sternly. "In this case you have lacked a proper penetration into character. That I could forgive, for characterization is my job, not yours; but you have also shown a want of your customary thoroughness in detail. Those library tickets: what was their use?"

Tarrant hesitated. "I'm not quite sure," he said.

"Precisely," said Miss Phipps, nodding. "Allow me, then, to inform you. Every reader in a library of the kind you describe has a ticket bearing his name and address; every book in the library has a ticket bearing its title, the author's name, and the class number. The reader enters the library, selects his book, then presents it — with his reader's ticket — to the assistant at the 'Out' counter. The assistant removes the book ticket, clips it to the reader's ticket, and retains both; the reader then leaves with his chosen book. When the reader brings the book back, at the 'In' counter, he receives his ticket again and the book receives *its* ticket again. Now do you see the picture? So long as the book is out of the library, the two tickets remain together *in* the library. They are filed by date — for example, all the tickets for books issued yesterday are kept under yesterday's date. And each day's tickets are arranged under the number which indicates the book's subject. Is that clear?"

"Clear *and* comprehensive," said Tarrant dryly. "But is it relevant?"

"Very," replied Miss Phipps. "For this reason. The row of tickets provides at any moment a register of the names and addresses of persons who have library books in their possession."

"Well?" said Tarrant irritably.

"The names and addresses of persons who have certain particular library books can thus be ascertained."

"Well?"

"The names and addresses of persons who have library books in their possession whose titles figure on Mr. Lancelot's list —"

Tarrant sat up suddenly. "That's an idea," he said.

"Mr. Lancelot was looking for a certain book," continued Miss Phipps calmly. "First he looked in the library, but he did not find it."

"So he visited all those persons who, according to the tickets, had books on his list!" cried Tarrant.

"Precisely," said Miss Phipps.

"But why didn't he simply consult the librarian and get him to do the job properly, by post?" demanded Tarrant.

"Secrecy was evidently essential," said Miss Phipps. "Besides, the poor old man didn't know which book he was looking for."

Tarrant stared.

"But clearly that is so," said Miss Phipps impatiently, "since he consulted the tickets which contained many titles. If he knew the title of the single book he sought, he would have had to visit only one house."

"But if he didn't know precisely which book he needed," complained Tarrant, almost angry with perplexity, "why did he need it?"

"He didn't."

"Miss Phipps!" cried Tarrant, purpling. "Upon my soul!"

"He needed," said Miss Phipps clearly, "something which was *in* the book — shall we say, a letter?"

"A letter?"

"Yes, my dear boy," said Miss Phipps, "a letter. Shall we say, an indiscreet letter? Shall we say, a letter left in one of those books of young Philip Lancelot's which his father gave away during the War? You said, you know, that he gave away Philip's possessions. What more natural than to give his books to the fine Brittlesea library? Yes, a letter, I think, left in one of Philip's books. Shall we say, an indiscreet letter from Lady Tabitha? Then a mere schoolgirl; today the wife of a man whose administration Philip has just been publicly praising. Shall we say, perhaps, an undated letter from Lady Tabitha? Imagine the effect on Philip's reputation, and on

Lady Tabitha's, of a sudden publication, at this particular moment, of an indiscreet note from Lady Tabitha to Philip, offering to meet him, perhaps, after a dance? Yes, I judge that is the kind of document, hidden away in a book, with which the poor old Vicar is so concerned."

"But why," began Tarrant, "why anticipate blackmail?"

"Oh, they aren't anticipating it," sighed Miss Phipps. "It's already begun. Lady Tabitha has already received a blackmailing communication stating that the writer has in his possession a letter saying so-and-so, which he means to send to the newspapers unless he receives a certain sum by a certain date. Lady Tabitha in a frenzy rings up Philip, whom she hasn't seen perhaps for years, and asks him how he could have been so stupid as to keep her silly schoolgirl notes, so mad as to lose one — obviously the postmark of the blackmailer was Brittlesea. And Philip, who hasn't kept her letters at all, racks his brains, and suddenly from out of the deeps comes a vague recollection. That day when War was declared, perhaps, and the fellows from the inn burst in on him before breakfast, and he stuffed Tabby's letter into the book he'd brought down from his bedroom; and then he went off to enlist and forgot all about it. Yes, that must be it. But which book was it? Philip can't remember, but he writes to his father at once and tells him the whole thing, and implores him to try to trace the blackmailer and regain the letter. He can't come himself because, as usual, there's an international crisis; besides, secrecy is essential. Don't you see it now?"

"It's the merest guesswork," objected Tarrant thoughtfully.

"It fits the facts," retorted Miss Phipps.

"There isn't a jot of proof," contended Tarrant. "And even if there were —"

"There is a psychological proof," urged Miss Phipps, "which also serves to identify the culprit."

"Identify the culprit?" exclaimed Tarrant incredulously. "And even if it does —"

"Yes. The culprit must have had access to Philip's books," said Miss Phipps. "He must know the Lancelot story well enough to know who wrote the note to whom; who Philip is and who Tabitha was and who she is today. The culprit also needs money. Now what person mentioned in this case fulfils all those conditions?"

"I've no idea," said Tarrant blankly. "And even if I had —"

"That's the third time you've begun an objection," remarked Miss Phipps. "Let's hear it."

"It's this," said Tarrant. "Your hypothesis only fits the facts if Mr. Lancelot was acting sensibly. Now I cannot believe that he was himself during these events; to me it seems certain that he was — well, in his dotage."

"Nonsense!" said Miss Phipps cheerfully. "There's nothing at all wrong with dear Mr. Lancelot's brain; I should say, to the contrary, it's exceptionally sound."

"You really think that," said Tarrant, with some indignation, "even though he gave those tickets to Dorothy Ames? Implicating a young girl in his misdemeanors! A parishioner! To me that is so completely unlike the normal Mr. Lancelot that I can't believe he was really himself when he did it. No," said Tarrant, shaking his head emphatically, "the old chap must have lost his reason — temporarily, at least."

"As it stood, the action was utterly incongruous," observed Miss Phipps. "I'm glad that at least you noticed that. But in reality, my dear boy, people very rarely act out of character. Action is the product of character and circumstances. When an action appears incongruous, we must look for circumstances which remove the incongruity. Let us assume, therefore, that the Vicar's action was what you would expect it to have been — delicate, generous, and kind. In what circumstances could such an action be so? Now consider the conditions which we said the culprit must fulfil. *Dorothy Ames fulfils them all!* She knows the Lancelot story — has heard it from father and grandfather and the Vicar himself. She needs money passionately, now that she missed her scholarship, to set her on her University career. She has access to all Philip's books. Remember, too, that the Vicar has coached her; presumably, therefore, she is studying the classics, and naturally she uses the books in the Brittlesea Library. In some Latin text of Philip's, unused all these years — for Brittlesea is not, you know, a seat of classical learning — she finds the letter. Old Mr. Lancelot, having checked up all Philip's books, having visited all the borrowers and found that none of them seemed guilty — he probably tested them with some key word — then guessed the truth. He's a wise old bird, as these simple, dreamy people often are. And so he gave Dorothy the library tickets, unconcealed, so that she would realize what he has been doing, and if she is guilty, know why; without a word to mar her moral façade, he gave her a chance to undo her wrong."

"The young minx!" exclaimed Tarrant. "And I saw her at the Brittle Manor Garden Fête only yesterday, laughing and talking to Mr. Lancelot. She told me she meant to try for a scholarship again next year, and the Vicar promised to coach her."

"But that's perfectly splendid, my dear boy!" cried Miss Phipps.

"Don't you see, that fête was probably the date and place appointed for Lady Tabitha to hand over the money — put it in a hollow tree, or something childish of that kind. But instead of that, Dorothy will try again to win what she wants by honest means, and the Vicar is willing to help her. Of course she's sent the fatal letter back to Lady Tabitha, and everything in the Brittle Manor Garden, though not yet quite lovely, is certainly on the mend."

"And what do I do about the Lancelot case?" grumbled Tarrant.

"Forget it," advised Miss Phipps.

"You're always right, Miss Phipps," said Tarrant, with a grin.

THE SPIRIT OF THE PLACE

"Southshire is a charming county," said Miss Marian Phipps, "and it is very agreeable to drive through it. One receives the impression of a spring frieze continually unrolling — a design of lambs, blossom, and daffodils repeated against a background of delicious green. I have almost stopped being ashamed of the cause of this outing."

The car's sudden swerve gave the measure of Detective-Inspector Tarrant's discomfiture. "Ashamed?" he queried.

"Ashamed," said the little novelist firmly. "Since our first meeting we have discussed three of your cases together," she went on, "and each time, by applying a knowledge of human nature —"

"Your knowledge of human nature," corrected Tarrant.

"— we reached a solution which later inquiry substantiated. But on this, the fourth occasion you have done me the honor of consulting me," continued Miss Phipps, "the application of our principle has proved inadequate. We have, or rather I have, been unable to elucidate the affair of the Watch House Café from your description of the persons concerned. I deeply regret my failure," said Miss Phipps, shaking her white head, "deeply. It distresses me all the more, because at the moment I am also at a loss in the short story I am writing. I am perplexed by one of my characters. I can't understand why my heroine at first declines to marry the hero, and later accepts him. I know she does so, but why I cannot tell. I will not conceal from you, my dear boy," concluded Miss Phipps mournfully, "that this double failure, indicating as it does a declining perceptive power, gives me a selfish distress in addition to my regret at being unable to help you."

Tarrant, somewhat abashed, stole a glance at his companion. Her hat, a mountain range of spiky bows, perched on her untidy white hair at an alarming angle; if her limp gray fur had never seen better days its life must have been grim indeed; her pince-nez drooped sideways, weighed down by the gold chain which attached them to the fat black button on her chest. Her pink face, now so downcast, resembled that of a rabbit even more than when she was in a cheerful mood. Decidedly she did not appear a likely person to assist a smart young detective-inspector. Tarrant sighed, and said in a would-be soothing tone:

"You'll feel differently when you've seen the place."

"It ought not to be necessary," mourned Miss Phipps. "The characters alone should be enough."

"But places have personality too, Miss Phipps," protested Tarrant's young American wife cheerfully, from the rear. "The Watch House certainly has plenty of that."

"Really?" said Miss Phipps, brightening. "Your husband didn't tell me that, my dear."

"It's one of the cutest little places I've ever seen," said Mary emphatically. "So very, *very* old."

"Indeed," remarked Miss Phipps. Her tone was noncommittal, for she thought the American view of architectural age might differ sharply from her own.

"It's just made up of archways and cellars and worm-eaten old beams," continued Mary with enthusiasm, "and mullioned windows with those tiny panes you call quarries."

Miss Phipps, more depressed than ever by her error in judgment, said mournfully, "Tell me more."

"The Watch House Café," chanted Mary, "has that name because it was formerly the watchman's house in the ancient city of Starminster, and was built in the Thirteenth Century, probably 1233."

"Can it have mullioned windows, then, dear?" queried Miss Phipps.

"The present street frontage was added in the reign of Queen Elizabeth, when the building became the residence of the first mayor of Starminster," said Mary. A slight frown marred her attractive forehead, and she added, "I forget the date."

"It doesn't matter," said Miss Phipps hastily.

"In the Eighteenth Century the building passed into private hands," continued Mary in her clear, even tones. "Since then it has been used for several purposes; as a house, a library, a shop, and so on. For the last ten years it has been a café, under the management of the proprietors, the Misses Harmond."

"Daughters of the late Dean Harmond," supplied Tarrant.

"Yes, yes," said Miss Phipps, nodding. "I see the place quite clearly now. Old oak tables — really old and rather wobbly on their feet; fine old jugs holding delicious wild flowers; good blue crockery; raffia mats; waitresses with good manners and clean frocks, who disdain tips and never hurry; fine China tea a speciality of the house; excellent homemade jam, superb honey, lots of fresh fruit; cakes a little stale; and the bill twice as much as you expected."

"That's right!" exclaimed Tarrant.

"Miss Phipps, you're a grand person," said Mary.

Miss Phipps preened herself and felt more cheerful.

"The doorways are very low and the light's so dim you can't see them," added Tarrant with feeling.

"The waitresses wear lavender linen," concluded Mary.

"And this charming place," said Miss Phipps thoughtfully, "has been invaded by a poltergeist."

"I don't believe in poltergeists," snapped Tarrant.

"But you must admit, Bob," argued Mary, "that the occurrences are very strange. The café closes every night at seven. The Misses Harmond lock up the premises and then bicycle out to their little cottage in a nearby village."

"Sloping roof, hollyhocks," murmured Miss Phipps.

"And in the morning, when they unlock the café to admit the char-woman," continued Tarrant, "the place is in a frightful mess."

"How in a mess?"

"As if a cyclone had blown through it," said Mary.

"Trays of buns scattered all over the floor; cakes standing on end as if they'd been rolled like hoops; vases upset, brasses fallen from the walls; chairs and tables knocked over; cutlery and silver thrown out of their baskets; milk streaming over the counter; dabs of margarine on the tables," said Tarrant.

"You have seen it in that condition, clearly," said Miss Phipps. "Did the Misses Harmond call in the police?"

"Yes and no," said Tarrant. "It was really Mary's doing that I came in."

"And he's not too pleased about it," said Mary. "You see, I often visit that café while I'm waiting for Bob to come off duty. I hang around there when he's due to come off, and then he knows where to find me and can buzz right along, or if his appointments have been switched and he can't come, he calls me up there. It's not so long since we were married, you remember," she added with a smile.

"He telephones you at the Watch House Café," said Miss Phipps. "Very proper. And so it was Mary who first heard about the poltergeist? I don't think I quite understood that before. Please tell me just how it happened, Mary."

"I was having a glass of tomato juice and waiting for Bob, about a quarter of one," began Mary, as the car passed a notice announcing that this was Starminster. "Or rather, I was waiting for a glass of tomato juice — you do a lot of waiting in that café — when Miss Harmond herself came up to me, and said she was so sorry I had to wait, but they were a trifle disorganized that morning. Had I heard of their unfortunate experience? I said, no, I had not; so then she narrated it to me. I asked her if she had any notion who was the guilty person, and she said she had none, but her sister had a strange idea. Just then Bob came in, so she smiled and withdrew. Well, a few days later I was at the Watch House again, buying a few crackers — I mean, biscuits — for Bob, and Miss Harmond was serving me, and she looked very depressed, and I asked her if she had traced the mischief-doer. And it appeared that the disorder had occurred again! And it has continued to occur, two or three times each week, ever since. The younger Miss Harmond thinks it's a poltergeist — she's rather fond of romance, you know, and goes to church a great deal. The older doesn't seem to know what to think. They have both grown thin and ill, worrying about it; so at last I said to them: 'Now, Miss Harmond, why don't you ask my Bob to help you? I'm sure he'd be delighted to solve your little problem.' They hesitated and said they would talk it over, and said they dreaded the publicity of calling in the police, but at last they agreed that if the mischief occurred again, they would ask for Bob's unofficial assistance. Next morning they called me up, very early, to say it had happened again, and we both went round right away, and there was the café, looking like it had been sitting in the path of a tornado."

"Thank you," said Miss Phipps. "A very succinct and significant account. Am I right in believing that no money is stolen on these occasions?"

"That's right. Luckily Miss Harmond always puts the day's receipts in the Southshire Bank's night-safe on her way home — you know, one of those slits in the bank wall," explained Tarrant.

"What one notices more and more in this case," mused Miss Phipps, "is the absence of any motive for these outrages."

Tarrant, guiding the car slowly along quiet narrow back streets, went on, "I've been thoroughly into the matter of effecting an entrance. The café doors have huge old keys, always carried by Miss Harmond, and enormous bolts as well. The windows are too small for a Pekinese to climb through, much less a child or a grown person. The only possible explanation seems to be that someone hides in the café at night, before it is closed, but Miss Harmond rejects that explanation. She says they now search the place each night before leaving it. I've tried putting a man outside and inside to watch the place, at irregular intervals," he continued. "I can't do anything on a large scale, as they seem unwilling to report it officially. When the inside man is on, the mischief stops, but the moment I take him off, it starts again."

"Remembering the case of the ubiquitous mannequin," said Miss Phipps, "I'm sure you have made searching inquiries as to the days when the poltergeist works."

"I have," replied Tarrant emphatically. "But it didn't tell me anything. The poltergeist, if you like to call it that, works irregularly, on different days of the week. The only common factors I could discover in the times of the different outrages — you see I'm learning from you Miss Phipps — the only common factor I could discover was that the mischief always took place on the morning following —"

"A fine day," suggested Miss Phipps softly.

Tarrant swung the car expertly into position beside the curb, applied the brake, and turned upon Miss Phipps.

"Now how did you guess that?" he said.

"I never guess," said Miss Phipps firmly. "I merely make use of my novelist's imagination."

Tarrant snorted. "You two go in," he said, helping Miss Phipps to descend, "while I park the car. The regulations are very strict in these narrow streets."

The two women slowly crossed the quiet sunny pavement to the café. As they climbed the steep stone steps into the ancient Watch House they were pounced upon by a small elderly lady, who told them their own names and their errand with much good will and excitement, before passing on.

"But if all the customers know about the poltergeist," began Miss Phipps.

"Some of the Starminster residents know," replied Mary, "but by no means all, from what I've seen. And none of the visitors. I just can't see Miss Harmond advertising her café as 'The Place Where the Poltergeist Plays.' Only her intimate circle is aware of her little difficulty."

"What a clear intelligence you have, my dear," said Miss Phipps admiringly. "It's a pleasure to work with you. You have the faculty of classification."

They took the only vacant table, which stood beneath one of the tiny windows, sat down, and ordered coffee. The dark little room was so exactly as Miss Phipps had imagined it that she smiled to herself as she looked around. She was observing with pleasure the crest in the window above her head when she heard her own name being spoken.

"It is exceedingly kind of Miss Phipps," said a gentle voice. "We know her books, of course, and we are honored by her interest. I greatly hope she will be able to help us, as otherwise I fear we shall be forced to leave our dear little Watch House."

Miss Phipps turned. The speaker was, naturally, one of the Misses Harmond. She loomed above the table, tall and stately, very thin, with aquiline features, mild gray eyes, and lustrous white hair coiled neatly about her head. Miss Harmond wore a high-necked gray linen dress, strong black-laced shoes with low heels, and a black velvet ribbon round her throat; she held her hands clasped lightly in front of her waist, and seemed to scent the air very delicately with lavender. "The English Gentlewoman, species now almost extinct," thought Miss Phipps, greeting her.

"It will be just too bad if you and Bob can't do something to keep Miss Harmond in the Watch House," Mary was saying. "She's an institution here, and we couldn't bear to lose her."

Miss Harmond smiled dolefully.

"It is too kind of you to say so, dear Mrs. Tarrant," she said in her gentle tones. "It would indeed be a terrible blow to my sister and myself if we were obliged to leave the Watch House, but we cannot endure this persecution much longer, I'm afraid. The senselessness of it all, the suspense of waiting for it to happen, the feeling that somewhere we have an enemy who wants to harm us —"

She broke off, and Miss Phipps, studying her sympathetically, saw that tears had come to her eyes.

"There's the pecuniary loss too," suggested Mary.

Miss Harmond gave a gentle smile, and moved quietly away to the counter, where a plumper and rosier edition of herself was giving change to a dapper little man in a gray suit.

"That is Miss Jessica Harmond," explained Mary, following the direction of Miss Phipps's eyes. "Very English types, the Harmonds, aren't they?"

"Yes," murmured Miss Phipps. "Sweet Williams. Rectory lawns. That's what makes it so strange."

"Yes — who could be such a brute as to want to hurt them?" said Mary.

"Who indeed?" sighed Miss Phipps. "They look very harassed, poor dears."

At this moment Tarrant entered the café, nodding to the dapper man in gray as he sat down.

"Who is that man, Bob?" asked Mary at once. "I often see him here."

"That's the manager of Quanders and Quanders," replied Tarrant. "You remember Quanders," he added, turning to Miss Phipps, "the big drapers at Brittlesea."

"I'm not likely to forget them," replied Miss Phipps, "seeing how long you talked to me about the Quanders' mannequin."

A look of inquiry blossomed in Mary's candid eyes, and Miss Phipps, repentant, explained hastily: "An earlier investigation, my dear, before he met you. We sometimes refer to it as the case of 'The Tuesday and Friday Thefts'."

"Miss Harmond," said Mary, "thinks mannequins are vulgar. She thinks Quanders are vulgar, she thinks lipstick is vulgar, she thinks women who smoke are vulgar. I'm never quite sure," concluded Mary with disarming candor, "that she doesn't think me vulgar. A very English type."

Miss Phipps surveyed her thoughtfully. "You should be a great help to your husband in his career, my dear," she said.

"Miss Phipps, you're a grand person," said Mary, "but I don't trust you when you make remarks like that. Unless I am altogether wrong, something is seething beneath your hat. Have you solved the poltergeist mystery?"

"I might guess the poltergeist's identity, or rather limit its identity to one of a known number of persons," said Miss Phipps. "I might also guess part of the motive. But the reason for that motive, the feeling behind it, I cannot fathom."

Tarrant showed the disappointment he felt. "Can't you at least advise me what steps to take?" he said.

"Yes, I think I might do that," said Miss Phipps. "But not here. Let us go." She drew her fur about her throat. "Is my hat straight dear?" she said.

Mary was trying to frame a reply combining both truth and tact when a sudden tremendous boom reverberated in the rafters above their head. Miss Phipps jumped to her feet. "What was that?" she cried.

"Only Big Edmund, the cathedral bell — it rings for ten minutes every day at noon," said Tarrant.

"Good heavens!" said Miss Phipps, sinking back as the deep note again rang through the air. "What a fool I am! What a noodle! What a ninny! Of course we are in Starminster, and Starminster is true to its name. Starminster has a cathedral."

"Yes, Starminster is a show place," said Tarrant, not without pride. "You should see the tourists here, on a summer afternoon."

"And a close, and gaiters, and a bishop, and a dean," continued Miss Phipps feverishly. "The Misses Harmonds' father was the Dean of Starminster Cathedral!"

"We told you so," said Tarrant.

"Oh, no, you didn't!" snapped Miss Phipps. "You said they were the daughters of *a* Dean. That," said Miss Phipps crossly, "is not the same at all." She jerked her fur into place. "Come along," she said. "There's no need for us to stay here any longer."

She stalked away — not out of the door, to her companions' surprise, but towards the little counter, where Miss Jessica Harmond, with her gentle melancholy smile, was selling a box of chocolates to a gentleman with a clerical collar. Miss Phipps positively pushed herself into the middle of the transaction. Her pink face was now wreathed in smiles, her voice at its blandest; for the first time since Mary had known her, Miss Phipps appeared The Literary Celebrity.

"Forgive me, Miss Harmond," she said, in a tone so firm and authoritative that the others in the little room fell silent, and Miss Phipps's words competed only with the booming of the bell: "Forgive me for interrupting you, but I am obliged to leave Starminster at once for another engagement, and I could not do so without communicating to you the results of my investigation. My advice to you — and I wish to express it in the strongest possible terms — is to leave the Watch House immediately. No nerves, however strong, could endure what you have had to suffer during the past few months, without being shaken. My friend, Inspector Tarrant, is fully aware," boomed Miss Phipps firmly, "of all the various factors involved, and you need dread no repetition of the trouble. But I fear the reaction for you after this great strain; my advice is — and I give it as one not without experience in these matters — that you and your sister should leave the Watch House as soon as the matter can be arranged."

"We are deeply grateful to you, Miss Phipps," quivered Miss Harmond.

"Grateful indeed, Miss Phipps," quavered the other Miss Harmond.

A composite gesture, which referred either to the shaking of hands or to the waving aside of Tarrant's bill, or both, was sketched by the sisters; then the Tarrants found themselves trailing after Miss Phipps into the noonday sunshine.

"Let us go out into the country," said Miss Phipps in a tone of command.

In silence Tarrant led the way to the car park. Still in silence he helped Miss Phipps to be seated. Still in silence he negotiated the narrow streets of Starminster, and, passing beneath the west front of the fine white cathedral, sped along the Brittlesea road. It was not a meek silence, however, for when he presently drew up beside a grassy verge and turned to Miss Phipps, his face was hot.

"Perhaps, Miss Phipps, you will now explain the amazing statements you made to Miss Harmond," he said stiffly.

"No, my dear boy," replied Miss Phipps, beaming, "I won't do that. I'll explain the whole case to you, and you shall explain my remarks yourself."

"Explain the whole case?" cried Tarrant, while Mary said, "Quiet, Bob."

"Yes. Here we have," began Miss Phipps, "a series of outrages, senseless or sensible, purposeless or purposeful. If senseless and illogical, then nothing can be deduced from them, and it is useless to waste time in ratiocination. Let us lay aside that hypothesis, then, not as disproved but to await psychical confirmation, and proceed on the assumption that the other is correct. If the outrages were purposeful, what was their motive? To inflict loss on the Misses Harmond? But, in fact, very little damage was done; for, as the outrages always took place between night and morning, first, there was no money in the till, and second, the cakes, buns, milk, and so on, that were damaged were always stale. And these outrages always took place after a fine day — that is, after a *busy* day, a day when the stock left on the counters was small, and the resulting pecuniary damage also small. We observe, therefore, the curious fact that the outrages did not inflict as much harm as they appeared to inflict. . . . Next, let us consider the behavior of the Misses Harmond. Did they summon the police?"

"Yes," said Mary.

"No," said Miss Phipps. "Why didn't they simply telephone to the police station, the first or second time the damage occurred?"

"They dreaded the publicity," said Mary.

"But they did tell all their Starminster friends," objected Miss Phipps. "And they deliberately approached you, known to be the wife of a detective-inspector, and told you the story and enlisted your sympathy. Yet your own clear judgment told you, Mary, that you are not the type to whom the Misses Harmond would easily turn. The inference can only be that they desired unofficial but not official interference by the police. Why?"

"They didn't wish to press a charge, to be forced to take the case to court," said Tarrant shrewdly.

"Exactly," said Miss Phipps. "And why not? One explanation of their reluctance to prosecute is that they guessed the identity of the culprit. When you add to that the bolted doors, the small windows, those small-paned windows through which nothing can be seen from outside, and the interesting fact that no outrage ever occurred when a plainclothes policeman was posted in the café then the identity of the culprit stares you in the face."

"Does it?" said Tarrant dryly.

"You mean it was a person hiding inside the building?" said Mary.

"I mean," said Miss Phipps, "that the poltergeist could easily be one of the Misses Harmond. The disorder could well have been arranged at night, before they bicycled home."

The Tarrants stared at her, too astonished to speak.

"I was fairly certain of that much," continued Miss Phipps, "even before I entered the café. The question which puzzled me was —"

"Why should they do it?" cried Mary.

"Exactly," said Miss Phipps. "But Miss Harmond herself set me on the right track. She told me twice in two minutes that if the outrages persisted, she and her sister would be obliged to leave the Watch House. But since the outrages were not serious enough to injure, but only to irritate, and since the Misses Harmond did not take prompt and strong measures to suppress them, and since they were in fact probably responsible for them, it seemed clear that the outrages were designed as an *excuse for leaving* the café. Why did they wish to leave the café? The answer to that question was provided by the most fortunate presence of the manager of Quanders, and Mary's remark that she had often seen him there. Miss Harmond wished to leave the café because she had the chance of selling it to Quanders at a good price. But why strive to conceal a wish so natural, so legitimate? That was what I could not understand — when suddenly the booming of the cathedral bell made it all clear to me."

"The booming of the bell?" said Tarrant, aghast.

"Yes. For it revealed to me the Spirit of the Place. I do not blame myself at all now," said Miss Phipps cheerfully, "for being unable to elucidate this problem in London, from your report alone, my dear boy; for your report left out Starminster, and an essential factor in the problem is the Spirit of Starminster. Imagine to yourselves, my dear children," urged Miss Phipps in a graver tone, "a woman brought up in the shelter of a cathedral close, in the seventies of the last century. To such a woman, to be ladylike is the eleventh commandment, to be vulgar the eighth and deadliest sin. Now, as Mary had already, with her acute observation, perceived, and told me, Miss Harmond regarded Quanders as essentially vulgar, all the more so because its vulgarity is rich, luxurious, successful. And then along comes Quanders, offering a good sum, which means peace and security to two tired old ladies. But the price of this security is the admission, into sacred Starminster, into the ancient Watch House itself (that very stronghold of refinement!), of vulgarity — Vulgarity with a huge glittering V. Quanders would put up a neon sign and hold mannequin parades! And Miss Harmond would be the traitor who let this vulgarity in. Miss Harmond, daughter of the late Dean, surrounded by her friends, must either refuse to sell to Quanders, or live the rest of her life among friends who know that she has sold the fort — sold out, as Americans would say. And so, poor tired lady, she planned to be *driven* into selling to Quanders. 'Poor dear Miss Harmond,' the gossip will go; 'such a tragedy, she was *forced* by some vulgar malicious person to give up her café to those *horrible* Quanders. My dear, it was too terrible for her, but what *could* the poor thing do? Sabotage, you know!' So Miss Harmond would be a martyr, not a traitor. So she wanted the damage to be known, talked about, taken seriously, but not, of course, to be taken into court."

"So that was why you urged them to leave the Watch House at once?" said Tarrant, starting the engine.

"Yes. The relief in those poor things' eyes as I advised them publicly to do just what they are longing to do! It was pathetic," said Miss Phipps. "Though not unpleasant in a way, because it proved that I was right."

"I can't understand such behavior all the same," said Mary, filled with scorn.

"The Spirit of the Place," said Miss Phipps soberly. "One is moulded by it. I shall make my heroine refuse the hero in an antique shop — and accept him," she added joyously a Tarrant put his foot on the accelerator, "in a car."

CHAIN OF WITNESSES

"I thought we were to kill the fatted calf tonight, Ruth, to welcome your Aunt Marian to Yelbeck," said Michael Dyer, serving out the cold ham. "Roast fowl and all the trimmings, what? Our daily help here for extra time and so on. Did something go wrong?"

"Our dear Mrs. Hoyle — she's our daily help — found she couldn't come tonight after all, so I postponed the bird till tomorrow. I hope you don't mind, Aunt Marian," said Ruth anxiously. "But Mrs. Hoyle is such a pet, you see — she was upset at the thought of me coping with a lot of cooking and washing-up all by myself. She actually rang up last night to let me know she couldn't come."

"Mrs. Hoyle is the comfort, support, and stay of this household — and don't make any mistake about it," said Michael with emphasis.

"I like Mrs. Hoyle," announced his small son Stephen staunchly (allowed to sit up late as a treat).

"I don't mind in the least, my dear," said Miss Phipps with a smile, replying to Ruth. "The more so since I believe the incident has given me an idea for a story."

"I keep forgetting you're a celebrated novelist, Aunt Marian," said Michael cheerfully. "You seem so normal, somehow."

"Really, Michael!" said his wife, laughing.

"I know what he means," said Miss Phipps. "I assure you, my dear, my withers are quite unwrung."

Mrs. Hoyle, plump, sturdy, graying, enveloped in a highly colored flowery coverall, was leaning over her kitchen table engrossed in the front page of Thursday's *Laire Post* — Laire was the city of which Yelbeck was a small suburb.

"Well, there!" said Mrs. Hoyle, raising herself on her huge round arms. "To think of you finding me wasting time like this, Miss Phipps! I'm right ashamed. But I was just reading about yesterday's awful murder. Seems to bring it home, like, happening at Yelbeck Junction."

Her eyes, which usually twinkled with glee even in the most adverse circumstances, were now solemn.

"What murder is that?" Miss Phipps, whose august and metropolitan morning paper had given no space to news about Yelbeck, conceded to Mrs. Hoyle the first choice of topic.

"It's poor Tom, the stationmaster at Yelbeck Junction. Or the porter, or the ticket-collector — I don't know which — he's all the lot, I reckon. You'll have seen him, Miss Phipps, I'm sure: a lame man with a stick — lamed in the first World War — a very kind, homely, helpful sort of body he was, always bustling about, up and down between the high level and low level platforms, helping people into trains and telling them about their connections and how they'd plenty of time for a cup of tea. Don't you remember him, Miss Phipps?"

This vivid portrait recalled Tom to Miss Phipps' mind very clearly. (She herself had been almost shepherded into the tearoom on more than one occasion.) "I do, indeed," she said. "I remember now I didn't see him last night when I arrived."

"He was dead," said Mrs. Hoyle portentously. "They found him at the foot of the steps between the levels, about half-past five, with his neck broken."

"Dear me! How did he come to slip?" inquired Miss Phipps. "Ah, he was lame, of course."

"He didn't. He was pushed," said Mrs. Hoyle.

"Does it say so in the paper?" asked Miss Phipps, curious. Drawing her pince-nez to the end of the thin gold chain which moored them to her bosom and perching them askew on her inquisitive nose, she bent over the *Laire Post*.

"It says that suspicion of foul play cannot be altogether ruled out," said Mrs. Hoyle, pointing to the words with a plump forefinger.

The position of the body on its back — walking-stick lying on top of the body as if thrown down later — bruise on temple — cup of tea he was carrying untouched on the ledge by the landing between two steps, read Miss Phipps, skipping down the column with a practised eye.

"Who would want to murder poor Tom, though? And why?" mourned Mrs. Hoyle. "Of course, I daresay you, Miss Phipps, writing detective stories like you do, can understand all about it at once."

"Well," began Miss Phipps, thus challenged, "let me see now."

She rapidly visualized the ill-lit, draughty, and howling desolation which was Yelbeck Junction, the product of competing railway companies in the Nineteenth Century. The lines on the lower level came from the north and east to Laire and those on the upper level approached a different Laire station from the south and west — so that changing trains at Yelbeck and hurrying up or down the long flights of stairs, to catch a connection on the other line, was a process well known to all Northshire travelers. The hill from Laire to Yelbeck was quite steep, so that engines thudded and plodded up the slope. Accordingly, some trains paused at Yelbeck to shed their mails; some flew past the platform arrogantly; some passed through the station without stopping but with a slowness exasperating to passengers, who yearned to board them; and all this took place simultaneously on two different levels and in four different directions. The result was a set of maddening railway activities — perfectly orderly and comprehensible, like the universe, when one understood the laws which governed them, but highly confusing to the uninitiated eye.

Miss Phipps coughed in embarrassment, struggled with her vanity and won.

"No, I'm afraid I can't guess the reason for the murder of poor Tom," she admitted honestly. "However, that isn't what I wanted to talk to you about."

"No, we did ought both to be getting on with our work, that's right," said Mrs. Hoyle, coloring a little. "It isn't like me to be standing talking like this first thing in the morning, I do assure you, Miss Phipps."

"I know that, Mrs. Hoyle," said Miss Phipps. "You are the comfort, support, and stay of this household, as Mr. Dyer was saying only last night at supper."

Mrs. Hoyle lowered her eyes, embarrassed.

"He's a young gentleman as likes his joke," she said. "Not but what he works hard too. Few people, as I often say to Mr. Hoyle, works harder nor what young Mr. Dyer does, bringing ledgers home at night and that, though things don't ever seem to turn out for him quite as he hopes. And Mrs. Dyer as well! They're a fine young couple and the little ones is lovely. I was right sorry to have to disoblige Mrs. Dyer last night after I'd given my promise like, but I couldn't help it."

"Mrs. Hoyle," said Miss Phipps, putting her hands on the kitchen table and leaning forward impressively, "*why* couldn't you help it?"

Mrs. Hoyle gazed at her dumfounded.

"Don't be alarmed — and please believe I'm not in the least questioning the validity of your reason. In this complex modern world of ours, Mrs. Hoyle," said Miss Phipps, thinking aloud, "the lives of all of us are very subtly and intricately interwoven. Our every action, however simple, has far-reaching consequences in the cosmic pattern."

"Of course I'm not one for much book-learning," murmured Mrs. Hoyle in anguish.

"But you would help me in the planning of a story, wouldn't you?" pleaded Miss Phipps. "Any story I conceived while visiting my niece I should regard as her property — a little gift," said Miss Phipps modestly, "instead of flowers or chocolates, you know, to one's hostess."

"Ah," began Mrs. Hoyle, brightening.

"And I need your help. To pursue a chain of cause and effect from end to end — if indeed it has an end," chanted Miss Phipps enthusiastically, "surely that is one of the primary functions of the novelist."

Mrs. Hoyle's brow darkened again to perplexity.

"To follow the results of one person's change of plan — through what diverse social and psychological strata would it not lead one! And here we have an example; a ripple which we can trace back from a point on the perimeter to its central impulse — a link at one end of a long causal chain."

Mrs. Hoyle continued to look flustered.

"Why, Mrs. Hoyle," concluded Miss Phipps, beaming, "*why* were you not able to come here last night though you had expected to do so? What alteration in your scheme of life had caused your change of plan? Did someone in your family group change *their* arrangements?"

"Oh, now I see what you mean!" exclaimed Mrs. Hoyle with immense relief. "Now isn't that clever? Yes, it was our Ted — my eldest grandson. You see," said Mrs. Hoyle in a confidential tone, "he'd been having a bit of trouble with his wife, had our Ted. She's having her first, you see, and she isn't settling down to it. Taken against Ted, she had. Poor Ted was right upset. So Ted, he wanted me to have a bit of a talk with her. But don't let's make it obvious, grandma, he says, or Carol will switch right off. I'll take you and Carol to this circus that's here this week, he says, and then you can stop in at our place for a bit of supper after, and I'll go out for some beer and you can have a bit of woman's talk together, see? So that's how it was, you see; we all went to the circus last night."

Miss Phipps, torn between respect for Ted's concern for his young wife and alarm at the exposure of Carol to the hazards of the circus, was somewhat at a loss.

"Was the circus — er — exciting?" she queried.

"Eh, it was lovely!" beamed Mrs. Hoyle. "And if there were any-thing a bit frightening, you know, lions and such, the way Carol snuggled up to Ted was lovely. I had a bit of a talk with her after, like Ted had said, but bless you, it wasn't needed. Them acrobats on the high wire had done the trick. She's a good girl really, is Carol, you know."

"But why was the night for the circus *changed?*" resumed Miss Phipps.

"Nay, I don't know. It was Ted. Thursday night it was to have been, and then on Tuesday night he comes round to our place and says it's got to be Wednesday — last night. Well, I told him about Mrs. Dyer and he was sorry but he couldn't change the night, he said, and you see I couldn't put him off about young Carol, could I? I mean, a baby!" said Mrs. Hoyle, as if that explained everything — as indeed it did. "So I said to Mrs. Dyer, I says, why not have the chicken tomorrow, I says? Your auntie may enjoy it better, I says, than after a long railway journey, five hours from London as

I understand, which is not very appetizing to some, Miss Phipps, if you understand me."

"But *why* did your grandson *change* the night for the circus from Thursday to Wednesday?" persisted Miss Phipps.

"Nay, I don't know. Why don't you go and ask him, Miss Phipps?" suggested Mrs. Hoyle. "He'd be right glad to see you. He reads your books, you know. He works in that big garage in Yelbeck High Street."

Stephen went to school nowadays, but Baby Pam accompanied Miss Phipps and Ruth to High Street in her carriage. The carriage, Miss Phipps noticed, was rather scratched as to its enamel, and while Pam faced the winter cold in warm bright blue, her gloves were mended and her mother's coat was shabby. Remembering a phrase of Mrs. Hoyle's, Miss Phipps tried delicately to probe the reason for this state of affairs, but was obliged to stop, for Ruth showed some sensitivity. She colored and hastily threw out a couple of apparently unconnected statements to the effect that Michael was working far too hard and that Mr. Caracass regretted that overhead was so high. (Mr. Caracass, of course, was Michael's partner in the firm of cloth merchants.) Miss Phipps, pretending to notice nothing of her niece's irritation, glided smoothly into arrangements for meeting half an hour later for coffee.

They parted at the entrance to the huge glass-covered shed which housed the Yelbeck Motor Company as Pam waved good-bye enchantingly.

Ted Hoyle, when extracted from a deep pit beneath a car, proved to be a large quiet young man in stained overalls, pleasant-looking in all such parts of his face and person as could be perceived between smears of oil and grease. He seemed to recognize Miss Phipps at once (could it be the pince-nez?) and said he was glad to do anything to oblige his grandma. Miss Phipps, looking up at him earnestly, explained her purpose.

"A single action may start off a chain of others," continued Miss Phipps.

"Like the combustion cycle," agreed Ted calmly, nodding.

Miss Phipps did not know what a combustion cycle was, but from the general opinion she had formed of Ted, she was sure he was right, and said so.

"I am tracing back one effect to its cause."

"The spark," said Ted.

"So would you kindly tell me why you changed the night of your circus party from Thursday to Wednesday? Unless it's too private a matter, of course," said Miss Phipps hastily, remembering too late that Carol might be concerned.

"Nay, it's not private," said Ted in his quiet drawl. "This is an all-night garage and we take turns at the late shift. Wednesday's my late night usually, so I fixed to take Grandma and Carol on Thursday. Then Mr. Langland asked me to change my late night to Thursday this week — to tonight. And that's all there was to it."

Mr. Langland being, Miss Phipps gathered, Ted's boss, and since the change did not matter much to anyone so far as Ted knew, Ted had agreed at once and went right off in his lunch hour and booked the circus seats for Wednesday. They were well booked up and he was lucky to get three good ones, and since Friday and Saturday were sold out, he didn't fancy it when his grandma wanted him to change — though of course he was sorry if he'd caused Mrs. Dyer any inconvenience.

"Not at all, I'm sure," said Miss Phipps, and if she was a little disappointed by the prosaic cause in the change of night, she strove not to show it. "Now, may I have a word with Mr. Langland, do you think?"

Mr. Langland, a thin tense forceful person of middle-age, with a pointed mustache, a white coat, and a supervisory air, was conducting a very acrimonious and sarcastic conversation on the telephone about the non-delivery of some promised tires. As the explanations at the other end grew longer, Mr. Langland's sneer grew more and more pronounced.

"Words, words, words!" said he. "Who was it said that the use of words is to conceal thought?"

Miss Phipps longed to inform him, but she did not dare.

"Well, never mind that!" barked Mr. Langland. "Where are those tires?"

His whole slight person quivered with rage as he fired shot after verbal shot at the dilatory tire manufacturers. By sheer persistence in insult, sheer unremitting rudeness, he finally achieved victory; on a firm promise of immediate delivery he banged down the receiver in triumph. He then for the first time noticed Miss Phipps, took her for a customer, and almost sold her one of the glossy monsters in the show window before she could put her question. This he received at first with some suspicion.

"Why do you want to know?" he barked.

"It's to go in a story in a magazine," drawled Ted, who was standing by, spanner in hand.

Mr. Langland's nervous countenance relaxed very slightly.

"Would the story mention the Yelbeck Boys' Club, then?" asked Mr. Langland.

"Why not?" said Miss Phipps.

Mr. Langland beamed.

"Well, you see, it was my Boys' Club committee," he explained. "Sir George Horsfall rang me up and asked if I could change the night — he's the chairman. I'm the Secretary, you know. Could you possibly make the meeting Thursday, he said. Well, it was a little awkward — such short notice, you see — it was Tuesday when he rang — but it's not a very large committee, only seven, so I rang round and managed to get all the members for Thursday — for tonight, that is. So then I asked Ted here to change night shifts with me, so I could be free tonight. We have a very fine Boys' Club in Yelbeck, Miss Phipps — yes, indeed!"

Miss Phipps felt ashamed. She had mentally relegated Mr. Langland to an inferior moral level as a snappy, aggressive little tyrant, and here he was spending his nights in good works.

"Why not drop into the Club tonight for a few minutes just before eight?" Mr. Langland was saying eagerly. "You'd be surprised, Miss Phipps, at the activities we have there. Table tennis and swimming and P.T. and woodwork — yes, you'd be surprised. You could see Sir George then, too."

"I should very much like to see your club," said Miss Phipps sincerely. "But I should prefer to make contact with Sir George before this evening, if I could."

Mr. Langland shook his head in doubt. "He's a very busy man, is Sir George," he said. "Very busy, indeed. Horsfalls' are about the biggest textile mills in Laire, you know, and that's saying something. Then he's on the Laire City Council, and Chairman of the bench of magistrates, and on dozens of committees in Laire and Yelbeck — he lives at Yelbeck Hall and exhibits chrysanthemums, you know. You'd have to telephone for an appointment, and I don't really know when you would get one, I don't indeed."

Miss Phipps, who already had her ideas of how to reach Sir George, smiled, thanked Mr. Langland for his invitation to the Boys' Club, promised to visit him there later in the week, and withdrew.

"I write detective stories," said Miss Phipps.

"Never read 'em," said Sir George.

"Then you have a pleasure in store," returned Miss Phipps with her blandest smile.

"H'm," said Sir George, looking at her with more interest from beneath his bushy brows.

Undaunted by the immense façade and towering chimney of Bridge Mills, Miss Phipps had passed boldly under the echoing archway and across the great courtyard, and stormed in turn the Inquiries Office, the General Office, the Chairman's Office, and Sir George's private secretary by the expedient of announcing that she had business with Sir George concerning the Yelbeck Boys' Club. Now, seated in a fine oak chair on a thick blue carpet in a large paneled room, she gazed across an expanse of desk on which lay nothing but a copy of the *Laire Post*, folded at the Yelbeck Junction story. Sir George was undoubtedly formidable. He had that short but sturdy and well-muscled build so frequently found in Northshire, a massive head thrust forward on a bull neck, untidy graying hair, a lined red face, and extremely shrewd blue eyes. He was admirably clothed in what Miss Phipps correctly judged to be some of his own finest worsted cloth, dark blue in color, with impeccable linen and a subdued tie. From time to time his secretary, a stern woman of about Miss Phipps's own age, entered the room with papers or queries. Each time she opened the door the strong, heavy hum of a vast collection of textile machinery throbbed on the air. Miss Phipps enjoyed this industrial scene, which was new to her.

"Well, what's it all about, then? You got in to see me by saying you came about the Yelbeck Boys' Club."

"If you didn't wish to see me about the Yelbeck Boys' Club then it was useless for me to see you at all," said Miss Phipps with a smile.

"Is that meant for flattery, eh?"

"Not altogether," admitted Miss Phipps.

"Is it a subscription you want?"

Miss Phipps emphatically shook her head.

"Is it about young Michael Dyer?"

"I see you know more of me than you choose to admit," said his visitor.

"I'm not a born fool, you know," said Sir George. "I don't let strangers in to see me without making some inquiries. You're Michael's wife's aunt, who makes her brass by telling women tales. I knew Michael's father pretty well when he was alive. Pity he died while Michael was in the war. How's Michael getting on, eh? Of course, cloth merchants aren't what they used to be — conditions in the trade have changed. But old man Dyer had a well-established firm in his day. What about this chap Carcase, or something such, that old Dyer took in as partner while he was ill and Michael was in Burma, eh?"

"Caracass is the name."

"It's not a Northshire name," said Sir George with a hostility only half pretended. "I never heard of such a name. How about this Caracass, then, eh?"

Miss Phipps was saved by the telephone from the necessity of inventing a reply. Sir George, picking up the receiver with the calm of a man well protected from casual callers, presently allowed his eyes to stray to the newspaper open on his desk.

"Aye, it's a bad do," he concluded the conversation.

"Murder?" ventured Miss Phipps.

"Well, that or manslaughter. There's not much point in murdering poor old Tom."

"You mean that the point, the motive, is not yet discovered," said Miss Phipps shrewdly.

Sir George stared at her.

"You're not such a fool as you look by any means," he said at length. "But you shouldn't wear cloth like that, you know. Doesn't do young Michael credit. I'd send you a length, but he'd be vexed. Now, what d'you want, eh?"

Miss Phipps explained.

"And what would you get for a story like that, eh?" inquired Sir George, affably contemptuous.

Miss Phipps told him.

"Would you indeed?" said Sir George, genuinely surprised. "It's a good-paying job, writing stories, eh?"

"It depends who writes them," said Miss Phipps laconically. ("With men of this kind," she said to herself, "one must keep one's trumpet constantly in play.") "Design, quality, finish, you know," she added, having read these words on an advertisement of the Bridge Mills product in the outer office.

"Know all the answers, don't you?" said Sir George with a muffled snort — probably, thought Miss Phipps, intended as a laugh. "Well, it was this way. I have to see the local textile Union representative, Fred Shackleton, about a Trade Union matter. We'd fixed late afternoon Thursday, but then —"

"He asked you to change to Wednesday?"

"Not exactly. He works here, you see, and as I was passing through the pressing room on Tuesday he stepped up to me and said, 'It was Thursday we fixed, wasn't it?' I knew by the way he said Thursday he wanted to change. And so —"

"To put him in a good humor for the negotiations you told him you found Wednesday would suit you better after all?"

"Something like that. I'm not a born fool, you know."

"May I go down and see this young man?"

"Fred? Aye. I'll have you taken down," said Sir George, pressing a button. "Now, mind what you say to him. He's a bit hot-headed, is Fred. I don't want to be splashed all over the press as making underhand inquiries into my employees' private affairs, you know."

"I'm not a born fool," replied Miss Phipps, rising.

Sir George snorted.

After an alarming journey through what seemed to be miles of clacking, clattering, thudding, banging machines, Miss Phipps emerged into the comparative calm of an electrically driven apparatus the size of a cottage, which purred gently in a room of its own. This giant was manipulated by Fred, who wore upstanding ginger hair, a fierce expression, and a smart pullover.

"I am conducting a piece of sociological research which I intend to use in a short story," stated Miss Phipps.

Fred diminished the monster's purr by turning a switch, and prepared to listen, hands on hips.

"I am tracing, step by step through the sociological field, the consequences of a single individual change of plan. This will reveal, I believe, the economic nexus which binds modern society so closely."

"It's an interesting idea," conceded Fred. "Of course, you've got to remember that once the initial act has taken place, all sorts of innocent people will be involved without their own volition — like puppets," he declaimed fiercely, "dancing to the strings pulled by big business in the seats of power."

Miss Phipps coughed gently. "You have an interesting point there," she said. "Now what made *you* ask Sir George to change the day of his appointment with you?"

"I never asked him!" exclaimed Fred, aggrieved. "I just mentioned the day to confirm it and he said Wednesday would suit him better. As it happened, it suited me better too."

"Why?"

"It wasn't as if I were delaying Union business by the change," continued Fred belligerently.

"No — of course not. But why did you prefer Wednesday?" murmured Miss Phipps in a gentle, soothing tone.

"Well, fact is," said Fred, "my young lady had a night off. From rehearsals, you know. She's a member of the Laire Thespians and they're doing Shakespeare. *Henry Fifth.* Been at it for weeks. It's a very imperialist play in my opinion, but as Doris says, you have to take the rough with the smooth."

"And Doris is playing a part?"

"That's right," said Fred. "She had Thursday booked for rehearsal, but then there was a change — some people are very inconsiderate, you know, never think how what they do affects anyone else. So she found she had Thursday — tonight — free after all. With Sir George changing his mind, like, me and Doris will have a night out together tonight in spite of all — first I've had with her for long enough."

"Now come, Mr. Shackleton," said Miss Phipps persuasively. "By a skillful use of your tone of voice you forced Wednesday on Sir George, didn't you?"

Fred scowled. Then he grinned.

"Happen I did. Doesn't do to let the old so-and-so have all his own way, you know," he said.

"Just so. And where could I find Doris?" inquired Miss Phipps.

"Miss Earnshaw teaches in Laire, at Morning Road school," said Fred stiffly.

He turned the switch down and the monster purred again.

Miss Phipps, late for lunch, rushed into Ruth's neat little dining room full of apologies. But these, she found, were scarcely needed. Michael, eating a boiled potato with a marked lack of enthusiasm, wore a somber frown; Ruth, feeding Pam in her high chair, seemed quiet and preoccupied, and Pam catching her mother's gloom looked ready to be tearful. Only Stephen appeared lively.

"Please forgive us for not waiting, Aunt Marian," said Ruth.

"Of course, my dear. I'm disgracefully late."

"Daddy couldn't wait because he has to rush back to see the police again," announced Stephen.

"The police!" exclaimed Miss Phipps, startled.

"A burglar broke into Michael's office last night after he had left," said Ruth in a choked tone.

"Good heavens! What did he steal?"

"He seems to have been interrupted in the job before he got hold of much," said Michael. "Not that there was much to steal. The safe door was open when I got there this morning, and some papers were scattered on the ground in a considerable mess, and the petty-cash box and one or two other things were gone. Probably the policeman on the beat passed by and the man took fright."

"The loss isn't very serious, then?" asked Miss Phipps.

"Well, it's all rather perplexing and silly," said Michael with a worried look. "You see, the Stock Book's gone."

"What's a Stock Book?" inquired Miss Phipps.

"It shows the inventory of cloths we have in hand."

"What is the significance of its disappearance?"

"Well, it's silly of course," said Michael as before, "but nowadays one is apt to have suspicions when a firm's Stock Book or Account Books disappear. It's a trick that's been played too often to get by. Those books would reveal any kind of — well, cheating, you see. And with our stock-taking due next week — well, it all seems odd. The worst of it is that the police seem to think it was an inside job. The outer door and the private office door and the safe showed no signs of having been forced. Apparently they had all been opened with keys."

"And who is suspected of this theft?" she said.

"At present," said Michael bitterly, "they appear to suspect me."

"What!"

"Michael! Not in front of the children!" exclaimed Ruth in anguish.

The meal went on in gloomy silence until the children had finished at last and were allowed to leave.

"Why do the police entertain this absurd suspicion?" said Miss Phipps then in a stern tone.

"Well, Aunt Marian, I'm bound to say I could easily have done it — though, of course, I haven't," said Michael unhappily. "No alarm was given last night. No stranger, nothing out of the ordinary, was seen. I was working late, and was the last to leave the warehouse. I locked up after all the rest had gone. The Town Hall clock struck 6:30 as I came down the steps. Nobody but myself and Simon had the necessary keys."

"Simon?"

"Simon Caracass."

"And where was Mr. Caracass during the period of the burglary?"

"He left for London last night by the 6:30 train. What he's going to say about it all when he gets back tonight," said Michael with a heavy sigh, "I'm sure I don't know. Or rather, I can guess. He always has plenty to say about everything. Well, I must go. Try not to worry too much, Ruth."

He kissed his wife and left the house, his pleasant young face drawn with anxiety.

Ruth, having dispatched Stephen to School and put Pam to bed for her afternoon nap, brought Miss Phipps a cup of coffee and then burst into tears. Mr. Caracass, it seemed, was so difficult, so severe. He was bound to blame Michael for the burglary — he blamed Michael for everything. He was very strict, and had cut down the amount Michael drew from the business until — well, really, until it was very difficult for the Dyers to manage on it. Michael had been working very hard indeed, lately, to see if economies could be effected in the business, but in vain. He dreaded the semi-annual stock-taking which was soon to begin. It was all very worrying. If things grew any worse, Ruth would be obliged to dispense with the services of Mrs. Hoyle, and that would be a tragedy. Mrs. Hoyle was so kind, so good, so experienced. . . . It was all very worrying indeed.

Miss Phipps soothed and comforted Ruth as well as she could before setting out to find Miss Doris Earnshaw. She was loath to leave her niece and loath to go out into the cold dark afternoon, but in view of Ruth's financial confidences, it seemed more than ever desirable that her projected story should be completed.

"Mr. Fred Shackleton gave me your address," said Miss Phipps to Miss Earnshaw, who was young and pretty, with brown curls and dancing eyes.

"Oh, him!" exclaimed Miss Earnshaw with a light irony in her tone.

Miss Phipps gathered that Miss Earnshaw had other suitors more favored than poor Fred. She tried another tack.

"The stage is your main interest, I believe?" she said.

"Well, yes and no," said Miss Earnshaw frankly. "The Children Must Come First, must they not? That's the teacher's slogan, you know."

Miss Phipps perceived that though Miss Earnshaw, in the modern fashion, mocked herself, she meant what she said. Miss Phipps looked around her at the great glass windows (on which rain now beat pitilessly through the dark), the wide corridors, the crayon drawings lining the cheerful pale blue walls.

"This school seems very well equipped," she said.

"It's not bad and that's a fact," admitted Miss Earnshaw. "New, you know."

"And which class — what age of children — do you teach?"

"I'm a specialist," explained Miss Earnshaw with a touching youthful pride. "I give speech training throughout the school."

"I see. And so naturally you belong to the Laire Thespians."

"Well, it's not as natural as falling off a tree," objected Miss Earnshaw. "There's an audition, you know, and quite stiff tests. However the chairman said he thought I was promising — though I didn't promise *him* anything, believe you me!" disclaimed Miss Earnshaw with lively relish.

"You have a part in the production of *Henry Fifth*?" pursued Miss Phipps, smiling.

"That's right. Mistress Quickly," said Miss Earnshaw cheerfully.

"Good heavens!" exclaimed Miss Phipps. "I can't imagine you playing that raddled hag."

"Oh, I love acting raddled hags. It's easier to play a character part than a straight one," explained Miss Earnshaw. "Something quite different from yourself, if you know what I mean."

"I wonder," said Miss Phipps with cunning, "if the story I am planning would make a play?" At this the gleam of interest she had hoped for lighted up in Miss Earnshaw's agreeable eyes. "I should like your opinion — but I must first ask you, why was your rehearsal changed from tonight to last night?"

"Oh, that I can't tell you. It was our beloved merry widow, our leading lady, who was responsible for the switch," said Miss Earnshaw sardonically. "Joan to some, Mrs. Ingram to me. I don't know if you know anything about producing plays, Miss Phipps — ah, I see you do," she said, catching herself up quickly. "Well, amateurs after all are only amateurs; they can rehearse only at night and they don't want every night for weeks and weeks engaged. They have their private affairs after all, you see," said Miss Earnshaw, her bright eyes sparkling. "So sometimes we have sectional rehearsals — act one or all the scenes with Bardolph on one night, and act two or no Bardolph the next. Well, we were rehearsing all the Bardolph scenes on Thursday, and I'm in a Bardolph scene; and on Wednesday we were doing the scenes with the French princess and Henry in camp at night. It had all been settled and put up on the notice board ages ago. Then suddenly on Monday night Mrs. Ingram, who is playing the Princess, said she couldn't come on Wednesday after all. Tony Harris — he's our producer — fumed and tore his hair, but then Ingram went all temperamental — no, stop me!" said Miss Earnshaw, holding up a hand in a charming gesture of self-admonition, "I'm being catty. Mrs. Ingram, I remember now, said she couldn't help her absence because it was due to business, and as a poor lone lorn widow she couldn't afford to alienate her boss, and so on. There was one of those frightfully involved and heated arguments which seem to be an inseparable feature of amateur theatrical life, and when the dust had subsided I found my rehearsal had been switched to Wednesday night — last night. So I had to give poor Fred the air for Wednesday. He came to the Playhouse to call for me on Monday night, and I told him then. And the foolish creature went and changed his own plans. So silly, really! As if he had a hope! Poor Fred! Of course it's time he got married," concluded Miss Earnshaw maternally, "so long as he doesn't marry me."

Miss Phipps's opinion of Fred's prospects suddenly improved greatly.

"I should like to attend the Thespian rehearsal tonight," she said.

"Why not? Just barge in and ask for Mrs. Ingram," said Miss Earnshaw, giving her the Playhouse address. "After all, Tony Harris can't eat you. Or can he? If he tries, butter him up a bit and he'll come round."

"It will need to be the best butter," reflected Miss Phipps in some dismay.

She felt tired and dispirited. The chicken which had been the cause of her long odyssey, though admirably cooked by Mrs. Hoyle, might have been sawdust for all the enjoyment it had brought that evening to the Dyer household. Michael had left in the middle of the meal to meet his partner's train in Laire; it was clear that he regarded their coming interview with apprehension. Ruth was pale with worry and could not eat; Miss Phipps, making admiring noises about Mrs. Hoyle's cooking, heroically stuffed down morsels for which she had no appetite. The night was cold, the rain had become a deluge, the stage entrance to the Playhouse was in a back street which her Yelbeck taxi-driver found difficult to locate. Now a flight of dark stone steps loomed and sounds of conflict rose to her ears.

"Quiet! Quiet, please! *LISTEN!*" bellowed an angry voice, male.

Miss Phipps sighed, negotiated the steps carefully, and pushed open a swinging door placarded with commands to keep it closed.

To her astonishment she found herself on a stage. The headquarters of the Laire Thespians consisted, in fact, of an extensive cellar, so agreeably decorated in shades of cherry and gray as to convey the complete illusion of a theatre, and fitted with a cyclorama and all that complicated lighting apparatus dear to a stage director's heart. Three or four Thespians on stepladders and chairs were painting a backcloth with the likeness of a Fifteenth Century French castle. In cherry-velvet stalls, from which the white covers had been pushed back, lounged a score of Thespians, male and female, whose interchange of gossip had provoked the plea for silence. On the stage with their backs to Miss Phipps stood a good-looking fair young man, a small, beautiful, dark and sophisticated woman, and a bouncing girl, who appeared to be Henry V and Katharine, with Alice in attendance, playing the wooing scene.

"*Les langues des hommes sont pleines de tromperies,*" coquettishly remarked Katharine, who was presumably Mrs. Ingram.

Her voice was sweet and low, and her French accent prettily assumed, but Miss Phipps was not sure whether she liked her. While Alice was explaining to Henry that the princess meant the tongues of men were full of deceits, Miss Phipps took a step forward in order to get a fuller view of Mrs. Ingram's face.

"This is too much!" yelled a very thin young man with a beaky face and long tangled hair, charging down the aisle towards the stage. "Who are you? What do you want? Coming on the stage during rehearsal like this!"

"Perhaps she's come to do some whitewashing, Tony," suggested Henry V in a soothing tone.

"Then let her go round by the other entrance," shouted Tony crossly.

Miss Phipps disclaimed whitewashing. "I just came to have a word with Mrs. Ingram," she said. "But I should like to watch you at work for a few moments, if I may."

At her name Mrs. Ingram turned quickly towards the speaker.

"Ah, no," reflected Miss Phipps, "I don't altogether like her. It's a beautiful face, but ravaged and unhappy. It's the face of a woman who has found the tongues of men full of deceits, certainly." Aloud she added, on a flattering note, "I write for the magazines."

Tony's face cleared. "Well — come down into the auditorium, will you?" he said. "Henry, give the lady a hand."

Miss Phipps was carefully lowered over the footlights by Henry V and one of the painters, and welcomed to a velvet seat and a cigarette. The rehearsal recommenced.

"Now let's have something a little more *soldierly* in your movements, Henry," urged Tony. "As though you were accustomed to wearing *armor*, you know."

Henry obediently clumped about the stage, while Mrs. Ingram played, with a good deal of finish and experience, a most enticingly demure French princess.

"I'm lucky to find you here tonight," said Miss Phipps when at length the scene was finished and cups of tea came in on a huge tray and the Thespians were gathered round her, all hoping to appear (with picture) in a glossy-papered, large-circulation magazine. "I had understood that Mrs. Ingram's scenes were to have been rehearsed last night?"

"So they were," said several Thespians in chorus, while others, by winks, nods, and shrugs, conveyed to Miss Phipps that she was on dangerous ground.

"So they were if Joan hadn't upset the whole schedule at the last minute," said Tony irritably. "Really it was too bad, you know, Joan."

"Now don't start all that again, Tony. I told you before," said Mrs. Ingram, her dark eyes flashing, "that I couldn't help the change. When your boss wants you to meet him at the railway station with some important papers he needs in London, you've got to do it or risk your job. If you'd let me be late I could have managed it."

"Boss my foot," said Tony crossly. "You know perfectly well he's your boy friend."

"If he knew on Monday he wanted the papers, surely he could remember to take them with him on Wednesday," argued Henry V, not, thought Miss Phipps, without some logic.

"He was in Northcaster all day and didn't want to cart them about with him. Now don't *badger* me," said Joan Ingram angrily, her beautiful voice taking on a shriller note. "I had to oblige my employer, and that's that. Give me another butt, Tony, if you've got any manners."

"And who *is* your employer, my dear?" murmured Miss Phipps, proffering her own cigarettes.

Mrs. Ingram told her.

Miss Phipps, taking off her macintosh in the Dyers' hall, heard unfamiliar voices coming from the lounge. She stood by the door and listened unashamedly.

"I think you must see, Mr. Dyer," said an official voice, "that the question of the keys is vital — especially since we have found the cashbox, still intact, in the river by Laire Bridge, not three minutes' walk from the front door of your warehouse. You were in your office alone, you had the necessary keys. Some explanation is obviously necessary."

"It is the disappearance of the Stock Book which troubles me most," said a voice more Oxonian than any Miss Phipps had yet heard in Northshire. "It appears to me, Superintendent — of course, I merely throw this out as a tentative suggestion — quite provisional, you understand, I don't wish to be thought to be making any accusation — but it seems to me — I'm sorry to have to say this, Dyer — it seems to me that the burglary, or shall I say the appearance of burglary, might well have been contrived to cover the disappearance of the Stock Book, that the disappearance of the book was, in fact, the prime object of the apparent burglary. We — the firm of Dyer and Caracass — are to take stock at the end of this month, Superintendent. Without the Stock Book the stock-taking must necessarily be a maimed rite. To a firm of the long integrity of mine, this will come as a very painful innovation."

"If there were to be any question of, say, bankruptcy," pursued the official voice carefully, "any disappearance of account books would be very suspicious. Otherwise, the matter would be primarily one for you two gentlemen, who are partners, to worry about. Now you, Mr. Caracass — you were out of town last evening, I believe? And your keys were on your person?"

"I left Laire at 6:30 P.M., carrying my keys," said the smooth liquid voice of Mr. Caracass. "My keys are always on my key chain."

"Mr. Caracass," interrupted Ruth's voice, harsh with pain. "Can you prove you left Laire at 6:30 last night?"

"As it happens, I can," said Caracass with a little casual-sounding laugh. "I was in Northcaster all day Wednesday, you remember, Dyer. Finding I had not brought with me some papers I should require in London, I phoned Mrs. Ingram, our secretary, and asked her to meet me at Laire station with the papers. She saw me leave on the 6:30 train."

"No, no!" cried Miss Phipps, bounding into the room. "That's a lie!"

"Aunt Marian!" exclaimed Ruth in horror.

"If this is your idea of a joke, madam," said Mr. Caracass coldly, "it strikes me as both ridiculous and tasteless."

Mr. Caracass, observed Miss Phipps, was one of those slim, tall, dark men whose careful tan gave them an air of distinction. His suit was impeccable both in cloth and cut — "It's as good as Sir George's — poor Michael looks shabby beside him," reflected Miss Phipps rapidly. "Yet why if they're equal partners —"

"Mrs. Ingram certainly witnessed my departure," concluded Mr. Caracass, eyeing Miss Phipps with icy distaste.

"Yes — and then you left the train at Yelbeck Junction as it crawled slowly up the hill, and you caught a train down to Laire and went back to the office and stole the Stock Book — and then caught a later train to London," said Miss Phipps rapidly. "And while you were changing trains the first time at Yelbeck, you met poor Tom the stationmaster on the stairs, and he knew you and could have broken your alibi. So you murdered him."

"Superintendent, you hear this public defamation of my character?" began Caracass in his eloquent way.

"Be careful, madam," warned the detective, watching her, however, with a good deal of interest.

"I can prove you arranged with Mrs. Ingram that she should see you off on Wednesday, thus giving you an apparent alibi, as early as Monday afternoon," said Miss Phipps.

"I think not. I'm sure Mrs. Ingram will not confirm that statement," said Caracass with cold conviction.

("That," thought Miss Phipps, "is only too likely, since she's probably your mistress.") "Luckily I have seven witnesses to that fact," said she, "who provide an unbreakable chain of evidence. A combustion-cycle springing from the spark of your need for an alibi."

"Nonsense!" said Caracass with contempt. But his accent had slipped a little. "How could you possibly have any such evidence?"

"You asked Mrs. Ingram to keep Wednesday evening free for you, so she changed her rehearsal with Doris Earnshaw. So Doris changed her outing with Fred Shackleton. So Fred Shackleton changed his Trade Union interview with Sir George Horsfall. So Sir George changed the Boy's Club Committee meeting with Mr. Langland. So Mr. Langland changed his late shift with Ted Hoyle. So Ted changed his circus night with his grandmother. So Mrs. Hoyle couldn't cook our supper on Wednesday. And they all," concluded Miss Phipps triumphantly, "made the change between Monday and Tuesday night."

"And what significance are we supposed to impute to all this?" said Caracass, rising to his feet.

"You've been cheating Michael Dyer for months — sales never seem to turn out as well as he expects. I daresay you cheated his dying father for years while Michael was in Burma," said Miss Phipps, reckless now. "You probably made love to Mrs. Ingram so she would help you, for she knows the tongues of men are full of deceit. Your flow of words is intended to conceal your thought. It's easier to play a character part than a straight one," Miss Phipps continued in a rush of inspiration, quoting some of the words of wisdom she had learned from her seven witnesses. "Caracass" — she reached her climax with Sir George — "Caracass sounds a made-up name."

Mr. Caracass sprang with hands outstretched.

He succeeded only in tearing Miss Phipps's pince-nez from their chain before the detective and Michael caught him and held him fast.

When he had been taken down to the Yelbeck police station for questioning, Miss Phipps, Ruth, and Mrs. Hoyle sat down to a happy cup of tea. Miss Phipps had to recount again and again to her admiring audience the chain of events which had led her to the truth.

"Of course it was a great piece of luck," she said modestly, "that one end of the chain lay in your own kitchen."

"Yes, in a way," agreed Ruth. "But if Mr. Caracass hadn't been so hard on us in money matters, you know, you wouldn't have troubled to go on with the story. You did it so as to be able to make me a present of it, Aunt Marian, you know you did!"

"Well," began Miss Phipps in an acquiescing tone.

"So it wasn't just luck," said Ruth. "It was that wicked man's own fault." She nodded righteously.

"There's a verse in the Bible as tells what it was," said Mrs. Hoyle with a chuckle. "*He that diggeth a pit shall fall into it*. Eh," concluded Mrs. Hoyle, beaming. "That's lovely, that one is!"

"You're right as usual, Mrs. Hoyle," agreed Miss Phipps.

A TELEGRAM FOR MISS PHIPPS

The telephone bell rang. Miss Phipps, leaving the hero of the story she was writing in mid-air as he fell from a mill chimney, uttered a savage imprecation and snatched up the receiver. "Hullo!" she barked, furious at the interruption.

"Miss Marian Phipps?" said a pleasant female voice briskly. "This is Messrs. Bookey and Bookey."

Miss Phipps's countenance underwent a lightning change, for Bookey and Bookey were her own publishers. Delightful thoughts of Book Society choices, wonderful reviews, reprints, and fresh commissions coursed through her mind, wiping the frown from her brow with the magic touch of hope.

"Yes?" she purred expectantly.

"This is Mr. Richard Bookey's secretary. We have a telegram for you. Would you like to take it down?"

"Uh — yes," said Miss Phipps, perplexed but still hopeful.

"The telegram runs as follows," said the pleasant voice: "*Charles died this morning funeral Applesham Wednesday eleven thirty Cissie.*"

Miss Phipps gulped.

"Should I read it again?" said the pleasant voice without any hint of impatience — Miss Phipps was one of Bookeys' "valued" detective authors.

"Do," said Miss Phipps.

The pleasant voice read the message again, carefully spelling all the names. "Have you got that satisfactorily now?"

"Look, my dear," said Miss Phipps. "How was this telegram addressed?"

"*Marian Phipps, care of Bookey and Bookey, London, W.C.2.* Handed in at Charing Cross, London, W.C.2. at 1:30 this afternoon. Would you like me to send it along to you by post?"

"Yes, please."

"I'll see to it at once, Miss Phipps. Goodbye."

"No, wait. I should like to speak to Mr. Richard Bookey, please."

"He's in conference at the moment, Miss Phipps."

"Then interrupt him."

The owner of the pleasant voice sighed, but obediently made the desired connection.

"Hullo, hullo, Marian! What do you want, my dear? I'm desperately busy this afternoon with my autumn list, not a moment to spare, three men hanging on my lightest word, please speak as quickly as you can, wouldn't a letter do instead? Yes, write me a nice long letter," urged Richard Bookey. His voice and mode of speech were quite inimitable, and Miss Phipps felt assured that she was in fact talking with the Richard Bookey she knew. "*The Mouse and the Lion* is going quite nicely. Nothing phenomenal, you know, but a good steady sale. Your next one coming along nicely, eh? Delivery date fixed yet? The end of October would give us nice time for the spring list. Has my girl told you about that telegram for you?" continued the publisher, suddenly infusing a suitable solemnity into his tone. "Hope it hasn't upset you too much? Not a near relative, I trust?"

"I never heard of any of them in my life," said Miss Phipps grimly.

"Eh? What?"

"I don't know Charles, Cissie, or Applesham."

There was a pause.

"That's a bit odd," said Mr. Bookey thoughtfully, for his bonhomous surface concealed an immense shrewdness. "There must be some mistake."

"Richard, you might get the post office to repeat and confirm all the names," suggested Miss Phipps.

"My dear, the girl's done that already. She's a conscientious sort of lass. New broom, you know. Energetic sweeper. Look, it must be some sort of hoax. You'd better take the telegram to the police. Or to your lawyer. Don't on any account go to Applesham — if there is such a place. You stay quietly at home and get on with your book. Remember, you promised it to us for the end of October."

"I did nothing of the kind, Richard," snapped Miss Phipps, banging down the receiver.

"The weather is certainly ideal for a country excursion," murmured Miss Phipps to herself on Wednesday as she drove along the winding roads which seemed to surround the village of Applesham.

She was entirely right. The sun shone, the sky was blue, the trees had that entrancing fresh green of early summer; the lilac and laburnum were in full bloom, the wide verges of the Southshire roads were gay with wild flowers, the grass in the gently sloping fields was deep and lush, and the brown and white cows swished their tails happily. Only Miss Phipps herself was out of harmony with the bright soft morning, for she was clad in mourning garments of a rather heavy style. All possible respect should be paid, she had decided, to Charles — whoever he was — and the natural grief of the unknown Cissie should also be properly deferred to.

Applesham, when at last she reached it, was one of those sweet little places which provide an epitome of English history. There was a Norman castle, in ruins; a Norman church, very little restored; a plain early Victorian vicarage fronted by a smooth lawn, a cedar tree, and a border of pink sweet williams and white canterbury bells; there was a wide main street with grass at the sides, a few tiny shops, some thatched cottages, and standing a little back from the road in a neglected lawn, a heavenly Queen Anne brick manor house in very bad repair. There was also the White Hart Inn, with a stone engraved 1443 over the door, which did not seem inclined to give Miss Phipps morning coffee, though a painted sign outside indicated its willingness to do so.

"Well, if you care to come into the lounge and wait, madam," said an old waitress with cheeks like a wrinkled apple, who emerged from a rear door when Miss Phipps rang the bell by the reception office, "I'll see what I can do. But we're all upset today, you see. Mrs. Carton said to me this morning, 'Tabitha,' she said, 'I don't know whether I'm on my head or my heels today.' "

"Ah," said Miss Phipps in a sympathetic tone. "The funeral."

"Yes." At this point Tabitha seemed for the first time to notice Miss Phipps's somber clothes. "You've come to attend? You knew him in London perhaps?"

Miss Phipps bowed her head silently.

"Poor Mr. Charles. It's a shame," said the old woman. "But perhaps you don't think so?"

She spoke with indignation, and Miss Phipps became aware of the difficulties of trying to pump people for information — one was far more likely, she discovered, to be pumped oneself. (Now if her friend Detective-Inspector Tarrant were there, he would know how to handle the matter properly.) Tabitha was gazing at her interrogatively.

"Ah," said Miss Phipps again, shaking her head in a manner to indicate that her thoughts about Charles were too deep for words.

"Do you believe it? What they say about him, I mean?" pressed the old woman.

"Not altogether," said Miss Phipps carefully.

"I daresay you're right," said Tabitha, nodding. "Things might look different if all had their due. I can't believe it of the young lady, either, can you? Though with such a husband, you could hardly wonder, perhaps?"

Acutely uncomfortable, afraid to say a wrong word that might damage some innocent person's reputation, Miss Phipps sought refuge in looking ostentatiously at the grandfather clock and comparing its time with that of her watch, which hung on her chest from a gold brooch in the form of a ribbon bow. This action luckily had the effect she desired — of sending Tabitha off in a hurry toward the kitchen to fetch her coffee.

During the waitress' absence, Miss Phipps examined the lounge. But she found nothing there of interest. It had been "done up" and was agreeably clad in chintz and lupins, with glossy country magazines scattered here and there on tables and settees. When Tabitha returned, Miss Phipps paid for the coffee at once and made a great show of being in a hurry, drinking the liquid almost scalding hot to escape any further questioning.

As she left the inn, Miss Phipps glanced up at the board above the door in search of the name of the licensee. *Hannah Carton*, she read. Well, that was neither Charles nor Cissie. Though in another sense it might possibly be Cissie, reflected Miss Phipps guiltily. Perhaps she ought to have — but how could one possibly explain such a matter to one's publisher? He was the last person in the world to understand a literary point of that kind, decided Miss Phipps, approaching the beautiful old church across the green.

The door stood open, and official-looking persons in black ties hovered around in the Norman porch. Miss Phipps observed that they looked more sincerely regretful than such persons often do at funerals. She entered, and choosing an obscure side pew knelt, and prayed that if these unknowns, Charles and Cissie, needed her she might not fail them in their need. Then she sat down and waited.

It was very quiet and peaceful in the little church, with the summer breeze wandering in through the open door and gently stirring the old banners hanging from the walls. Miss Phipps was not bored. There was plenty to look at near at hand: brass plates and stone plaques and even a tomb with the effigy of a Norman knight and his lady, all to the honor of the de Coulcy family — or rather, the name was de Coulcy at first, but had become Coulcy by the time generals died in the Crimea under Queen Victoria and second lieutenants perished in the 1914 war. Was Charles a Coulcy?

"Probably," decided Miss Phipps. "Lived in that decaying manor house, I shouldn't wonder. Poor. Several sets of death duties in the last two wars have nearly wiped out the estate. I still don't see what he had to do with me, however."

But now the church bell began to toll, footsteps sounded outside, and the organ began to play. Miss Phipps, looking about her, perceived that while she had been reflecting on the Coulcy misfortunes, a considerable number of persons had entered the church. They were of all kinds — "gentle and simple," reflected Miss Phipps. Proud of her power of observing character, she amused herself by picking out the doctor, the lawyer, the tenant farmers, the "county" friends from a distance with their respective daughters, the sisters and wives, and the inevitable pewfuls of middle-aged spinsters of the parish, clinging to each other and rather in a twitter. A large hot elderly woman puffed in at the last moment who was almost certainly Hannah Carton, since she was accompanied by the wrinkled Tabitha. All these had arranged themselves, with that natural decorum so characteristic of the English, in descending order of their acquaintance with the deceased, leaving a great swath of empty pews in the front for the accommodation of the relatives.

The Vicar, old, lean, silvery, sad, came out of the vestry and walked down the aisle; then, pronouncing solemn and beautiful sentences, he turned and led the cortège towards the altar. Miss Phipps observed it all keenly.

The coffin was handsome, the flowers superb.

The chief mourner was a tall fair good-looking young man of military bearing, who walked alone looking thoroughly miserable. Next came a thin, stooping scholarly man with a sweet-faced elderly lady at his side; both had aquiline, distinguished faces and agreeably silvered hair. The same lean handsome face — no doubt a Coulcy heritage — was to be seen on the man of the next couple, who was tall, dark-haired, fortyish, and very much alive, with a large expressive mouth and sparkling dark brown eyes; his wife, as tall and handsome as himself, was clearly expecting a child very shortly, but carried this off with calm assurance and the aid of a good dressmaker.

"What a lovely girl!" thought Miss Phipps in admiration as the next couple passed by.

Indeed she was exquisite: small, fair, slender, very young, with immense gray eyes and a dazzling complexion, beautifully dressed and groomed. She walked steadily, held her head up, kept her face still, but there was no mistaking the fact that she was struck to the heart with grief. Beside her walked a much older man, tall, fleshy and sallow — good-looking enough if you liked that slightly gross, self-satisfied, dominating style.

"I don't," decided Miss Phipps.

All these mourners went without hesitation to the front pew; the others — a mass of second cousins and aunts, decided Miss Phipps, dismissing them after a shrewd look — milled about, politely yielding precedence to each other, and at last sorted themselves out and sat down.

Miss Phipps had never in her life seen a single one of those present in the church — that is, not before today.

"Forasmuch as it hath pleased Almighty God of His great mercy to take unto himself the soul of our dear brother Charles Ranulf here departed," began the Vicar.

"Ah, it's Charles all right," reflected Miss Phipps.

Presently the Vicar delivered a little address. It was not his custom on such occasions, he explained, but today he felt impelled to do so. Charles, it seemed, had shown splendid courage in the recent war; he was generous, loyal, friendly, honorable, of great prowess in all manly sports, and very much beloved; his faults, which he himself would be the first to admit, sprang from the excess of his good qualities.

"Wine, women, and song, I suppose," thought Miss Phipps, sighing. "I wonder how old he was and how he died?"

The service ended; the Vicar led the way to the graveside. Miss Phipps followed and concealed herself behind a nearby marble slab. At that terrible moment, always so cruel to those who really care, when the handful of dust rattles upon the lid of the coffin, the beautiful girl could not restrain a sorrowful exclamation. The tall man took her arm in his grasp — a very strong grasp, thought Miss Phipps, watching it all from the rear, if it were meant to support and console her.

The chief mourners now withdrew, but the rest seemed inclined to linger, examining the wreaths and discussing the deceased. But, the decorum of the occasion preventing gossip, Miss Phipps could learn little more of Charles than the Vicar had already told her. Not relishing the prospect of another interview with Tabitha, she withdrew to the next village for lunch, and returned later in the afternoon to investigate privately.

Yes, Charles was a Coulcy. Aged thirty-nine. There were very handsome wreaths from Captain Gerard Coulcy, Mr. and Mrs. Stephen Coulcy, Dr. Everard and Miss Hermione Coulcy, Sir Richard and Lady Quinberry, Canon and the Misses Bingham; these from their position close by the open grave were obviously regarded as coming from those nearest to the deceased. There were wreaths too from Charles's old regiment, from all kinds of groups and associations in county and town, from "his old nurse Hannah Carton," from friends galore. There were no flowers from anyone called Cissie, or Cecilia, or any cognate appellation. But in a corner there lay a bunch of fine yellow roses — "what is known as a spray, I believe," reflected Miss Phipps — which bore no card, no name.

"That's from Cissie," thought Miss Phipps.

She climbed into her car thoughtfully. She was no nearer to understanding the mystery of the telegram than when she had first come to Applesham, but somehow she now felt deeply involved and pledged to its solution. She liked Charles, grieved for the beautiful girl, disliked the sallow bossy man, felt troubled for the unknown Cissie.

She drove down the wide village street and was about to turn right to return to London when suddenly she saw that the left arm of the signpost announced *Brittlesea 16 miles*. Now Brittlesea was the home of Detective-Inspector Tarrant, in whose cases she had often been associated. On a sudden impulse she swung the wheel to the left.

That a crash did not result was due chiefly to the excellent driving of the young woman in the large dark green van just turning the corner, but partly to Miss Phipps's own capacity for keeping her head. There was an alarming moment when the van and Miss Phipps's little car appeared to be charging each other head on, then Miss Phipps wrenched her wheel, the van driver wrenched her wheel, Miss Phipps found her hat in one hedge and the van young woman found hers in the other. They dismounted and examined their respective vehicles — Miss Phipps in the carefree spirit of an owner whose car has been scratched before, the van young woman in some anxiety.

"Are you marked at all?" called Miss Phipps cheerfully.

"I don't know yet," snapped the young woman.

She bent over the rear fender. Miss Phipps approached her.

"No. It's not marked, thank goodness. I beg your pardon for sounding so bad-tempered, but you see the van's the property of the Southshire County Council, and you know what these public bodies are."

"I do indeed. The affair was entirely my fault and I apologize," said Miss Phipps. "I changed my mind suddenly and decided to go to Brittlesea instead of London."

She laughed. After a moment, when the girl looked disapprovingly at her from beneath raised eyebrows, the girl laughed too.

"Pleasant girl," thought Miss Phipps. "Modern type. Educated. Speaks well. Stands straight. Thick dark hair. Good brown eyes. Cotton frock and sandals, cheap but tasteful. Lady. Virtuous. Salt of earth. Worried."

"Are you by any chance Miss Marian Phipps?" said the van girl.

Miss Phipps colored with pleasure.

"Now how did you know that?"

"Oh, it's not too difficult," said the girl airily.

She moved round to the back of the van and pulled a lever. The doors swung open. Miss Phipps gave a cry of delighted surprise. The van was lined with shelves of books, and on a tiny table lay boxes of index cards.

"Why, it's a traveling library!" she exclaimed.

"Yes. County Council Mobile Library Service. We visit the outlying villages. Here's your latest detective book, you see."

She picked up the brightly jacketed *The Mouse and the Lion* and turned it over, so that Miss Phipps saw her own bespectacled countenance smirking up at her from the back flap of the wrapper. Not for the first time she indulged the wistful hope that she looked less idiotic in real life than in her photographs.

"It's in good demand," said the library girl.

"Do tell me about your work," said Miss Phipps. "I'm really interested."

The library girl began to describe her routine in an offhand way, but perceiving from Miss Phipps' questions that her interest was genuine, warmed up and revealed her real enthusiasm. Miss Phipps adored anything to do with libraries. Accordingly, it was several minutes later when they were roused from an absorbing talk by the sound of violent hooting, and looking out from the back of the van they saw that their vehicles were impeding the progress of a young man in a jeep with a netted trailer full of pigs. They parted hurriedly and Miss Phipps drove away.

"I am not exactly a fool, my dear Bob," said Miss Phipps to Detective-Inspector Tarrant. Remembering the photograph on her book jacket she added hurriedly, "However much of one I may appear."

The Inspector gave a deprecating cough.

"And therefore I can guess why Cissie sent me that telegram."

"Can you indeed?" said the Inspector, somewhat startled.

"Yes. By the way, my dear boy," said Miss Phipps in a casual tone, "have you read my latest novel yet?"

"Oh — no. Not yet," admitted the Inspector, coloring. "Mary has," he added, looking across at his young American wife, who had just come downstairs from putting the baby to bed. "Haven't you, dear?"

"Yes, indeed. I'm one of Miss Phipps's most enthusiastic fans," said Mary. "I thought *The Mouse and the Lion* was one of your best, Miss Phipps. It was so neat the way that insignificant little typist Cissie said the word which started unraveling the whole mystery."

"Cissie?" said the Inspector, really startled now.

"Yes. The person who sent the telegram inviting me to Charles Coulcy's funeral took the name of a character in my own book — the character who started the investigation of the murder."

"Oh, come, Miss Phipps," said the Inspector uneasily.

"Obviously the person who sent me the telegram did so because she thought Charles Coulcy was murdered. She is the insignificant little person in the background who gives the warning which eventually will catch the murderer."

"Oh, come, come!"

"She relied on my intelligence to perceive this, and," said Miss Phipps, beaming over her pince-nez, "I shall not fail her."

There was an awkward silence.

"But Miss Phipps," objected Mary, "in your book it was an old woman who was murdered by poison by her grandson — the circumstances aren't in the least the same."

"No, no, of course not," said Miss Phipps impatiently. "Only the character of Cissie, and her role in the tragedy, are the same."

"But why should she appeal to *you*? Why not inform the police? And why not use her real name?"

"My dear Mary," said Miss Phipps. "It's such a pleasure to talk to you — you always pierce through the cluttering detail to the essentials of a problem. The answer to all three of your questions is the same: *she is too close to the murderer*. So, from the shelter of anonymity, she sets me on the trail."

There was another silence.

"Look, Miss Phipps," said Tarrant at length, in a soothing tone. "I don't want to be unkind or to offend you, you know, but I must state my honest opinion. All that stuff about Cissie is so far-fetched as to be quite preposterous."

"You think so? That's a very helpful observation, Bob," said Miss Phipps thoughtfully.

"How so?" said the Inspector, puzzled.

"To me the Cissie theory isn't preposterous at all. To you it is. Therefore, to my kind of person it isn't preposterous, to your kind it is. Therefore, Cissie is *my* kind of person — that is, a writer, or a keen reader, somebody in some way familiar with books. Now, that's very helpful, Bob — it narrows the field, which otherwise would be distressingly wide."

"Isn't that a little — I mean, will so many people have read —"

"You think I'm exaggerating the size of my public? You forget the mobile library, Bob. Anyone in the whole of East Southshire could have read *The Mouse and the Lion*."

"But surely you don't seriously think Charles Coulcy was murdered?"

"He fell from the balcony of the London house of that highly publicized financier Sir Richard Quinberry while drunk. See the *Southshire Gazette* for last Saturday. There is some scandal about a young lady and Charles in London. See Tabitha of the White Hart Inn. Cissie asks a detective novelist — who is known, by the way, to have solved real cases — to come and investigate. I think that's enough to rouse suspicion, don't you?"

"No," said Tarrant bluntly. "Don't you see, Miss Phipps, the whole thing's a mare's-nest? A mistake made by some telegraph clerk in the Charing Cross post office. The address of one telegram has accidentally been put on the contents of another. Somewhere there is a Coulcy relation who received no telegram about Charles's funeral because the telegram meant for him went to you. And somewhere somebody is furious because you have not replied to the telegram he sent you, because you never received it."

"In that case," inquired Miss Phipps blandly, "who is Cissie?"

"Of course she must be a Coulcy, or connected with the family."

"There's no Cissie or Cecilia or any similar name in the Coulcy family tree," said Miss Phipps.

"A pet name," grunted Tarrant.

Miss Phipps picked up her notebook and read out emphatically: "Captain Gerard Coulcy, seconded to War Office, younger brother and heir to Charles, unmarried. Dr. Everard Coulcy, uncle to Charles, Master of Southstone College, Oxbridge, unmarried. Sister Hermione Coulcy lives with him. Stephen Coulcy, cousin to Charles, barrister, married to Ruth, with issue Stephen, Henry, Philip — and another one coming," she added. "You'll have some difficulty in finding a Cissie amongst those names, Bob."

Tarrant snorted. "A secretary or housekeeper," he suggested.

"Secretaries or housekeepers don't allude to their employers by their first name only and sign by their own first names only, in solemn telegrams," said Miss Phipps.

"You've got something there, Miss Phipps," agreed Mary.

"On the other hand, I don't see a Cissie of *your* kind amongst that crowd," said Tarrant crossly. "Barristers and Masters of Colleges and Captains in the Guards don't send telegrams to unknown novelists — to novelists they don't know, I mean," Tarrant corrected himself hastily — "signed by the name of a fictitious character in the novelist's latest detective story."

"You're quite right, Bob," said Miss Phipps without resentment. "To discover the identity of Cissie is likely to be a difficult task. I take it I have to do it without your aid?"

"I'm afraid so," said Tarrant.

"How will you begin, Miss Phipps dear?" asked Mary solicitously.

"Bob has unintentionally furnished me with an excellent plan," beamed Miss Phipps.

"I am not quite clear what you wish to ask me, Miss — uh — Phipps," said the barrister, Mr. Stephen Coulcy, in his full mellow tones, "and I am afraid I cannot give you very much time — I am due in court in half an hour. So if you would be as explicit as possible, I should be grateful. The message on your card mentioned a telegram and the Coulcy family."

"Yes. I received a telegram addressed to me and purporting to come from someone named Cissie, informing me of Mr. Charles Coulcy's death and inviting me to his funeral. *Charles died this morning funeral Applesham Wednesday eleven thirty Cissie.* As I was not acquainted with Charles Coulcy, I thought there must be some mistake."

"Good Lord, yes!" said the barrister, staring. "That must have given you a considerable shock. Didn't you know Charles at all, then?"

"No."

"He was one of the most lovable fellows I ever knew," said Mr. Coulcy emphatically. "However — Cissie, you say? A curious set of mistakes on the part of our great G.P.O.! Address and sender belong to one party, you; message belongs to another party, presumably some Coulcy."

"No — Cissie is unknown to me."

"Well, she's certainly unknown to *me*," said Mr. Coulcy. "There's no Cissie in the Coulcy family — or even among our friends and acquaintances. But perhaps the name was a misprint, a misinterpretation? Cissie, Coulcy — same number of letters. A not impossible confusion? What do you think?"

"The name was checked. You, yourself, then," went on Miss Phipps, "have not received some telegram mysterious to you, which might have been intended for me?"

"Certainly not at home — and not to my knowledge here in chambers. But I'll ask my clerk."

He pressed a bell on his desk and asked for the clerk to come to him.

"You can understand," pursued Miss Phipps, "that I am anxious to find this missing telegram addressed to me."

"Of course."

"I am rather disturbed lest I am losing some royalties by its non-delivery."

"Royalties? I can see, Miss Phipps," said Mr. Coulcy, bending towards her genially, "that I ought to know who you are and what you do. But I don't, you know. Will you forgive me and enlighten my ignorance?"

"You don't read detective stories, then?" said Miss Phipps. "I write them."

"I never read anything but briefs, nowadays," smiled the barrister.

"I congratulate you on the size of your practice. And your wife?"

"Ruth? She's a musician, you know. Piano. In her spare time — when she has any. Children keep her busy. Never reads fiction."

"That takes care of her, then. But in any case," reflected Miss Phipps, "Ruth, as I remember her in Applesham Church, would never regard herself as Cissie."

"If I may advise you, Miss Phipps," continued the barrister, resuming a formal courtesy. "I suggest you take this matter to the police. They could probably make the Post Office show the original form on which the telegram was written. On the back would be found the name and address of the sender. You could then get in touch with that sender."

"Thank you," said Miss Phipps. "That's very helpful."

"I myself," continued the barrister, "neither sent nor received a telegram concerning my cousin's death or funeral. His younger brother, Gerard, telephoned me late at night from Salisbury Plain, where he was engaged on War Office business and informed me that Charles had fallen from the balcony of Sir Richard Quinberry's house and was lying seriously injured in the Thameside Hospital. I went there immediately and remained through the night, and was joined there by Gerard as soon as he could reach London. But poor

Charles was unconscious and died the next morning. I was in touch with young Gerard all the time. I mention this because, so far as I can see, only one person could properly have sent a telegram in such terms as you describe — namely, my cousin Gerard — and only one person could properly have had such a telegram addressed to him — namely, my uncle, Dr. Everard Coulcy of Southstone College, Oxbridge. You could perhaps ask them. But in my opinion the police are best able to handle your problem. Ah, here comes Mr. Sitherside, who will give you a definite answer to your question about mysterious telegrams here. I'm afraid I myself must now leave you."

Mr. Sitherside, small, neat, dried-up, with very shrewd blue eyes, listened with his head on one side to Miss Phipps's explanation, and replied, "We have received no telegram which was not perfectly comprehensible to us."

"Do you read detective stories, Mr. Sitherside?" inquired Miss Phipps impishly.

She fled away from the clerk's look of horror in such discomfiture that she almost fell down the uneven stone stairs of the old legal Inn.

"Your best plan," said one of the agreeable young ladies behind the Charing Cross Post Office counter, "is to telephone from one of the boxes over there. Of course you have to pay for the service, you know."

Miss Phipps did the necessary dialing, explaining, and inserting of coins.

"*Marian Phipps, Bookey and Bookey, London, W.C. 2,*" read the voice from Enquiries. "That the one?" She read out the whole telegram.

"Yes. I want the name and address of the sender from the back of the telegram, please."

"The sender's name is: A. Cissie," read the girl. She spelled it letter by letter. "The address is Applesham."

"Thank you," said Miss Phipps.

"That all you want to know?"

"That's all."

It was a warm, sunny day, but Miss Phipps felt a chill down the back of her neck as she left the telephone box. So Bob Tarrant thought her idea about Cissie preposterous! Well, well . . .

"But we are delighted to see you, my dear Miss Phipps," said Dr. Everard Coulcy, the Master of Southstone. "Delighted to have the opportunity of meeting one who has given my sister and myself so many hours of pleasure. I read your detective stories aloud to my sister while she embroiders."

"Tapestry," put in Miss Hermione, raising her head from a very fine example of that kind of work.

"We enjoy them because they are exercises in pure ratiocination," continued the Master.

"No foolish thrills," said his sister, returning to her work.

"We found *The Mouse and the Lion* particularly good. The various threads of the mystery resembled a hopelessly entangled net, yet when the young typist said the key word, she pulled on the one thread that made the whole series of events and motives come out straight and clear. What was her name, Hermione?"

"Cissie," said Hermione. "And the key word was *string*."

Miss Phipps started. Hermione raised her eyes. Miss Phipps stared full into them; they met her gaze calmly, clear and untroubled.

"However, this is not to the point," continued Dr. Coulcy. "I regret very much that we are not able to help you, Miss Phipps. We have received no telegram which might have been intended for you. Indeed the news of poor Charles's accident and subsequent death came to us not by telegram but by telephone. Sir Richard Quinberry, in whose house the unfortunate accident occurred, telephoned us that night after the ambulance had taken poor Charles away, and my nephew Gerard telephoned us on the following morning after Charles's death. Poor Charles never regained consciousness after the fall, you know."

"I don't know why you keep saying *poor* Charles, Everard," said his sister with sudden asperity.

"My dear, in spite of all his faults, I was very much attached to him, and he was a young man, with half his life yet to live."

"But very little to live for. The girl to whom he was engaged was killed by a flying bomb in the war," said Hermione, addressing Miss Phipps. "And he had recently decided that the Manor House would have to be sold to keep the Applesham estate solvent. What had he left for which he cared? He was slipping into habits of unworthy dissipation. When I last saw him, at Christmas, I was shocked by the change in his appearance and personality. His fatal fall was perhaps a merciful dispensation of Providence."

"He had Gerard to care for, and Gerard cared greatly for him. He might have pulled himself up and even married somebody else. But these family affairs cannot interest Miss Phipps, my dear," said Dr. Coulcy. "I am truly sorry we cannot be of service in your search for the missing telegram, Miss Phipps. If you will accompany me to my study, I will instruct my secretary to look again through all my recent correspondence, but I fear the result will be negative."

Dr. Coulcy's secretary, a rather tousled but mild and erudite gentleman who declared himself personally unacquainted with Mr. Charles Coulcy, confirmed this verdict.

"Dear, dear! I wish we could have helped you. But meanwhile, Miss Phipps, my sister and I hope you will stay to tea?"

"Thank you very much. Are these family portraits?" asked Miss Phipps, gazing in awe at the walls of the stately corridor as they returned to the drawing-room.

"No, no. Just previous Masters," explained Dr. Coulcy. "A long tradition." He began to recount their names, dates, and histories with great precision; his memory could certainly be relied upon.

"And you *sent* no telegram about Mr. Coulcy's death?" Miss Phipps slipped into the stream.

"No, no. I had no occasion to do so, since Gerard and Stephen already knew of it. Now this Master," said Dr. Coulcy with relish, "must have been a very odd old boy, because . . ."

"I must try the non-literary ones next, I suppose," thought Miss Phipps with a sigh. "Still, one learns a little here and a little there."

Mrs. Hannah Carton had told Miss Phipps the whole history of Charles Coulcy's birth, infancy, teething, childhood, boyhood, schooldays, war service, and the tragic loss of his fiancée, and had now reached the present decade. Born in the north of England, she had accompanied Charles's mother to Applesham on her marriage, and brought up the two boys, Charles and the much younger Gerard, till her own marriage to the Coulcy butler; then with Carton's sister, the parlormaid Tabitha, they had left the Coulcy service and took over the White Hart Inn.

"So you see, love, his death is a great grief to me," said the good old woman with tears in her large brown eyes. "The manner of it too! Falling drunk off a balcony! What would Lady Honoria have said to that? Poor Mr. Charles! He's never been the same since he lost poor Miss Bingham."

"Ah, Miss Bingham," said Miss Phipps, vaguely remembering a wreath which bore that name.

"Yes, love — Miss Caroline Bingham, the eldest of the Vicar's girls. Handsome she was — oh, yes, handsome and spirited — it was a treat to see her on a horse. The Vicar's youngest, now, Miss Elizabeth — her that's Lady Quinberry — some say she's very beautiful, but she isn't a patch on Miss Caroline, not a patch, I tell you straight. Miss Bingham was in the Army in the war — the A.T.S. or the W.A.A.C.'s or whatever they were called — very high up she was at headquarters in London, and she was in St. James's Church that Sunday morning when it got a direct hit. Yes, killed outright. Poor Mr. Charles! Poor Miss Caroline! A fine young lady if ever there was one! Straight as a die! It's no use telling me," said Mrs. Carton on a peevish note, "that Miss Elizabeth's a patch on her, because she isn't. Throwing Mr. Gerard over the way she did, for that Sir Richard Quinberry who is old enough to be her father! Some say it was just a lovers' tiff, but I say it was because that Sir Richard had a couple of million pounds. Pity Mr. Charles ever invited him down here. Miss Elizabeth has always been spoilt, that's what I say, with her mother dying when she was born and her elder sisters making such a fuss of her. I grant you she's the only fair one and pretty enough like a doll on a Christmas tree, but she's not a patch on Miss Caroline. That's why I can't believe it — I just can't *believe* it — when they say Mr. Charles has been running after Lady Quinberry up in London."

She looked in anxious question at Miss Phipps, who replied firmly, "I shouldn't believe it for a moment if I were you."

Mrs. Carton's honest face beamed with relief.

"There now! Didn't I say so to Tabby? It isn't likely he would, is it? After Miss Caroline. And with Miss Elizabeth, Lady Quinberry I should say, having been his brother's girl and all. He was much too fond of Mr. Gerard to do any such thing — he always looked after Mr. Gerard, him being so much younger. But it's been said about in the village, Miss Phipps — it has indeed! They've been seen in London — dining together, you know. And then to fall off Sir Richard's balcony, drunk! Whatever would Lady Honoria have said? As for telegrams, I didn't send any nor yet receive any, Miss Phipps. The Vicar himself came across and told me about Mr. Charles, Miss Georgiana being off as usual like, with her van."

"With her van?" exclaimed Miss Phipps.

"Her library van, you know," said Mrs. Carton. "Young ladies all work nowadays, you know, times not being what they were, Miss Phipps. Of course the Vicar is a Canon now and I daresay that helps, but Miss Georgiana and —"

At this moment the clock struck, the bar had to be opened, and Miss Phipps took the opportunity to escape.

It was an action she was to regret.

"My father," said Georgiana Bingham firmly, sitting very erect on one of the broken-springed Vicarage armchairs; "is writing a commentary on the Book of Job, and this is one of the very few hours when he is at leisure to devote himself to it. I really don't want to disturb him, and I assure you that all business matters in this house go through my hands."

"I'm sure they do — and very capable hands too," thought Miss Phipps, observing them as they lay, slim and brown, in their owner's lap, and remembering their swift accurate wrench on the van's wheel.

Aloud she said, "If you could just assure me that you neither sent nor received a telegram about Mr. Charles Coulcy's death, then I could pursue my researches elsewhere."

"We neither sent nor received any telegram about Mr. Charles Coulcy's death," said Georgiana Bingham steadily.

Miss Phipps was staggered. She could not believe that this girl with the honest eyes, the erect carriage, the good plain face, the vicarage background of faded chintz and Sunday School classes and early service, would lie.

And yet! Surely she *must* be Cissie? Everything fitted: her appearance, her character, the position of her home so near the Manor House, her sister's marriage, her access to *The Mouse and the Lion*.

"When I met you the other day in the van," began Miss Phipps.

"You didn't mention this telegram affair to me then," said Georgiana sternly.

"I didn't know who you were, then," countered Miss Phipps.

Georgiana's face cleared. "No, of course you didn't — how stupid of me! I beg your pardon," she said.

"When I met you and you showed me your delightful mobile library," began Miss Phipps again, "there was a copy of my latest novel, *The Mouse and the Lion*, lying on the desk."

"Yes."

"Forgive me — excuse me — I dislike this inquiry very much," panted Miss Phipps, "but it is essential. Have you read *The Mouse and the Lion?*"

"No," said Georgiana.

"What?" gasped Miss Phipps. "No?"

Georgiana shook her head.

"Word of honor?"

"Word of honor. It must sound very rude of me," said Georgiana, coloring. "I'm truly sorry. But you see archeology is my real subject, and my library work gives me all too little time for it. So you see —"

"I see perfectly," said Miss Phipps. "So you don't know Cissie?"

"I'm afraid I don't."

"Oh, Lord," cried Miss Phipps in great distress. "That really knocks me flat! Bob Tarrant must be right after all. Unless of course the Quinberrys —"

Georgiana Bingham frowned.

"Miss Phipps," she said earnestly, leaning forward, "is it really so important to you to find this missing telegram?"

"Well, it might be, you see," said Miss Phipps feebly.

"Because if it is not — I should be rather glad," said Georgiana carefully, "if my sister need not be troubled in the matter."

"She was much distressed at the funeral, I noticed," said Miss Phipps, recovering a little.

Georgiana scowled.

"If you have heard any gossip about my sister and Mr. Charles Coulcy, you should disregard it as totally mistaken," she said sternly. "Mr. Coulcy and my sister had, it is true, met each other frequently of late, but it was to discuss a matter of business."

"Oh, my dear, I know all about it," said Miss Phipps in a gush of sympathy. "Elizabeth, who hasn't a very strong character, had a tiff with Gerard, who was too high-minded to ask her to marry him because the estate's in a mess and he has no money. Sir Richard caught her on the rebound. She's wretched with him and weeps out her wretchedness to Gerard. Gerard confided this, as he confided everything, to Charles. Charles, who was devoted to his brother and had a good deal of influence with your father, tried to find some way of making that beastly Quinberry give Elizabeth a divorce so that she can marry Gerard. Then Charles broke his neck and there seems no hope for poor Elizabeth. Isn't all that true?"

"One thing at least is true," said Georgiana, and her eyes were bright and hard. "Sir Richard Quinberry is a beast of the first water — a loathsome, sensual, cruel, clever devil."

"Yes, I could see you were worried about your sister. It strikes me as odd, you know," said Miss Phipps more calmly, "that when Charles fell, Sir Richard telephoned Captain Gerard Coulcy on Salisbury Plain and Dr. Everard Coulcy in Oxbridge, but did not telephone Mr. Stephen Coulcy who is on the spot in London. Stephen did not hear of the accident until Gerard telephoned him. The result was a delay before Charles was seen by any of his relatives, and by the time he was seen, he was quite unconscious, and never spoke again. His silence was convenient."

"Miss Phipps, don't go to see my sister!" exclaimed Georgiana. "Richard will worm it all out of her, and be furious. When he is vexed for any reason, he makes Elizabeth suffer for it. Please don't go!" Georgiana was pleading and Miss Phipps forced herself to be stern.

"I must. You see, my dear," said Miss Phipps, shaking her head, "you haven't read *The Mouse and the Lion*. You're not Cissie. I can't give up my quest until I've found Cissie. Cissie has something important to tell me about Charles's death — I feel certain of that. I *must* find Cissie."

"Though who on earth Cissie can be," she reflected as she drove rapidly back to London and Sir Richard Quinberry's elegant Mayfair address, "I simply cannot imagine. Unless it's Elizabeth Quinberry. If so, she must have more intelligence than all the others give her credit for."

By the time Miss Phipps reached London the summer twilight was falling; by the time she drew her little car up in front of Sir Richard's house, a white crescent of moon was riding in the darkening sky. It was absurdly late to make a call, and the butler who answered the door clearly took this view. But Miss Phipps, though she always looked an odd old trout — she had heard a young thing call her this once, and retained the memory as a salutary self-discipline — could on occasion produce an air of convincing authority. She produced it now; the man admitted her, showed her to a handsome drawing-room on the first floor, and went in search of Lady Quinberry.

"How do people still manage to have money like this?" wondered Miss Phipps, looking about her. "Can it be acquired honestly nowadays?"

The long high room, painted throughout in clear white, was furnished with some beautiful examples of Chippendale. The upholstery was white; a superb jar of early Wedgwood Queensware held masses of gorgeous blue and orange "Bird of Paradise" flowers against the wall. One pair of the long French windows stood open.

"Ah, the balcony!" said Miss Phipps, advancing towards it.

The balcony had an ironwork railing of an agreeable pattern, painted pale green. It was not a high railing, but neither was it particularly low.

"I don't quite see how anyone could fall over it," thought Miss Phipps grimly, "even if drunk. Charles was a tall powerful fellow, too, to judge from the size of his coffin. The best way, I suppose, would be to make him trip and then seize his back leg and heave."

She stood on the balcony, her hands on the railing, and looked down. Below lay a small plot of garden, fringed by trees. It was, certainly, a small garden compared with those of the Manor House and the Vicarage at Applesham, but Miss Phipps, who knew that the ground rents of Mayfair houses were fabulously high, registered the existence of any garden at all as one more indication of Sir Richard's wealth. The garden was quiet and secluded, and edged all round by an asphalt path.

"Convenient," reflected Miss Phipps.

Behind her a door opened. She slipped back into the room.

"Poor little Elizabeth! Poor young thing!" thought Miss Phipps in heartfelt sympathy.

At first sight her pity seemed uncalled for. In a striking full-skirted dress of rustling white — "one of those new materials," reflected Miss Phipps — Lady Quinberry looked even more beautiful than in the elegant black suit she had worn at the funeral. The lovely lines of her throat and arms, the dazzling purity of her complexion, the gleam of her wonderful pale gold hair, were enough to make any girl proudly happy. Diamonds sparkled in her charming ears and in a magnificent bracelet round her slender wrist. But her eyes were dull with anguish.

She smiled — the troubled, pleading smile of a little girl afraid of a scolding — and held out her hand.

"I'm afraid I didn't quite understand what you wanted? My sister knows you, of course."

"So Georgiana telephoned!" thought Miss Phipps, a little surprised.

"I'm afraid I haven't read any of your books," continued Lady Quinberry in her sweet wistful tones. "I don't seem to have much time for reading."

Miss Phipps had met this excuse a thousand times before. Her usual tart reply rose to her lips: "We can always find time to do what we want." But she repressed it — the child looked so very forlorn. As for sending Miss Phipps a telegram under the name of one of Miss Phipps's characters, poor Elizabeth might just possibly have read *The Mouse and the Lion* and be lying about it, but she simply wouldn't have had the brain to work out such a plan. She wasn't the telegraphing Cissie.

"It was just that a telegram addressed to me became mixed with a telegram concerning the death of Mr. Charles Coulcy," explained Miss Phipps in her kindest tones. "I am trying to find my telegram."

"Charles?" exclaimed Lady Quinberry. "He's dead, you know."

"What is this about Charles?" said an angry voice.

Lady Quinberry started aside, and her husband was revealed behind her.

"What is this about Charles?" repeated Sir Richard, advancing into the room.

"Sir Richard Quinberry? My name is Phipps —"

"A telegram about Charles's death," fluttered Elizabeth, interrupting her.

"What?" barked Sir Richard. "What is the meaning of this? Who is this person? What has she to do with Charles? Is this an attempt at blackmail, madam?"

"Certainly not!" exclaimed Miss Phipps, turning scarlet. "I have lost a telegram addressed to me, and —"

"Leave us, Elizabeth," commanded Sir Richard, turning to his wife.

"Catherine knows her, Robert," faltered Elizabeth.

("Catherine? Who in the world is Catherine?" marveled Miss Phipps.)

"Leave us!"

Poor Lady Quinberry gave Miss Phipps a deprecating smile, then, hanging her head, went out of the room. Her pale gold hair fell on each side of her perfect face. "She really is exceptionally lovely, poor child," thought Miss Phipps.

In watching her, Miss Phipps had forgotten Sir Richard, whom she now discovered to be towering close beside her. He looked well in his admirably tailored dinner jacket, and appeared taller and more powerful than in the Applesham church — there was muscle beneath the smooth black cloth. His face however had the sagging flesh, the fatigued color, and the deep telltale lines, of the roué, and Miss Phipps disliked him heartily.

"And now kindly explain yourself."

"I received a telegram about Mr. Charles Coulcy's death —"

"From whom?"

"I have no idea."

"What! Nonsense! It was Gerard Coulcy who sent you here," said Sir Richard in a low tone of fury. "Admit it, you come from Gerard."

"No."

"Yes, Gerard sent you," repeated Sir Richard. "He sent you to my wife. You think there was something strange about Charles's death — is that what it is? Is that it?" he shouted suddenly.

His yellow eyes blazed with a strange wild fire, and Miss Phipps thought, "The man is mad."

"You came to investigate? That is right? Look," said Sir Richard, seizing her arm in an iron grasp and impelling her towards the open window. "I will show you exactly how Charles's death happened. Then you can tell Gerard, and Gerard can tell my wife."

"The man's mad with jealousy," decided Miss Phipps. "He loves that child and knows she loves Gerard."

She found that she was on the balcony. Sir Richard swung her towards the railing. She was like a stuffed doll in his powerful hands.

"Charles tripped — he stumbled," said Sir Richard, his tone now smooth, his yellow eyes gleaming. "The effect was like so." He kicked her right ankle sharply. Miss Phipps involuntarily withdrew it and was left standing on one foot. Sir Richard then stooped. He seized her left ankle, he heaved, he threw.

Miss Phipps plunged over the railing.

Her glasses fell off. She grabbed at the ironwork and managed to secure a hold. Sir Richard kicked at her knuckles. Miss Phipps, wishing she weighed less, hung on grimly. Sir Richard tried to kick her, but fortunately the pattern of the ironwork was too close to let his foot through. It was all most unpleasant. With an exclamation Sir Richard rushed away into the drawing-room.

"Help!" shouted Miss Phipps at the top of her voice. "Though it's no use calling for help to that sweet silly Elizabeth," she thought, and on an impulse she screamed, "Catherine! Catherine!"

Sir Richard came back with a footstool in his hands. He leaned over the railing, the footstool raised high, and prepared to smash it down on Miss Phipps's head. Miss Phipps, looking up into his frenzied face, could not decide whether to let go her hold and fall, or hang on and wait for the blow from the footstool; but an instinctive tenacity caused her to clutch the railing tightly.

Then suddenly another face appeared beside Sir Richard's distorted mask. It was a perplexing face, reflected Miss Phipps, for it was like the face of Georgiana Bingham and yet not quite like it. It resembled Georgiana's in feature, in coloring, in intelligence, in honest plainness, in troubled integrity; but this face was urban where Georgiana's was rural. It was made up with cosmetics, and had a sophisticated haircut, and its owner, though quietly and inexpensively dressed, wore an essentially London black frock, utterly unlike Georgiana's country prints.

("I suppose," thought Miss Phipps in a dream, "that this is Catherine, that at long last this is Cissie.")

"Leave her alone, Richard!" cried this newcomer strongly, laying her hand on the madman's shoulder.

Sir Richard shook it off and turned on her with a savage snarl. The action threw him off balance, and with an awful cry he staggered, then fell over the railing, and the footstool and Miss Phipps fell with him.

Miss Phipps, however, fell on top and was unhurt save for a few bruises. Sir Richard, underneath and horribly entangled with the legs of the footstool, had broken his neck and was dead.

The police had at last gone, knowing all that Miss Phipps knew about the Quinberry-Coulcy case except her real motive for tracking down the telegram, which she thought it unnecessary to mention. She now rested on a white settee in the Quinberry drawing-room, bandaged in various portions of her person. Elizabeth was in bed upstairs, after a sedative administered by the Quinberry family doctor. Catherine sat beside Miss Phipps, pouring out coffee.

"Don't tell me," said Miss Phipps, accepting a second cup. "Let me work it out for myself. You're another of the Bingham sisters."

"Yes. There were four of us. We used to say, jokingly, that there were two Binghams with beauty, and two with brains."

"The eldest and the youngest, Caroline and Elizabeth, were the beauties."

"Yes. They resembled my mother, you see."

"You and Georgiana take after your father and have the brains."

"Something like that."

"I ought to have deduced a fourth sister," said Miss Phipps, shaking her head.

"I don't see how."

"My dear, I should have remembered the wreath. The card said: *Canon and the Misses Bingham*. Misses. Plural. But Elizabeth, being married, was no longer Miss Bingham, and Caroline was dead, so there must have been another Miss Bingham beside Georgiana. I believe Hannah Carton was just going to mention you, too, now I come to think of it," said Miss Phipps thoughtfully. "Miss Georgiana and Miss Catherine both work for their living, she was about to say, when the bar opened and I stupidly fled." She took a sip of coffee and asked diffidently, "So you are Cissie?"

"Yes."

"And you sent me the telegram?"

"Yes."

"But I had it fixed in my mind that the anonymous spray of yellow roses had been sent by Cissie," said Miss Phipps.

"You were quite right. I wanted to send a tribute of my own, apart from the wreath I shared with father and Georgiana. You see, I always loved Charles Coulcy," said Catherine Bingham quietly. "He never took any notice of me, of course — he never had eyes for anyone but Caroline. I didn't grudge him to her, because she deserved him. But I couldn't bear that devil Richard Quinberry killing Charles and getting away with it. I was in the house that night — I had a standing invitation to dine here, because Richard thought I acted as a kind of chaperon to Elizabeth against Gerard."

"You were in the house and heard Charles fall?"

"Yes. He wasn't drunk. He was made to trip over a string — I'm sure of it. Elizabeth and I rushed into the room when we heard the crash, and I saw Richard putting a neat coil of string into his pocket. But can you imagine what he would have done to Elizabeth if I had spoken of the string to the police?"

"I can indeed," said Miss Phipps fervently. "And you had just been reading *The Mouse and the Lion* and saw yourself as Cissie?"

"I was very familiar with the book," said Catherine after a slight hesitation. "I had even written letters about it."

"Are you a regular reader of my work, or was it just an isolated chance which led you to *The Mouse?*" purred Miss Phipps, deliciously flattered.

"Miss Phipps, you still haven't *quite* worked it all out," said Catherine. "Didn't my voice sound at all familiar to you when you heard it on the balcony this evening?"

"As a matter of fact it did," admitted Miss Phipps. "But I attributed that to its family resemblance with your sisters' voices. Have I ever heard your voice before?"

"Yes."

"Where? Tell me quickly," urged Miss Phipps. "Don't let me burst with curiosity.

"I'm Mr. Richard Bookey's new secretary," said Catherine Bingham.

MISS PHIPPS GOES TO SCHOOL

"Diddle diddle dumpling, my son John," sang Mary Tarrant happily, "went to bed with one shoe on."

Young Master John Tarrant, agreeably clad in his own charming birthday suit and held firmly round the waist by his mother's loving hands, laughed and crowed and stamped gleefully about her knee. Miss Phipps watched smiling from a nearby chair.

"My darling," whispered Mary fondly, kissing him. "Well, I guess I'd better go and make that coffee. Mrs. Brooke did say she'd call for you at eleven, didn't she, Miss Phipps?" She laid her son down on her lap and began what appeared to the detective novelist the impossible task of inserting his waving arms and legs into various small garments.

"Yes, at eleven," agreed Miss Phipps, looking at her watch. "Let's hope she'll be late. I don't want to tear myself away from your offspring's antics."

"Yes, isn't he precious? Such a piece of luck, your being invited to lecture at Star Isle College, Miss Phipps," said Mary. "I was so anxious for you to see the baby as he is now. He changes almost every week, you know."

"My dear, I only accepted the engagement because it gave me the chance of visiting you in Brittlesea *en route*," said Miss Phipps truthfully. "Boys' boarding schools, however well-known and reputable, are not really in my line."

"But Star Isle is really a very fine school," said Mary, clasping a safety pin. "John says so. The buildings have all been modernized, and they have a beautiful beach. The new Headmaster, Dr. Brooke, is very progressive and energetic, and his wife is young and intelligent, and she coaches the boys in drama. And the Brookes have a baby about the same age as Johnny," concluded Mary triumphantly, offering this last fact as a supreme token of the Brookes' desirability.

It occurred to Miss Phipps to wonder whether Detective-Inspector Tarrant had ever been over to Star Isle College in his professional capacity, and if so, why; but knowing his discretion on all matters connected with his work, she forebore to put the question, and just then the doorbell rang. Mary placed the baby on the settee, wedging him in with cushions, then went to answer it. Miss Phipps, shy but determined, crossed over to the settee and did a little baby worship on her own, and was rewarded by having one finger tightly clasped in a delicious miniature fist. She was thus in a good position to observe the look which young Mrs. Brooke turned on the baby when she entered the room. This look startled, even shocked Miss Phipps, for it was one of fear and anguish.

Introductions were performed. Mrs. Brooke's hand trembled in Miss Phipps's clasp.

"I'll just slip out and fetch the coffee," said Mary.

"No! No, thank you," said Mrs. Brooke hastily. "It's most kind of you, Mrs. Tarrant, but I'm afraid I really can't stay. The ferry across to the island, you know, has only limited service on Saturday mornings. We shall just have time to catch the 11:30 boat if we leave now."

"But couldn't you stay and catch the next boat?" urged Mary.

"I'm afraid it's impossible," said Mrs. Brooke.

She spoke with so much authority and decision that there was nothing to do but obey, although Mary was upset by the rejection of her hospitality and Miss Phipps was grieved on Mary's account. Miss Phipps's overnight bag was hastily thrown into the back of Mrs. Brooke's car, Miss Phipps herself was hustled into her coat and almost thrust into the front seat, farewells were curtailed, Mrs. Brooke took the wheel, and they were off for Star Isle.

During the next twenty minutes Miss Phipps, observing her companion with the shrewd eye of a novelist and listening with a novelist's ear, discovered that Mrs. Brooke was tall, slender, dark, neat, dressed in good tweeds, intelligent, a University graduate, and a skillful driver. But she wore an angry frown down the center of her forehead, and snatched every advantage on the road which offered itself. Her story about the ferry was clearly not a mere snobbish excuse to refuse Marys' hospitality; she was obviously motivated by some painful urgency.

The ferryboat—no doubt a landing-craft from wartime days, reflected Miss Phipps—was at the pier with its blunt bows open and lowered when they arrived. Mrs. Brooke jumped the queue of waiting cars and drove up to the boat, at which the attendant seaman and policeman gaped in astonishment. She made no comment on her action to the sailor who collected her ticket, although he gazed at her reproachfully. As the ferry waddled slowly along the winding course marked out by numerous posts and buoys, she tapped her foot impatiently.

"A sandy coast?" said Miss Phipps politely, merely making conversation.

"Yes—with quicksands here and there. Very treacherous."

"Is it like that all around the island?"

"Oh, no! To the south, by the College, we have cliffs and bays."

"Is it far from the harbor to the College?"

"About four miles," said Mrs. Brooke. Her foot kept tapping, and her hands clenched themselves about the wheel of the car.

Miss Phipps was so affected by this impatience that whereas ordinarily she would have much enjoyed the process of disembarkation—the throwing and securing of lines, the dignified lowering of the stern, the parade of foot passengers along a gangway surrendering tickets, the laying of planks for the car's wheels, and the bumpy ticklish drive from ship to shore, solemnly superintended by an elderly policeman—today she found it almost unbearably slow and tedious. Once they were on land, however, they flew along the russet autumn lanes, rushed through the old stone gateway of the College, and drew up sharply with a squeal of brakes in the gravel circle in front of the Headmaster's residence. Mrs. Brooke leaped out and ran up the shallow steps to a handsome cream perambulator with a fringed awning, which stood on the terrace beside the door. Bending over this she lifted out a sleeping infant, then returned to Miss Phipps with the baby in her arms and the frown quite gone from her face, which now looked very young and yearning.

"Will you come in? They'll fetch your bag later," she said, and led her guest into a large, pleasant sitting room with French windows

on two sides, one set overlooking the terrace with the baby carriage, the other, on the opposite wall, having an agreeable view of
beach, cliff, and sea to the right, with the long row of gray College
buildings on the left.

Miss Phipps sat down, feeling a trifle ruffled. A middle-aged
woman with bluish hair, a rather superior expression, and dressed
in white, was arranging a large tray of glasses and sherry on a
table nearby; it appeared that a rush of masters, invited to meet the
great lecturer, was imminent. The older woman was introduced to
Miss Phipps as Miss Bellivant, the College housekeeper.

"I've read one or two of your books, Miss Phipps," said
Miss Bellivant in a condescending tone. "Just as light reading, at
night."

"I hope you enjoyed them," said Miss Phipps, commending
herself for keeping her temper.

"Oh, yes, quite. Other people enjoy them too—I can't seem
to keep them on my shelves," said the housekeeper in a rather
puzzled fashion. "They keep disappearing."

"I do beg your pardon, Miss Phipps," said Mrs. Brooke when
Miss Bellivant had gone, and still rocking her sleeping child gently
in her arms, "for rushing you along like this. It was unforgivable.
And that sweet Mrs. Tarrant. I'm afraid I was rude to her—I am
most truly sorry. But you see—I was so anxious about Tommy."

"Why?" said Miss Phipps bluntly.

"Leaving him alone," said Mrs. Brooke, hanging her head.

"But surely you have plenty of staff here," objected Miss Phipps,
"to keep an eye on him?"

"Yes, in a way. But—oh, well, a young mother, you know," said
Mrs. Brooke, laughing falsely. "One gets these fancies."

"What fancies?" said Miss Phipps. Mrs. Brooke was silent. "What
kind of fancies?" pressed Miss Phipps. "You're too intelligent, too
well-educated, to indulge in groundless fancies, I'm sure," she
continued. "You feared some danger for the child?"

"It was so strange," began Mrs. Brooke hesitantly. "Such a
mysterious little incident." She stopped. "I'm ashamed to trouble
you with it."

"What did your husband say when you told him of the incident?" inquired Miss Phipps.

"Henry? He laughed. But I think he was worried. He's rather worried about a good many things just now," said Mrs. Brooke.

There were occasions when Miss Phipps, usually the mildest and most modest of women, found it useful to play the celebrated novelist. She did so now.

"My dear," she said in the commanding resonant tone which she used to impress fans at literary cocktail parties, "you had better tell me all about it. I have had a good deal of experience in solving these small mysteries, both as a detective novelist and as an occasional assistant to the police. Confide in me. You may trust in my discretion absolutely."

"Well," said Mrs. Brooke, still hesitating; then she plunged: "It was like this. It sounds so silly, but really it was strange. Last Sunday morning I'd just put the baby in his pram on the terrace. I was upstairs in our bedroom, putting on my hat and coat, meaning to slip late into Chapel. I heard the baby begin to cry. I looked out and saw that he had thrown his rattle out of his pram."

"They often do that," said Miss Phipps, nodding her head wisely. "Throw things away and then want the discarded objects back again. Just like adults."

"So I ran downstairs and out to the terrace," Mrs. Brooke went on, "and the rattle was in his pram."

"*In* his pram?" exclaimed Miss Phipps stupidly.

Mrs. Brooke nodded. "Lying on the coverlet."

"But somebody must have put it there!"

"Agreed. But who? All the boys, the teaching staff, the secretarial staff, Miss Bellivant, and several of the masters' wives—everybody, in fact—were in Chapel. We have our own College chapel, you know. We had the Bishop of Southshire over here that morning, as a matter of fact, and he's a very good preacher, so everybody was there."

"One of the domestic staff?"

"We have no domestic staff of our own; nowadays all that work is done by the College domestic staff."

"Then one of them?"

"Miss Phipps," said Mrs. Brooke very earnestly, "believe me, it was *nobody*. I've asked *everybody*. After all, it was kind action; nobody need be ashamed to own up to it, need they? But nobody admits to having put the rattle back in the pram."

"My dear," said Miss Phipps in her most soothing tone, "don't be vexed with me when I tell you I really think you are making a mountain out of a molehill. The postman passed by, perhaps—oh, no, not on a Sunday. The milkman—no, not by your private front-entrance. Well, somebody," concluded Miss Phipps pettishly. "It's a very small matter, after all."

"Not when taken in conjunction with other small matters which have been happening here," said Mrs. Brooke. "There seems a jinx on the school this term. And Henry cares so much, you know. Everything was going so well—till now."

"What other small matters?" demanded Miss Phipps.

"Here we are, my dear," said Henry Brooke, entering the room with a flock of masters behind him.

He was one of the new type of Headmasters, Miss Phipps observed with interest—short, slight, fair, utterly unpompous, but with a dynamic energy informing his whole personality. His gray eyes were shrewd and bright.

"Ah, Miss Phipps," said he, shaking hands.

His tone was courteous but noncommittal; it was clear to Miss Phipps that his judgment on his visiting lecturer was as yet suspended.

"And why not?" thought Miss Phipps honestly. "He knows nothing of me as yet."

She exerted herself to make intelligent conversation.

"My dear boy," said old Mr. Pryce in mild, sad, mellifluous tones. "My dear Deighton, if you would only understand that I am not reproaching you in the least for upsetting the pile of reports. It's the easiest thing in the world to do, especially as my desk stands under the common-room window. I entirely acquit you of any desire to wound or annoy me."

"But, Mr. Pryce," began young Mr. Deighton, who was short and gingery, wore a pullover stained with chemicals, and spoke with a decidedly less well modulated accent, "I give you my word—"

"I am well aware," Mr. Pryce flowed on, his long gray mustaches quivering with wounded feeling, "that to young scientific men like yourself, classics masters are mere useless survivals, a sort of dinosaur. I have no quarrel with that attitude. I understand well how it can be so. I do not complain. Also, I appreciate your desire for fresh air. Young people like open windows; they do not suffer from draughts as we old fogeys are apt to do. In opening the common-room window, you dislodged the pile of my half-term house reports, which, no doubt in complete conformity with some law of dynamics familiar to you, fell to the ground in hideous confusion. They had been carefully alphabeticized in order of the boys' names; this order was destroyed by the fall and some forty minutes were required to restore it. But what of that? Such an accident might happen to anyone," said Mr. Pryce with noble acceptance. "I do not claim exemption from misfortune. But—"

"Another glass of sherry, Pryce?" put in Henry Brooke, proffering the decanter.

"Thank you, Headmaster. I am aware that you are trying to divert me from a painful subject," said Mr. Pryce. "But your sherry is good and your thought a kind one, tee-hee!" He laughed gently and held out his glass, his innocent old eyes beaming. "So I accept with gratitude."

"He's rather a pet, after all," thought Miss Phipps, who from her place beside Mrs. Brooke on the settee was watching the uncomfortable little scene.

"But, Mr. Pryce, I assure you I did *not* upset your pile of reports," said young Deighton in a tone of greatly suppressed exasperation. "I never went near your desk. And I didn't open the window."

"It was open when I entered the common-room," said Mr. Pryce with a mild, meditative air. "It is your lack of trust in my good fellowship which grieves me, Deighton. Have I proved myself so harsh a colleague that you cannot confess to me a small peccadillo, an accidental injury? That wounds me, my dear boy, wounds me deeply. I had not thought that my younger colleagues held me in such dread."

"Mr. Pryce, I don't hold you in any dread. I feel for you only respect and affection!" shouted young Deighton. "But I didn't knock over your reports!"

"Well—let us dismiss the matter. Let us forget it," said Mr. Pryce sadly. His sadness was genuine, Miss Phipps noted; the gleam in his old eyes faded, his mustaches drooped. "I raise my glass to you, Deighton. I drink to you and Science."

"Mr. Pryce," began Deighton in a high shrill voice, which reminded Miss Phipps of steam escaping from an overcharged boiler, "I—"

Henry Brooke laid a hand on his arm, and the young man turned away, crimson with rage.

"But wouldn't it be better *not* to forget the incident? To probe it to the core?" said Miss Phipps boldly, rising and going toward the group.

On all their faces, as they turned to her, she read that male expression of distaste which means "Women!" Nevertheless, she persevered. She liked kind old Pryce, able Brooke, and struggling young Deighton; she wished them all well, and in her opinion the truth is the best gift one can wish for anyone.

"Such little mysteries, at first sight inexplicable, are my stock in trade as a detective story writer," she went on blandly. "Could I have the details of this one, please?"

"My dear madam," said old Mr. Pryce, bowing courteously, "I shall of course be most happy to serve you in any way. Without troubling you with the details of our routine, let me give you the essential facts. Yesterday morning during a free period just after break, I was working on a pile of reports in the common-room. I was alone in the room. The window was shut. I left the room, for a few moments only, to go out to ring a certain bell. As I went out, I encountered Mr. Deighton coming in. As I returned, I met Mr. Deighton coming along the passage from the common-room, which is, so to say, situated in a cul-de-sac. I entered the common-room and found my reports scattered over the floor, and the window slightly open."

"Perhaps the draught from the window scattered the reports?" suggested Miss Phipps.

"A substantial paperweight rested on them," said Mr. Pryce with his air of serious musing.

"And now you, Mr. Deighton," said Miss Phipps in a friendly tone.

"Well—I don't know anything about his reports, though I don't suppose you'll believe it," snapped Deighton in his brash, aggressive manner. "I went into the common-room to fetch a dictionary from the shelves. It took me a minute or two to find it. I found it and left with it in my hand. I met Mr. Pryce in the corridor. That's all."

"Were the reports on the floor when you left the room?"

"No. Emphatically, no."

"Was the window open?"

"I don't know. I think not, but I couldn't swear to it. At any rate, I never went near the window."

"Perhaps you banged the door, and the vibration upset the reports?"

"I don't bang doors, even if I didn't go to Oxford or Cambridge," cried Deighton angrily. "And on my word of honor I never touched Mr. Pryce's reports."

"An interesting little problem," said Miss Phipps in her blandest tone. Apart from the possibility that one of the two men was mistaken, she had not the faintest idea of any solution, but she did not intend to let the staff of Star Isle College know this. "It is these everyday *minutiæ* which offer the greatest scope for keen ratiocination," she continued.

The Headmaster gave her a shrewd look.

"And what would you suggest," he began in a quizzical tone, when suddenly to Miss Phipps's relief the sound of an immense bell clanged long and loud through the air. "Ah, lunch. On Saturdays we lunch in hall with the boys," said the Headmaster. "Are you coming, Ella?"

His wife shook her head. "I'll stay with the baby," she said nervously.

The Headmaster was not pleased, but accepted her refusal with an urbane little bow, then ushered Miss Phipps out of the seaview windows. He took her at a smart pace along a path, under an archway, up some steps, across a huge kitchen—where Miss Bellivant amid rows of steel cookers and enameled refrigerators directed a scurrying crowd of white-coated girls—and through a pair of swing doors.

"Short cut," he said briskly as they emerged on a dais by a long refectory table.

Miss Phipps nodded, too breathless to speak. The other masters streamed in their wake. Evidently punctuality was *de rigueur* at Star Isle College.

In the large dining hall, however, there was a long pause. Something, thought Miss Phipps, glancing down from the dais to the long rows of boys standing silent and attentive by the tables on which dishes already steamed, seemed to have gone wrong. The other masters did not look in the direction of Dr. Brooke, who stood silent and motionless, his face carefully blank. Then suddenly in the gallery at the far end of the hall appeared an older lad with a silver badge in his buttonhole. He was crimson and breathless, but managed to utter a Latin grace without stumbling. At its conclusion the school sat down and fell to, and several silver-badged lads sitting on the opposite side of the high table from Miss Phipps passed her meat, vegetables, and gravy with great politeness. Dr. Brooke's brow remained frowning, however, and he did not speak.

The lad from the balcony now appeared at the Headmaster's elbow.

"Well, Crawford," said Dr. Brooke in a chilling headmasterly tone.

"I must apologize, sir, for being so late," said Crawford, who was still somewhat breathless. "I was working in the library, and my watch disappeared."

"Disappeared, Crawford?" said the Headmaster with a tinge of irony.

"Yes, sir. I was taking notes at the table at the far end, and I'd laid my watch in front of me so as not to be late. Then I went up the iron stairs into the gallery, sir, to look for an old issue of *Nature*, and when I came down, my watch was gone. I was still busy hunting for it when the luncheon bell rang. I ran all the way, sir."

"Very well, very well," said the Headmaster in a forgiving tone. "Sit down and eat your lunch. Miss Phipps, this is F. X. Crawford, our head prefect," he went on as the lad went round the table and seated himself opposite Miss Phipps. "Scholarship boy. Native of the island. Captain of football. Mathematician. Going up to Cambridge when he's done his national service—just won a place."

Miss Phipps bent her writer's eye on the lad. He was strongly built, with broad shoulders, a pleasantly plain face, straight dark hair, and highly intelligent brown eyes. Not wishing to keep him from his meal she contented herself with a smile at the introduction, and did not speak until after the first course.

"It must be agreeable to have such a fine swimming beach so near the school," she said then.

"Yes. It's actually part of the school grounds," said Crawford in a friendly tone. "The beach and the cliff on the left, that is. But the cliff is out of bounds except with a master. There's a cave there which is rather dangerous—it has an inner chamber with a very low entrance; you can get cut off in there at high water."

"And how is the swimming arranged?" pursued Miss Phipps. "By house or class?"

"By class."

"I suppose you prefects," said Miss Phipps, smiling at the row of silver badges opposite her, "are allowed to swim whenever you're free."

"Oh, no!" said Crawford. "The rules are very strict—"

"Never less than three boys are allowed to be in the water together," boomed the Headmaster in her ear. "And to become a three-swimmer, as we call them, a boy has to pass very severe swimming tests. We have a swimming pool as well, you know. He has to do two lengths of the pool, two breadths underwater, and a life-saving test."

"And are you a three-swimmer?" inquired Miss Phipps of Crawford.

"Only this term—I've never had time before to work up for the tests," said the lad without embarrassment.

"Life is real, life is earnest, for those who want to reach scholarship standard in mathematics," said the Headmaster. "Isn't that so, Crawford?"

"It is indeed, sir," said Crawford, laughing.

"However, there are compensations. Football match this afternoon," continued the Headmaster.

"Yes. It's strange about my watch, sir, isn't it?" said the boy.

"We'll have a word about that this evening, Crawford," said the Headmaster, dismissing the subject.

"Yes sir," agreed Crawford readily.

"Star Isle! Star Isle!" shouted Miss Phipps encouragingly. "Well passed, sir! Good heavens, what a fumble! Look out, Star Isle! Oh—" her voice changed to satisfaction—"Crawford's got it. A very reliable player, Crawford," she added in her normal tone, turning to the Headmaster.

Muffled to the eyebrows, she sat between the Headmaster and his wife, watching the football match. The Brooke baby lay asleep in his pram behind the white-painted seat. The College buildings provided shelter on the sea side of the field, but the other sides were open to the briskly blowing breeze.

"Crawford," said the Headmaster with emphasis, "is very reliable in any activity he undertakes. A strong, steady character. Humble circumstances at home, you know. Excellent head prefect. Very much respected. Good bowler, too. Ah!" he exclaimed.

"He's hurt!" cried Miss Phipps in a tone of anguish.

Indeed, in tackling an opposing forward, Crawford seemed to have suffered an injury, for a group had gathered round him as he lay on the ground. He got to his knees and tried to rise, but bent double again in evident pain.

"Oh, dear!" wailed Miss Phipps.

"Probably just winded," said the Headmaster.

A group of boys wearing First Aid armbands now ran up bearing a stretcher. Crawford waved them impatiently aside and again tried to rise, but again fell to his knees. The First Aid detachment, obviously eager to show their skill, stood no more nonsense from him, but rolled him onto the stretcher and carried him off. The Headmaster laughed.

"Poor Crawford!" he said. "He'll be furious."

"But isn't he hurt?" cried Miss Phipps. "Look, there's an ambulance!"

"Yes. They'll take him off to the Sanatorium for a check-up," said Dr. Brooke. "Being winded can be a trying and painful experience, you know—I've been winded myself in the days when I played scrum-half. But it isn't serious. He'll be all right tomorrow. He'll be the first case in the San this term, won't he, Ella?"

"Yes. So far we've been lucky in that respect," said Mrs. Brooke.

"Where is the San?" enquired Miss Phipps.

"Up there toward the cliff," said Dr. Brooke, pointing.

"Odd about Crawford's watch, wasn't it?" said Miss Phipps.

"Very," said the Headmaster shortly.

The whistle sounded. Star Isle had won handsomely. Miss Phipps walked off the field with Mrs. Brooke, assisting her occasionally with the pram. The Headmaster, accosted by several friends, parents, and well-wishers, fell behind.

At the entrance to the College, Mrs. Brooke and Miss Phipps were met by Miss Bellivant. The housekeeper was in such a state of agitation that for a moment Miss Phipps feared that Crawford was seriously hurt after all, and Mrs. Brooke obviously thought the same, for she quickly spoke his name.

"No, no, he's just winded—he'll be all right tomorrow, they say," said the housekeeper. "It's the ice cream, Mrs. Brooke. I'm sure I'm most terribly sorry—I know how much the boys look forward to it. I'd made it striped with the College colors as a special treat—just for the two competing teams, you know—we do so like to give our visitors a really *good* tea, Miss Phipps. It's all so disappointing, I could cry!" Her face quivered, tears actually came to her eyes, and her usual superior, martyred expression had quite vanished. She looked genuinely distressed.

"I don't quite understand, Miss Bellivant," said Mrs. Brooke soothingly. "Has something gone wrong with the ice cream?"

"Ruined!" exclaimed Miss Bellivant dramatically. "The door of the small refrigerator has been left open, and the ice cream is all melted."

"Who left the door open? Surely it was very careless," said Mrs. Brooke, frowning.

"That's just it, Mrs. Brooke! I can't find out *who* left it open," wailed Miss Bellivant. "It was closed at half-past two when I put the ice cream in—I closed it myself. And all the girls are off duty this afternoon until four. I put the ice cream in, I made sure the door was closed, and I set the freezer," she detailed, performing the movements with her empty hands. "Then I went out to watch some of the match. I left a few minutes before the end and went straight to the fridge. The door wasn't latched and I pulled it open wide and there was all the ice cream completely melted. All the stripes run into each other," she wept, "they look really horrid. I hardly think we shall be able to use the ice cream even after it's frozen again, it looks so horrid! So wasteful, Mrs. Brooke! It seems like carelessness on my part, but really the door *was* closed when I left it—"

Her lamentations continued.

"Miss Bellivant," interrupted Miss Phipps, "have you missed any food from the College kitchens lately?"

Miss Bellivant, tear-stained and disheveled, gazed at her.

"Well, Miss Phipps, when you cater for three hundred boys three meals a day, it's not easy to say whether any food's missing or not," she said. "I mean, what's a bun or two among three hundred? But once or twice I have thought—but I couldn't say for certain. But the ice cream! I'd made it striped in the College colors as a special treat—"

It was some minutes before Miss Phipps could detach herself. She went up to the room that had been assigned to her thoughtfully.

That evening Miss Phipps lectured to the boys on *The History of the Modern Detective Novel*. The lecture proved a huge success, and as Dr. and Mrs. Brooke and Miss Phipps sat together round the fire afterward, sipping coffee, the Headmaster's manner was a good deal more cordial than it had been earlier in the day.

"You know Detective-Inspector Tarrant pretty well, I believe?" he said, passing Miss Phipps the sugar.

"Yes."

"Did he happen to tell you that we recently consulted him at the College?"

"No, he did not," said Miss Phipps.

"But you have helped him on some of his cases, haven't you?"

"When he has asked me, I have offered one or two suggestions," said Miss Phipps in her primmest tone.

"I perceive you are a woman of intelligence and discretion, Miss Phipps," said the Headmaster, smiling.

Miss Phipps bowed her head in acknowledgment, curious to know what the Headmaster wished to confide to her.

"I should be very grateful for your advice," Dr. Brooke went on. "We have had here lately—we have suffered—really if one could credit such nonsense, one might imagine a poltergeist has been at work here."

"I had a case once, in your cathedral city of Starminster, in which an alleged poltergeist figured," said Miss Phipps. "But of course the agency proved to be human—*very* human. But please go on."

"We have had in Star Isle College during the last few weeks a series of curious happenings," said Dr. Brooke, speaking in a quiet, precise way, as though teaching a class constitutional history. "To begin with, there were several thefts."

"Of what?"

"Small sums of money. An odd feature of the thefts was this: the whole of the sum available was never taken. If it was money from the pocket of a boy's coat, only one or two coins would be missing; if it was notes from a master's wallet, again, some notes would always be left."

"As if the thief hoped the theft might not be noticed," said Miss Phipps thoughtfully.

"The same sort of thing happened with sweets and biscuits in the boys' tuck-boxes and lockers," continued the Headmaster. "It was then that I asked Inspector Tarrant's advice. But he couldn't attempt to find the thief, he said, unless I would give him freedom to tackle the boys openly. I was considering this, when the thefts ceased. Then odd things began to happen—"

"The replaced baby's rattle, the upset reports, Crawford's missing watch, the ruined ice cream, for example," said Miss Phipps.

"Yes—and all the contents of our drama wardrobe wicker baskets tumbled about and creased," added Mrs. Brooke.

"It is certainly difficult to reduce such varied incidents to any orderly motivation," said Miss Phipps thoughtfully. "They appear to lack coherence."

"There is *no* sense whatever in the incidents," said the Headmaster warmly. "Stealing money and sweets is detestable, but at least it is understandable. But why upset poor old Pryce's reports? Why ruin the ice cream? Why steal a watch you'd never dare to wear? Even supposing some items of the theatrical wardrobe have been removed, what could a boy do with period clothes?"

"And why pick up, then put back the baby's rattle?" said Mrs. Brooke with a shiver.

"I own that perplexes me particularly," said the Headmaster. "All the other incidents might be attributed to some form of malice—but to do any hanky-panky with a baby's rattle seems—well, I confess I'm disturbed."

"Yes, it is queer," said Miss Phipps slowly. "To get to the truth in this affair, we must distinguish, I believe, between actions which accomplished their object, actions which failed or were left uncompleted, and actions which were merely incidental. Sometimes one can discover the motive for an action quite simply by considering its effect."

"But what effect had the replacement of the rattle, in heaven's name?" said the Headmaster impatiently.

"Ah, I think it didn't have the desired effect," mused Miss Phipps. "It was done too late—it was one of the failures."

The Brookes gazed at her open-mouthed.

"Miss Phipps," said the Headmaster at length, "you alarm me even more."

"I think you have every right to be alarmed," said Miss Phipps gravely. "I believe it would be well to summon Inspector Tarrant at once."

"I'll ring him up immediately," said the Headmaster, starting toward the telephone.

The Brittlesea police station said that Inspector Tarrant was engaged in conference with the Governor of the County Gaol and could not be disturbed, but he would come out to Star Isle first thing next morning.

Miss Phipps wondered if that would not be too late . . .

First thing next morning, Miss Phipps was wakened by Mrs. Brooke, bearing a cup of tea in her hand and a look of disaster on her young face.

"The baby?" queried Miss Phipps in alarm, shooting upright. "Your husband?"

"No. Crawford."

"You don't mean his—or—being winded has taken a serious turn?"

"No. He was perfectly all right when Henry went over to see him late last night. No, it's not that. He's disappeared."

"Disappeared? This is very serious indeed," said Miss Phipps, throwing back the bedclothes. "What clothes has he disappeared in? He had pajamas and bedroom slippers and a dressing gown in the sanatorium, I suppose?"

"Yes. They're all gone. But, oh, Miss Phipps," said young Mrs. Brooke, weeping, "we've found them all on the beach just above high-water mark."

"We must get Inspector Tarrant here at once," said Miss Phipps. "I will dress instantly. How does your husband explain the matter?"

"He thinks Crawford must be responsible for all the strange things which have been happening this term—"

"Nonsense!" exclaimed Miss Phipps with vigor.

"—the poor boy must have had a breakdown from overwork."

"Do you mean you think he has drowned himself?"

"That seems most likely. Or, of course, he may just have decided to take a swim in the middle of the night, being nervously unbalanced."

"Preposterous! A boy who is head prefect, to break one of the strictest rules of the school! I don't believe it," said Miss Phipps. "Besides, my dear, consider. Crawford was in Chapel when the baby's rattle was replaced. He was on the football field when the refrigerator door was opened."

"He could have done the other things," said Mrs. Brooke doubtfully.

"Yes. But not the rattle or the fridge. A problem is not solved unless the solution fits *all* the conditions."

Mrs. Brooke's face cleared a little. "I do so hope you're right," she said. "It would be terrible to have to tell his parents he was a thief. They were so proud of him."

"Let us hope they will continue to be," said Miss Phipps, energetically donning her dressing gown. "The tide is pretty high, I see, but on the ebb."

By the time she was dressed and ready to go downstairs, Inspector Tarrant had arrived from Brittlesea. The large police car, she noticed from the staircase window, was standing in the gravel circle by the Headmaster's terrace, with a plain-clothes constable at the wheel. She entered the sitting room and found Dr. and Mrs. Brooke and Inspector Tarrant in grave consultation, with a sergeant taking notes.

"Dr. Brooke," rapped out Miss Phipps sharply. "Is there a room available which does not look onto your terrace? Your study? Then please let us go there."

The Headmaster colored a little at being thus ordered about in his own school, but said politely, "This way," and led the party along a corridor.

"Meanwhile, John," said Miss Phipps to Inspector Tarrant, "oblige me by summoning your constable indoors on some pretext."

Inspector Tarrant raised his eyebrows.

"Have you some idea about this troubling affair?" he said.

"Yes. It may be wrong, but if it's right, it will be much better for your constable to come in here for a few moments," said Miss Phipps firmly.

Tarrant sent the sergeant on the errand.

"Now," said Miss Phipps when they were all assembled, "as I said just now, my solution to this problem may be completely wrong. But it is worth trying. I write detective stories. One of my methods is to invent a series of strange incidents—at first sight, inexplicable—and then try to think out a set of circumstances which will explain them. That is what I have done here. I set myself to invent something or somebody that will explain *every* strange incident that has happened at Star Isle College."

"And you have succeeded?" inquired the Headmaster, obvious irony in his tone.

"Yes," said Miss Phipps with quiet confidence. "Here is the solution I have deduced. The thefts of food and money are easily explained by the presence of somebody on the College premises who is without resources. He is hiding here. He needs food. He needs money for later on—after he has escaped from the island. He needs a watch, so as to know when he may expect the various classrooms to be empty. He is a man, I think, belonging to a lower income bracket, for he is unaccustomed to refrigerators, he cannot drive a car or manage a boat. He likes the lighter forms of litera-ture to read. He climbs in and out of the masters' common-room, opening the window and upsetting poor old Mr. Pryce's reports, on the chance that the masters have left some coffee over from their elevenses—something to drink during the day," said Miss Phipps thoughtfully, "and even something to drink *from*, may well have been one of his most serious problems."

"Why did he pick up the baby's rattle?" said his wife.

"And why does he stay here?" said the Headmaster.

"How do you know he can't drive a car?" said Tarrant.

"He is a small man," continued Miss Phipps, "and Star Isle is an island."

"For heavens' sake, Miss Phipps!" exclaimed the Headmaster. "Please explain yourself."

"The channel of water between Star Isle and the mainland," said Miss Phipps, "is too deep to wade and too wide for any ordinary man to swim. Moreover, it has dangerous currents, and quicksands near the mainland shore. As I said, it must be postulated that this man cannot manage a boat. *So how is he to get off the island?*"

"How did he get on it in the first place?" asked Tarrant grimly.

"My dear John," said Miss Phipps, delighted. "From the tone of your question I gather that my deductions are not totally wide of the mark. Am I not right?"

"Possibly," said Tarrant. "But please answer my question. How did this man get on the island in the first place?"

"In the luggage compartment of a car, of course," said Miss Phipps triumphantly. "He was a criminal, you see—a prisoner escaping from the County gaol—and being hard-pressed by his pursuers he climbed into the trunk compartment of a temporarily unoccupied car. The car then moved off and came to this island. Imagine the poor little man's horror when he cautiously peeped out, perhaps, and found himself on the ferry! The car brings him to the College. So here he is, with plenty of food in the kitchens, and money to steal for his needs to come—but in moderation, for he doesn't want to excite suspicion while he's here by taking too obviously or too much. Clothes from a heap of old wicker baskets would seem to him unlikely to be missed. He has a handy cave to hide in when it's low tide, and the extensive College buildings to roam in at night. When the tide is high in the daytime, life isn't quite so easy for him; it's dark and damp and eerie in that inner cave, so he has to risk coming ashore in daylight. Naturally he's anxious to get off the island and rejoin his friends. But how is he to get off the island? If he tries the ferryboat, there will be the ticket collectors to face, perhaps even the police. His best chance is to get off *the same way he came on*. So he is continually on the lookout for cars."

"But all this doesn't explain the baby's rattle!" cried Mrs. Brooke.

"Yes, it does, my dear. The Bishop of Southshire preached here that morning, you said."

"Yes, yes."

"He came over in a car—a large car?"

"Yes!"

"He drove himself?"

"No—his young chaplain drove him."

"Same thing from our point of view," said Miss Phipps. "The chaplain attended the service in your Chapel, of course. The car stood unattended in the circle of gravel by your front door. The criminal approached. And then your baby dropped his rattle and began to cry. Now what happens when a baby cries?"

"One goes to the baby, of course," said Mrs. Brooke.

"Exactly. So the criminal puts the rattle back in the pram to stop the baby crying—for crying is bound to bring someone to the pram, and he will be seen. But unfortunately—from his point of view—he is too late! You are already running down the stairs to your baby. The criminal quickly hides himself—it is touch and go, a matter of split seconds—so he has no time to open the trunk compartment."

"Ah!" said Mrs. Brooke with another shudder. "To think of that odious little man being so near to the baby!"

"My dear," said the Headmaster, "remember, this is all mere supposition. And how," he added, turning to Miss Phipps, "does your theory explain the disappearance of poor Crawford?"

Miss Phipps shook her head gravely. "I'm afraid poor Crawford saw the criminal. You see, the Sanatorium has been empty save for the staff, hasn't it? There have been no previous cases this term, you said, Headmaster. The criminal has been accustomed to regard the Sanatorium sickrooms as safe. Crawford saw him there."

"The criminal ran off to the cave," suggested the Headmaster, interested now in spite of himself.

"And young Mr. Crawford followed him," put in Tarrant. "The tide would be at halfway."

"The criminal knocked Crawford out and tied him up there."

"But he knows he has to make a getaway before the next low tide, when Crawford, having recovered consciousness meanwhile, will come back and reveal the criminal's presence."

"So the escaped prisoner may make an attempt in your car, now that it's unobserved," warned Miss Phipps.

"Surely not in a police car," objected Tarrant.

"None of you is in uniform," said Miss Phipps. "He may not notice the small blue police sign. And besides, he is now desperately anxious to get off the island."

"So all we have to do," said Tarrant, smiling, "is to arrest Simthwaite in the trunk compartment of my own car—"

"Simthwaite!" exclaimed the Headmaster. "Who's Simthwaite?"

"He's a petty thief, a kind of cat burglar—he escaped from the Southshire County Gaol a few weeks ago," began Tarrant.

"What!" cried the Headmaster. "Do you really mean there *is* such a man as Miss Phipps describes loose on the premises?"

The men were glaring at each other when suddenly all four of them hurled themselves from the room. Shouts and a high yell in an unfamiliar Cockney voice seemed to indicate that something exciting was taking place outside. The two women ran to the front door.

The trunk compartment of the police car stood open; half in, half out, a chubby, balding little man with the beginning of a fluffy beard, clad in a pair of tight black Victorian trousers and a frogged velvet smoking jacket, was just having handcuffs clasped on him by the sergeant, who had removed a watch from the little thief's wrist to facilitate the operation.

"But what about poor Crawford?" cried Mrs. Brooke. "Has that little brute hurt him?"

"No, no, lady," said the little man earnestly. "I ain't 'urt 'im. Never no violence from Slippery Sim. Just knocked 'im out and left 'im in that inner cave—'e'll be as right as rain when the tide goes down. Shouldn't wonder if 'e ain't hollerin' out there right now. I didn't do no 'arm to your baby neither—just give 'im back 'is rattle. *I* didn't wanter stay in your high-falutin' College, I can tell you. I'll be glad to see the back of it, and that's the truth, lady."

"Allow me to congratulate you, Miss Phipps," said the Headmaster, shaking her hand warmly, "on an admirable piece of ratiocination."

"Elementary, my dear Doctor," said Miss Phipps, smiling brightly.

A MIDSUMMER NIGHT'S CRIME

"I adore Stratford!" exclaimed Miss Phipps, taking her foot off the accelerator as the spire of the church which houses Shakespeare's bones came into sight across the green Warwickshire fields. She reflected joyously on the two tickets for the Shakespeare Memorial Theatre which nestled in her purse. *"Soul of the Age! The applause! delight! the wonder of our stage! My Shakespeare, rise!"* quoted Miss Phipps rapturously, *"Sweet Swan of Avon—"*

At this moment a van drew level with her and prepared to pass. Miss Phipps frowned. It was an insult to her new little Cardinal (in two shades of rose) that she should be passed by a small trades-man's van. Flouting the voice of conscience and the Highway Code, she put her foot down firmly on the accelerator. The Cardinal leaped forward, and Miss Phipps had a swift but compelling view of the driver of the van and his companion.

The driver, who leaned forward to scowl at her, was a roughish type in a turtle-neck sweater of dirty grey, with the largest, ugliest, most peculiarly shaped ears Miss Phipps had ever seen; his companion wore a mauve silk skirt, a rather too decorative tie, and had varnished black hair.

Miss Phipps kept her foot hard down, but the van gained and presently drew level again. For a few uncomfortable seconds the van and the Cardinal rode side by side and Miss Phipps had time to observe the vehicle, which was of a rather unusual kind. It seemed to be a box made of cream-painted boards, on which some biblical texts appeared in large black capitals. *PREPARE YE THE WAY OF THE LORD,* read Miss Phipps. *THE HOUR COMETH. EXCEPT YE REPENT YE SHALL PERISH.*

"A Gospel van!" exclaimed Miss Phipps.

She had heard of these itinerant preachers, but had never met one before. It was not a form of missionary activity which commended itself to Miss Phipps, but she had too much respect for the religion of others to scoff at the van, or to hinder its work by refusing to yield the right of way. She was raising her foot from the Cardinal's accelerator when the van rendered this unnecessary by suddenly shooting ahead.

"Curious," said Miss Phipps.

The back of the van was now presented to her view. Its glossy doors read:

THOU	*BLESSED*
SHALL	*ARE*
DELIVER	*THE*
ME	*MEEK*

"Curiouser," said Miss Phipps.

Then she rebuked herself for her cynicism. One could be truly religious without handsome ears or a knowledge of grammar, and silk shirts were not a crime, particularly in this lovely summer weather.

The van flew round a bend in the road and disappeared, and Miss Phipps drove on to Stratford-upon-Avon.

"I *adore* Stratford," said a pretty, drawling, petted voice of a type which always sent shudders down Miss Phipps' spine because it so often belonged to a discontented person. "I *adore* Stratford, Michael, but I do think this is a most *disgusting* hotel."

"It was you who wanted to come here," said a muffled male voice.

"I can't help it if I don't like it, can I?"

Miss Phipps sighed. Her novelist's psychology had not misled her, she reflected, as she drew the Cardinal carefully into line. Only a very fretful spirit would find fault with the Hathaway Hotel, for it was certainly one of the best in the town.

"Look at this alleged garage space, I ask you," continued the petted voice. "How we're ever going to get *out* of it again, I don't *know*. Oh, and here's *another* car to block us in!"

She turned and scowled at Miss Phipps, who smiled back cheerfully as she got out of her car and locked the doors. Yes, just the type I'd imagined, decided Miss Phipps: fair-haired, pretty, slender, with rather exceptionally good legs, dressed in a charming blue and green summer frock cut very low, but with a face rather too liberally made up; and she was wearing entirely too much costume jewellery (necklets and bracelets) for really good taste. Also, Miss Phipps observed with her novelist's eye, whereas the two young men and the second young woman, a pleasant bright-eyed brunette, were all helping to take the luggage from their old but well-cared-for little car, the blonde girl stood aside and did not lift a finger to help them.

"Spoiled and selfish," reflected Miss Phipps sadly. Aloud she said, "Yes, these old inn yards present quite a parking problem, especially now that modern cars have grown to such a length. I think I've left you space enough, however," she continued, stepping aside to estimate this more accurately.

"Why, it's Miss Phipps!" exclaimed the shorter, plumper, and fairer of the young men, withdrawing his head from the luggage compartment.

Miss Phipps looked affable but interrogative.

"Don't you remember me? But of course you wouldn't. But surely you remember the Laire murder trial? In Northshire, you know? Your niece's husband's partner? You pinned it on him through a member of the Laire Thespians, don't you remember? Our amateur dramatic society, you know. I was doing a production of *Henry V* for them—"

"Tony Harris!" exclaimed Miss Phipps.

"That's right. Ruth, Linda, Michael—this is Miss Marian Phipps. Detective, novelist, and detective-novelist. Sorry—I've introduced you the wrong way round. My sister Linda," continued Tony, indicating the blonde. "Her husband Michael Lynn. Ruth Armstrong. We're all Laire Thespians."

"We're doing *A Midsummer Night's Dream* for our summer show, so we've all come to see the Stratford production," explained Michael.

"Tony's producing, and Linda and I are doing Helena and Hermia," added Ruth.

"How do you do?" concluded the blonde coldly, tilting her pretty little nose in the air.

"She hates anyone but herself to receive any notice," thought Miss Phipps, shaking hands warmly all round. "Poor Michael."

Michael was a kind, honest-looking young man, tallish, with ordinary brown hair and ordinary brown eyes; but that was the trouble—he was too ordinary ever to satisfy the ambitious Linda, and at present his eyes showed unhappiness.

"What about a drink to celebrate our meeting?" suggested Miss Phipps.

This was well received, and they all trooped into the Hathaway by the back entrance, Michael carrying Miss Phipps' luggage and Linda's as well as his own. They then separated to their several rooms after agreeing to meet in the bar at six o'clock prompt—but not before Miss Phipps heard Linda complain, "I don't see *why* we should have such a *wretched* little room when we booked *ages* ago; you must excuse my *saying* this, Michael, but I really *don't.*"

Miss Phipps of course understood the reason perfectly: the Hathaway was an expensive hotel and Michael's resources did not stretch beyond modest accommodations.

The Hathaway, like all other Stratford hotels, served dinner at a quarter past six for the benefit of theatre-goers, and although they had barely a hundred yards to walk, most guests were punctual, for they liked to get to the theatre early—the theatre exercised so great a fascination that nearly everyone wanted to share in its excitement as quickly as possible.

Miss Phipps came down promptly at the dinner hour, and Tony and Ruth followed her very shortly. Michael appeared later, but without Linda. He looked wretched, and chain-smoked three cigarettes without speaking. They drank a round at Miss Phipps' expense, and a round at Tony's; then it was time to dine.

"You'd better go in without us. I'll wait here for Linda," said Michael, looking miserably at his watch.

"Don't make it too late, old man," said Tony.

"I'm not sure whether Linda will come to the play at all," blurted Michael.

"What, after coming all this way to see it?" exclaimed Ruth.

"Is it the same trouble as before?"

"Yes. She seems as if she just can't get over it."

"I'm afraid my sister isn't showing at her best," said Tony, turning to Miss Phipps. "You see, she hoped to play Titania for the Laire Thespians and she hasn't been cast for it."

"And wasn't it a reasonable hope?" said Linda, suddenly swishing up behind them.

She certainly looked extremely pretty and fairy-like in her ethereal white dress, which billowed quite delightfully from her small waist. It was spangled in some way with silver, which her silver shoes agreeably matched. The whole effect was striking, though perhaps a little over-elaborate for an ordinary midweek occasion.

Miss Phipps found herself hoping that Michael's income could stand all this finery, but from the appearance of his car she had a shrewd notion that it couldn't.

"Why can't you be satisfied with Helena, Lindy?" said her brother with some irritation. "It's a longer part."

"Oh, don't be silly, Tony. I *wanted* to play *Titania. Any* casting director but Michael would have cast *me* for it."

"I can't give every leading part in the season to my own wife!" exclaimed Michael in obvious agony.

"I don't know what Miss Phipps will think of your *callous* disregard for my *happiness*, Michael," said Linda.

"*I could not love thee (Dear) so much, Lov'd I not honour more.*" murmured Miss Phipps.

A tide of hot but delicate colour flooded Linda's clear cheeks.

"Please don't let Michael's excessive preoccupation with his very unimportant responsibilities make us ridiculous," she said in a haughty tone.

"Nobody can make one ridiculous but oneself," said Miss Phipps briskly.

Linda gave her a glance of unmitigated hate and led the way into the dining-room.

"Have a drink first, dear," urged Michael.

"No."

"You could take it in with you."

"No!"

Miss Phipps firmly rejected the attempts of the head waiter, who was short of tables, to seat her with the Laire Thespians, and was placed in a corner alone; it might be selfish of her, but she declined to have her evening at Stratford spoiled by Linda. For the same reason she nipped out very quickly after dinner, hoping to avoid the Laire party.

"I adore Stratford!" said Miss Phipps, strolling along happily through the balmy summer air.

Beneath the pink and white chestnuts in full flower, with the river Avon flowing softly, decked by the pure white elegance of swans, a thousand people were making their way eagerly to the great theatre. There were people of all ages, religions, colours, nationalities, from all over the world. Or at least, thought Miss Phipps, shaking her head, from all over the free world. There were Indians in their lovely gauzy saris; there were French, Germans, Italians, Japanese, Malays, Americans, Canadians, Australians, Africans, Spaniards—oh, there was just everybody!

All of them looked happy and excited; all of them were talking about Shakespeare. "This is the fifth time I've seen the *Dream*"—"I'm told the rustics are particularly good"—"The *Observer* critique was rather severe"—"It's the best children's play ever written"—"You see, my dear fellow, it's such an essentially English play; a wood near Athens is all my hat, it's English countryside really"—"Is it a play to be taken seriously? Is there any philosophic significance?"— "No, no, just sit back and enjoy the sheer fun and beauty of the thing"—"I always think this place is the quintessence of the drama."

Miss Phipps, as a novelist enjoying everybody else's enjoyment as well as her own, could have wept for sheer bliss.

Alas, she had not counted on the difference in walking speed between the young and the old—the Laire party caught up with her and it was only by slipping away onto the grass that Miss Phipps avoided them. Even so she heard occasional echoes of their talk, for Linda's high voice carried through the babble of the crowd.

"An *ugly* building—outdated now, quite *old-fashioned* really . . ."

"*Far* too many swans—they're trying to get *rid* of them . . ."

"I *do* think they might do something about these *pebbles* . . ."

"Quite a *cold* breeze . . ."

To Miss Phipps' regret they all reached the great foyer, and queued to buy the huge scarlet programmes, together. Linda was now in the process of delivering a scathing attack on the choice and dating of the five plays to be performed that year.

"It's *impossible* to see *all* the plays in *one* visit unless you stay *forever*," she said. "Why do they so *often* perform the *same* play on *consecutive* nights?"

Michael mildly suggested the problems of staging which such an arrangement might minimize.

"Well, I think it's *too* bad. And what a draught there is in this foyer!"

"You ought to have brought a coat or at least a stole, Linda," suggested the sensible Ruth, looking at the expanse of bare, though undeniably pretty, back which Linda was offering to the evening air, and glad, Miss Phipps thought, of the opportunity to terminate Linda's diatribe, which was attracting unfavourable glances from other members of the queue.

"Yes, I do hope you won't catch cold, darling," said Michael apprehensively. "I wanted you to bring your coat."

Miss Phipps guessed at once that Linda's coat was not equal in chic to her dress.

"Would you like me to slip back to the hotel and fetch it?" went on Michael.

"No."

"It wouldn't take me more than a few minutes," pleaded Michael.

"Don't *fuss* so, Michael!" said Linda crossly.

"You needn't have frozen in your best bib and tucker tonight, Linda," said Tony in a brotherly tone. "*She* won't be here until tomorrow."

"How do you know?" said Linda quickly.

She spoke with real eagerness, forgetting her languid drawl, so that Miss Phipps wondered what woman could have aroused in her such unaffected interest.

"They told me at the reception desk at the Hathaway."

"You might have told *me*," said Linda angrily, with an involuntary glance at her fluffy skirts, which in spite of their modern uncrushability would no doubt lose some of their freshness by being squashed in a theatre seat for several hours.

The five minute bell sounded.

"Well, here we go!" exclaimed Tony.

A smile of excited happiness spread over every face, even Linda's, and the crowd surged forward. The Laire party went up to the dress circle, Miss Phipps noticed, while she had treated herself to an expensive stall.

In the moments before the play began, Miss Phipps discovered on her right two Oriental gentlemen of great decorum, who did not obtrude speech upon her but bowed and smiled in a welcoming way as she pushed pass them. She was vexed with herself for having made this necessary by approaching her stall from the wrong direction; she had imagined her place nearer the centre and was just a trifle disappointed to find herself only one seat from the left aisle. But with postal booking, and a theatre habitually filled every night of the season, one just had to take what the box-office sent and be grateful.

Miss Phipps then turned to her left and received the shock of her life.

Her left-hand neighbour was Mr. Mauve Shirt from the Gospel van.

"If I used a coincidence like this in a story, Ellery Queen would never swallow it," thought Miss Phipps. "But in real life such things are always happening."

She smiled affably at Mr. Mauve (as she decided to call him), and received a somewhat chilly and uncertain contortion of the features in reply.

"You must excuse my behaving as if I knew you," said Miss Phipps in her friendliest tone—after all her white hair defended her from any imputation of attempting a pick-up—"but I saw you in your Gospel van this afternoon. On the Warwick road."

Mauve Shirt said nothing. He merely tightened his lips and glowered.

"You passed me. I was driving a little Cardinal in two shades of rose," persisted Miss Phipps, somewhat abashed and feeling the need (though she knew it was absurd) to defend herself. "Don't you remember?"

Mauve made a slight movement which might have been taken, by a friendly critic, as an inclination of his head.

"Is your mission part of some spiritual campaign?" enquired Miss Phipps. "Or is it entirely undenominational and independent?"

"It's nothing to do with me, see?" broke out Mauve Shirt in shrill Cockney tones. "It's my friend's wot I was driving with. S'nothing to do with me reelly, see."

"Oh, I see," said Miss Phipps. She felt at once relieved and amused—relieved to know that the spiritual destinies of Stratford were not to be linked with Mr. Mauve and amused by his perky speech. "An interesting experience for you, no doubt."

Mauve Shirt gave a snort so derisive that Miss Phipps was startled, and turned to give him a longer look. But at that moment the stage lights came on and there was applause for the simply majesty of the steps and columns which set the scene. Theseus and Hippolyta entered with dignity and an attendant court, Miss Phipps was enthralled—and Mauve Shirt was forgotten.

The play flew along on the iridescent wings of Shakespeare's exquisite poetry. Titania was, of course, adorable, Oberon magnificently sinister. Ordinary mortals, it seemed, were clothed in Grecian white, royalties in white with scarlet cloaks and ornaments; rustics in whatever it had pleased God to send to their obscure abodes, thought Miss Phipps, paraphrasing Gogol; fairies in a most ethereal, incredibly transparent and beautiful tulle of deepest indigo blue, so that their every movement seemed to shimmer moonlight.

As the audience rose to go out for coffee at the interval, Miss Phipps explained this sartorial scheme to the Oriental gentlemen, who were scanning their programmes with an earnest intensity which seemed to implore guidance. They all waited, standing, for the crowd in the aisle to diminish. The Orientals were a little shocked, it seemed, by the frivolous modern levity with which Helena and Hermia were being played—such tit-for-tatting females were not their idea of Shakespeare's heroines.

"That's what *I* say," broke in an American voice, which emanated from a blue-haired lady in the row behind. "It's throwing Shakespeare out the window, that's what I say, but my niece here says this is the first time those two girls ever made any sense to her, and she has a point there, you know."

"She has indeed," approved Miss Phipps. "What is your view?" she inquired, turning to Mr. Mauve Shirt.

"Well, it's not wot I was led to expeck from Shakespeare, and that's a fack," said Mauve. "That Bottom fellow is the man for my money—he's the smart one."

At this moment the crowd yielded an opening and they all surged out into the aisle. Mauve at once slipped away like an eel and vanished.

"I'm sure she's not here tonight," said the American lady to her niece.

Miss Phipps, intrigued by this second reference to an unknown woman of importance, turned round and enquired courteously, "Excuse me, but who were you expecting?"

"Why, our Miranda Lee, of course," was the reply. "Maybe she isn't as well known to you Britishers as she is to us, but—"

"Oh, but she is!" exclaimed Miss Phipps.

"—in our country we regard her as a very great actress," concluded the American lady in a rather hurt tone.

"So do we. I've seen several of her films," said Miss Phipps hastily. "She has a very real talent."

"She's planning to do a Shakespearean series on American television, so she's visiting Stratford for new production ideas," explained the blue-haired tourist, mollified.

"At the hotel it was expected that she would arrive here tomorrow."

"Is that so? Do you hear that, Monica? Miranda Lee is expected tomorrow."

"Which hotel would that be?" asked the crisp young niece eagerly.

"The Hathaway."

"My niece would naturally like to see Miss Lee," said the American lady. "She is something of a heroine on the college campus, you know."

"I understand," said Miss Phipps. They exchanged smiles, and understood each other to have the same views on the charming susceptibility of youth.

Miss Phipps went out to the terrace overhanging the river. It was a breath-taking spectacle. Dusk was just falling, stars began to gleam, and in the darkening Avon the lights of the theatre and the distant bridge were softly reflected. A few belated swans and a solitary boat gave variety to the scene. Happy people in gay clothes crowded the terrace and balcony, talking with animation, not of private grievances nor public problems, but of the greatest poet of all time.

Mr. Mauve Shirt was leaning over the railings in the far corner. Miss Phipps smiled a little at the sight, and feeling happy and dashing, went in to the snack bar and bought herself, not coffee but a youthful glass of orangeade. She was imbibing this through a straw with considerable gusto when over the rim of her glass she caught sight of the Laire party, seated at a distant table. They all looked more cheerful than Miss Phipps had yet seen them, and Miss Phipps, feeling good will toward all men, waved a greeting and made her way to them.

"And what do you think of this way of playing the lovers?" enquired Miss Phipps. "It brightens the girls up a good deal, don't you think?"

"Yes, indeed. There's a lot more scope in Helena than Linda thought," said Tony. "You must see that, Lindy."

"Small thanks to Michael," said Linda, pouting. But she was clearly pleased. "Ruth doesn't like it," she added.

"Oh, yes, I do," said Ruth quickly. "It's only that I doubt my ability to play the part that way. It's Linda's line, not mine."

"I should very much like to see the Laire production," said Miss Phipps diplomatically.

The bell rang and the audience trooped back into the theatre. Mr. Mauve arrived in his seat late and a trifle breathless, and seemed, Miss Phipps thought, rather bored with the proceedings until the rustics' play at the end, when he applauded Bottom's playing of Pyramus very heartily. The fairies spoke the lovely epilogue and left the stage empty in moonlight; the curtains came down and went up again many times while applause thundered from all over the house; and then the national anthem brought the audience to their feet.

Miss Phipps went out with the crowd streaming away in eager talk beneath the lighted chestnut trees. The darling *Dream* was over.

"I adore Stratford!" said Miss Phipps, lolling in a deck-chair beside the gentle Avon next morning.

The sun shone brightly, the river glittered; families with young children and every imaginable breed of dog disported themselves on the grass, the customary early morning queue outside the theatre hoping for tickets for the evening performance had just dispersed, the theatre cafés were crowded. Rowing-craft flew up and down the river, ice-cream was sold from a nearby float, and the big motor-boats waited throbbing till their quota of passengers should be complete.

Miss Phipps' happiness was not quite perfect, however; she had had a theatre ticket for last night, and she had a theatre ticket for tomorrow night, but she had no ticket for tonight. It had seemed absurd, months ago when she booked, to see *A Midsummer Night's Dream* twice, on two consecutive evenings, so she had booked once for the *Dream* and once for *Coriolanus*.

But now that she was here in Stratford, she had come under the spell; and she was beginning to feel that she would give a great deal to be going to the theatre again tonight. On an impulse she climbed out of her deck-chair and approached the box-office. But there were no tickets left, not even standing-room tickets.

"Oh, well!" said Miss Phipps wistfully.

To cheer herself up she decided to take a trip on one of the motorboats. There was one called *Titania*, and one called *George Washington* ("Why?" wondered Miss Phipps), and one called *Swan of Avon*. It was *Titania*, however, which bore her downstream to a superb view of the church. At this point the engine was stopped and the boat drifted while fares were collected. Miss Phipps' eyes wandered, and in a quiet distant field on the far bank she was suddenly sure she saw the Gospel van parked by a grassy slope.

"I am sure I saw it," mused Miss Phipps. "That's one of those odd locutions which mean the opposite of what they say. *I'm sure I saw it* means really that I'm not sure at all. Why should the van be there? How did it get there? Was it really there? I shall walk along the left bank and find out."

When she stepped off the boat, however, it occurred to her that its name, *Titania*, was a good omen; surely it meant that she would see Titania tonight. Miss Phipps really despised all such superstitious fancies, but her longing for this to be a true portent was so great that she visited the box-office again—in vain.

"Serves me right," said Miss Phipps regretfully. "I should stick to facts, not fancies."

So she trotted off across the bridge and along the path on the far bank, to check whether the presence of the Gospel van in a remote field was fact or fancy.

It was fact; but Miss Phipps had a good deal of trouble to verify it. She turned into one or two narrow lanes and climbed one or two fences before she actually set eyes on the van, for it had been parked—"Accidentally? Intentionally? Skillfully?" wondered Miss Phipps—behind a grassy knoll.

Only from one or two widely separated spots where trees and slope connived could the van be seen. Miss Phipps approached the gate leading into the field, with the intention of walking past the van towards the river bank, for she was curious to know how a Gospel van carried on its mission from so remote a position. One could not harangue a crowd that distance.

But perhaps the van was driven back into Stratford when the urge to sermonize overtook the man with the ugly ears. The gate clicked beneath Miss Phipps' hand and the sound must have been audible in the van, for when Miss Phipps turned towards the field again after closing the gate, the man with the ugly ears stood by the back wheel. From this distance his ears were not, of course, clearly visible, but his dirty turtle-necked sweater and something in the way he stood and looked at Miss Phipps convinced her that he was the same man.

Miss Phipps paused. She took a step forward into the field. The man, motionless and silent, regarded her. Miss Phipps hesitated. The man took a step towards her. Miss Phipps turned and fled.

She was heartily ashamed of herself for doing so.

"Disgusting cowardice!" she told herself angrily. "The onset of old age! You'll be afraid of cows next! A perfectly harmless, well-meaning citizen—a bit of a crank, perhaps, but doubtless a truly religious man—and you run away from him as if he were a thug!"

"He *is* a thug," replied Miss Phipps' inner self in a subdued tone. "His whole personality is teaming with menace. As for that Gospel van, I don't believe a word of it! The way he looked at me!"

She glanced over her shoulder apprehensively, and quickened her step. Though she had now reached the river bank, a good many of the visitors had gone to lunch and this side of the Avon seemed quiet and lonely. To her relief, the ferry was working; she crossed thankfully to the theatre side. She felt quite nervous and shaken, and accepted this as an excuse to lunch in the theatre restaurant.

As there was no matinee that afternoon, the terrace restaurant was not its usual seething mass of theatre-goers waving scarlet programmes; only a few tables were occupied and Miss Phipps easily secured a place. Under the influence of the good food and charming décor (white, black, and shocking pink), Miss Phipps grew calmer; her heart quietened, her powers of observation returned.

The head waiter now ushered into the restaurant, with great respect, a party of three. There was a man whom Miss Phipps recognized as one of the important theatre officials; there was another man, tall, handsome, dark, highly silvered at the temples, elegantly dressed in grey with a white carnation in his button-hole; there was a woman who Miss Phipps knew at once must be Miranda Lee.

Oh, yes, there was no doubt of it—she was Miranda Lee. Although she was dressed in jeans and sweater, with a band of white chiffon tied carelessly round her blonde hair, her beauty blazed, and she had that look, indefinable but unmistakable, of world-wide celebrity. Her aquiline face, her wonderful pale glossy hair, her exquisite figure, her starry violet eyes, her friendly smile revealing how perfectly at ease she was in every milieu—as Miss Phipps observed all these, she felt a pang for Linda. This was what the poor child wished to be and never would achieve; her small-town prettiness was a candle to the sun of Miranda's beauty.

"But candles are very charming and useful things to have about the house," reflected Miss Phipps. "Easier to live with—if they are content to remain candles."

All the same she could not keep her eyes from Miranda. And a certain regret crept into her gaze.

"How difficult it always is to properly assess people of another nationality," she thought sadly.

The tall handsome man, whom Miranda called Maurice, was to Miss Phipps, indubitably and at once, a fake. Quite a few of the other guests in the restaurant must have thought the same, especially the men, as Miss Phipps saw from their embarrassed looks. The Official showed by his chilly politeness when he addressed Maurice that he despised him. Even the Laire contingent, provincial though they were, reflected Miss Phipps, would not have taken long to assess Maurice as a phony. Michael and Ruth would have seen through him in an instant, Tony in an hour—even Linda would have suspected him in a day or two.

But here was this gorgeous Miranda girl, who must have met men of every kind in her seven years of fame, taken in by this shoddy piece of work simply because he sported what she probably thought was a genuine Oxford accent.

"Smooth," thought Miss Phipps, scowling at Maurice resentfully. "Clever. Insinuating. A cadger. What is the girl thinking of? Of course," she admitted, "one can hardly blame dear Maurice for making up to Miranda. What man wouldn't, if he had the chance? It's she who ought to have more *sense*. But there," repeated Miss Phipps sadly, "it's as I say. She'd see through him at once if he were her fellow-countryman."

Alas, Maurice continued to describe the vicissitudes of their drive down from London in Miranda's powerful hired car in his liquid, resonant, imitation-upper-class tones and Miranda continued to turn those marvellous eyes admiringly upon him.

"Moving accidents by flood and field," snorted Miss Phipps. "It's an old dodge, but as Shakespeare knew, it always works—it catches the Desdemonas."

She felt so vexed that she did not wait for coffee, but stalked out and went back to the Hathaway in a huff. The result of all this—of sitting hours in the fresh air, a boat trip, a walk, a fright, a big meal, and no coffee—was that when she sat down in her bedroom and picked up a detective novel, she fell asleep and did not wake till it was late afternoon.

By the time she had had a cup of tea and was strolling beneath the chestnut trees again, the car-parks were filling, the coaches arriving, the crowds already beginning to arrive for the evening performance.

In the distance she saw the Laire party, still in day clothes, and waved to them. They turned and came towards her.

"You're still here, then?" said Miss Phipps, a little surprised after Linda's angry harangue the previous day.

"Oh, yes. We're here till Sunday, I'm glad to say," said Michael.

"The boys took two days' leave," said Ruth.

"We're seeing the *Dream* again tonight—we came to *study* the production," said Tony earnestly.

"By the way, Linda," said Miss Phipps, "your Miranda Lee has arrived. I saw her at lunch in the theatre restaurant."

"What was she wearing?" asked Linda eagerly.

Miss Phipps told her. Linda's face clouded with disappointment.

"Never mind—she'll be *en grande tenue* for the theatre tonight, I'm sure," said Miss Phipps. Linda's face brightened. "Oh, how I *wish* I had a ticket for tonight!" mourned Miss Phipps. "How foolish it was of me not to get one."

"You might still get in," said Tony with sympathy. "There's always a queue for cancellations, you know—tickets sent back at the last minute. Sometimes motor coach trips will bring back as many as six! But you'd have to go now—the queue's already forming."

Miss Phipps hesitated.

"Would you like me to go and stand for you, Miss Phipps?" offered Michael. "I'll gladly do so."

"You'd miss your dinner, Michael!" Linda protested.

Michael muttered something about that being of no consequence. Miss Phipps made up her mind.

"You're a kind boy, Michael," she said, "but I'll queue for myself, thank you."

"You'll miss your dinner," said Ruth.

"I ate a big lunch."

"Why not buy a snack and take it along with you?" suggested Tony.

"Why don't *we* buy her a snack and take it to her in the queue?" suggested Michael. "Yes, that's what we'll do. You go straight to the queue now, Miss Phipps, and we'll come to you. Girls, you go along to the Hathaway and get dressed. We'll follow later."

"Don't you dare to be late, Michael," said Linda warningly.

Miss Phipps, excited and gleeful, found herself twelfth in the queue which began on the settee in the foyer and gradually spread out through the door and round the side of the building.

"Even if I don't get a seat for the performance," she decided, munching on a sausage roll, "it's worth it as a spectacle."

For, standing at one side in a fixed position, she saw and heard more clearly than before, the polyglot audience as it poured through the great doors.

At last it was seven o'clock and the cancellations began to come in. Miss Phipps moved to tenth in the queue. Ninth. Seventh. Fifth. A young man ahead took a cancelled standing-room ticket, and Miss Phipps was then second in the line.

The Laire party arrived. Linda in her white and silver had an unhappy yearning expression on her face, and Miss Phipps did not need to be told that she had seen Miranda Lee in the Hathaway dining-room. The other three congratulated Miss Phipps on her good chance of securing a ticket. The five minute bell rang.

"We'd better be getting to our seats," said Michael.

"Oh, no! Let's wait and see her come in," said Linda.

"But why, if it makes you unhappy to see her?"

"Don't be silly, Michael! She *doesn't* make me unhappy!" said Linda, stamping her foot.

"Well, I'm going in. Come along, Ruth," said Tony impatiently.

They had just crossed the emptying foyer and were mounting the steps when Miranda Lee arrived. Maurice accompanied her, a red carnation in the lapel of his dinner jacket. Miranda was certainly worth waiting for, thought Miss Phipps, as the actress glided across the foyer to the officials waiting to receive her, with the floating gait which was one of her special graces.

As Miss Phipps had prophesied, she was *en grande tenue*. Like Linda she wore white and silver, but the similarity of colour scheme only made the difference between the girls more cruel; the diamonds at Miranda's throat and wrists, the superbly tailored bodice, the white chiffon which swirled about her shoulders, the mere cobwebs of silver thread which were her shoes—all pointed to the difference between the Parisian couturier and the Laire dressmaker, the famous beauty and the pretty little girl. Linda stood wide-eyed, the corners of her mouth drooping wistfully.

"Poor Linda!" thought Miss Phipps with a pang.

Michael evidently had the same feeling, for under the guise of urging his wife towards the stairs he put his arm around her protectively.

At this moment the girl from the box-office who had been issuing the cancellations to the queue suddenly appeared before Miss Phipps, beaming, with four back-stalls tickets in her hand. Nothing could have pleased Miss Phipps better: she had a place, yet need feel no remorse in taking it since she was not the last to benefit.

She paid and rushed to her stall just a few seconds before the performance began. The last thing she saw in the auditorium before the lights faded was Mr. Mauve Shirt, down in front, sitting in the same left-aisle seat he had occupied last night.

"Curiouser, and curiouser," thought Miss Phipps.

She forgot Mr. Mauve until the end of the interval, but then remembered his late and breathless return to his seat after the interval last night. Of course drinks, coffee, cloakroom, might easily have detained him, but Miss Phipps standing at the back of the stalls and watching shrewdly, saw that he was still absent, again late in returning.

On impulse she left the auditorium, pushed through the crowd beating back in the reverse direction, and went out through the bar towards the darkening terrace. The bar, fast emptying, was almost cleared by the time Miss Phipps reached the outer door. The terrace was quite empty—except for Mr. Mauve, who in the dim far corner was leaning over the railing.

"So you're here again tonight?" called Miss Phipps cheerfully, advancing upon him.

Mauve gave a violent start and turned towards her.

"Wot if I am?" he cried. "No business of yours, lady, is it?"

Miss Phipps had never seen a cornered rat, but what she saw now was what she had always imagined. From a perky little Cockney, Mauve had turned into something dangerous. His eyes had a sudden reddish gleam, his small pale face was contorted and savage.

"Er, no," said Miss Phipps, halting suddenly. "I was just interested, that's all. Because—"

"Then keep out," said Mauve Shirt fiercely. "Out of my way, see?"

He looked round him. The terrace was empty. Miss Phipps suddenly realized that it was, indeed, quite horribly empty. She was afraid to turn her back on him. She thought of screaming, but doubted if the bar attendants would hear her in time.

She saw that Mauve was aware of her distress. He also perceived the emptiness of the terrace. His little rat eyes gleamed. He grinned. He put his hand in his pocket and advanced upon her.

"Hi-de-ho!" called a cheerful American voice from the wire gate at the other end of the terrace.

"Hi-de-ho!" shouted Miss Phipps, running madly towards it.

The niece of the blue-haired American lady—the girl who had found Hermia and Helena making sense the night before—was standing on the steps just outside the theatre precincts.

"I hope I didn't interrupt," she said politely. "We were just passing along and saw you. I wanted to thank you for telling us Miranda Lee was to stay at the Hathaway. We dined there tonight and had a wonderful view of her."

"Thank *you*," said Miss Phipps fervently. "Must go—bell has sounded—see you tomorrow perhaps!" she cried, rushing away to the safety of the crowded foyer.

"I almost wish I were *not* in Stratford," mused Miss Phipps sadly. "If I were in Southshire, I could go and tell my suspicions to Inspector Tarrant. But to a strange policeman they would sound altogether too nebulous. In fact, they *are* altogether too nebulous," concluded Miss Phipps with a sigh, picking up her book again.

She was lying in her comfortable bed at the Hathaway, trying to soothe her harrowed nerves by reading (as usual) a detective story. She had taken care to keep amongst the crowd on leaving the theatre and had thankfully joined the Laire group as they approached the hotel. Linda was at her worst, snapping and whining, but Miss Phipps would gladly have put up with someone far worse than Linda, for the sake of the protection her company afforded. Besides, poor Linda's self-confidence had been badly shaken by her glimpses of Miranda Lee, and Miss Phipps, from previous encounters with critics of her novels, knew just how painful the experience of mauled self-confidence could be.

"Oh, well!" sighed Miss Phipps again. "It's not my affair, I suppose."

In her mood of frustration she found herself dissatisfied with the development of the plot in the novel she was reading.

"These heroines, really!" exclaimed Miss Phipps.

The telephone at her bedside rang.

"Yes?" said Miss Phipps.

"Is your car a Cardinal in two shades of rose, madam?" enquired a male voice politely, giving her the registration number.

"Yes."

"Then I am afraid I must ask you to come down and move it, madam," said the voice. "A London gentleman who has to leave very early tomorrow morning is unable to get his car out."

"I left plenty of room," began Miss Phipps.

"No doubt, madam. But other cars have probably moved in since. We have so much trouble with cars parked in the yard, madam, you wouldn't believe it."

"A few well-placed white lines would eliminate your difficulties," said Miss Phipps grimly.

"Now that's an idea worth consideration," said the voice.

"Oh, very well, I'll come down. But you'd better warn the London gentleman that it may be five minutes or so before I get there. I'm in bed—I'll have to get dressed."

"I'm exceedingly sorry, madam," murmured the voice.

Miss Phipps banged down the receiver and climbed out of bed. She surveyed herself with distaste in the mirror and began reluctantly to undo the night preparations she had so recently completed. She took the net from her hair, wiped the cream from her face, threw off her nightgown, put on a dress and coat, pulled on an easy pair of shoes, and extracted the car key from her purse. She still looked pretty frightful, she decided, but sufficiently reputable to glide through the Hathaway passages without causing too much surprise.

"Luckily the weather is fairly balmy," she thought, emerging from her room.

At the foot of the stairs, in the otherwise empty hotel foyer, sat Michael Lynn, alone and smoking moodily.

"Linda's been so hateful he dislikes the thought of going to their room," thought Miss Phipps compassionately. "Hullo, Michael!"

"Miss Phipps!" exclaimed Michael, springing to his feet. "Is there anything wrong?"

"I must look even worse than I imagined," reflected Miss Phipps sardonically. She explained the circumstances.

"Why not let me move the car for you?" suggested Michael, crushing out his cigarette. "I'm familiar with Cardinals."

"Why, how kind of you, Michael I should be most grateful," said Miss Phipps, handing him the car key. "Leave the key at the reception desk, will you? I can pick it up tomorrow morning."

She returned to her room, performed all her night preparations for the second time, lay down in bed, and again took up the mystery story.

"I have no patience," she said, re-reading a paragraph, "with these heroines who are deceived by false messages. It's a gimmick for getting the heroine into the hands of the villain, which is hopelessly out of date in the modern detective story and should never be used again. No sensible woman would ever be deceived—"

"Good Lord!" cried Miss Phipps, springing out of bed. "And I've sent Michael!"

She snatched a coat, some shoes, her electric torch, and flew downstairs. The foyer was still empty, with no clerk at the reception desk, though voices could be heard coming from a room labelled *Manager's Office*.

Miss Phipps rushed through the passages to the back entrance and burst out into the long yard, a place now almost completely in shadow, filled with darker shapes. She switched on her torch and groped among the cars to her Cardinal. She knelt down.

Yes, she was right.

The false message gimmick, stale though it was, had proved successful.

A body lay on the ground, from whose head blood was slowly oozing. Owing to Michael's kindly disposition and Linda's fretfulness, however, the body belonged not to Miss Phipps, as the assailants had planned, but to Michael.

"Help! Help!" shouted Miss Phipps, rushing back into the hotel. "A man has been murdered!"

The door of the manager's office was flung open and a confused cluster of people tumbled out. There was the plump balding manager himself; there were Miranda Lee and her Maurice; there was a uniformed police sergeant, massive and rather Dogberryish in appearance; there was a lanky gingerish young constable; there was a very neat, lean man in plain clothes whom Miss Phipps, from her long experience of her friend Robert Tarrant, recognized as a Detective-Inspector.

"Quick! Telephone for an ambulance! Michael Lynn has been attacked and wounded."

The reception clerk flew to the telephone, the sergeant to the hotel yard.

"Is he dead?" enquired the smooth tones of Maurice.

"I don't know," said Miss Phipps. She felt fairly certain that Michael lived, but thought a good fright would hasten action.

"Can this have anything to do with the other matter?" said the manager anxiously.

"What other matter? Yes, I'm certain it has," said Miss Phipps. "It was I whom they meant to knock out, not that poor boy Michael."

"Oh? Why?" said the Detective-Inspector, giving her a sharp look.

Miss Phipps was well aware that her appearance offered nothing reassuring to an Inspector's eye. She therefore became the celebrated novelist, put on her V.I.P. manner, and said firmly, "My name is Marian Phipps. I am a writer. If you will telephone the Southshire County police, Detective-Inspector Tarrant will vouch for my *bona fides*."

"Will you all please go in there and wait," said the Inspector, indicating the manager's office.

He herded them in and closed the door firmly. Miss Phipps at once opened it.

"Poor young Mrs. Lynn must be told," she said. "And her brother, Tony Harris. Though I think her friend Miss Ruth Armstrong will probably be more useful. They are all staying here."

"We shall attend to all that, madam," said the Inspector curtly. "Please go in there and wait."

This time he put the constable in the room with them. The man stood with his back to the door and glowered. Miss Phipps looked about her. The manager sat in the chair behind his desk, harassed and preoccupied; he was obviously wondering what on earth his directors would say to all this. Miranda Lee, looking beautiful and calm but weary, sank gracefully to a settee. Maurice seated himself beside her and lounged back against the cushions as if he had not a care in the world; yet it seemed to Miss Phipps' shrewd eye that the hands about his knee were too tightly clasped, as if to control any nervous quivering. Miss Phipps chose a seat near the door.

"May I know what was the other matter you referred to?" she asked the manager.

He hesitated, but Miranda Lee said at once, "My diamond necklace has disappeared."

"Ah!" exclaimed Miss Phipps. "Did you lose it at the theatre?"

"Yes," said the manager quickly.

"No," said Maurice.

"Opinions differ, I see," said Miss Phipps mildly. "But you, yourself, Miss Lee—when did you first miss the necklace."

"Not till I went up to my room," replied the actress.

"Oh, I couldn't swear to that," said Maurice.

"When she was leaving the theatre, then? Could you swear to that?"

"No—how could I? It's not my habit to gaze at Miss Lee's jewelry—I prefer to look at her face."

"Very pretty," smiled Miss Phipps. Then she added mentally, "But a lie, I'll bet my Cardinal. He had a telephone call, which could have been from Mauve Shirt about me, and he was absent from Miranda's observation twice. It could have been he who telephoned me and struck down poor Michael."

At this point in her meditations the lean Inspector, followed by the massive sergeant, came in.

"Now, madam," said the Inspector sternly to Miss Phipps. "I have checked with the Southshire police about you by telephone. Just to make certain that you really are Miss Marian Phipps, would you mind telling me the name of Detective-Inspector Tarrant's second child."

"But he has no second child!" burst out Miss Phipps indignantly.

"Just a little test question, madam," said the Inspector drily. "I think we may accept that you are, in fact, Miss Marian Phipps."

"Very kind of you, I'm sure," said Miss Phipps, ruffled.

"Will you now please give us your account of this affair. Why did you say the attack on Mr. Lynn was meant for you? Why did you say the attack was connected with Miss Lee's necklace?"

"Well," began Miss Phipps, taking breath for her story.

"Please be brief," Miss Phipps," put in the Inspector.

"I shall be thoroughly succinct," said Miss Phipps, annoyed, "because you, Inspector, have no time to lose if you wish to apprehend the thieves and recover the necklace. Briefly, then. Yesterday I was passed on the road by what is known as a Gospel van, manned by two people who looked like knaves if ever I saw knaves. The van had on its back some very familiar biblical texts, wrongly and ungrammatically quoted. And this alleged van had a far greater speed than such a van would normally have. These three observations led me to believe that it was in fact not a genuine Gospel van but a powerful car, camouflaged.

"At the theatre last night I saw one of the van men, whom I nicknamed Mr. Mauve from the colour of his shirt. Mauve, a ratty little man of a type one would not usually find in an expensive stall, was completely ignorant of Shakespeare; he mistook that delightful fool Bottom for a sharp shrewd fellow. Unfortunately I let him know that I had seen him on the van that afternoon. Mauve returned late and breathless to his stall after the interval. This morning I saw the van parked secretly in a field, some distance from the town but close to the river. When I attempted to approach it the driver became menacing. This evening I saw Mauve again in the theatre, which struck me as curious."

"Why?" barked the Inspector.

"He was completely ignorant of Shakespeare."

"Even an ignorant man might, to lessen his ignorance, attend two consecutive performances."

"Of the same play? Highly improbable," said Miss Phipps confidently. "It occurred to me that Mauve's procedure on the previous evening had been a sort of *rehearsal* for an incident which was to occur tonight. The incident, whatever it was, had been carefully planned—Mauve's two stalls must have been booked some time ago. And a controlling intelligence superior to Mauve's seemed clearly indicated.

"I followed Mauve onto the terrace. I saw him in an attitude that suggested he was dropping something over the railings. I spoke to him. He resented my presence violently. I thought he was about to attack me, but I was saved by the unexpected approach of American acquaintances.

"Clearly Mauve disliked my presence. Why? Because I, and I alone, knew that the man who dropped something over the railings was connected with the van. Therefore, it was dangerous to him that his connection with the van should become known.

"Presently Mauve's accomplice, a man with an educated voice—not Mauve or the driver—telephoned me pretending to be the hotel clerk and lured me down to the dark car park with a message asking me to move my car. Michael Lynn, in the kindness of his heart, poor lad, went out to do the errand for me and was struck down in mistake for me. Why? Again, because it was dangerous that Mauve's connection with the van should become known, and so any possibility of evidence from me must be eliminated.

"Why was I dangerous? Obviously because the over-speedy, falsely-religious van was nothing but a fake. Yet if it were only a means of escape, it was a clumsy fake, for it was so very noticeable. Therefore the appearance and size of the van were necessary to the plan.

"It then occurred to me that the van could hold a small boat. Or hearing of the theft from Miss Lee it further occurred to me that Mauve had dropped Miss Lee's necklace over the railing of the empty terrace to someone in a boat below."

There was a dumbfounded silence.

"But I didn't see any horrid little man like this Mauve near me in the theatre," objected Miranda Lee.

"No? I think somebody else stole the necklace and passed it to Mauve," said Miss Phipps. "The man with the smooth voice, you know. And then off the necklace went, over the railing, and down the Avon. So that if the theft were quickly discovered and a search made, it wouldn't be found anywhere in the theatre."

"It's a strange story," said the Inspector.

"It's fantastic," said Maurice with contempt.

"You'd be surprised how fantastic human beings are, sir," said the Hathaway manager, shaking his head with a knowing air. "In my profession we learn to be surprised at nothing."

"It hangs together, however," continued the Inspector, disregarding their interruptions. "And parts of it are susceptible of proof. You might get that van traced, Sergeant."

"It probably won't be a van now. The boat and the text-painted boardings will have been left in the field, and a fast car will now be on its way to London," said the manager sadly.

"Perhaps," agreed Miss Phipps. "But Mr. Mauve Shirt and his driver think they've knocked me out, you know. So there's nobody about, they think, to put two and two together. And then again," she added with a sly smile, "I gave Mauve such a start on the terrace that I rather believe he may have missed his aim, and the necklace may now be at the bottom of the Avon. What were you saying?" she enquired of Maurice, who had given an irrepressible start.

"I said nothing," replied Maurice hoarsely.

Everyone looked at Maurice—the Inspector and Sergeant in sober calculation, Miranda Lee from wide horror-stricken eyes, the manager with a sudden impish grin. But there came an interruption. A wild scream sounded from the foyer outside. So wild, so agonized was this scream that everyone in the room sprang to their feet and the Sergeant threw open the door.

Miss Phipps ducked nimbly under his arm and ran out. Two policemen were carrying Michael to the ambulance on a stretcher. His body was limp beneath the grey blanket, his eyes closed; nevertheless Miss Phipps, to her ineffable relief, saw that he lived, and that the comparatively natural colour in his cheeks indicated his injuries were not as serious as she had feared. Linda was kneeling beside the stretcher, impeding its progress and trying to raise Michael's head.

"My poor child!" said Miss Phipps, raising her from the ground. "You must let them take him quickly to the hospital."

Linda threw herself into Miss Phipps' arms.

"I can't bear it! I can't bear it!"

"You love him very much," said Miss Phipps softly, taking the opportunity to make a point on behalf of Michael's future happiness.

Linda raised a tear-stained face, which to Miss Phipps' surprise was contorted, not with grief but with terror.

"I can't do without him," she said.

Miss Phipps sighed. Even at this moment, she reflected sadly, Linda could experience only a selfish emotion—she merely dreaded the thought of life without the continuing kindness, the ever-present protection of her husband.

A hoarse breath at Miss Phipps' shoulder caused her to turn. It was Maurice who had followed her and who now tried to edge out of the door.

"I thought so," said Miss Phipps. "And where are you going, pray? To the van and your two accomplices?"

With an angry exclamation Maurice shoved her roughly aside and ran down the street.

"Inspector!" cried Miss Phipps, tottering backwards. "Catch him!"

She might have spared her breath, however, for the whole scene had already burst into violent action. Police whistles shrilled. Several constables seemed to appear from nowhere and sprinted off at the double. Late homeward-going revellers were scattered on the street outside the hotel, and threading his way through these delayed Maurice's headlong course. The lanky constable put on speed and gained on him. Miss Phipps, riding along sedately in the ambulance with Michael and Linda, witnessed the capture.

"You've nothing on me," cried Maurice angrily, his artificially smooth tones now rough and sharp. "I haven't got your blasted diamonds."

"What about this blood on your shirt-sleeve." said the Inspector, arriving at the appropriate moment. "Assault and battery, that's yours, my man—at the least."

"I adore Stratford!" exclaimed Miss Phipps, as from a bend in the road she caught a last glimpse of the church which housed Shakespeare's bones.

Stratford had certainly done her proud on this occasion. The mystery was solved, the three villians were in custody—Maurice, it turned out, was a jewel thief well known to the London police, Mauve Shirt and Big Ears equally well known for petty offences. The diamond necklace had been dredged up from the bottom of the Avon. Michael and Linda were reconciled, and Linda had an anecdote of a great theatrical star on which she could live for the rest of her life. Linda had something more tangible, too.

"I shall never forgive myself for being the cause of your husband's injuries, Mrs. Lynn," Miranda Lee had said to Linda. "I'm more than thankful he is convalescing so well. I'm so very deeply indebted to him."

"I don't see that *you're* indebted to him," objected Linda, nevertheless delighted. "Miss *Phipps* is indebted to him, but not *you.*"

"But if he had not gone out to Miss Phipps' car, Miss Phipps would have been attacked and knocked unconscious, and then the thieves would have escaped. They would simply have raked my necklace from the bottom of the river and gotten away with it, and Maurice would still be an accepted member of my intimate circle," said Miranda with a sad little smile. "I understand that hospitalization is free in this country, or of course your husband's medical expenses would be my responsibility. As it is, you must allow me to offer you some token of my gratitude. I say you, because from what I have seen of you and Michael, I guess your husband would prefer you to benefit rather than himself. Now is there anything which would give you special pleasure?"

"Well," said Linda, colouring happily and looking at Miss Phipps for guidance. "Well! I don't know *what* to say, I'm *sure!* I don't know whether Michael would—"

"Some small personal thing, perhaps," suggested Miss Phipps. "Something which has belonged to yourself personally, Miss Lee."

Miranda smiled her beautiful, world-famous smile.

"Take this," she said, unclasping from her wrist a platinum and sapphire bracelet. "Yes, Linda, I insist . . ."

So the mystery had been solved and the necklace restored and the thieves apprehended and Miranda Lee rescued from a scoundrel and Michael and Linda made happy. And all this had been accomplished with the air, curiously enough, of the greatest poet of all time.

"Soul of the Age!" declaimed Miss Phipps. *"The applause! delight! the wonder of our stage! My Shakespeare, rise!* And take a bow," added Miss Phipps, pressing the accelerator.

"Sweet Swan of Avon . . ."

MISS PHIPPS IMPROVISES

It was a wet afternoon in Brittlesea. The sea looked like lead and the rain poured from a sky of unbroken gray. Detective Inspector Tarrant had not come home for lunch. Young Johnny was upstairs engaged in his afternoon nap. Mary Tarrant and Miss Phipps sat beside a bright fire, each with a cup of Mary's excellent coffee beside her. Mary was knitting a pullover for her husband and Miss Phipps held a detective novel in her hand. The general effect was intimate and cosy.

With a sigh Miss Phipps threw down her book.

"Come to the end?" said Mary.

"Only to the end of my interest," said Miss Phipps.

"Why so?" inquired Mary.

"No suspense," said Miss Phipps.

"How does one create suspense, Aunt Marian?" asked Mary, beginning another row.

"The best way to create suspense in a detective story," declared Miss Phipps, "is to employ two characters, each of whose integrity appears to vary inversely with that of the other."

"I don't find that as clear as your usual pronouncements, Aunt Marian," Mary remarked with a smile.

"Let us suppose we have two characters—A and B."

"Arthur and Bob," suggested Mary.

"Just so. If Arthur is to be believed, Bob should be a scoundrel. If Bob is to be believed, Arthur must be the scoundrel. For a few pages the reader is led to believe in Arthur. Then some slight but significant incident occurs, which appears to reinstate Bob. Can Bob be innocent after all? If so, Arthur must have been telling lies; therefore he must be the scoundrel. The reader's suspense is drawn tauter and tauter by these alternate hooks—if you see what I mean."

"Who is found guilty in the end?" asked Mary.

"Well, there lies the peculiar advantage of that kind of story," said Miss Phipps, beaming. "There are no fewer than four

171

possible answers to your question. One, Arthur can be guilty. Two, Bob can be guilty. Three, both can be guilty. And four, neither can be guilty. The final choice is open to the author and prevents the solution from becoming obvious until the end, or very late in the story."

"Certainly a complicated structure would be necessary to maintain the situation in doubt until the last page," said Mary, counting stitches.

"Oh, I don't know," said Miss Phipps confidently. "It would need some skill in invention, of course."

"Now you're boasting, Aunt Marian. I challenge you to produce such a story, here and now."

"But, my dear Mary—" began Miss Phipps.

"Start!" commanded Mary firmly.

"Well, let me see now," said Miss Phipps, half flustered and half flattered. "Arthur—a rather old-fashioned name. Yes. Arthur, let's say, was cashier of the Laire Woollen Company, a small but reputable firm manufacturing tweed cloth, in a rather quiet valley outside the city of Laire in Yorkshire."

"You've begun well. A cashier suggests at once the possibility of embezzlement or theft," said Mary.

"Doesn't it? Well, Arthur was a man in his late fifties, thin, gray-haired, meticulous, with a habit of looking over his spectacles in a rather crushing style at any younger person who ventured to disagree with him—even, we'll say, if that person were the junior partner. Slow in his bookkeeping, was Arthur, but sure—at least, the Laire Woollen Company had found him so for upwards of a quarter of a century."

"But such a man could not possibly be guilty of any crime," objected Mary.

"That," said Miss Phipps, "is precisely the impression the reader is intended to receive—at first."

"Go on," said Mary.

"It was the custom of the Laire Woollen Company to have the wages of the employees fetched from the bank in Laire on Thursday afternoon. Arthur then prepared the pay envelopes, which were distributed on Friday morning. The money was fetched from the bank by Arthur and Bob—"

"Ah, ready to be stolen," said Mary.

"Bob being the junior partner of the firm—"

"I thought so," said Mary.

"—and Arthur and Bob naturally traveled to and from the bank in Bob's car."

"Tell me more of Bob," said Mary.

"Bob's grandfather, old Mr. Denison, was the head of the firm."

"*Grand*father?"

"Bob's father was killed in World War II."

"I see," said Mary thoughtfully. "A gap of two generations, and a gap in sympathy, huh?"

"Exactly. Bob had been sent to a good public school, and then to the textile department of Laire University."

"I suppose he was rather wild there, and got sent down without taking his degree."

"On the contrary—and who is inventing this story, Mary? Bob wasn't especially brilliant, but he took a good solid second-class. He also played rugby for the University."

"Oh, no!" said Mary. "We can't have the criminal being good at *football*."

"Who said Bob was the criminal? He was—or appeared to be—a nice ordinary young man, strong though stocky in build, with brown hair and brown eyes. Quite knowledgeable about textiles, and fond of athletics and amateur dramatics."

"That last item strikes a rather suspicious note," commented Mary. "The ability to act is often found in a criminal plot."

"Oh, he never took leading roles," said Miss Phipps reassuringly. "Only minor parts—one of the two policemen at the end who arrest the villain, and that sort of thing, you know. What he really enjoyed was building the set—whacking about with a hammer and so on. He had a good deal of physical energy which had to be expended somehow."

"He still sounds quite innocent," said Mary.

"Moreover, he was in love with Arthur's daughter."

"The plot thickens! Was she a nice girl?"

"Both Arthur and Bob thought so. She worked with the Laire Woollen Company as old Mr. Denison's secretary."

"Pretty?"

"Yes, certainly. Very fresh and neat, with those attractive legs and full skirts one sees about so much nowadays. I haven't worked out yet whether she was a blonde or a brunette," said Miss Phipps thoughtfully. "Blonde, I think. Yes, fair hair, very well cut. Fine gray eyes. She was not a fool, you know. Intelligent. Sensible. Full of go. Kind to her father and mother."

"The heroine, in short."

"Exactly."

"Had she any other admirers?"

"Oh, yes, one or two."

"I think you ought to be more specific," objected Mary.

"Very well. Let's say, two. One of the clerks in the outer office, and a childhood friend, the boy next door. Her name was—let's see, Catherine?"

"Agreed. Her father calls her Kitty in private?"

"I prefer Cathy. Arthur was a trifle old-fashioned, you remember."

"In that case he's probably rather strict with Cathy about dates and young men and coming in late, and doesn't approve of Bob's attentions."

"I agree. Now we come to the day of the crime. A bright, pleasant day in October."

"Thursday or Friday, no doubt."

"Thursday afternoon, just after working hours. Arthur was just completing the preparation of the week's pay envelopes when the mill buzzer sounded."

"Buzzer?" queried Mary.

"Well, a hooter, a siren—whatever you like to call it. Some loud noise used to mark the beginning and ending of the work day."

"Proceed."

"The mill rapidly emptied of its employees, who poured out of the gate. Arthur finished his task and was just placing the pay envelopes in the office safe when a man came in and asked for work."

"But don't men in this country usually obtain employment through a Labour Exchange?"

"Exactly Arthur's reaction. 'You'll have to go to the Labour,' he said. 'Any way we haven't any vacancies here. Try so-and-so's,' he said, giving the name of a neighboring firm. 'I did not,' said Arthur when giving his evidence later—you understand, this is Arthur's account of the affair—'I did not altogether like the appearance of the man. He didn't look very respectable to me, and he held a handkerchief to his face in an unbecoming manner.' "

"*Unbecoming* is good," said Mary with relish. "Just the right word for Arthur. What happened then?"

"The man said, according to Arthur, 'I'd like to see old Mr. Denison, all the same.' To which Arthur replied stiffly, 'Mr. Denison has left.' He looked into the inner office, and added, 'Mr. Bob is not here either.' 'Good enough,' said the man with the handkerchief, and drawing some implement from his pocket he whacked poor Arthur hard on the back of he head. Arthur fell down, but in falling grabbed hold of the man so that they rolled about together on the floor. The man disentangled himself, treading on Arthur in the process, and rushing to the window, shouted, 'Come on in!' and waved his arms, clearly beckoning to an accomplice. He then sprang back to the dazed Arthur, wrapped a scarf round his head, and sat heavily on him, holding him face down to the ground. Arthur passed out—I believe that is the expression. When he came to some time later and tore off the scarf, he found the safe empty and the men gone. Fortunately, some of the wage envelopes were still lying on Arthur's desk—the men had overlooked these, or perhaps found them too scattered to collect in their haste. Arthur rang the police and old Mr. Denison, and very soon an able and conscientious Detective-Inspector—shall we call him Tarrant?—"

"Why not?" said Mary, smiling.

"—very soon Detective-Inspector Tarrant was at the Laire Woollen Mill, conducting a vigorous and detailed investigation."

"How much money had been stolen?" asked Mary.

"Fifteen hundred pounds."

"Not a big haul, as hauls go."

"No. Inspector Tarrant noticed that immediately. The criminals were either small-time thieves, or they were—"

"Somebody in desperate need of such a sum."

"Exactly. You've learned a good deal from your husband, my dear."

"It seems to me, too," said Mary thoughtfully, holding up the pullover to judge its length, "that a good deal of local knowledge was required for this robbery."

"Just what the Inspector said, my dear."

"I'm sorry. I can't listen any more for a minute or two," said Mary. "I have to narrow now, for the armhole."

"I'm delighted to hear it—it gives me time to plan the next development," chuckled Miss Phipps.

Presently Mary said, "I'm ready now."

"Old Mr. Denison and Bob have now joined Arthur in the Laire Woollen Company's office and are listening to Arthur's evidence."

Miss Phipps coughed to clear her throat and began to act her various characters.

" 'I suppose the two thieves went out by the side door,' said Bob thoughtfully.

" 'They can't have done that—I locked it when I left,' said old Mr. Denison.

" 'But they can't have left by the front door,' exclaimed Bob.

" 'Why not?' said the Inspector sharply.

" 'Because I was standing at the gate, with the front door in full view, for at least ten minutes after the buzzer sounded,' said Bob.

" 'What were you doing there all that time?' said old Mr. Denison.

" 'I was waiting for Catherine, and when she came I was talking to her,' said Bob.

"At this both Mr. Denison and Arthur scowled at him, and the Inspector gave him a searching look. . . . How do you think it is developing, Mary?" Miss Phipps inquired.

"Arthur is certainly under *my* suspicion," said Mary firmly. "That business about the second man—the accomplice—struck me as rather unconvincing. Why have an accomplice? Why not just knock Arthur out yourself and take the cash?"

"You would need to hit Arthur much harder to carry out that plan," said Miss Phipps. "As it was, a tap that merely stunned and a muffling scarf sufficed."

"That's exactly what I mean," said Mary. "Arthur had to invent some reason for his lack of severe injury—so he concocted this thin story of the second man."

"And how did he get rid of the money, if he stole it himself?"

"He had a few minutes alone, while he was supposed to be lying unconscious on the floor, you remember. And also while he was waiting for the police. However," said Mary, "you are telling this story, Aunt Marian, not I."

"At present, then, your suspicions rest on Arthur?"

"They certainly do."

"So did Inspector Tarrant's. Until he found the scarf in which Arthur had been muffled, lying in a corner of the office. It was what you would call a collegiate scarf, Mary—a scarf with huge stripes in pink, black, and gray. It was a Laire University scarf. In fact, it was Bob's scarf."

"I don't see that proves anything," objected Mary. "Those young men drive about in sports cars wearing huge gloves and enormous woollen collegiate scarves, I grant you. But Bob could easily have left his scarf hanging on a peg in the office. In fact, he must have done so, and the thief simply snatched it up to muffle Arthur."

"Unfortunately," said Miss Phipps gravely, "the evidence seemed to indicate that Bob left the office just before the buzzer went, *wearing* the scarf."

"Whose evidence?"

"Arthur's."

"I don't believe it. He was simply trying to implicate Bob and support his weak story about the accomplice."

"And Catherine's."

"*Catherine's?*" exclaimed Mary. "You mean *Catherine* said Bob was wearing the scarf?"

"Yes. While waiting for the police to arrive, Arthur telephoned his home to explain to his wife that he would be late and she was not to worry. Hearing the agitation in his voice, she asked what was wrong. He told her in general terms that there had been a robbery and he was awaiting the police. As soon as Catherine reached home and heard this news, she came straight back to the Laire Woollen Company. The Inspector saw her hurrying across the yard, intercepted her, and asked about her talk with Bob at the mill gate."

"She probably thought Bob had been hurt."

"Probably—let's say he aimed at some such impression."

"Then it was mean to trap the poor girl like that," said Mary.

" 'Do I understand you and Mr. Bob left the mill together, Miss Catherine?' said the Inspector.

" 'No. He left before I did and was waiting for me at the gate.'

" 'And you stood there and talked for several minutes?"

" 'Yes.'

" 'And then what happened?'

" 'I walked away towards the bus stop at the top of the road.'

" 'And Mr. Bob?'

" 'I don't know what he did then. I presume he walked towards the right of the mill where his car was parked.'

" 'Still wearing his muffler?'

" 'Yes, of course. Is he hurt, Inspector?'

" 'No, no. I take it that he did not offer to drive you home, then?'

" 'He did offer to do so, but I declined,' said Catherine.

" 'Was there a quarrel between you, Miss Catherine?'

" 'There was a slight disagreement,' admitted Catherine. 'But why do you want to know all this, Inspector? What has happened? Is Bob hurt? Is my father hurt? Has there been a robbery?' . . . And so on." Miss Phipps paused. "Poor Catherine was very much upset."

"No wonder!" exclaimed Mary. "This is dreadful, Aunt Marian! It would seem that Bob is guilty."

"If Arthur's evidence is truthful, perhaps so. Do you think Bob was the unseen accomplice, then?"

"Presumably. Yes. Yes," said Mary. "He did not wish to be seen in the act of robbery by Arthur, so he remained outside until Arthur was knocked out. His guilt would explain, too, why Arthur was not severely injured—Bob did not wish to hurt Catherine's father."

"Bob gave his scarf to the young thief who had first entered the office, then?"

"I suppose so," said Mary, but there was a doubtful note in her voice. "It seems a silly thing to do, I must admit. What did Bob say about the scarf?"

"At first he could not account for its presence in the office at all. Then he remembered that he had found the battery of his car run down, and had had to use the starting-handle. It seemed to him that he probably threw off his scarf while using the handle, but he could not remember with certainty."

"Foolish, misguided young man," said Mary sadly. "Why did he ruin himself by committing this crime? He was in debt, I suppose."

"The Inspector investigated that matter promptly. Bob was not in debt at all. The date was shortly after the beginning of the month and all his bills—garage and so on—were paid."

"You mean he didn't do it?" asked Mary. "Then Arthur must have done it. He'd been stealing from the firm—fiddling the books, you know—and he stole this money to make gool his shortage."

"A very possible solution," agreed Miss Phipps. "The Inspector, however, had the firm's books closely investigated by a chartered accountant. They were in perfect order."

"So we're thrown back again to Bob. What about that quarrel between Bob and Catherine? Another girl, perhaps? He had seduced her and needed the money to pay her off?"

"Again a possible solution. Arthur, I may say, hinted at it. By this time he was in a towering rage against Bob and swearing he should never marry his daughter."

"The Inspector investigated the 'other girl' possibility?"

"He did. There was no such girl."

"What about Grandfather Denison? Could he be involved somehow?"

"Oh, he had an unbreakable alibi. He was being driven home by his elderly chauffeur during the entire period of the robbery. No, he definitely does not come into the mystery."

"I wonder if Arthur and Bob could have been in it together?" suggested Mary thoughtfully. "Perhaps the Laire Woollen Company's finances were unsound. Maybe the money wasn't there at all, and Arthur and Bob faked the theft to conceal its absence."

"The money was withdrawn from the Laire bank that afternoon," replied Miss Phipps. "Inspector Tarrant investigated the Laire Woollen Company's finances and found that the firm, though not a gold mine, was solidly prosperous."

"Aunt Marian," said Mary with determination, "will you please tell me at once who committed this robbery, and why? I can't stand this suspense any longer. I'm on tenterhooks."

"A very textile metaphor, my dear. So you admit that my recipe for suspense—two characters each of whose integrity appears to vary inversely with that of the other—is a valid one?"

"Yes, yes, I agree."

"And that it is valid because there are four possible solutions? You have already advanced three of the four—that Arthur is guilty, that Bob is guilty, that Arthur and Bob are both guilty."

"The fourth possible solution is that neither Arthur nor Bob is guilty," Mary remembered. "I'd prefer that to be the correct answer, Aunt Marian, if it is at all possible. I've grown quite attached to these people, and I certainly want that nice Catherine to be happy. She can't be happy if either her father or her future husband is guilty."

"Well, let us see what we can do," said Miss Phipps, smiling. "Let us assume that both Arthur and Bob are telling the truth."

"Hurrah," said Mary.

"Arthur is a slow, precise, elderly man; Bob is a vigorous impetuous young one. The sense of time could vary considerably between two such persons. I suggest that Arthur was a good deal longer in finishing his pay envelopes than he thought. On the other hand, Bob had a few sharp words with Catherine; she whisked away in a pet; he hurried across the yard, tried the self-starter of his sports car, leaped out, threw off his scarf, finally started the car manually, and drove off, all in a fury. By that time the mill yard was empty, the thieves arrived, and the scarf, forgotten by Bob, lay on the ground."

"Oh, quite," said Mary. "I can accept all that. But it doesn't give us a clue to the identity of the thieves."

"I think it does," said Miss Phipps.

"Really?"

"Yes. Remember that this scarf was very noticeably striped in the colors of Laire University. Nobody in the mill was likely to have a similar scarf. Everybody in the mill would know the scarf as Bob's."

"You mean that whoever took the scarf into the office did so to implicate Bob?"

"I do."

"But who could that be? Surely not Arthur?"

"No, of course not. Arthur was a good man, a little too strict perhaps—a nonsmoker and teetotaler and all that kind of thing—but thoroughly honorable."

"Then who? I don't see anybody else in the story."

"My dear," said Miss Phipps with something of a smirk, "it is not required of a detective-story writer that she *thrust* the guilty person into view. The man is there, however. You can find him if you think back to one small incident in the story—an incident which you dismissed too casually after a single question."

Mary paused. At length she said, "The quarrel between Bob and Catherine."

"Exactly."

"What was it about?"

"What indeed?"

"Did the Inspector investigate it?"

"Eventually."

"Was it about Arthur?"

Miss Phipps shook her head.

"About Bob's old grandfather? He disapproved of the match?"

"No. The grandfather was a rather fine old man, saddened by having lost his son in the War, a little perplexed by the strange modern world, but anxious only for Bob's happiness."

"Then who—oh!" cried Mary suddenly, dropping her knitting. "I've got it! Of course! Catherine's other suitors. The clerk in the outer office. Bob was jealous of his attentions and said so rather too possessively to Catherine, who tossed her head and walked off. It all happened just as you said—about Bob and the scarf and the car—and this clerk, who of course knew all about the pay envelopes in the office—by the way, what was his name? Did you ever mention it?"

"No—but let's call him Eric."

"A name I've never had a fancy for. Eric picked up the scarf and gave it to his confederate in the office, deliberately intending to implicate Bob. Eric must have planned the theft beforehand."

"Oh, yes, he had."

"Gambling debts?"

"Dogs. And then a money-lender."

"I see. Tight trousers and a mop of hair?"

"No, older than that. Sideburns and a fancy waistcoat."

"And his partner in crime?"

"A bad companion from Laire's underworld, I'd say."

"Would they be caught?"

"Yes—you know that detective stories are the most moral of all stories. The numbers of the notes were known to the Laire bank—quite a customary precaution."

"So Arthur and Bob and Catherine and Grandfather Denison were able to live happily ever after."

"Yes. After a good deal of suspense, I hope you agree?"

"Oh, I agree. You win, Aunt Marian. Heavens, there's Johnny moving already How time flies!"

She ran upstairs to her little son. Miss Phipps, with a sigh, picked up her book again.

"No suspense," she murmured.

MESSAGE IN A BOTTLE

Miss Phipps, with Detective-Inspector Tarrant's wife Mary and the Tarrants' small son Johnny, emerged from the lane onto the narrow Rylan Bay beach. Johnny, smartly clad in a jodhpur suit of white wool brightened by a canary-colored sweater, trotted along holding Miss Phipps's hand; his fair hair blew in the breeze, his cheeks were rosy. Mary was carrying the picnic basket; Miss Phipps, who was paying her annual summer visit to the Tarrants, bore a rug.

The sea came into view.

"Ohohohohoh!" cried Johnny joyously. He snatched his hand from Miss Phipps's and plunged down the beach.

Miss Phipps dropped the rug and ran after him, for the shore was so haphazardly covered with rocks sand, and pebbles that it seemed impossible for those small eager feet to reach the water's edge without a stumble. Sure enough, Johnny tripped at the high-water mark, where seaweed and jellyfish and strips of rotting wood lay entangled, the flotsam and jetsam of the tide. He fell and sprawled, scrambled up manfully, then stood with flushed face regarding his hands and knees, now encrusted with seaweed, distastefully.

"Oh, what a shame," said Miss Phipps in a consoling tone, brushing him down.

Johnny gave her a glance of severe reproach, and the corners of his mouth turned down. He was deciding to cry.

"Look, Johnny!" said Miss Phipps hastily, pointing. "There's a bottle floating in the sea!"

Johnny forgot about crying, and stretching out his hand imperiously, demanded, "Bottle!"

Thus committed, Miss Phipps, aiming pebbles rather skillfully, drove the bottle near the shore. In this long narrow cliff-bound bay the water was deep and the tide came in vigorous and splashing; Miss Phipps became damper than was altogether suitable to her dignity as a best-selling novelist before she at last clasped the bottle in her arms. Laughing, and not really minding the amused glances of the other holiday-makers—the beach was crowded with families who had come, like the Tarrants, on the afternoon bus from the neighboring seaside resort of Brittlesea—she took Johnny's hand and ran along to Mary.

The rug was already spread, the basket opened. Johnny lost interest in the bottle and rooted for the chocolate biscuits.

"Look, Mary!" cried Miss Phipps triumphantly.

"Is there a message from a shipwrecked mariner in it?" said Mary, smiling.

"Well, oddly enough—believe it or not!—there *is*," said Miss Phipps. "There's a piece of paper inside, anyway."

She wrestled with the swollen cork, got it out at last, and tried to extract the piece of paper which lay curled inside. But the paper adhered damply to the sides of the bottle.

"I need some kind of implement or other," murmured Miss Phipps, looking about for help.

Just above the tidemark of the once remote little bay stood two old fishermen's cottages, thatched and whitewashed, which had been converted by modern enterprise into a store-cum-café for visitors' entertainment. *KELLY'S RYLAN BAY CAFE—Teas and refreshments—Lobsters For Sale*—was freshly painted across its wall in brilliant blue. Miss Phipps scrambled up and went toward the little building.

A tall, large man in his shirt-sleeves, with thick graying hair and the wreck of a handsome face, overtook her and strode round the side of the café. He held a bucketful of blue-black squirming lobsters in each hand. His glance swept Miss Phipps's plump form—perhaps a little plumper than usual in her flowered summer frock—with sardonic amusement; his fine gray eyes, Miss Phipps noticed, had a harassed, angry look.

Glancing over her shoulder, Miss Phipps saw a white rowboat pulled up on the shore, its stern still partly afloat in the waves; clearly the man with the lobsters, who was probably Kelly, had just arrived in it.

Miss Phipps went into the café, passed between the clustered tables where passengers from the bus were partaking of tea or ice cream according to age and taste, entered the store part of the establishment and approached the counter. Here lolled half a dozen customers of various ages.

A pleasant-looking young man, fair and stocky, ostensibly examining a stand crammed with picture postcards, was glancing shyly at the girl behind the counter, who was quite beautiful. At least, decided Miss Phipps, she would have been beautiful if one could have seen her face through the make-up. Her silvery blonde hair, her huge long-lashed gray eyes, her oval face, were all highly agreeable in spite of the overdone artifice of green eye-shadow and mauve lipstick.

"Excuse me," said Miss Phipps. "Have you a long pin of any kind—an old-fashioned hatpin would do—to poke out the paper from this bottle?"

"No," said the blonde flatly.

"A hairpin might do."

"We haven't any hairpins."

"Or a knitting needle."

"We haven't any knitting needles," said the blonde, whose beautiful face was now contorted by a scowl.

"What about a pencil?"

The presence of pencils could not be denied, as cards full of them, in many bright colors, were propped against toy boats, buckets, spades, and shells on the counter.

"These are a shilling," said the blonde, proffering a card.

"You've some cheaper ones over there, Maureen," said a pleasant cockney voice in Miss Phipps's ear, and a pointing finger came over her shoulder.

Miss Phipps bought a threepenny pencil and tried to poke out the piece of paper, but without success; it clung stubbornly to the inside and would not be dislodged. The owner of the cockney voice, who proved to be the fair young man, then tried his hand, also without success. So did several other customers, till there was quite a hubbub round Miss Phipps.

Suddenly a huge deep bellow boomed, "Shut up! *I'm* speaking."

Astonished, everyone turned and gaped. The man whom Miss Phipps had seen carrying the lobster buckets stood there, his face crimson with rage. With his great height, his massive shoulders, and his flashing eyes, he awed the crowd into silence.

"What's going on here, Maureen?" he demanded angrily.

"It's just this lady trying to get a piece of paper out of a bottle, Grandpa," said Maureen.

Her voice was timid; it struck Miss Phipps that she was really afraid.

"Give it to me," commanded Kelly, stretching out his hand for the bottle.

Miss Phipps laid it in his powerful hand.

"It just came in from the sea," she said weakly.

"Everything for miles round comes in here," said the man. "The currents bring everything in. You just want to put a spoonful of water in the bottle—"

He strode out of the café, Miss Phipps and the customers trailing after him. He made for a rock pool, dipped in the neck of the bottle, swirled the water round inside, put in a finger, and withdrew the floating paper.

"There you are," he said impatiently, handing the paper to Miss Phipps. "I hope it does you some good. It'll be back here next tide." With a powerful gesture he threw the bottle far out to sea, and strode away.

The paper was a half sheet from a pocket-size engagement diary. It had been torn from the bottom half of a page, and therefore the names of the month and year were not visible, but *2 Wednesday (245-120)* defined the date and day of the week. In the space below *2 Wednesday* was written in pencil, in the large careful capitals of someone writing under difficult conditions, an address: *6 Hill Road, Brittlesea.*

The final letters of the last word were a trifle blurred by sea water, but the name was unmistakable, and Miss Phipps felt a childish pang of disappointment. There was no mystery in her cherished bottle, only a Brittlesea picnicker's joke.

"I'm sorry you're so disappointed, Aunt Marian," said Mary Tarrant. (Miss Phipps had been promoted to this rank in the Tarrant family since the birth of Johnny, who was her godson.)

Mary's voice held a trifle of amusement, and Miss Phipps quickly explained: "I was hoping to find a plot for a detective story."

"Oh, I see," said Mary with respect—the sales of Miss Phipps's detective novels were not to be sneezed at. "Can't you manage to make something out of it?"

"I don't see how," said Miss Phipps dolefully.

She turned the half sheet over, and read in pencil on the other side:

HELP ME

"The first thing," said Miss Phipps eagerly to Detective-Inspector Tarrant that evening, "is to ascertain the date when it was written."

"I see no way of doing that," replied Tarrant crossly. "The page belongs, as you can see at once if you subtract 120 from 365 and count back, to the month of September."

"Obviously," agreed Miss Phipps, who had not previously seen this at all.

"As regards the year," continued Tarrant, ruffling the pages of his own engagement diary and doing a few rapid mental calculations, "September 2nd was a Wednesday last year, 1959. Before that—let's see—allowing for Leap Years—September 2nd was a Wednesday in 1953."

"The pencil writing looks too fresh for 1953," put in Mary.

"Yes. It was probably written last year or this year, don't you think?" said Miss Phipps in a pleading tone.

"What of it?" said Tarrant, his voice still cross.

"The writer," said Miss Phipps, pink but persistent, "may be living at 6 Hill Road, Brittlesea, perhaps kept in restraint, in dire need of help."

"Then why didn't he apply to the police? Why—and indeed how—could such a person throw a bottle into the sea? Hill Road is a good ten minutes' walk from the shore."

The telephone rang and Tarrant hurried off to answer it.

"Don't take any notice of his bad temper, Aunt Marian," said Mary. "He's very worried at present about a big burglary case. Emeralds stolen from Lord Southshire. It happened the week before you came to Brittlesea, but the police have made no progress yet. So John's not quite himself, you see."

"My dear," said Miss Phipps gravely. "Everything John says is completely sensible and well-founded. The whole thing is probably just a picnicker's joke. Nevertheless, because there is just a remote chance that it is not so, I should feel myself lacking in humanity if I did not make myself acquainted with the people who live at 6 Hill Road."

The door was opened by a quietly handsome woman in her early thirties, dark, slender, and admirably dressed. Holding her hand was a merry little girl with large bright brown eyes, who danced up and down with great enjoyment and beamed at Miss Phipps. The resemblance between the merry face and the quiet one was strong; they were surely mother and child.

"Number 6 Hill Road?"

"Yes."

"Mrs. Hesseldine?" said Miss Phipps, who had made inquiries.

"Yes." There was reserve in the reply.

"I've called to ask you a few questions," began Miss Phipps.

She broke off, startled; the look of alarm which sprang to Mrs. Hesseldine's fine eyes was so vivid, her sudden pallor so complete. She has something to conceal, thought Miss Phipps. Her interest quickened.

"It's just this questionnaire," resumed Miss Phipps with an apologetic smile, producing some sheets with mimeographed headings with which she had provided herself. "About the new traffic arrangements in Brittlesea."

"Oh!" said Mrs. Hesseldine. She gave a quick sigh of relief, then smiled. The smile lighted up her face and made her look warmhearted and friendly. "It's probably my mother-in-law you want—Mrs. Robert Hesseldine. She is the householder here. I'm Mrs. Philip Hesseldine—my husband and I are just living with his widowed mother till we can find a house. I'll fetch her."

She hesitated, however, obviously not quite certain whether to invite Miss Phipps into the house.

"I should like to have your opinion too, if I may. This is not an official survey, you understand—just an unofficial investigation by a private group who desire an entirely impartial opinion," babbled Miss Phipps. "The new arrangement of one-way streets and pedestrian crossings, the diversion of the through traffic, and so on."

"You should see my husband on that point," said Mrs. Hesseldine. "He says that the street beside the library has become a perfect deathtrap in the last few years. He is the Chief Librarian of Brittlesea, as you know."

"Of course," lied Miss Phipps affably. "That is just the kind of impartial reaction my group is seeking."

"Do come in. Vicky, take the lady into the front room—I'll go and fetch Grannie."

Vicky took Miss Phipps's hand and led her into a pleasant bay-windowed room, with books and newspapers lying about, and a distant glimpse of the sea. A piece of sewing hastily thrown down on a settee, and a disheveled doll with some toys and papers strewing a larger table, showed that Mrs. Hesseldine and Vicky had been sitting here when Miss Phipps rang the bell. Miss Phipps sat down on the settee.

"Can you draw?" inquired Vicky.

"Not very well," confessed Miss Phipps.

"Could you draw a dog for me?"

"I hardly think so. I might manage a cat in a sitting position."

"I can draw a cat myself, thank you," said Vicky, shaking her head in polite refusal. "What else could you draw?"

"I might try a daisy?" suggested Miss Phipps after some thought.

"A daisy, a daisy!" cried Vicky gleefully.

She bounded away, and bounded back with an old drawing book and a handful of pencils which she thrust on her guest. To the best of her ability Miss Phipps proceeded to draw a daisy. From the artistic point of view it was not a first-class daisy. Vicky viewed it doubtfully, then brightened.

"I'll just print *daisy* below, and then everybody will know what it's meant for," she said, suiting the action to the word.

"She's a darling child," thought Miss Phipps. "I hope to goodness that whatever is wrong here does not concern her. I am glad I came."

"I hope Vicky hasn't been troublesome," said Vicky's mother, advancing into the room accompanied by an older woman.

"Not in the least," replied Miss Phipps, rising.

Introductions were effected. Miss Phipps volunteered her surname. Mrs. Robert Hesseldine was a sturdy, comely woman in the sixties, her manner brisk, firm, emphatic, but not unkind. It struck Miss Phipps that she was a woman accustomed to authority; she had been a hospital Sister, perhaps.

"Jancis tells me you're taking a poll about traffic problems in Brittlesea," she boomed.

"Not quite a poll. A questionnaire," murmured Jancis.

"Same thing. Time, too. My husband—he was surgeon here all his life, you know—would have been horrified by the rise in casualties. What about Vicky's road to school, Jancis?" said Mrs. Hesseldine.

"Vicky and I have lived only a few months in Brittlesea, so I imagine our opinions are not of great value," said Jancis in her quiet tones.

Vicky is not Philip Hesseldine's child then, guessed Miss Phipps.

"Our first consideration must be safety," said Mrs. Robert Hesseldine. "If you had ever taken charge of a casualty ward, as I have, Miss Phipps, you would agree."

"I agree with all my heart," said Miss Phipps, privately preening herself on the accuracy of her deduction.

The talk grew friendly. Tea was proposed. While Jancis went to prepare it, Vicky under the elder Mrs. Hesseldine's directions placed a small table for the convenience of the guest. The table belonged to a nest of three, and Vicky, who had enjoyed the duty of placing it, took up another and looked around.

"Will you have a table as well as Miss Phipps, Grannie?" she said eagerly.

There was a pause—a very slight pause, but long enough for Miss Phipps to see in her hostess's eyes a look of pain, heartache, and fear—before Mrs. Robert Hesseldine replied in her hearty tones. "Yes, Vicky. Put it here."

Oh, dear, thought Miss Phipps sadly. I'm afraid whatever is wrong here *does* concern little Vicky. It was the word *Grannie* which obviously upset the senior Mrs. Hesseldine. Vicky is not her granddaugher by birth, but surely she does not resent the child calling her so? The junior Mrs. Hesseldine had been frightened at the thought of being asked questions, before she had been told what the questions concerned.

Yes, there is something wrong here. But what? And which woman wrote *Help me?* And why?

"Money?" wrote Miss Phipps in her notebook as she and Mary sat waiting for Inspector Tarrant to come in to supper. "Cruelty?"

The Brittlesea Central Library, as became that opulent seaside resort, was an impressive building, large, new, and admirably staffed. Miss Phipps, inquiring for Mr. Philip Hesseldine to aid her on a point of research, was at first gently and politely but firmly put off by ascending grades of library assistants, who endeavored to ascertain her errand and deal with it themselves. But the moment she declared specifically her requirements, pretending that she needed information on the coastline between Brittlesea and Rylan Bay, she was whisked immediately through private doors and into the Chief Librarian's presence.

Philip Hesseldine, thought Miss Phipps approvingly, was exactly the husband she would have chosen for Jancis. Tall and slight, with fine slender hands, gray eyes, and smooth mouse-colored hair, his long intelligent face was at once refined, judicious, and distinguished—it had the look of a man who had suffered much, yet kept his ideals and his self-discipline intact throughout.

"But surely you are Miss Marian Phipps, the detective novelist?" he said in surprise.

Miss Phipps at once threw aside her cloak of silliness and became herself.

"Yes. I'm ashamed to trouble you with my small query, but I need the information for a story I am writing. Absolute accuracy, as you know, is essential."

"It will be a pleasure to assist you," said Philip Hesseldine courteously, placing her in a comfortable armchair.

"I am interested in the workings of the sea tides and currents round Rylan Bay," Miss Phipps invented rapidly. "Flotsam and jetsam and that kind of thing."

She observed him keenly as she spoke. He did not look in the least uneasy or as if the fate of a floating bottle concerned him.

"I don't know that we have anything on those lines," he said thoughtfully. "It is true that the set of the tides towards Rylan Bay is rather remarkably strong, owing probably to the curious Warren structure—"

"Ah, the Warren structure," said Miss Phipps, keeping her end up strenuously. "That interests me greatly. How exactly would you describe it?"

"It's an ancient landslide—a kind of cup between two headlands, seamed with caves and chasms. But as to the tides, I don't think they have gained any widespread literary notice. Would official mariners' charts be helpful. Is it just the Rylan Bay area? Or the Warren?"

"Well—all the coast between Brittlesea and Rylan," said Miss Phipps.

A keener interest showed in Philip Hesseldine's eyes.

"Perhaps a book dealing with the topography of the Southshire coast might be useful?"

"Possibly," agreed Miss Phipps.

"If you will give me your address, I will instruct my staff to find some suitable books and notify you."

"I am staying with Detective-Inspector Tarrant," explained Miss Phipps.

Philip Hesseldine appeared a trifle puzzled. He wrote down the address in a firm beautiful calligraphy in the modern style—much more literate, observed Miss Phipps, than the bottle-note handwriting.

"My staff shall notify you," he said, rising.

Miss Phipps rose too, and turning with a certain deliberate vagueness, found herself in front of a photograph frame of light plain wood, standing on the Chief Librarian's desk. It held a very charming study of Jancis and little Vicky, looking at a book together.

"Oh!" exclaimed Miss Phipps in a gushing tone which even to her own ears rang false. "Are you by any chance—that is, you must be—Mr. Philip Hesseldine who lives at 6 Hill Road?"

"Yes," said Philip Hesseldine coldly.

"I was there yesterday afternoon," babbled Miss Phipps with a gesture toward the photograph, "and met your wife and mother."

"Yes," said Philip Hesseldine.

"And little Vicky, of course. What a sweet girl!"

Philip Hesseldine looked straight into Miss Phipps's eyes and stated in an icy tone, "My stepdaughter. I intend to adopt her."

"A very good idea, I'm sure," approved Miss Phipps heartily.

Yes, he too has something to conceal, and Vicky is at the center of it, thought Miss Phipps as an assistant came in response to a touch on a bell and led her away.

"What a charming photograph of Mrs. Hesseldine that is on the Librarian's desk!" gushed Miss Phipps to the young assistant. "A very good likeness!"

"Yes. She's always very elegant," said the girl admiringly. "She lived in London—Mr. Hesseldine met her while he was working for a time in a library there, you know."

Miss Phipps sighed as she bade farewell and moved out into the sunshine through the handsome library portico.

"I'm not an inch farther with my investigation," she reflected. "No, no, that's not true," she replied to herself staunchly. "I have achieved some certainties and some eliminations. All three Hesseldines have something to conceal, and this something probably concerns Vicky. Philip is not the kind of man to write a *help me* note. He is not affected by the mention of sea tides, but he responds when the coastline is brought up. Odd. We narrow the authorship of the note down, therefore, to Mrs. Hesseldine senior or Jancis. On the whole, I incline to Jancis. She looks as if she had been through a good deal. But against whom could she need help? Her mother-in-law? Why? Her husband?"

Miss Phipps snorted angrily. Few men looked less dangerous than the honorable and intelligent Philip, who wished to adopt

Vicky. Was one of them being blackmailed? Had Vicky some money which the Hesseldine were trying to lay their hands on?

"Oh, bother the Hesseldines," said Detective-Inspector Tarrant angrily. "I really must request you, Aunt Marian, and in the strongest terms, not to busy yourself about this absurd Hesseldine story any longer. The whole thing is a mare's-nest and not of the slightest importance."

"Four people's happiness perhaps," murmured Miss Phipps.

"It is no concern of yours."

"A child's happiness is everyone's concern."

"You are known to be connected with me, and you go about poking your nose into people's private affairs, making your way into their houses under false pretenses, invading their professional premises—"

"Oh?" said Miss Phipps. "How did you know that?"

"Philip Hesseldine telephoned me, of course."

"Really!" said Miss Phipps, astonished. "Why?"

"Do try to show some sense!" shouted Tarrant.

"John," murmured Mary.

"It's all very well, Mary," said her husband irritably, "but here is the whole town in a state of tension, and—"

"*You* are surely in a state of tension, John," said Mary mildly.

Why is the whole town in a state of tension?" asked Miss Phipps. "Wouldn't it be better if you told me all about this Southshire emeralds affair? The Hesseldine business might be mixed up with it."

"Rubbish," said Tarrant rudely.

"Will you tell me, or must I go to the library and read it all up in back issues of the *Brittlesea Herald*?" demanded Miss Phipps.

"For heavens' sake don't go near the library again!" cried Tarrant.

His distress was so real that Miss Phipps was mollified. She sat down and said in a serious, reasonable tone, "John, please tell me the details of the emerald mystery."

"There's no mystery about it—that's the trouble," said Tarrant gruffly. He propped himself on the corner of the table and swung one long leg. "A ducal cousin of Lord Southshire is shortly getting married in Scotland with a good deal of ceremony—balls, dinner parties, that sort of thing. Lady Southshire naturally wishes to wear the famous Southshire emeralds. Lord Southshire brought them down from London—"

"They were stolen near the Library?"

"No. Please don't interrupt, Aunt Marion. Lord Southshire, back in his study, which is in one of the newer wings of the Brittle Keep building, opened the case and looked at the emeralds. The setting of one stone seemed to him a trifle insecure. He went into the next room to fetch a magnifying glass, intending to give the setting a closer examination. He was absent only a minute or two at the outside. When he returned the emeralds were gone."

"Any suspects?" murmured Miss Phipps.

"The thief was perfectly obvious," said Tarrant. "Window cleaners were busy on the Keep windows at the time. One man was occupying a ladder at the next window, invisible to Lord Southshire when he left the room. Obviously, this cleaner moved the ladder to the study window, saw the emeralds, was tempted—Lord Southshire's desk stands beside the window—and stole them."

"Window cleaners!" exclaimed Miss Phipps in amazement. "You mean a commercial firm of window cleaners, from Brittlesea?" Tarrant nodded. "You mean the Earl of Southshire has his windows cleaned by an outside firm, not by his own staff?" Tarrant nodded again. "I gather," said Miss Phipps drily, "that the Earl of Southshire belongs to the new poor."

"Quite right," said Tarrant. "A lot of death duties during the last war."

"How valuable were the emeralds?"

"As such things go, not tremendously. Still, they had diamonds between the stones. Quite a number of thousand pounds," said Tarrant cautiously. "Unique historical setting. Family associations. Huge sentimental value."

"Insured?"

"Of course."

"Then, John dear," said Miss Phipps soothingly, "why worry so much about their recovery? Surely to the Southshires nowadays the insurance money would be infinitely more useful than the jewels?"

"But that's just the point!" shouted Tarrant. "The insurance company hasn't said openly that Lord Southshire disposed of them himself in order to get the cash, but it's clear they're suspicious. They're offering a reward and sending an investigator."

"Ah!" exclaimed Miss Phipps. "I see."

"Brittle Keep has a good system of burglar-alarm bells," went on Tarrant more calmly. "Lord Southshire pressed the bell, the alarm sounded, the courtyard gates were immediately closed, police cars rushed up the hill. Two window cleaners were inside the courtyard, but they are irrelevant—they were too far from the study and under observation at the time. Two more were outside. One of these was quite a distance from the study, round the other side of the castle. One was near the study, as I told you. We questioned him. He denies seeing the emeralds. We questioned everybody. They all offered to be searched. We searched them. We searched the whole castle. It's perfectly clear to me," concluded Tarrant, "that this window cleaner snatched the emeralds through the window, then when he found the police so promptly on the spot, he got rid of them, hid them somewhere. But where?"

"What sort of a man is the window cleaner?" asked Miss Phipps.

"My dear Aunt Marian," said Tarrant. "Believe it or not, he's your old friend Slippy Simthwaite. You remember the Star Isle College case? He finished his prison sentence for that little episode a month or two ago. The other window cleaners are angry with him for involving them. He took those emeralds, I'm sure of it," said Tarrant, rising and pacing the room impatiently. "I can see it in his eye. But he hasn't them in his possession now—I'm also sure of that. There's a sort of cocky impertinence in his manner—he may be speaking the truth when he says he doesn't even know where they are. 'I'm as sorry as you are about it, Inspector,' he said to me. 'I'd help you if I could, upon my word I would.' We can't hold him for anything, of course."

"Most people think he just dropped them over the edge of the cliff into the sea," suggested Mary.

"The sea?" exclaimed Miss Phipps, startled. "Where is Brittle Keep?"

"Really, Aunt Marian!" bellowed Tarrant.

"It's that massive old Norman castle on the cliff to the west of Brittlesea Bay," said Mary hastily.

"Oh, dear," said Miss Phipps. "Do you really think—"

"It's highly probable. The cliff path is only a few yards away from the Keeps walls at that point," said Tarrant. "And then you, Aunt Marian, go to the Brittlesea Public Library and ask for books about the Southshire coastline!"

"I'm sorry, John," said Miss Phipps meekly. "If I'd known all this before, of course, I wouldn't have done so."

Tarrant growled and continued to pace.

"What kind of man is Lord Southshire?" inquired Miss Phipps. "Elderly fuddy-duddy?"

"Certainly not. He's a man of my own age. Went through the war in the 4th Southshires. Burma. Prissoner of war. Health severely damaged by privations. Recovered now. Recently married a very nice girl who adores him. No children yet."

"I gather," said Miss Phipps drily, "that you too went through the war in the 4th Southshires."

"I did. And therefore I shall be very much obliged, Aunt Marian," said Tarrant emphatically, "if you will kindly lay off all detective work in Brittlesea for the time being. Your activities are embarrassing to me."

"Emeralds," said Miss Phipps, "are as nothing compared with a child's possible unhappiness."

"I agree, I agree!" said Tarrant impatiently. "But what about Lord Southshire's unhappiness? He's a right to justice, you know, even if he is an earl. By these foolish activities you are confusing the issue, Aunt Marian, muddying the waters, directing suspicion where it cannot possibly lie. Besides, all this Hesseldine business is nonsense—you've nothing at all to go on. You just like to preen yourself on your powers of observation and deduction. It's simple vanity on your part."

"John!" exclaimed Mary.

"I'm sorry," said Tarrant. "But this business is getting me down."

A subdued Miss Phipps was wheeling young Johnny Tarrant down the ramp to the Brittlesea beach in his push-chair, leaving Mary free to do some shopping. Johnny, who thought the push-chair childish and wished to walk, was silent, pouting.

"Oh, there's Miss Phipps with a little boy!" cried Vicky, dancing up suddenly from the crowded beach. "What's your name, little boy?"

Johnny, as susceptible as most males to flattery, remained silent but surveyed her with some approval.

"My name's Vicky. What's your name?"

After protracted consideration Johnny made his decision. "Johnny," he said, with an effect of male gruffness so like his father's that Miss Phipps smiled.

"Come and sit by us. Grannie's coming down later. Shall we make a sand castle, Johnny? Mummy, Johnny and I are going to make a sand castle."

Miss Phipps found herself settled without choice in the shelter of a small stone pier with Jancis at her side, while Vicky and Johnny made a sand castle a few yards away.

"Very well!" thought Miss Phipps, accepting the situation. "Now for it!"

She drew out of her handbag the bottle message and without comment handed it to her companion.

"What is it? Oh! This is Vicky's handwriting," said Jancis, smiling. "6 Hill Road, Brittlesea. Yes—my husband has taught her to write our address—in case she is ever lost, you know. Is anything wrong, Miss Phipps?"

"No," whispered Miss Phipps, almost choked by surprise and disappointment.

"It looks like the piece of paper she put in a bottle when we were at Rylan Bay last week."

"Yes," stammered Miss Phipps. She explained briefly how she had retrieved the bottle from the waves.

"The currents bring everything back to Rylan Bay, my husband says. Vicky!" called Jancis.

Vicky obediently ran to them.

"Is this the paper you put in the bottle at Rylan Bay last Tuesday afternoon?"

"Yes! Yes!" cried Vicky gleefully. "Did you find it, Miss Phipps? I hoped it would sail right away to France or the other side of the world. But if you found it I don't mind, Miss Phipps."

"Did you write anything on the other side of the paper, Vicky?" asked Miss Phipps hesitantly.

"No."

"Not—this?" said Miss Phipps, turning it over.

"Help me," read Vicky. "No, I didn't write that."

"Where did you get the paper, Vicky?" asked her mother, leaning a little forward to read the message.

"It was just blowing about on the shore," said Vicky.

"Vicky! Vicky!" called Johnny, and she danced away.

"Did *you* write this appeal for help, Mrs. Hesseldine?" asked Miss Phipps.

"No, of course not. Are you not well, Miss Phipps?" said Jancis.

"Quite well. A trifle disappointed, that is all."

"I see it all!" cried Jancis suddenly. "You read that and you thought it a real appeal for help, and you came to the address to see if you could help. That was why you went to see my husband too—to find out what help was needed, and by whom."

"Yes. It was just—well, vanity on my part," said Miss Phipps.

"I don't think so," said Jancis warmly. "To take so much trouble for utter strangers! It was good and kind. Miss Phipps!"

"Yes?"

"I didn't write the message, but I need help all the same. Or rather, I need advice. I feel," said Jancis, "that I can trust you."

"I am entirely at your disposal, my dear," said Miss Phipps. "But do not tell me anything you may possibly regret later."

"It's about Vicky," said Jancis, looking away. "She's illegitimate, you know. I was not married to her father."

"My dear," said Miss Phipps gently. "Youthful indiscretions of that kind have happened before in human history and been forgiven."

"Yes. But Philip wants to adopt her legally. And I want him to do so. It will be so much better, so much easier for her in later life."

"I agree."

"The sooner it is done, the better."

"Quite right."

"But there will be formalities, papers to sign. Her parentage will have to be stated. It will become known that she is illegitimate. Shall I hope to conceal it, or shall I tell?"

"Absolute truth between husband and wife is the only sound foundation for married life," said Miss Phipps.

"What do you mean? Of course *Philip* knows!" exclaimed Jancis angrily. "It's *Mrs.* Hesseldine."

"You and Philip are keeping the truth from her?"

"Yes, at the moment."

"That accounts for your distress and your husband's. But what accounts for *her* distress? Believe me, it is as strong as yours."

"Really? I haven't observed any distress on her part."

"She is as preoccupied with concealing it as you are preoccupied with concealing yours."

"But what are you suggesting?" said Jancis, puzzled. "Surely you don't mean—"

"Here you are!" said Mrs. Robert Hesseldine, walking briskly down the little pier. "I've been looking for you all over. You're not in view from the prom. I caught sight of Vicky at last."

She seated herself by Jancis and glanced at Miss Phipps distrustfully.

"My little godson Johnny Tarrant," said Miss Phipps, waving an introductory hand.

"Mrs. Hesseldine," cried Jancis, cutting across this. "You have perhaps wondered why I continually postpone Philip's adoption of Vicky."

Mrs. Hesseldine hesitated. Her rather artificial look of brightness was suddenly gone.

"It is because Vicky is an illegitimate child. I was not married to her father. He was a married man. He left me and I don't know where he is—and I don't want to know. Vicky's parentage will have to be stated on the application form. I did not want you to know all this," panted Jancis.

"Jancis," said Mrs. Hesseldine slowly, "I have known it for several months."

"Known it?"

"Yes. You forget that I was a nurse before my marriage, and have many friends in the nursing profession. One of them attended you when Vicky was born. She recognized you in photographs I showed her of you and Philip on your wedding day."

"Do you feel very bitterly towards me, Mrs. Hesseldine?"

"My dear," said Mrs. Hesseldine painfully. "What I feel is of little consequence. It is what Philip will think when he hears, which has so distressed me."

"First Miss Phipps insults me and then you!" cried Jancis, the angry color flying to her cheeks. "Do you suppose I should marry Philip without telling him? He has known for years. He knew Vicky's father. That's how I met Philip. He begged me to marry him before Vicky was born. I refused, and I refused many times because I thought I ought not to spoil his life by bringing my troubles into it. But at last he convinced me—perhaps I was wrong—I hope not—that I was necessary to his happiness. Philip's happiness is all I care for except Vicky," faltered Jancis.

"Oh, Jancis!" began Mrs. Hesseldine, weeping.

"Johnny, come and get your coat!" cried Miss Phipps loudly. "It's time we went home."

The weather was gray and misty next morning, and Miss Phipps's spirits matched the weather as she doggedly climbed the cliff path toward the Warren.

Inspector Tarrant had snorted with derision on the previous evening when she told him of the happy denouement in the Hesseldine family.

"Your detection went for nothing," he said.

"That's not quite fair, John," said Mary. "If Aunt Marian hadn't followed up the bottle clue, if she hadn't discerned that something was wrong in the Hesseldine family, if she hadn't shown the paper to Jancis, the discovery that each Hesseldine knew Jancis's secret, and was trying to hide it from the other, would never have been made."

"They would have discovered it for themselves. Outside interference in family affairs is always a mistake. However," conceded Tarrant, "I withdraw my laugh, Aunt Marian. But I still allow myself a smile."

He looked so tired as he sat there eating a late supper after another fruitless day that Miss Phipps smiled too, though not too happily.

For she felt he was right. She was ashamed of her interference, of the lies she had told—especially to Philip Hesseldine. She decided on the spot to make one of her lies to him true—by taking a real interest in the Warren. So here she was, doggedly climbing the path to which Mary had directed her, in a chilly mist.

Somewhat unexpectedly the massive gray walls and towers of Brittle Keep loomed up before her.

There was a man in a raincoat and a uniformed policeman strolling about the grassy cliff-top, and Miss Phipps perceived that this side of the Keep was under observation. It was easy to see where the new wing had been built (a couple of hundred years ago, judged Miss Phipps), which was the study window, where the window cleaner's ladder had rested.

"Looking for the emeralds?" she called jokingly to the policeman.

"Who isn't?" he said, giving her a shrewd look nevertheless.

He made a slight gesture toward the cliff edge. Miss Phipps, peering over, saw below on the gray sea a vessel which was obviously a police launch, and two or three smaller boats. The mist swirled. The height was dizzy. Miss Phipps drew back and walked on.

For five minutes the path was broad and clear. Then, amid masses of gorse and heather, it divided. On the left a tiny track descended abruptly. On the right a sandy path went evenly forward. Miss Phipps, her usually high spirits daunted by her Hesseldine experience, decided timidly that the tiny track was not a path, and went to the right.

It was a long, long walk, and not a very interesting one. The mist began to clear away; from time to time she caught glimpses of a jumble of heather, gorse, and rock on her left, from which rose the sound of surf—inexplicably, for the sea seemed far away. On her right the road from Brittlesea was now visible, running at a distance below hedges and sloping fields.

She had walked a mile or so away from the sea, a mile parallel to the road, and then a mile toward the sea, when suddenly she found herself on top of a grassy headland, in blazing sun.

Far down to her right lay Rylan Bay. Below her to the left stretched the tumbled mass of rock and heather which was now, clearly enough, the Warren with its caves and chasms. Below the Warren, on the distant sea, appeared Kelly's white rowboat, approaching from the direction of Brittlesea. He ceased to row and began to haul in lobster pots, empty them of their victims, and weight and return them, dropping them from a buoy into the rocky crevices. Beyond the Warren rose a headland which now looked close enough to throw a pebble onto it. And sticking up above this headland was an odd stone conformation.

"What's that? Good heavens!" exclaimed Miss Phipps. "It's the top of Brittle Keep Tower!"

She now perceived that she had been walking for these last two hours round the edge of the Warren, across which a short cut would have brought her in a mere ten minutes. As bird flew or fish swam, Brittle Keep was barely half a mile away. Still, perhaps it had been wisest not to tackle the Warren chasms in a mist.

Miss Phipps turned right and hurriedly thankfully down the long slopes of bracken to Rylan Bay.

Hot, hungry, and exhausted, she went into the café, which was empty, the morning bus having gone, the afternoon one not yet come. Maureen, looking very beautiful in spite of an even heavier make-up than before, came out of the back room to greet her. A look of fear crossed the girl's face; it was clear she recognized her.

"Some luncheon, please."

"We don't serve lunches. There's only lobster," sulked Maureen.

"*Anything* will do," said Miss Phipps.

She ate an enjoyable lobster caught by Maureen's grandfather Kelly yesterday, tea, bread and butter, chocolate biscuits, and calling Maureen, drew out her purse to pay.

"Let's see," said Maureen. "There's lobster. That's three and six, and tea that's tenpence, and how many biscuits did you have?"

"Three," said Miss Phipps. "And bread and butter too."

Maureen sighed, and fetching a notebook and pencil from the counter, began to write down the items.

Miss Phipps's eyes goggled. The little book was a last year's diary. The *help me* message had been written on just such a page.

"Maureen! *You* wrote that message!" she cried.

"What do you mean?" blustered Maureen.

"You wrote *help me* on a page of that diary. You meant to give it to that nice young man who comes here to admire you. Then your grandfather came in and you didn't dare. You quietly dropped the message out of the window behind your back. The paper blew away. Why do you want help, my dear?" said Miss Phipps firmly.

"Boo hoo!" bellowed Maureen, bursting into tears.

She threw herself into Miss Phipps's arms and wept cosmetics all over her clean blouse.

"Tell me about it, Maureen," urged Miss Phipps.

"Grandfather didn't know what they were," wept Maureen defensively. "He thought they were cheap stuff—costume jewelry, you know. He gave them to me to wear. Then next day there was a long piece in the newspaper and he took them back and said I mustn't say a word."

"Oh!" exclaimed Miss Phipps. She had suddenly remembered how near, by sea, Brittle Keep was to Rylan Bay; she had remembered old Kelly hauling up his lobster pots. "Oh," she repeated. "The Southshire emeralds."

"That's right. They were tangled in the top of one of his lobster pots—in the wickerwork, you know, when he pulled it up out of the sea."

"But there's a reward offered for their recovery, you silly child!" cried Miss Phipps. "Your grandfather has only to tell the police at once—"

"He's afraid the police mightn't believe him. He has a record, you see. He was in the County Gaol at the same time as that Slippy Simthwaite, and he thinks the police will think it's a put-up job between them. Slippy must have snatched those emeralds and thrown them over the cliff when the police came so quick. But Grandpa wasn't in on it—honest he wasn't! He's been running straight ever since he came out of gaol and we came here."

"He hasn't thrown the emeralds away into the sea?" cried Miss Phipps in sudden alarm.

"No. He can't bear to do that, he says, now he knows how valuable they are. He keeps them in his hip pocket—won't put them down for a minute. Oh, Lord!" cried Maureen, sobbing and pointing, "there he is coming in now."

The white rowboat was heading straight toward them down the long narrow bay. Miss Phipps observed Kelly's easy powerful strokes, remembered his strong body, his impatient speech and angry eye, and wondered what argument a plump elderly lady like herself could possibly find to make him tell his story to the police. Her heart sank.

"I didn't ought to have told you," wailed Maureen. "Oh, there's the busload now," she went on as a hum of voices rose through the sunny air. "Grandpa tries to come in when they're arriving, so they'll see how fresh the lobsters are. I must do my face," she concluded, scurrying to the mirror.

Miss Phipps longed to advise her to wash the face first, but not liking to be unkind, went out of the cottage instead. As she stood there, with the hum of voices swelling behind her and Kelly rowing fast inshore, she saw that infuriating bottle again, bobbing up and down on the incoming tide. If only she'd never seen it!

"Maureen! Maureen!" shouted Miss Phipps, rushing into the café. "Quick, quick, before the bus people come!"

She thrust the largest bucket and spade she could see into Maureen's hands and dragged her down the beach to the tide wrack.

"Dig! Quickly! Put a jellyfish and a heap of seaweed in the bucket," urged Miss Phipps.

"Why?" said Maureen.

"Because you've just found the emeralds caught in the sea wrack deposited by the tide!" cried Miss Phipps.

She snatched up the bucket and ran to the water's edge. Kelly, who had driven the nose of his boat ashore, now leaped out and began to pull the boat up on the beach.

"Mr. Kelly! Maureen has just found the Southshire emeralds tangled in the seaweed!" cried Miss Phipps, waving the bucket at him. "Look! In here! I'm Detective-Inspector Tarrant's aunt." she added in a low, penetrating voice. "Put them in here at once and let Maureen earn the reward, you silly fellow."

The bus passengers peered into the bucket with awe.

"However did you find them, dear?"

"She saw the gleam among the seaweed," prompted Miss Phipps.

"I saw the gleam among the seaweed," repeated Maureen. Her natural quickness of wit then reasserted itself, and she added, "And I ran back and picked up the first bucket and spade I saw."

"But how could the emeralds get *here?*" queried another passenger.

"All the flotsam on this coast is drawn into this bay by the tide," explained Miss Phipps. "It's something to do with the Warren, you know."

"That's true enough," croaked Kelly, wagging his head.

"Your picture will be in all the papers, Maureen," said the Cockney young man admiringly.

For the first time in Miss Phipps's acquaintance with Maureen, the girl smiled.

"I don't believe a word of it," said Detective-Inspector Tarrant. His tone, however, was mild. "You fixed it somehow, Aunt Marian."

"It is absolutely true in essentials, John," said Miss Phipps.

"Well, at least it's taken you away from the Hesseldines," said Tarrant.

"On the contrary. The bottle led me to the Hesseldines, and the Hesseldines led me to the emeralds," said Miss Phipps with a smile.

MISS PHIPPS DISCOVERS AMERICA

"What first put you on to me?" asked the murderer. "It was a matter of literary history," said Miss Phipps. She explained. "I get your point, and I'm sorry," began the murderer, "because as it is—"

"That's the trouble, you see," said Miss Phipps sorrowfully, shaking her head. "One murder so often leads to another. I felt some sympathy for you about the first. I must warn you that I'm wearing a life-jacket," she added hastily.

"That won't help you any after a hard crack on the head with this paddle."

"A dangerous drifting log? I see. But my body will float."

"Not after my well-meant but futile attempts at rescue."

Miss Phipps plucked a whistle from her capacious bosom and blew three loud blasts . . .

On Wednesday morning Miss Phipps had wakened with a start. Whether it was the reflection of the lake water moving in silvery ripples across the bedroom ceiling, or whether it was some sound which had broken her slumber, Miss Phipps was not sure.

Her sleep had been heavy, for she had flown from London to New York the night before, then traveled by another plane, a car, and at last her host's new speedboat, to join her friends, the Stones, in their summer camp in the Adirondacks.

Waldo Stone—short, dark, square, hairy, and friendly—the editor of one of those glossy American magazines which pay such delightfully fabulous sums for serials and short stories, and his small blonde wife Louella, who wrote some of the stories, had been friends of Miss Phipps' ever since a tale of hers had first appeared in Waldo's "book." When Waldo and Louella had married a few years ago, after previous matrimonial misadventures, Miss Phipps had rejoiced greatly.

Now some kind of mixup had arisen about her new serial for Waldo and its television rights, and Louella had cabled her: WHY

NOT COME OVER AND TAKE CARE OF IT AND PLAY ON OUR LAKE—and here she was. So far the Adirondack scenery was all that had been claimed for it. The mountains, the lakes, the huge pines, the chalk-white birches, the graceful spruce . . . Miss Phipps slipped out of bed, put on her spectacles, and went to the window.

The landscape visible from the Stones' handsome "camp"— this was the proper word, Miss Phipps had discovered, though she tended to think of these lakeside summer houses as wooden chalets—had been lovely in hot sunshine yesterday afternoon, when the lake waters were deep blue and the unbroken slopes of surrounding trees deep green; it had been lovely last night when a moonlight path lay across the black lake; it was lovely again now, in still another different guise.

The hour was very early, not quite full dawn, and as Miss Phipps watched a gleam of sun cut a narrow swathe of light across the lake through one of the stretches which divided the Erwins' pine-covered island from the mainland, wreaths of mist still swirled and brooded over the calm silver water. The Stones' wooden boat-dock lay full in this ray of light, but dark patches of mois-ture—footprints pointing to the shore—still remained on it here and there, undried.

Even as Miss Phipps gazed, however, the mist curled in on itself and gracefully withdrew. Across the water, to the left, on the point of their long private island, the Erwins' smartly painted white camp gleamed in the sunshine. Then suddenly the green of the trees brightened, and the lake water took on a delicate tinge of blue.

"Heavenly!" exclaimed Miss Phipps.

She slid back into bed and fell asleep.

It seemed only a moment—though in reality it was some three hours—before she was wakened again, this time by shouts of "Phippsy!"—for this was the name by which she went in the Stone household.

"Coming for a swim, Phippsy?" called Louella, putting her head round the bedroom door.

With some reluctance Miss Phipps heaved herself from the warm bed, squeezed her curves into a sea-blue swim suit, and went down to the boat dock, where Louella (in smart white) and Waldo (in scanty red) were already waiting.

"Hurry up, Randall!" cried Louella to the young man who, in a dark blue bathing suit sporting the white insignia of an athletic club, was neater than Miss Phipps had expected from his tousled appearance the night before. The young man was coming through the trees.

"Don't wait for me!" he called out.

There was more urgency in his tone than the occasion seemed to require, and Miss Phipps looked at him with some interest as he approached. He was tall, dark, and very thin, with a haggard aquiline face, a mass of tumbled black hair, and brilliant brown eyes. It had emerged last night that Waldo regarded him as one of the new young poets of whom America might hope one day to be very proud.

Louella had known Randall's mother at school, so they were both glad to invite him up to the camp for a month and had bedded him in one of their outlying cabins where he could be alone and work to his heart's content. He had felt like working last night soon after Miss Phipps' arrival—so that she had been able to settle the serial and television matter with Waldo at her ease, and had seen little of her fellow guest.

Now as he scrambled down the uneven bank she perceived that Martin Randall limped, and she remembered that Waldo had told her of the childhood riding accident which had crushed the bones of his left foot.

At this point Waldo, looking owlish without his glasses, splashed into the lake in a flat but vigorous dive. Louella lowered herself carefully down the vertical ladder from the dock into the lake, gave a girlish scream at the water's low temperature, and then floundered off in a somewhat spasmodic breast stroke. Miss Phipps followed with a similar scream and stroke, for the water was cold and deep. Randall, she observed, came down the ladder too; possibly his leg injury made it difficult for him to dive.

The day's program proved entirely delightful. After a quick dip, they sipped hot coffee beside a crackling log fire, ate an ample breakfast, dressed at their leisure, then began to make plans. Waldo and Louella decided to invite their lakeside friends for cocktails the next afternoon. As they had no telephone, the invitations must be given in person, and the quickest route was not by the distant and winding road, but by water.

Louella and her two guests went down to the boathouse and stood around while Waldo discussed which of the families who had camps around the lake were in residence with Ben Hunter, the guide employed by Waldo. With his lean height, long curly gray hair and beard, and rather impish blue eyes, he appeared to Miss Phipps the image of James Fenimore Cooper's Natty Bumppo in old age, and she listened to his calm ironic drawl with much enjoyment.

"Are the Erwins in, Ben?" inquired Louella.

"I wouldn't know anything about the Erwins, Mrs. Stone," said Ben. "But I've heard they came two days ago."

"Their flag isn't up," objected Waldo.

A gleam of amusement crossed Ben's blue eyes.

"I did hear as how Mr. Erwin was rather mad about that, Mr. Stone. Seems his flagstaff broke in a blow last winter. He ordered a new one from town, but they haven't delivered it yet. Seems he didn't pay his last bill there in full. Had an argument about an item, or something."

Miss Phipps gave a sympathetic murmur.

"Don't waste any sympathy on John Clayton Erwin, the third, Phippsy," said Louella tartly. "He's a rich playboy who never did a stroke of work in his life. Isn't that so, Ben?"

"I never heard of his working any," drawled Ben. " 'Course, my testimony ain't impartial, ma'am," he added, turning to Miss Phipps.

"Ben worked for the Erwins at one time," explained Louella. "But they didn't see eye to eye on various matters, did you, Ben?"

"It was chiefly deer, Mrs. Stone," murmured Ben.

"Clay shot more deer than his license entitled him to," said Louella. "He was fined heavily and his license revoked—after Ben left him."

Ben gazed across the lake—possibly, thought Miss Phipps, to hide the spark of satisfaction which brightened his elderly eyes. "He's not what you'd call a good shot, Mrs. Stone," he murmured.

"We shall have to ask the Erwins all the same, Louella," said Waldo testily.

"That might spoil the party for your other guests, Mr. Stone," said Ben. "Professor Firbaum and those young Normans, it seems they don't feel very neighborly to Mr. Erwin."

"Why not?"

"I couldn't say, I'm sure, Mrs. Stone," said Ben. "Will that be all, Mr. Stone?"

"Yes, Ben," said Waldo.

"He's a native of these parts and knows everything about everyone," Waldo added to Miss Phipps as Ben disappeared among the trees.

"So I gathered," said Miss Phipps.

A considerable discussion followed as to who should fetch the mail, who should give the invitations, and which boats should be used for these errands. It seemed that Waldo and Louella were both proficient paddlers, and Randall a promising pupil; Miss Phipps declined to attempt a paddle, but was eager to ride in a canoe. So one was drawn down from its rack and launched by Waldo with some noise and splash, but then rejected by Louella as too slow.

Miss Phipps was content to listen idly to the talk, lounging in the now blazing sunshine, and gazing out over the rippling blue lake. From time to time a boat or two passed in the distance; in the mountain peace every sound carried far and accurately across the water. All at once a loud bang nearby caused Miss Phipps to jump in alarm.

"A squirrel, Mr. Stone," said Ben, appearing with a long gun in one hand and a limp gray form in the other.

"Good," said Waldo.

"Why do you shoot squirrels?" asked Miss Phipps, her voice full of distaste.

"They eat the birds' eggs, ma'am," said Ben, disappearing again among the trees.

Miss Phipps sighed. She was familiar with the anomaly by which some people adored horses and dogs but hunted foxes; to love deer and birds and hate squirrels was part of the same perplexing paradox. But then all life was perplexing, mused Miss Phipps, since all animals, in order to sustain life, must destroy other life. Man, however, had imposed laws on this ruthless scheme—at least, to some extent.

"Dreaming up a plot, Phippsy?" shouted Waldo in her ear. "Your royal barge awaits you."

They all climbed into the speedboat and roared off down the lake.

Miss Phipps studied the customs of the lake with great interest. One slowed the speedboat when approaching canoes or persons fishing. One shouted, "Hi, there!" or waved, to every boat or person one passed. It was permissible to blow a whistle to attract attention, and Waldo explained, without demonstrating, the arrangement of long and short blasts which meant a call for help.

They swerved, turning toward the Erwins' handsome boathouse.

"Clay and Virgie are there—I see them," said Waldo.

"Virgie's wearing a hat and a town suit. They must be going somewhere. Perhaps they won't be able to come for cocktails," said Louella—it seemed to Miss Phipps that she spoke with relief.

"Erwin isn't wearing town clothes," observed Randall.

The contrast between the dress of the Erwin pair was certainly marked. Clayton was wearing the typical lake uniform of shorts and T-shirt—of the very finest quality, Miss Phipps observed—while Virginia had a suit of gray corded silk and a little hat to match which, though of the most expensive simplicity, certainly belonged to town.

The Stone speedboat drew up jerkily alongside the dock, for dear Waldo was not the most expert of navigators, thought Miss Phipps; he had not been born to inherited wealth, but had achieved a lake camp recently, the hard way. Miss Phipps saw a look of contempt cross the fair, well-chiseled features of the handsome young Clayton Erwin, and she disliked him on sight.

"Hi, Clay! Hi, Virgie!" cried Waldo, beaming.

"Hi, Waldo," replied Erwin. The deliberate calm and level cadence of these two words had an effect of mockery, and Miss Phipps disliked him even more.

"We came to ask you up for cocktails tomorrow," said Waldo.

"Virginia can't. Her father's ill again," said Erwin.

His slight emphasis on *again* indicated that in his view the health of his wife's father was an unmitigated bore.

"We're just off to see if I can get a seat on the afternoon plane," said Virginia.

Miss Phipps heard in her voice that she was anxious to leave at once. "But to show her anxiety to her husband is a mistake," she thought.

Sure enough, Erwin said promptly, "Oh, there's plenty of time. Come up and have a drink, Waldo—Louella. Oh—and you, Randall." His glance raked Miss Phipps, who had never felt plumper and plainer in her life. The introduction was effected. "I'm afraid I haven't read any of your books," said Erwin with a cold smile.

"I don't believe we've time, Clayton," said Louella, with a glance to Miss Phipps to call her attention to Virginia's unease.

"Oh, come, Louella!" urged Erwin. "Virgie will think she's been inhospitable if you don't stay a while."

The speedboat party disembarked and trailed unhappily up the rocky woodland path to the white camp. Miss Phipps took it slowly for Randall's sake, and Virginia hung back with Miss Phipps.

"Clayton won't have a telephone when he's on vacation, you see," explained Virginia. "We received the telegram about father's illness only yesterday afternoon when we fetched the mail. It was no use trying for a place on the morning plane, Clay thought."

Her voice was wistful. Poor child, thought Miss Phipps, she's a sweet, simple person—she really believes she's been inhospitable. She believes all her husband's gibes. She's desperately unhappy. And very beautiful, added Miss Phipps, surveying the wings of dark hair, the lovely gray eyes, the clear fine skin, the delicate profile.

"As a matter of fact," lied Miss Phipps in a loud cheerful voice so as to be overheard by the three in front, "we really mustn't stay long. Both Mr. Randall and myself have manuscripts which must be posted in time to catch the plane. Isn't that so, Mr. Randall?"

"It certainly is," lied the poet promptly.

A faint color tinged Virginia's cheek. She turned. "Hi, Martin," she said.

"Virginia and I are old schoolmates," said Randall quickly. "She and I and Louella come from the same home town."

"Oh, lord, he's in love with her and the riding accident was in some way her fault and he was too proud to take advantage of it and she feels guilty," diagnosed Miss Phipps rapidly.

"The Stones' camp used to be my father's, you see," said Virginia. "Waldo and Louella bought it after—"

"Virginia!" called her husband imperiously.

Virginia hurried meekly ahead.

Louella and Miss Phipps sat on a log outside the neat little white wooden building, in a grassy clearing framed by pines, which to Miss Phipps's delight had proved to be the nearest U.S. Post Office. Randall, who did not relish the mini walk from the foot of the lake down the road, had remained in the speedboat, and Waldo was inside the Post Office. A huge salmon-pink car flashed by; Virginia Erwin waved, her husband lifted a disdainful finger, in greeting.

"Horrid man!" exclaimed Miss Phipps with emphasis.

"You don't have to tell me," agreed Louella.

"Possessive. Wants his wife at his beck and call every moment. I wonder he allows her to go home alone," said Miss Phipps.

"That's how he holds her. They've no children. Through her father's comfort, I mean. Her mother died some time ago. Her father took a financial tumble, and Clayton rescued him—more or less."

"Less rather than more, I should think. Keeps both of them on the end of a chain. Emotional blackmail, I'd call it. Don't let him blackmail you, Louella."

"What makes you think he does?" said Louella quickly, flushing.

"Oh, just a vague indication here and there—it's surprising what an intonation or pause can suggest . . ."

"Waldo has always said how keen your observation is, Phippsy," said Louella drily. She hesitated. "It's really too absurd," she said. "After all, I'm almost old enough to be Clayton's mother."

"But still handsome, Louella," murmured Miss Phipps, glancing admiringly at the charming petite figure and thick blonde curls.

"It was at a party at our camp. I was getting some more liquor from the closet, when Clayton came up behind me and kissed my neck."

"But did that matter so much?" marveled Miss Phipps. "Everyone kisses and calls darling nowadays."

"No, of course it didn't matter," said Louella angrily. "I disliked it because I dislike Clayton Erwin, but I never thought of it again until he began hinting about it, referring to the incident as if it were something important between us."

"Ah, I see," said Miss Phipps thoughtfully. "You didn't tell Waldo."

"Why on earth should I? It wasn't worth telling."

"But with the lapse of time and these continual hints—"

"Waldo," said Louella, busily lighting a cigarette, "in spite of his editorial airs, is basically not very self-confident. He always tends to think of himself as poor and plain."

"Louella," said Miss Phipps earnestly, "tell Waldo tonight."

"No, I won't!" said Louella. "It's too late."

"You're running a foolish and unnecessary risk, Louella."

"On your way, girls," cried Waldo, emerging from the Post Office with a handful of mail. "We've three invitations to deliver before lunch."

The speedboat swerved, straightened, ceased to roar, and drew up rather neatly beside the boat dock of Colonel Merriam, retired. Waldo climbed out and Randall quickly followed.

Instantly pandemonium reigned. Six small children, clad in six life preservers of varied colors, mingled with six golden retrievers, rushed out on the dock. Waldo and Randall almost disappeared in a confusion of yapping and barking, of screaming and laughing, of a flourishing of tails and paws, a waving of small bare arms and a tossing of curly heads.

Suddenly a voice from above boomed out a word of command, unrecognizable by Miss Phipps, but completely efficacious, for the noise ceased at once. Louella and Miss Phipps, somewhat impeded by several friendly dogs who wished to lick their faces, were at length hauled out of the boat and followed Waldo up the path to the camp, Randall trailing behind. The Colonel, tall, broad, gray-haired, neat in slacks and shirt of becomingly pale khaki, met them halfway. Miss Phipps and Randall were introduced.

"Grandchildren," said the Colonel, indicating them with a wave of the hand. "Come for a month. My sons won't be here again till the week-end and my daughters-in-law have gone marketing with my wife. So I'm in charge. Always put 'em all into life preservers right away—safer, you know. Only two of these dogs are mine, but my sons have two each. Boo-ya!" he shouted—or at least it sounded like that to Miss Phipps.

The dogs and children sat down at once, and Miss Phipps marveled at the similarity of Colonels of all nations. Drinks began to be administered and invitations issued.

"Glad you've dropped by, Waldo," said the Colonel seriously. "Here's Fritz and Ruth come with an awkward problem. Professor and Mrs. Firbaum, Miss Phipps—lake neighbors."

Professor Firbaum (white-haired, fresh-complexioned, probably a Hitler refugee) and his wife (university lecturer, younger, with a spark in the brown eyes behind her spectacles) reminded Miss Phipps strongly of Professor Baer and Jo March in that childhood classic of Lousia Alcott's, *Little Women Wedded*. As these two characters had always been favorites of Miss Phipps's—indeed, the youthful literary efforts of Jo had helped to confirm Miss Phipps's own ambitions—she listened with great sympathy to their account of their troubles.

The details were somewhat too dependent on local topography for Miss Phipps to grasp completely, but she understood the general problem well enough. Clayton Erwin wished to "buy in" part of the Firbaums' land, which faced his own on the mainland on the opposite side of the lake from the Stones—to protect his view, Erwin said. The Firbaums did not wish to sell any of their smallish holdings. Erwin therefore was causing trouble by throwing doubt on their title to their land. Surveyors had been summoned, and lawyers called in.

"But why protect his view? We do not threaten his view. Our camp can scarcely be seen from his windows. We do not even go often on the lake in a boat. We are not good with the boat," explained the Professor, turning to Miss Phipps.

It occurred to Miss Phipps, and she could see that the thought was present in the minds of the others, that the explosions and roarings involved in the inefficient starting and conduct of an outboard motor boat might well disturb a neighboring island's peace. But what arrogant selfishness on Clayton Erwin's part—to be unable to tolerate an infrequent noise! Just like him, however, thought Miss Phipps.

"Fellow's a damned little dictator," boomed the Colonel. "Thinks he rules the earth because he owns a few bonds. Like to have him under my orders for a day or two. Why don't you and I go into town with Fritz, Waldo, and tell the surveyors' office a few things, hey?"

"Be glad to," said Waldo. "All the same it would be better to tackle Clayton privately and try to get him to call it off. Bound to cost Fritz a lot of money if he has to go to court to establish his title."

"I certainly wish I hadn't asked the Erwins for tomorrow," said Louella in distress.

"Might be a good opportunity—I might say a few words to him on Fritz's behalf," said the Colonel, a gleam of battle in his eye.

"He might turn nasty," objected Louella.

"Wouldn't frighten me," boomed the Colonel with obvious enjoyment.

It was agreed to await the result of the Colonel's "few words" before taking any public action.

"We must go—it's late—we still have to call on the Normans," said Louella.

The Normans' camp pleased Miss Phipps greatly, because it was so neat and so obviously homemade. The small house looked exactly like the illustration of the log cabin in the book *From Log Cabin to White House* which Miss Phipps had enjoyed in her teens. A small patch of grass in front was green and well kept.

The boat dock, where a canoe and an outboard motorboat were tied up, was clean and new. What Miss Phipps called a nice normal young man, American married-postwar type, was sawing a log by hand on a sawhorse, watched by a healthy-looking ten-year-old boy.

"Hi, Les!" called Waldo.

"Hi, Waldo," replied Leslie Norman. "Come on in."

He put down the saw carefully and came toward the dock. Miss Phipps noted that his tone, though friendly, seemed subdued. Waldo and Louella evidently noted it too, for they spoke together, with the same intent.

"Sorry—no time," said Waldo. "Just dropped by to ask you and Fran to come in for a drink tomorrow about five."

"Is anything wrong, Les? Where's Frances?" said Louella.

"You haven't heard, then? Tom and Ed here were nearly drowned yesterday morning. Canoe overturned."

The four in the speedboat exclaimed their concern.

"Sure were. 'Course they can both swim, and I went after them pretty quick when Ed blew his whistle—he kept his head and blew it fast, I'll say that for him," said Ed's father, ruffling his son's already tangled hair with a proud hand. "But Tom being younger got a bit of a fright, and he isn't feeling so good this morning. So Fran's kept him in bed and she's staying near him."

"Very wise," said Miss Phipps.

Leslie seemed to find this sympathy agreeable, for he relaxed and said, "But come on in," in a more energetic tone.

"But how did it happen, Les?" said Waldo. "I thought your kids were too well trained on the water to turn over a canoe."

"It was that blasted Clayton Erwin!" growled Leslie, suddenly crimson. "He came past the kids in his speedboat, far too close and far too fast, and naturally the waves of his boat's wake upset their canoe. Of course," said Leslie, swallowing and clearly making a great effort to be fair, "I don't say he saw it happen. He'd be round the point before the wake reached them. But all the same, I'd like to tell Mr. John Clayton Erwin the third just what I think of him."

"You ought to report it to Colonel Merriam as chairman of the Lake Association," suggested Louella.

"Yes, that's the thing to do," urged Waldo. "It was a clear violation of our lake-navigation laws."

"Well," said Leslie doubtfully, "that's what Fran says. But for myself, I'd rather take a poke at that arrogant, condescending—"

"No sense in putting yourself in the wrong, Les," warned Waldo. "Frankly, as an up-and-coming young architect in this neighborhood, you can't afford to make enemies."

"And think of Fran," urged Louella.

"Come round tomorrow and we'll talk it over," said Waldo. "Bring the kids, of course. 'Bye, now!"

" 'Bye now," echoed the young father.

As their boat left the shore Miss Phipps observed that Norman stood looking after them for some time.

"Just tell me, Waldo Stone, what we shall do with Clayton Erwin if he turns up at five tomorrow evening," said Louella.

"We'll turn him over to Phippsy," said Waldo, grinning.

Miss Phipps groaned . . .

A swim, a nap, and a short stroll through the woods filled the afternoon very pleasantly.

"*This is the forest primeval. The murmuring pines and the hemlocks,*" quoted Miss Phipps, gazing up at the towering trees.

"Longfellow!" snorted Randall with derision, while Waldo murmured deprecatingly that the trees were not in fact primeval, but second or third growth.

"Why jeer at Longfellow?" said Miss Phipps. She knew several answers to her question, but wanted to make the young man talk. "Arnold Bennett called him the chief minor poet of the English language."

"What did he know about poetry?" scoffed Randall.

"What do you think of modern English poetry, Mr. Randall?"

"There haven't been any English poets worth mentioning since Shelley and Keats," said Randall, his eyes sparking as he threw out this challenge.

"Wouldn't you include Lord Byron?"

Randall muttered something that Miss Phipps could not make out. The young man was obviously annoyed.

"Tell me about modern American poetry," said Miss Phipps encouragingly.

At first sulky, Randall presently recovered his spirits and talked enthusiastically.

But the best part of the day proved to be the evening, when in two canoes—Louella and Randall in one, Waldo and Miss Phipps in the other—the party set off to the remoter stretches of the lake in search of deer. The canoes glided silently through the calm water in which the huge trees were mirrored with astonishing exactness; in the twilight hush came a sudden *swish-swish* noise, and a red deer bounded suddenly away into a thicket.

The purpose of the excursion being thus achieved, the canoes turned homeward. They had quite a long way to go, and the moon was silvering the black water before they rounded a point of land and saw the lights of the Stones' camp in the distance.

"This is the Erwins' island," said Miss Phipps, proud of the local knowledge she had acquired in only one day. "Oh, no, it can't be," she added, disappointed. "There are *two* lighted houses."

"It's the Erwins' all right," said Waldo. "The other building is where their butler and cook live. In the old days when Clay's father was alive, they had scads of guests and scads of servants, four or five big guest cabins and huge servants' quarters. Even Erwin can't do that nowadays—he just has a married couple. They've a lot of cabins still on the island, though."

"Don't talk to me about that young man," said Miss Phipps. "He spoils the view."

On Thursday morning Miss Phipps woke late and happy, feeling that she had her new environment well in hand. She was now well acquainted with canoes, speedboats, inboard and outboard motors, boat docks, squirrels, deer, gunshots, beaver, chipmunks, trees, drifting logs, guides, camps, and navigation laws. The day began with the agreeable routine which now seemed familiar. After breakfast Randall decided to work and retired to his cabin;

Louella entered into consultation with her elderly housekeeper; Waldo and Miss Phipps were sent down the lake to the nearest small town, to fetch additional liquor for the party.

"That's Les Norman ahead with our local doctor," said Waldo. He put on speed and overtook the Norman outboard, in which an elderly man in more formal clothes than those usually worn by the lake dwellers was sitting rather stiffly. "Hi there, Les! Isn't young Tom feeling well this morning?"

"He's had a very restless night—so Fran wanted the doctor here to have a look at him," said Leslie.

"He has been in shock, and has a cold," said the doctor in a professional tone. "But all he needs is slight sedation and the comfort of his mother's presence. Nothing seriously wrong."

"Glad to hear that," said Waldo, roaring away.

On their way back from town Waldo and Miss Phipps called at the little Post Office to collect the mail.

"I was just wondering, Mr. Stone," said the neat young postmistress, "if you would be so kind as to deliver a telegram to Mr. Erwin. He hasn't been in this morning . . . and . . . as it *is* a telegram . . . it might be important."

She blushed; it was clear that, of course, the contents of the telegram were known to her.

"I'll be glad to," said Waldo.

"I suppose Virginia's father has died," said Miss Phipps.

"I guess so. Clay will need to catch the afternoon plane," said Waldo soberly.

"Shall I stay in the boat?" suggested Miss Phipps a little later, as they tied up at the Erwin dock.

"Certainly not," said Waldo. "Clay is a good character-study for you, and as your editor I insist that you give him the full treatment."

Miss Phipps climbed meekly up the path behind him. At the top they were met by a dignified butler, bald, lined, and adipose, who led them into the large airy living room of the Erwin camp.

"Good morning, Pearson," said Waldo.

"Good morning, sir. I regret that Mr. Clayton is not up yet," said Pearson in an accent which revealed his origin.

"You're English—a fellow-countryman," said Miss Phipps.

"Yes, madam," said Pearson, bowing. "I encountered the late Mr. John Clayton Erwin in France in the First World War and have been butler in the family ever since. My wife too is English."

"I hate to interrupt you two at your old-home week," said Waldo, "but I have an urgent telegram for Mr. Erwin."

The butler hesitated. "It is beyond my instructions to waken Mr. Clayton before he summons me," he said.

("He's accustomed to his master lying blotto with a hangover," decided Miss Phipps with malice.)

Waldo exclaimed impatiently and strode toward an inner door.

"Would you care for a little refreshment, madam? A cup of coffee? A pot of tea? My wife would be happy to prepare it," said Pearson.

Miss Phipps was about to decline when she was interrupted by a loud shout from Waldo, who came rushing out to them in obvious terror, his face white.

"Clayton's dead!" he cried.

"Oh, no, sir," said Pearson calmly. "Mr. Clayton often appears somewhat lifeless after a little over-indulgence the previous night. Last night, Mrs. Clayton being absent, he was a trifle—under the weather, shall I say—when I took him another bottle of whiskey about eleven o'clock."

"Don't be a fool, man," panted Waldo. "His brains are strewn all over the pillow."

The butler, his face a mask of horror, rushed into the bedroom. Miss Phipps followed. Both soon withdrew; the facts were as Waldo had stated them. It was an unpleasant sight.

"He's been murdered!" gasped Pearson.

"What makes you think of murder?" demanded Waldo roughly.

"Mr. Clayton would never kill himself, sir—he likes himself too well. It might have been an accident, perhaps?"

"I don't see how you can have an accident with a deer rifle, while lying horizontally in bed in silk pajamas," said Waldo. "The gun's on the floor at the foot of his bed. Was it his own gun, I wonder? Yes, probably it was," he answered himself, pointing to an empty place in the rack beside the hearth. "Did you hear any shot during the night, Pearson?"

"Not to distinguish from other shots in the woods, sir," stammered Pearson. "There will be fingerprints on the gun, perhaps?"

"I doubt it," said Waldo. "I must ask you, Pearson, to stay here on the island, with your wife, while I go down the lake and notify the police. I shall lock the bedroom door and take the key with me. Don't touch anything."

"Certainly not, sir," said Pearson.

"This dock is under observation, clear if distant, from my camp," continued Waldo, "so any attempt to leave would be instantly noticed."

"I have no desire to leave, sir," said Pearson with dignity.

"Were you attached to your master, Pearson?" asked Miss Phipps.

The butler hesitated. "Mr. Clayton was very charming as a little boy," he said. "After his father died and he inherited so much wealth, he became spoiled. Of late years my wife and I would, I own, have been glad to leave his service, but we should have found it difficult to obtain fresh suitable posts at our age. We are very fond of Mrs. Clayton," he added wistfully.

"I feel this is all wrong, Phippsy," said Waldo as they hurried down the path. "I oughtn't to leave the body, I oughtn't to leave the Pearsons alone. But you can't drive the boat, so I can't stay there myself, and I don't fancy leaving you there alone with the Pearsons. Suppose one of them is the murderer? Not that I think it likely—what the old chap said about the difficulty of finding a new place at his age is true enough, so why should he kill off his present employer?"

"How old is his wife?" inquired Miss Phipps.

"Every month as old as he is," said Waldo, casting off, "and plainer if possible. Erwin hasn't been playing round with her, if that's in your mind. Now if their daughter had been living here—but she hasn't; she married years ago and went to California. And their son is in England—married and stayed there after the war. No, I can't see either of the Pearsons firing a bullet into Erwin's head. But who else could it have been? This is an island, you know—a murderer can't just drop in and out . . . I think I'd better take you back to our camp, Phippsy, before I go for the police—I may be hours with them."

The roaring of the engine made further conversation difficult.

"How far is your camp from Erwin's, Waldo?" shouted Miss Phipps.

"About two miles," shouted Waldo.

When they approached the Stone camp, they saw Louella at the window, with Randall at her side, both waving to them cheerfully. Waldo cut off the engine.

"This is going to be a very unpleasant affair, Phippsy," said Waldo. "So many people round the lake have reason to dislike Clayton Erwin. The police will ferret everything out. It will be a mess."

"Still, as you say, the Erwins' camp is on an island," said Miss Phipps.

Waldo glanced at her sharply. "If you have any bright ideas about solving the murder, Phippsy," he said, "produce them—and fast!"

"I think I know who the murderer is," said Miss Phipps thoughtfully.

"What!" barked Waldo.

"Only there are one or two details I should like to check first." She outlined her plan.

"Well, okay, why not?" said Waldo. "What do we have to lose?"

Miss Phipps, leaning forward, surreptitiously took possession of the whistle which lay in the dashboard compartment.

The murderer paddled the canoe toward the Erwin camp.

"Though I don't see what we're going to do when we get there."

"Neither do I," said Miss Phipps thoughtfully. "I don't think the Pearsons murdered Clayton Erwin, do you? No motive."

"They had a strong motive *not* to do so," said the murderer emphatically. "Besides, to point a gun at a man's head from a yard away, and fire, takes more nerve than an old fellow like Pearson is likely to have."

("The usual pathological conceit of the criminal showing its ugly head," thought Miss Phipps. "He means: 'Pearson couldn't but *I* could'.")

Aloud she said, "He was a soldier once."

"Forty years ago."

"We acquit the Pearsons then, do we? Although they did have the best opportunity . . . Perhaps it would be well to consider all the suspects under the headings of motive and opportunity?"

"It would be better," said the murderer, "to leave it all to the police."

"I'm hoping to clear up the case before the police arrive," said Miss Phipps. The murderer gave her a sudden grim look, and she continued rather nervously, "The people with motives are Louella, the Firbaums, the Normans, Randall, old Ben. Of these, the motives of the Normans and Ben belong to the past; the murder, if committed by them, would spring from revenge for wrongs already inflicted. Now old Ben, I think, has had his revenge: I think it was he who reported Clayton Erwin to the authorities, resulting in the hunting license having been revoked."

"Your analysis so far is excellent," said the murderer. "I agree."

"As for Leslie Norman, it's true he expressed a desire for revenge on Erwin. But he had no opportunity, I think. The boy Tom had a restless night—a statement confirmed by the doctor who had heard the child's own account—so the Normans must have been up several times during the night to comfort him. Therefore, Leslie Norman could not have slipped away to murder Erwin without his departure being noticed. Of course the whole question of opportunity is a very difficult one," said Miss Phipps. "The Erwins' camp being an island, you know."

"You are omitting Colonel Merriam from consideration?" said the murderer.

"I acquit Colonel Merriam on grounds of character, and his sons because they were absent," she said. "His wife and daughters-in-law of course I haven't met. But I acquit the whole family from lack of opportunity. Imagine any murderer trying to slip away quietly in the night from that camp! Those dogs! Whoever tried to leave or return, at least four of them would bark their heads off! The Colonel's command to stop them is a pretty loud bark too."

"True," said the murderer.

"As for Louella," began Miss Phipps.

"Louella surely has no motive."

"I'm afraid she has," said Miss Phipps soberly. "But, I am glad to say, no opportunity. If she had tried to start a motor at our camp, we should all have been wakened by the noise. As for a canoe—the two canoes are on stands and they make a grating noise when pulled across the dock. I doubt, too, if Louella has the strength to launch one. Yes, it is this question of transport which is decisive," she continued. "Consider the Firbaums, for example. Their motive is clear. But they are 'not good with the boat,' you remember? Can you imagine either of them making their way *quietly* across the lake in the dark? Their motive rests on Erwin's objection to the noise they make when they attempt to boat. Yes, the question of transport is, I repeat, decisive."

"How did the murderer reach the Erwins' island, then?"

"He swam. I woke up early on Wednesday morning and saw damp footprints, pointing inwards to the camp, on the Stones' dock. The sun had not yet risen to dry them."

"But Erwin was alive later that Wednesday morning—we all saw him."

"Quite. Wednesday's swimming performance was your *rehearsal*. For some date when you hoped Virginia would be safely absent—for you love Virginia, don't you? I didn't realize the significance of the footprints on the dock at the time, of course."

"What first put you on to me?" asked the murderer.

"It was a matter of literary history, my dear Randall," said Miss Phipps. "You were so sensitive about Lord Byron yesterday afternoon. Byron was a poet, like you, and lame, like you. Because other sports were closed to him he made himself into an exceptionally strong swimmer. So did you—I noticed when I first saw you at the dock that your bathing suit bore the insignia of an athletic club. Byron swam the Hellespont, you remember—the strait between Asia Minor and Europe, the one Leander swam in classical times to see his girl—about four miles."

"I get your point, and I'm sorry," began Randall, "because as it is—"

"That's the trouble, you see," said Miss Phipps sorrowfully, shaking her head. "One murder so often leads to another. I felt some sympathy for you about the first. I must warn you that I'm wearing a life-jacket," she added hastily.

"That won't help you any after a hard crack on the head with this paddle."

"A dangerous drifting log? I see. But my body will float."

"Not after my well-meant but futile attempts at rescue."

Miss Phipps plucked the whistle from her capacious bosom and blew three loud blasts. At the Stones' dock the speedboat started with a roar.

Randall was silent, then he said with surprising calm, "You win, Miss Phipps." He sprang up, tilting the canoe, and threw himself into the lake. "Give my love to Virginia," he said.

He disappeared from view and did not rise again.

MISS PHIPPS GOES TO THE HAIRDRESSER

Brittlesea was having itself a Festival—the Brittlesea Summer Festival of the Arts.

"It's quite a nice coat, Mary," faltered Miss Phipps in a deprecating tone. "I really can't see why you fear for my appearance at the Festival."

"It's a *lovely* coat, Aunt Marian," said Mary Tarrant. For indeed it was lovely—a longish Oriental-looking coat of white satin embroidered in silver with intricate arabesque designs. Worn over the matching white satin gown, plain and sleeveless, which Miss Phipps had acquired as a complement, the effect would be most handsome. At present the two garments lay extended on the bed in the Tarrants' spare room of their house in Brittlesea, which Miss Phipps was occupying as a guest. "Yes, it's lovely. But that only makes it worse."

"Worse?" faltered Miss Phipps again, increasingly dismayed.

"Yes, worse. Aunt Marian," said Mary, with all the appearance of one nerving herself to utter a terrible truth, "You can't go to the banquet tonight, you can't wear that beautiful coat, with your hair in that condition."

"My hair?" murmured Miss Phipps, dumfounded. She raised one hand to her short unruly mop, which she was accustomed to wash herself, hastily and often, and then run a comb through strongly in a backward direction. "What's the matter with it?"

"Everything! No, that's not true. The hair itself is splendid—thick and a nice creamy white and with a broad natural wave. But it's a *mess*, Aunt Marian! It's all different lengths, it's got no shape—one doesn't know whether that zigzag part is intentional—it looks as if different parts belonged to different persons. In short," said the American-bred Mary, producing this English idiom triumphantly, "it looks as if you had been pulled through a hedge backwards. It's an insult to our Mayor, the first woman in Brittlesea to hold the office, to attend her Festival dinner with hair like that; it's an insult to women; and it's an insult to that superb coat."

Here Mary, whose voice had risen almost to a scream, broke off and burst into tears. At this young Johnny, hitherto a placid bystander, also broke into tears and flung his arms round his mother's knees.

"I'm sorry, Aunt Marian," wept Mary, burying her face in Miss Phipps's shoulder. Being much taller than Miss Phipps, she had to stoop to do so, which made it somehow—to coin a word, thought Miss Phipps ruefully—worse.

"But it's all true?"

"Yes, it's all true," Mary sobbed.

"You've been wanting to tell me this for some time?"

"Well—yes," admitted Mary.

"There, there," said Miss Phipps soothingly, patting her shoulder. "Don't cry, Johnny, Mummy isn't hurt. Let's all go downstairs and have a cup of tea."

Mary stopped weeping, but she did not move.

"But what can I do about it?" said Miss Phipps, sensing that there was more to be heard.

"You must go to a really good hairdresser and have a really good set," Mary insisted.

She took her head from Miss Phipps's shoulder, but did not meet her eyes—stooping down instead to attend to Johnny's eyes and nose.

"But surely all the Brittlesea hairdressers will be booked up today," said Miss Phipps hopefully. "If I take your implication aright, every woman attending the Festival banquet will be busy cutting and curling, so—"

"Aunt Marian," said Mary firmly, raising her head, "I'm ashamed to tell you this. I agree I've behaved badly, but the truth is, I've booked an appointment for you at three o'clock this afternoon—at Basil's on the Promenade."

"You should have told me sooner, Mary," said Miss Phipps. She spoke sadly; the thought that she had become intimidating to Mary distressed her.

"Yes, I should have—but I got all hot and bothered about it. In case you'd be annoyed. I seem to get hot and bothered about lots of things nowadays," said Mary shakily.

A sudden delightful idea coursed through Miss Phipps's active brain.

"Perhaps there's a special reason for that?" she suggested.

"Perhaps there is," said Mary meekly, smoothing Johnny's curls with great care.

"Well, I hope it's a little girl this time," cried Miss Phipps joyously.

"Aunt Marian, you're a *brick!*" cried Mary.

"Is this your usual line, madam?" inquired the pleasant young man in the white coat, pressing the waves above Miss Phipps's ears with knowledgeable fingers.

Miss Phipps, dropped by Mary at the white-painted establishment labeled *Chez Basil* in cursive golden script, had entered it with a good deal of alarm and despondency. However, she was soon reassured. Everything was brilliantly clean and extremely comfortable, and the comely young creatures who stood about (on marvelous legs) and attended to customers were clad in coveralls of a charming deep shade of rose.

But Miss Phipps attached less importance to their coveralls than to their courtesy; they guided her through the preliminaries of reception and hat removing (the day was too hot to wear a coat) without stressing her unfamiliarity with these, suggested that she remove her spectacles, shampooed her hair backward (as Miss Phipps thought of it) without allowing water to run down her spine, restored her glasses, and put a cosy warm towel over her head while she waited for her allotted young coiffeur to be free— all the time smiling kindly and speaking in quiet friendly tones.

It was while the young man put up her hair in rollers that Miss Phipps began to be reconciled to her sojourn in *Chez Basil*. The airy rollers were of different sizes and different colors; this intrigued her, and she began to wonder, and to find amusement in wondering, which of them would be used where, and why. But when, the roller installation completed, she sat under the drier in a mauve wrapper, with a glossy woman's magazine in her lap, her enjoyment became actually positive. The magazine she disregarded, but the customers were fascinating.

There was the young girl with very dark smooth hair whose tresses were being sheared off, Miss Phipps thought, far too lavishly. As the rose linen sheet which had been spread beneath her chair became strewn with dark strands and tufts, the girl's expression, which Miss Phipps could see in the mirror, became one of mingled triumph and fright; it was an expression that would take a couple of paragraphs—and not short ones either, mused Miss Phipps—to elucidate and describe.

"I might make a story out of this," reflected Miss Phipps, and at once the keenness of her observation increased.

Presently the rose linen sheet was taken up, the tufts were collected in an elegant rose-colored paper bag inscribed *Chez Basil*, and handed to the girl. She put the bag into her purse, moved to another chair, and took on the ugly, soap-smothered appearance common to the shampooed. Miss Phipps lost interest in her. But there were others to engage her attention.

There was an elderly lady, very cheerful and talkative—an American, Miss Phipps guessed, who was attending the Brittlesea Festival after a quick tour of Europe. As her gray hair was neatly coiled about her head she delivered a monologue which Miss Phipps, under the tyranny of the drier, could not hear; but she guessed it to be a shrewd travelogue.

There were three highly respectable ladies in middle life—"Councillors' wives, I feel sure," thought Miss Phipps—who with frowning absorption consulted pocket notebooks, made out shopping lists, and read letters. They kept their heads down virtuously and knew nothing of what went on around them; they were obviously interested only in themselves.

There was the altogether delightful young married woman in rather crumpled white who came in with a deep round box in one hand and the leash of a white poodle in the other—a nice poodle too, not oddly clipped (this Miss Phipps detested) but wearing his own charmingly curly coat in its natural growth. The girl had a very agreeable face—not brilliantly beautiful, not even conventionally pretty, just young and fresh and good. Her hair, straight, thick, cut fairly short, lay in a shapely bell about her head.

"How difficult it is to find the right word for that color of hair," mused Miss Phipps. "*Blonde* is too pale, *fair* is too insipid. It's not saffron enough for *yellow*, and not quite lustrous enough for *golden*, and too delicate by far for *straw*. It is, *tawny*, perhaps? I don't know. At any rate, a good color. Warm, sunny, honest. Shaded here and there. Good gray eyes, too. A nice girl. Obviously, from the way the assistants greet her, a regular and valued customer."

A man now came hurriedly out from behind a curtain at the back of the shop, which concealed a staircase. It did not escape Miss Phipps's novelist's eye that he had been summoned, for he was followed by one of the rose-clad attendants, who came out with the air of an errand well performed, smiling.

A small, dark, large-eyed, well-groomed, pale little man, forty-ish, in a spotless white short coat, lavender shirt, and bow tie, he hurried at once to the sunny-haired girl, in short springy eager steps.

"This," decided Miss Phipps, "is obviously Basil."

He began to cut the tawny girl's hair, employing, Miss Phipps thought, considerable skill, gentle handling, and a great deal of care. Though she could not hear a word he said, his eager gush of speech was plain to see and it struck Miss Phipps as pathetic, for the girl appeared to give only a vague occasional murmur in reply, and was otherwise silent.

"He adores her and she doesn't know he's there," decided Miss Phipps.

The hair styling finished, the girl made a quiet gesture toward the deep round box she had brought with her. Basil untied its gold cord and took off its lid (inscribed *Chez Basil*) with much *empressement*. Miss Phipps could not, however, see what was inside the box since Basil blocked her line of sight. After a few minutes of animated talk the lid was replaced and Basil took the box reverently away into a small room at the rear.

At this point one of the rose-clad attendants came and released Miss Phipps from the drier, led her to a seat before a mirror, and began to dismantle her rollers. She became aware of her restored ability to hear when a new customer entered the shop.

"Lesley!" drawled the newcomer, advancing at once upon the tawny girl.

"Hello, Sybille," said Lesley pleasantly. "Preening for tonight, like the rest of us?"

"Of course," said Sybille with just a touch of scorn.

Though she doesn't look as if she needed any preening, thought Miss Phipps, observing in the mirror before her Sybille's complex and elegant hairdo, every dark strand smooth and intact.

"She's very elegant altogether. Beautiful slim figure, superb complexion, long dark lashes—artificial, though, I think—a really interesting dress of a strange pale bronze hue, shoes and gloves and bag in gleaming bronze that match exactly. She makes dear Lesley look a little sloppy," thought Miss Phipps ruefully.

"And you?" drawled Sybille.

"Just a trim," said Lesley.

"And how is dear Canon Floyd?" inquired Sybille.

Strange how one word can create a hostile impression when it is excessive in sentiment, thought Miss Phipps, disliking Sybille instantly. *Dear* Canon Floyd, indeed! Insincere pussy! She doesn't care a row of pins for Canon Floyd, whoever he may be.

"My father is not convalescing quite as well as I could wish," replied Lesley. Her tone was formal, reserved, and she turned her head aside rather sharply; from this Miss Phipps deduced that the Canon was seriously ill, and that his daughter loved him.

Basil returned, and bowing politely but without enthusiasm, greeted Sybille as Mrs. Mortimer, and withdrew again to the rear. Miss Phipps's young hairdresser now approached and began to brush out her curls, and Miss Phipps temporarily lost interest in Lesley and Sybille, especially as her view of them was now somewhat obscured by the lad behind her.

"Is this your usual line, madam?" he inquired, adjusting the waves above her ears with knowledgeable fingers.

Miss Phipps gazed at herself in the mirror, aghast. A distinguished-looking, well-groomed, haughty, totally unrecognizable person gazed back at her.

"Well," she began timidly, "perhaps a little less—"

She was interrupted by a disturbance behind her. Turning quickly, she saw a tall, handsome, brown-haired, scowling young man stride furiously through the shop. There was a sharp bark, a confusion of voices, a scrape of chairs, then the tall athletic young man strode through the shop again, dragging the alarmed poodle, who looked backward appealingly at Lesley following hastily behind him.

"I must pay," objected Lesley, looking flushed and disturbed as she opened her purse.

"There's no time," said the young man sharply, continuing his angry stride.

"Another day, another day," said Basil soothingly, approaching at a run and waving his hands.

In the background Mrs. Mortimer smiled with some malice, and raised her eyebrows as man, dog, and Lesley rushed out of the shop.

"Is this madam's usual line?" persisted Miss Phipps's coiffeur.

"Well—yes, I suppose so," said the reluctant but intimidated Miss Phipps.

The American lady, who had now belatedly decided to have a manicure, nodded at her approvingly.

Inspector Tarrant in his dress uniform with a couple of medals, Mary in a primrose silk which enhanced the luster of her brown hair, Miss Phipps in the white and silver Oriental coat, stood in the reception room of the Brittlesea Town Hall, drinking cocktails amid a crowd of equally well dressed persons, similarly engaged. Miss Phipps thought their trio made a very good appearance, and beamed happily.

In the distance she saw Lesley, again in white (not new in fashion). At her side stood the handsome young man, in the uniform of an Army officer. Miss Phipps was interested to see that signs of mutual acquaintance passed between Lesley and Mary.

"Who is that fair-haired girl? With the good-looking Captain, over there?" she asked.

"That's Mrs. Carey. We attend the same cookery class at the Brittlesea Technical Institute—that's how I know her. Her husband is with her."

"He's stationed at the barracks just outside Brittlesea—his regiment is the Southshire Buffs. Very nice chap. A bit hot-tempered at times," enlarged John Tarrant.

"And a bit jealous too, from all I hear," said Mary disapprovingly. "So silly—his wife's as good as gold, and so devoted to him."

"But very attractive," said Inspector Tarrant.

"Captain Carey's very attractive too," said Mary.

"But a decent fellow," repeated Inspector Tarrant. "I have to deal with him sometimes, you know, when some of the men of the regiment get into a spot of bother."

"And who's the slinky beauty in skin-tight black standing next to them?" inquired Miss Phipps, gazing disapprovingly at Mrs. Mortimer's smile. "I know her name."

"Mrs. Mortimer is a rich widow who has a bijou residence on the Promenade," said Mary drily.

"She seems rather interested in Captain Carey," commented Miss Phipps, observing Sybille's play of lip and eye.

"She's interested in any man," said Mary as before. "Any man, period."

"But perhaps especially in Captain Carey?"

"I don't really know," said Mary. "Perhaps."

Dinner was announced. The speeches were perhaps slightly better than the average of Mayoral-banquet speeches. Miss Phipps's response to the toast of "The Guests" was well received.

The next night was the occasion of a concert given in Brittlesea's Pavilion by an orchestra of international repute. The vast Victorian structure of glass and iron, situated on the outer end of Brittlesea's pier and built, of course, in pre-automobile days, presented parking problems of quite staggering proportions. Cars were, of course, not allowed on the wooden-plank pier.

Inspector Tarrant dropped his wife and Miss Phipps at the land end of the pier, and drove off, like everybody else, in search of a place to leave his car. The two women walked along the pier—fortunately the night was fine and warm—entered the foyer and stood waiting for him. They had no wraps to check and therefore nothing to occupy their time. In the bustle and chatter of the foyer Mary began to wilt.

"Let us go into the auditorium, dear," suggested Miss Phipps.

"John gave me all the tickets," hesitated Mary.

"You go in. Give me John's ticket and mine, and I'll wait for him."

Mary agreed with relief, and Miss Phipps was left alone.

The incoming audience swelled to a crowd, eased off to a comfortable throng, thinned to a slow stream, became a mere few latecomers rushing up the steps. Among the last arrivals were Captain Carey and Inspector Tarrant.

"Where's Mary?"

"She went in."

"Good. Come along."

Captain Carey reached the ticket taker ahead of them.

"Has my wife gone in, Bradshaw?" he demanded. His voice was loud and harsh, and his face flushed.

"I don't think so, sir," said the elderly Bradshaw, who had the look of an ex-soldier.

"You mean she hasn't, don't you," shouted Captain Carey.

"I couldn't say for certain, sir," replied Bradshaw firmly. "Best go in and see, sir."

With an angry mutter Carey swung away, outward toward the steps. Unluckily, at this moment Basil came running up the steps into the foyer. Without a word of warning Captain Carey hit him hard across the mouth. Basil stumbled sideways and fell on his hands and knees.

Miss Phipps rushed to him and pulled him upright; Inspector Tarrant seized Captain Carey by the arm; with one accord they pushed the combatants—not that poor Basil was much of a combatant, reflected Miss Phipps—into a side room, and the Inspector with his free left hand closed the door behind the four of them.

Miss Phipps dumped Basil into a velvet chair and began to dab his mouth, which was bleeding, with her all-too-small lace-edged evening handkerchief.

"I'm an officer of the police," said Inspector Tarrant in a stern official tone. "Do you wish to prefer charges, Mr. Basil? The assault was entirely unprovoked, and there were witnesses."

"No, no! Of course not," panted Basil. "On no account."

"It wasn't entirely unprovoked, Inspector," said Carey grimly.

"I saw no provocation."

"I don't wish to discuss it here."

"Then I must ask you to accompany me to the Brittlesea police headquarters."

"No, no!" exclaimed Miss Phipps, viewing with horror the prospect of the young officer's career being wrecked.

Basil stood up. "I slipped and fell against the wall of the foyer, Inspector," he said, his light voice unexpectedly firm, "and that will be my testimony."

"If you are certain of that, sir, of course there's no more to be said."

"I should prefer to be charged," raged Carey. "The man's a blackguard and a scoundrel."

"I don't know what grounds you have for saying that, Captain Carey," said Basil in a tone of astonishment.

"Yes, you do. You know perfectly well."

"Believe me, I have no idea."

"I don't believe you."

The door of the room was flung open, and Lesley Carey came in. She ran straight to her husband and took his arm.

"Bradshaw told me you were in this room, Gerard," she said. "What's the matter? What has happened?" Looking quickly round the room, she saw Basil, his mouth still bleeding, and gave an "Oh!" of dismay.

The Captain disengaged his arm from her hand.

"Where have you been this last half hour, Lesley?" he said. His utterance was now quiet, but ominous.

"I went across the Square to look in on father," said Lesley. "You *knew* I was going to see him—I *told* you, Gerard."

"Liar!" burst forth Carey in furious anger. "I saw you at the entrance to this little whippersnapper's flat."

"Oh, rubbish!" exclaimed Lesley.

"Yes. The small porch entrance at the side of his shop, which leads up a staircase to his flat. I *saw* you, Lesley."

"That's absolute nonsense, Gerard," said Lesley.

"I tell you I *saw* you."

"I have not seen Mrs. Carey since yesterday afternoon, when you called for her at my salon," said Basil quietly.

"Of course you would say that to defend her."

"It is true I have much respect for Mrs. Carey," said Basil. "Too much, I assure you, to lie about her."

Really the little man came out of this clash extremely well, thought Miss Phipps. It is not easy to retain one's dignity with a lip cut and swollen, a bow tie under one's ear, and a collar blood-stained; but he achieved it.

"I saw her at your door," insisted Captain Carey.

"We are keeping these good people from the concert," said Lesley, suddenly icy. "I shall go and stay at my father's and await your apology, Gerard. You are really too insulting. I can't stand this endless silly jealousy any more."

Her voice quavered on this last sentence, and she left the room in a rush, as if fearing the collapse of her composure.

"Please go into the auditorium, Miss Phipps—Mary will be anxious at our absence," said Inspector Tarrant formally. "I will ring for an ambulance for you, sir; you must have that cut attended to at once."

He left the room, followed by Basil.

"But I *saw* her! Don't you understand, I *saw* her!" said Captain Carey, turning to Miss Phipps. "Does he think I don't know my own wife? It's not as if it were twilight, or autumn, or something of that sort; it's high summer, only seven o'clock, bright daylight, golden sunshine, and I wasn't fifty yards from her. I *saw* her."

He spoke the word *golden* with a wincing emphasis which revealed to Miss Phipps's novelist's ear that he thought of his wife's hair by that loving epithet, and his handsome young face was so contorted with anguish that Miss Phipps felt extremely sorry for him. She believed every word he said. Unfortunately she also believed Lesley and Basil.

"I'm sure there must be an explanation which will make everything clear," she said soothingly.

But she could not for the life of her think what it might be as, next morning, she visited all the locales of this regrettable triangle.

The previous evening had been decidedly uncomfortable. As the orchestra had begun to play by the time Miss Phipps was finished with Captain Carey, who suddenly flung himself out of the building, she was not allowed to enter the auditorium, but was ushered politely back into the same side room to await the end of the Beethoven symphony. Miss Phipps, who had particularly wished to hear this orchestra's performance of the *Eroica* (very familiar but still a great favorite), was vexed, and her vexation was not diminished by the behavior of the car drivers, men and women, who, late because of parking difficulties or mere unpunctuality, were likewise confined to the side room. Apparently untroubled by missing the Beethoven, the others had argued so vigorously about the parking problem in Brittlesea that the wearied Miss Phipps felt she knew every back street, road, and square in the vicinity of the pier.

Among these late-comers was Mrs. Mortimer, who swept in impressively clad in a white sheath which made poor Lesley's full chiffon—which she had worn the night before—look decidedly outmoded. This again had vexed Miss Phipps, and she observed rather crossly with what admiring attention (quite insincere) Mrs. Mortimer had turned her brilliant dark eyes (belladonna drops) on all the males and had roused their admiration for her hair by raising a hand in a languid gesture to smooth it.

When at last the symphony was finished and the prisoners were released, Miss Phipps found Mary white and anxious, but had to wait for the intermission before she could tell her the whole story. In the foyer they had been met by Inspector Tarrant, who found them seats and coffee with masterly competence, but then stood in front of them without a smile.

"How I dislike that woman!" Miss Phipps had exclaimed irritably as the beautiful Mrs. Mortimer strolled by, a man on either hand. "Really, rich young widows are a menace to the community."

"That's rather too sweeping, Aunt Marian," Inspector Tarrant had objected heavily.

His gloomy mood was still with him next morning. When Miss Phipps asked him at breakfast where he had parked the previous night, where Captain Carey had parked, and had he seen Mrs. Carey in the doorway leading to Basil's flat, he replied shortly, even snappily; if Miss Phipps had not listened to the parking talk last night she would have been completely at sea.

"No, I did *not* see Mrs. Carey," he said with irritable precision. "I parked in Smith Street, which runs from High Street into the Promenade, at right angles; I walked up to the Promenade and along the Promenade and I saw Captain Carey emerge ahead of me from Taylor Street, a street parallel to Smith Street, some hundred yards or so nearer the Pier. I followed him along the Promenade, gradually narrowing the distance between us. *Chez Basil*—" he had pronounced the words with immense disgust—"is farther along the Promenade, nearer the Pier. At the entrance to the Pier, Captain Carey paused and looked back along the Promenade, and I drew near to him."

"And where does Canon Floyd live?"

"In Taylor Square. The Square is to the left of Taylor Street. Nearer the Pier."

"Then Mrs. Carey could hardly have reached *Chez Basil*—"

"Yes, she could. There are streets parallel to the Promenade, leading out of Taylor Square, and other streets leading up at right angles to the Promenade. If Carey had as much difficulty finding a parking space in Taylor Street as I had in Smith Street, which is all too probable, she could well have reached *Chez Basil* by another route, before him. Mrs. Mortimer, whom I saw later approaching the Pavilion, as I went with Basil to summon the ambulance," added Inspector Tarrant drily, anticipating Miss Phipps's question, "lives on the Promenade, at the corner of Taylor Street. She could well have seen Captain Carey coming up Taylor Street from her corner window, watched him pass, and followed him. But in that very tight shift, or whatever you call it—"

"Sheath," put in Mary.

"She probably couldn't walk fast enough to catch up to him. Indeed, she couldn't have done so, because she didn't catch up with me, and I was some yards behind Carey. So if you think she persuaded Captain Carey to believe he saw his wife at Basil's entrance, Aunt Marian, you are wrong. Is there anything more you want to know?"

"No, thank you," said Miss Phipps meekly.

"I'm glad of that. Let me say that I shall be extremely displeased if you attempt any interference in the Carey affair, Aunt Marian. It would be most uncalled-for, and most unwise."

"They are two good young people, unhappily estranged," said Miss Phipps, firing up.

"Never interfere between a man and his wife," pronounced Inspector Tarrant, gloomier than before.

"Just let them remain unhappy, eh?"

"I believe Captain Carey—that he did see his wife."

"So, so do I. But I believe Lesley and Basil too."

"How can you?"

"That's what I propose to find out," said Miss Phipps.

"They contradict each other."

"Not necessarily," said Miss Phipps staunchly.

"How do you make that out?"

"We shall see."

Inspector Tarrant gave a hollow laugh and left for headquarters.

"Will you come with me, Mary?" said Miss Phipps. "I must see these places for myself."

"I think I'd better not," hesitated Mary. "John seems so upset. Of course he never tells me anything about his work, but I think— I *think* it's just *possible*, you know, that he may have seen Lesley Carey—just a glimpse, you know."

"Oh, *no!*" said Miss Phipps.

"I think John caught just a glimpse of her in the distance," repeated Mary.

Miss Phipps refused to believe it. But when she had seen Smith Street, Taylor Street, Taylor Square, and various other smaller streets, which were all laid out in rectangles as Inspector Tarrant had said, she perceived that his account of the movements of the characters (for she thought of them that way) was not only possible, but probably true. She felt daunted. Bracing herself, however, she walked along to *Chez Basil*, observed the little white porch at the side which covered the doorway of Basil's flat, and entered the shop next door firmly. The establishment, naturally enough for any morning, particularly a morning after two important evening functions, was rather empty.

"Madam," said Basil, bowing. "I believe I have reason to be grateful to you."

He looked pale and sad, and wore a strip of plaster at one end of his mouth. There was a touch of gray, Miss Phipps observed, above his ears.

"I should like to have a few words with you about last night's incident, if I may," she said.

Basil shrugged, and led her up the stairs behind the curtain.

The flat was extremely pleasant, with white paint, gray carpet, mauve-patterned gray curtains, mauve linen furniture covers, long white shelves of books—poetry, plays, biographies, intelligent fiction—on each side of the handsome inset radiator, a large record player and television set, and two startling but attractive modern paintings, originals. The view of the sea was, of course, delightful. Miss Phipps was alarmed. He's much more intellectual than poor young Captain Carey, she thought; but then, I don't suppose Lesley is very intellectual either.

"There are two entrances to your flat—one direct from the Promenade, one through the shop," she said, coming at once to the point.

"Yes. And there is a back exit from the shop into a lane behind," said Basil drily.

"Oh, dear. Then Mrs. Carey's visit to you, and her disappearance before her husband reached your porch, was perfectly possible."

"It was possible," said Basil, "but it did not take place. Any suggestion that it did is totally untrue. Do you believe me, Miss—Phipps, is it?"

"I believe you. How did you come to follow Captain Carey to the Pier Pavilion?"

"I had a ticket for the concert, of course, since music is one of my great pleasures. I saw Captain Carey's car drive down the Promenade, looking for a parking place. I waited for him to come back, for I hoped that Mrs. Carey would be walking with him. It is a pleasure to me to see her. I intended to follow them at a distance. When he returned alone, I gave up hope of seeing her and left for the Pavilion. Yes, it is a pleasure to me to see her, but all the same, Miss Phipps, she did not visit me."

"She says she went to visit her father."

"Whatever Mrs. Carey says is true. Her father is very ill. Rest assured, Miss Phipps, that I shall make no charges against Captain Carey for his assault on me. I would not give Mrs. Carey such pain."

Miss Phipps was silent for a moment.

"Can you give me the names and addresses of all the customers who were in your salon the afternoon before the banquet?" she said at length.

"I can and will. My girls have orders to take the names and addresses of all new clients, and we already know those who have formerly visited us. I see no purpose in this, however."

"Anything is worth trying," said Miss Phipps.

Basil shrugged.

Miss Phipps, who while on lecture tours had traveled quite extensively in Mrs. Seaton's native State, found her very friendly and conversational. Indeed, she found herself lunching at the admirable hotel where that lady was staying, and discussing the capitals of Europe at length. The problem was to get her hostess back to the incidents at *Chez Basil*, which naturally held less interest for her than the Champs Elysées or the Colosseum.

"I came really to ask your help," said Miss Phipps, having truthfully agreed that the hotel coffee was not bad but not as good as that obtainable in the States. "Will you spare me a moment of your time?"

"Why, surely," said Mrs. Seaton. (Her face, however, fell just a trifle.)

"It has nothing to do with money," pursued Miss Phipps.

(Mrs. Seaton brightened.)

"We were in that hairdresser's called *Chez Basil* at the same time, the day before yesterday in the afternoon."

"We were," agreed Mrs. Seaton.

"Though you remained there longer than I did because of your manicure. Do you remember a rather good-looking young woman, with a white poodle?"

"Yes, indeed. A very fine head of hair. Very English-looking. My granddaughter's is similar, my eldest granddaughter that is," began Mrs. Seaton, reminiscing. Miss Phipps listened patiently, and presently brought her back to *Chez Basil*. "But that noisy young man, I guess he was her husband! What terrible manners! What a way to behave! He must have been out of his mind! Do you know why he was so mad, Miss Phipps?"

"I think he was troubled by jealousy."

"Men!" exclaimed Mrs. Seaton putting a world of feeling into just one word. "My son-in-law—my younger son-in-law, that is—but you don't want to hear about him. My husband always says, 'Elvira, you talk either too much or too little.' He's right, you know. He wouldn't come to Brittlesea with me. 'No, Elvira,' he said, 'you go ahead and enjoy your night; I haven't finished with London yet.' I wanted to come to the Festival, you see; I wanted to see Sir Mervyn—" here Mrs. Seaton mentioned the name of a very famous actor—"in the play tonight. *Twelfth Night*. Yes. I do *love* your Shakespeare," said Mrs. Seaton, beaming. "He's ours too, of course."

"We have tickets for the first night, tonight," murmured Miss Phipps hastily. Having got into the conversation, she went on hastily, "Did you notice anything—well, significant—about that fair-haired girl, anything which might indicate any—connection—any intimacy between her and the hairdresser?"

"Why, no! What are you thinking of?" cried Mrs. Seaton in dismay, shocked to the depths of her Bostonian soul. "My thought was that he had a kind of reverence for her because of her beautiful hair, but she was quite unconscious of it. The only thing I noticed about her was that, being dragged off in a hurry like that— Colonel's tea party or no Colonel's tea party, but I think myself that was just her husband's excuse—she forgot her box; for which her husband will probably scold her, though it was all his fault."

"Ah, yes, I remember that deep round box," said Miss Phipps. "What—"

"Oval," Mrs. Seaton corrected her. "That dark beauty, her friend, took it for her—Basil gave it to her to deliver. I don't mean the young girl, the actress, who was having her hair trimmed. I mean the older woman, rather feline, wearing a Dior dress."

"Oh, it was a Dior—"

"Yes, indeed. I think Miss Jackson will make a charming Viola, don't you?"

"Oh, is she to play—"

"Yes, yes. The young girl who was having her hair trimmed. The boy who dressed my hair told me. I guess that was the reason for the very short hair. Well, I hope you won't think I'm rushing you, Miss Phipps, but I'm afraid I must leave you now. I must have my rest in the afternoon, so Dr. Braun says. He's quite the best psychiatrist in the States; I go to him every Wednesday. Goodbye, Miss Phipps. We shall perhaps see each other at the theater tonight. Goodbye."

"Goodbye—and thank you immensely," said Miss Phipps.

But Mrs. Seaton was already disappearing up the stairs.

The receptionist at the quiet but reputable hotel which Miss Olive Jackson had given *Chez Basil* as her address looked grave when Miss Phipps inquired for the actress.

"She's at the theater. The Pavilion, you know," said the receptionist. "They're having some trouble with the scenery. It doesn't fit. A door's position may have to be changed, and that, I'm told, will alter the acting positions. Sir Mervyn is very cross about it."

Miss Phipps, wandering peacefully into the Pavilion auditorium, beheld the sight, always so fascinating to a theater-lover, of a bare stage in the process of being transformed into a scene.

"A permanent set," she thought as she stood in the center aisle, enjoying her own familiarity with theatrical terms. "Those steps are good. And that balcony. But oh, dear! That flat containing the door won't go in at the side. I can see that. I wonder what—"

"Who are *you*?" demanded a furious voice.

Miss Phipps turned in a flutter and found herself face to face with the great Sir Mervyn in a towering rage.

"Marian Phipps," she stammered.

"What are you doing here?" shouted Sir Mervyn, contracting his heavy eyebrows in a fearsome scowl.

"Well, I just wanted to see—" began Miss Phipps.

"Get this woman *out* of here!" roared Sir Mervyn to the young man beside him. "How often have I told you, idiot, that I will *not* have any outsiders present at rehearsals?"

The unlucky assistant stage manager, looking pale and scared, seized Miss Phipps's arm and hustled her out of the auditorium.

"I just wanted to see Miss Jackson," said Miss Phipps.

"Straight up those stairs, turn to the right, first along the corridor," whispered the A.S.M.

Miss Phipps, knocking at the door and entering the indicated dressing room, found Miss Jackson sitting in front of her mirror, wearing a huge woolen pullover and very tight pants, both of a dreary color and rather dirty. She looked despondent.

"Who are *you*, then?" she threw crossly over her shoulder, seeing Miss Phipps in the mirror and not troubling to turn.

"My name," began Miss Phipps, "is Marian Phipps. I—"

"Ought I to know it?"

"It would be nice if you did," said Miss Phipps, "but of course I don't expect—"

"What have you played?"

"I am a writer," said Miss Phipps, "of detective stories. I make no—"

"I haven't read them. Are any in paperback?"

"Six," snapped Miss Phipps.

"Oh. Sorry, I'm sure. What can I do for you, then?"

"I'm trying to right a wrong done to a young wife—" began Miss Phipps.

"The best of British luck to her, I'm sure."

"You may have noticed her in *Chez Basil* on Monday afternoon," persevered Miss Phipps. "She has very fair hair, quite noticeable."

"Oh, Goldilocks. Yes, I saw her, and dear Basil bowing at her feet, and the slinky dark lady hovering nearby, vulturewise."

"I'm glad you noticed her," said Miss Phipps, pressing on. "Because—"

"Oh, you noticed me, then?" said Miss Jackson with interest. "Are you coming to see us, then? Eh? Have you booked? You should, you know. You won't get in otherwise. I don't expect you've booked. Later on, of course, you'll try. Dickens said—in *Nicholas Nickleby*, you know, though I don't expect you do—that the British public never want to go a theater until they think they can't get in."

"I have already booked my seat for tonight," said Miss Phipps with some dignity. "And I certainly did notice you. I was interested by so much shearing off of your hair. I understand that now."

"You don't, you know."

"If you're playing Viola—"

"Oh, you know the play, do you?"

"Really, Miss Jackson, you are being extremely rude," said Miss Phipps, now in a rage as towering as Sir Mervyn's, though she lacked his resonant means of vocal expression. "I noticed you only because it intrigued me to see all your discarded tresses being gathered up and given back to you. I wondered why. That was all; I have no personal interest in you whatsoever."

"It was for my wig, of course," said Miss Jackson, a trifle disconcerted.

She pulled open a drawer in her dressing table, snatched the lid off a cardboard box which lay inside, and revealed a great mass of black hair, short and long. "See? I've got quite a lot now; be enough for a good wig quite soon now."

"Oh, I see!" said Miss Phipps in a friendlier tone. "As an actress, of course—"

"Nah, nah!" said Miss Jackson. "Not for the stage. You're not with it, my dear. Every smart girl has a wig nowadays. If she can afford it, that is. Head always in good trim. Swim in the sea, let the wild winds blow, put on the wig, hair keeps its line, waves not to and fro. Rather neat, don't you think? Of course you have to take it in for a set occasionally. Now, if you don't mind, would you please scarper? I'm supposed to be running through my lines."

"Yes, I will leave you gladly," said Miss Phipps. "It is useless to expect any help from you, since you are interested only in yourself."

She sailed out of the dressing room and descended the shabby stairs with a quick and angry step.

"Miss Phipps!" called a voice from above.

Miss Phipps looked up. Over the railing leaned Miss Jackson, her slender legs asprawl.

"I'm sorry I was such a beast to you," she said. "Fact is, I'm all in a twitter about tonight, you know."

Miss Phipps, remembering the blackbrowed Sir Mervyn, forgave her at once.

"I don't wonder," she said sympathetically.

"Oh, well, not to worry. I was a bit narked, you know, about your nose in the air over my wig. Nowadays a wig isn't the sign of a scarlet woman, Miss Phipps. Your Goldilocks pal has one, you know. In that handsome box. On a proper stand and all. I bet she got it at a reduced price from her doting Basil."

"She has a what?" said Miss Phipps excitedly.

"A wig, of course. Golden-brown, made of her own *bee*yutiful hair."

Miss Phipps rushed for the door and took a taxi to the nearest telephone booth.

After last night's experience in parking, the Tarrant party took pains to arrive at the Pavilion early. Nearby parking was easily achieved.

"Miss Phipps?" sad Bradshaw, beaming. "I have a note for you, madam."

The note read simply: *We shall be delighted if you and Inspector and Mrs. Tarrant will join Mr. Basil and ourselves in our box. Gerard and Lesley Carey.*

"But we have our own seat tickets," demurred Inspector Tarrant.

"The box office will gladly sell them for you—there's a full house and a long queue waiting for returns," said Bradshaw.

"When you urged me on the phone to confront Mrs. Mortimer and ask her what she had done with my wife's wig, I thought you were entirely mad," said Captain Carey, beaming happily. "But the Colonel had heard about your clever detection at Star Isle school—the Headmaster's his brother, you know—so I risked it. She made a frightful scene, sobbing and throwing herself around, wailing all sorts of silly things about me, and 'How did you find out?' and so on. It seems she told Basil she would deliver the wig to Lesley, and she meant to do so, but this idea came into her head, you know. She saw Lesley and myself getting out of our car in Taylor Street, and Lesley going off toward Taylor Square, and she guessed Lesley was going to see the Canon, and she herself—Mrs. M., I mean—was wearing white like Lesley, and she just had this kind of compulsion to stir up trouble between myself and Lesley—I can't imagine why!"—his handsome face flushing—"and she popped on the wig and nipped off to Basil's porch and then nipped round the corner when a big van came by, so I didn't see her disappear."

"I didn't see her from above," said Basil quietly, smiling as he turned to assist Mary Tarrant with her wrap.

"Well, I hope this will be a lesson to you, young man," said Miss Phipps to the Captain with mock sternness.

"Oh, it has. It has indeed," said Captain Carey. "You see," he murmured in Miss Phipps's ear, "I was always angry about that wig. I thought it was a present from Basil. But I didn't like to question Lesley about it, for fear it would look as if I didn't trust her. It turns out now, when we got it all out into the open, that her father paid for it, and she didn't like to tell me because I'm always a bit edgy about presents from her father, he being much deeper in the pocket than I am. Basil had *suggested* the wig, of course, but nothing further."

"Marital frankness," said Miss Phipps mildly, "often pays dividends."

"I am so grateful to you, dear Miss Phipps," said Lesley, smiling, and she leaned forward and kissed Miss Phipps's cheek.

"Olive Jackson's Viola," said the *Southshire Post*, "had a rare quality of youthful sweetness. The young actress justly received a floral tribute from a member of the audience—the famous novelist, Miss Marian Phipps, guest of Inspector and Mrs. Tarrant—at the close of the first performance."

MISS PHIPPS AND THE NEST
OF ILLUSION

"Now be passionate!" said one of the technicians.

At this mock-serious command the whole company roared with laughter. Even Miss Marian Phipps, seated uncertainly on her shooting-stick, which she had installed near a few rough stones to keep her feet dry, chilled to the marrow by the moorland wind and disciplined to silence, could not forbear a snicker. A couple of young passers-by, hikers with knapsacks on their shoulders, colored and started, fearing that the laughter was directed toward them. Miss Phipps gave them a kindly smile, but they did not seem altogether reassured.

"But of course, poor pets, they haven't a clue to what it's all about. How could they? Even I, noted as I am for my succinct descriptions, my swift creation of atmosphere," mused Miss Phipps with a sardonic chuckle, "even I would require several pages to explain this setup."

In fact, this company of persons, which included director, camera crew, lighting crew, clapper-boy, actors male and female, wardrobe mistress, make-up girl, script girl, various secretaries, dogsbodies galore, five large blue trucks, cars to taste, and a long motor coach, comprised a film unit which was making a four-part television serial out of one of Miss Phipps's detective stories.

Uniformed policemen looking grave in order to conceal their real enjoyment patrolled the road at each end of this nest of illusion, halting cars whose occupants, at first vexed by the delay, presently grew so interested that they wouldn't move on. Fictitious policemen clustered round the coach, comparing their buttons with the real thing. Two St. John's First Aid men, one short and one tall, in uniform, and one female ditto, hovered in the background in case anyone suffered injury. For Miss Phipps's story required a murder to be committed in this wild moorland landscape, and however careful actors were with weapons and so on, accidents sometimes occurred.

It was not the first time that Miss Phipps had accompanied the group "on location," and she had got over her first astonishments. It did not surprise her now to find that she was no longer in command of her own characters; girls she had described as fair and silly turned up as dark and strong, while darkly elegant women in middle life appeared youthfully blonde. Her own dialogue was not always used, but she had seen the script and had grasped the probable reason for this; the script for today's shooting kept closely to her original story, and she guessed that this was because her dialogue was short and snappy. On the whole, however, she was well satisfied; the story line emerged clear and strong; there was no doubt that these young men knew what they were doing.

They were serious, they were dedicated, they were completely engrossed in their work. They rehearsed a dozen times, they rolled the heavy cameras here or there, nonchalantly putting down and moving heavy planks for the purpose, they altered a door or a light by an inch without a murmur, they repeated a comic moment without a smile. To the hordes of children who clustered round them in street scenes they behaved with a cool kindness which quelled.

Miss Phipps was indeed so much interested by them as a professional group that she had scarcely got around yet to her customary study of persons as individual characters. Perfectly courteous to her, as the author of the work in process of translation, they greeted her politely—"Good morning, Miss Phipps," "Nice to see you here," and so on; they gravely fetched cups of tea and coffee, sandwiches, biscuits, cake, for her from the interiors of the blue trucks; they politely indicated to her where she could or could not stand—"You'll be out of camera here," or "Just a yard this way"; they listened to her appraisals or criticisms of the shots just taken, without cutting her short, with attentively bent head and reserved smiles. But all without the least real interest or enthusiasm. In a word, they did not care two hoots what she thought because the story had become theirs; but they were obviously nice lads and wished to show this elderly author a proper respect. When they found that she unreservedly accepted these conditions of their association, the technicians became warmer—Miss Phipps never ventured to speak to the actors, who seemed to be regarded as a race apart.

Well, "never" was perhaps rather too strong a word; she had spoken to one of them on location the previous day. It was a scene in which a large number of extras had been required; in a small blue truck an official of some kind waited to pay them for their day's work. Miss Phipps, extremely tired of sitting on her shooting-stick, sank down on the step of this truck. Inside, exchanging a few words with the payer, was a young man whose swarthy complexion, smooth dark hair, and fiercely jutting nose gave him a decidedly sinister appearance.

"If you aren't playing my villain, you ought to be!" exclaimed Miss Phipps.

"Oh, I am," said the young man. He smiled, which improved his looks considerably. "This isn't quite my own nose," he continued with diffidence.

"It suits you," said Miss Phipps.

"It suits Verney," corrected the young man, naming the villain.

"That's what I meant," said Miss Phipps.

"It's a great part," said the young man with feeling. "I'm enjoying it. Quite a chance for me, really."

Miss Phipps was pleased. "You find Verney's motivation adequate," she said.

"Er—yes. How do you like having your story filmed?" said the young man, rather in a hurry, Miss Phipps realized, to get away from questions of motivation, which seemed unfamiliar to him.

"Very much. It's irritating at times, of course, to have one's characters and language altered," said Miss Phipps.

"Oh, I do think we should keep to the *script*," said the young man earnestly. "I mean, if you don't get your cues, where are you?"

"Where indeed?" agreed Miss Phipps, amused again by the difference between the author's point of view and the actor's. She decided not to upset his faith in the script by mentioning any of the changes.

At this point "Verney" was called for. "You can rely on *me* to speak your lines, Miss Phipps," the young man reassured her as he departed promptly.

Today called for Verney's big scene, the murder, and Miss Phipps looked forward to it with particular anticipation. The dialogue in the script was her own, word for word, and she couldn't help wondering how it would "play."

Delia and Roger, the main characters, had been filmed driving up the long steep hill in Roger's convertible; they parked at the side of the road and got out of the car. Roger attempted a love passage, but Delia, whose thoughts were not inclined that way (at any rate, not with Roger), stood gazing at the wild moorland landscape—the somber hills rolling away on every side into the clear evening sky, the rough tawny bents blowing in the relentless wind, the stretches of brown ling patching the long slopes, the row of shooting butts along a nearby edge, the shaggy sheep determinedly cropping here and there. This landscape was particularly dear, because native, to Miss Phipps, and she was pleased that the director had decided to film the most important incident where she had originally placed it.

"An unusual locale—it will give a certain freshness," he had said, smiling pleasantly, his long hair blowing in the wind.

He seemed never to feel cold, rain, fatigue, or hunger. Of course, he was clad from head to foot in the wool and leather devised by modern skill for style, ease of movement, and protection, with knee-high boots; but Miss Phipps thought his protection was mental rather than physical; he was so totally engrossed in "Never the First"—this was now the title of the film, quite different, of course, from Miss Phipps's title—that all other sensations passed him by.

Delia said something poetical about the moorland. Roger, a rather poor fish in the story, excellently acted as such by a lively blond young man, gave the rather innocuous reply which Miss Phipps had written for him. Or at least, she presumed that he did so; a microphone suspended overhead caught and recorded the words of Roger and Delia, but at this distance Miss Phipps did not hear them. She was accustomed by now to this "microphone voice," but hoped she had taken up a position sufficiently near to the site of the murder to hear all that went on there.

Delia now ran down a slope, sprang gracefully over a small stream, and made for a large flattish rock inclined against the face of a knoll from which there was a superb view of distant mountains and valleys. Thus far the action had been successfully filmed. Now Delia threw herself down on the rock, and then, clasping her hands about her knees, gazed out with keen enjoyment. Her rich dark hair and fine eyes, enhanced by long dark eyelashes, looked particularly beautiful.

Roger, following her devotedly, stumbled on a stone in the beck and splashed his ankles, drew out an elegant handkerchief and dried them; then he descended to the rock with uncertain steps, surveyed its damp surface with distaste, but finally sat down by Delia's side and put his arm round her. She laughed good-humoredly but pushed it away.

"They're both very good," approved Miss Phipps to herself.

Verney, in a long dark cloak and wide-brimmed hat, now sprang out from behind the knoll and with a cry of rage held a knife over the amorous Roger. The villain's hat, striking a rocky projection, fell off.

"No, no!" cried the director, rushing forward. "Your hat can't fall off. It would look comic."

"It's a wonder my head didn't fall off," said Verney, rubbing it ruefully. "That rock is sharp."

A long and dreary interval followed—dreary at least to Miss Phipps—while the director strove to rehearse the scene so as to convey the exact effect he wanted Verney having entered three times and knocked his hat off or side ways each time, was instructed to enter from the other side of the knoll. But Delia was in his way there. Delia, who kept putting on yet another garment, for the wind was certainly piercing, obediently moved to the far side of the rock. Roger now objected; he disliked putting his right arm round a girl.

"It's unnatural," he said. "I mean, one needs one's right hand for other activities."

An appreciative titter from the company—the girls in their neat white boots quivering like butterflies—was sharply silenced by the chief cameraman, who announced gloomily, "The light's going."

The scene in the story required twilight, but of course one secured that, Miss Phipps knew, by glazes in the lens, not by reality. A frenzy of experiment and rehearsal followed, while vehicles and pedestrians were allowed to pass by.

Miss Phipps became bored, and directed her gaze to the oncoming sunset and to the lights which now began to twinkle in the little town far below in the valley. Occasional utterances reached her ears and recalled her attention.

"But it throws my nose away," lamented Verney, who now wore a stocking over his face. Miss Phipps agreed with him, and was glad to see him rush back to the dressing-room truck and emerge with his slouch hat replaced.

"This rock is hellishly cold," said Roger. "To sit on, I mean."

"No central heating here, my boy," said a technician.

"It really *is* cold," observed Delia mildly.

Roger sat down beside her gingerly, with a grimace. "Icy," he groaned.

"Now be passionate, lad," urged a technician in a kindly tone.

Everybody roared with laughter, and even Miss Phipps, though chilled to the marrow and extremely tired of sitting on her shooting-stick, could not forbear a snicker. A pair of youngsters passing by looked alarmed, and Miss Phipps gave them a reassuring smile.

At this point a pale thin young man wearing a police-uniform costume, with a peevish look and an excessive bush of golden hair over his eyes—an actor whom Miss Phipps had not much noticed before—suddenly rushed forward with a rug of artificial grass in his arms and threw it with a grand gesture on the rock. Miss Phipps slid off her shooting-stick at the sight, for anything more artificial, more phony, than this bright green nylon herbage against the dun moorland background, could hardly be imagined. She opened her mouth to speak, but this was not necessary; the director had already swooped down on the rock, snatched up the grass carpet, and flung it aside.

"I just thought it would make the rock warmer," said the young man in an injured tone.

The director gave him a smile. Possibly this was meant to be kindly, but its effect was tigerish; the young man, muttering in an angry tone, retreated. Glances were exchanged among the company, but nothing further was said, and everybody suddenly became extremely busy about something else. Miss Phipps resumed her uncomfortable perch on the shooting-stick and her appreciative gaze over the valley. After a few moments conversation rose again.

At length the road traffic ceased and a kind of hush descended on the company. Miss Phipps, turning to the scene of the action again, became aware that a shot was imminent. Delia quietly shed an overcoat, a scarf, and a sweater, and emerging in a very skimpy miniskirt which displayed her charming figure to perfection, sat down without murmur or grimace on the rock, which in the cool evening air looked even wetter, in exactly the same pose she had adopted before.

"A real actress," approved Miss Phipps.

"Is the blood in position?" inquired the director.

Roger felt his bosom. "Blood okay," he said.

"Everyone quiet, please," boomed the loudspeaker.

The hush became absolute.

"Roll them."

"Shooting."

The clapper-board boy, standing in front of the camera, made the appropriate gesture, and said, "Episode Two. Incident Three. Take One."

A pause, then from the director: "Action!"

Roger put his arm round Delia in a thoroughly lecherous fashion. Delia laughed and pushed him away, but he bent to kiss her. The figure in the dark cloak and hat leaped round the knoll, and crying, "Drop dead!" drove his dagger at Roger's heart and vanished.

Delia screamed and rose in panic. Roger staggered to his feet; he clutched at his heart, blood spurted out of his shirt, his face seemed to blanch and distort into a look of hideous surprise; then he bent forward, swaying as if in agony.

"This may be corny, but it's frightfully effective," thought Miss Phipps, who had leaped to her feet and only just caught her shooting-stick in time to prevent it falling with a clatter to the stones.

Roger fell violently sideways. His weight knocked Delia off balance and she slipped from the rock into the stream below and lay motionless.

"Cut! Cut!" yelled the director, bounding forward in a fury. "What the hell are you doing, Roger? You've knocked her out of the shot, you dolt! We shall have to do it all over again. I hope you've got a clean shirt. Have we plenty of blood? Get up, idiot! Are you all right, Delia?" he said with a sudden change of tone.

Several technicians and the First Aid woman rushed to the stream and helped Delia to her feet. She was as white as chalk, her mouth hanging open, her eyes rolling. They pulled her out of the stream and up the bank; she fell from their arms to the grass, and fainted. The First Aid woman produced smelling salts and applied them, tugged at the pitiful little skirt, and sharply ordered the would-be helpers to keep their distance.

"Is she hurt? You don't think she's hurt, do you? If she's hurt everything's ruined! She's in nearly every scene!" exclaimed the director. "That idiot Roger!" He stepped aside to reprimand the unfortunate Roger, but found the two First Aid men confronting him.

"Are you in touch with the town by radio, sir?" said the tall one.

"Of course not," said the director, keeping his rage firmly under control.

"The police may be," said the short one.

"Try them," said the tall one.

"If not, someone must drive at once to the nearest telephone."

"What the hell are you talking about?" shouted the director.

"We need an ambulance at once. I'm afraid Mr. Anstruther—it's he who's playing Roger, I believe—is seriously injured."

"Don't be silly," said the director, laughing to conceal his exasperation. "That was just a well acted murder scene—only Roger overdid it."

"I'm afraid not, sir."

"Roger!" said the director, pushing the First Aid men apart so that he could see the actor's recumbent form. "Get up, man."

"I'm very much afraid he may be dead, sir," said the tall St. John's man, somber.

"What! Absurd! That isn't real blood, you know."

"I'm afraid it is."

"Yes. And that's a real knife," said the other St. John's man.

"No, no. It's impossible! This is just Roger's excessive realism," said the director in a soothing tone. He knelt beside the fallen actor and stretched out his hand to take the usual trick property knife that appeared to be sticking out of Roger's chest.

"Best not touch it," advised both First Aid men at once.

"The actor in the cloak was wearing gloves, though," added one.

The warning came too late. But the knife did not yield to the director's hand; it was not, in fact, a property knife and it was not adhering in the usual theatrical style to Roger's breast; the knife was a real one, sunk deep in his flesh.

The short man stooped and took Roger's wrist. "I can't feel any pulse," he said.

There was a long and frightful silence. Everyone stood motionless, and gaped.

In the hush a thudding, banging noise became audible in the distance.

"Officer!" cried the director suddenly, recovering his habit of command and springing to his feet. "Sergeant! Here! To me! A serious accident has occurred, we need an ambulance and a doctor at once. See to it. You First Aid men, bring something to cover poor Anstruther."

"Will this do?" said the pale fair young man, once more offering the artificial grass rug.

"Yes. Excellent. Thanks. What's the noise? Somebody stop that confounded banging," said the director irritably. "No, not you, Jack," he added seizing the cameraman's arm as he made to move off. "You move the camera back to the recording truck and stay there. And you, Constable, stand beside the truck. Don't you see," he went on impatiently as everyone stared at him, "the stabbing will be on film. The film will show the whole incident. It will be evidence. Where the hell is Verney? Somebody find him. He must have got hold of a real knife by accident somehow. What a mess! What a *mess.* Let's see the film now."

"I don't think it was Verney," murmured Miss Phipps as they all moved off toward the recording truck.

"Why not?" said the director sharply.

Miss Phipps had no chance to reply, for at this moment the group drew level with the dressing-room truck, and it became evident that Verney was inside.

"Help! Help! Let me out!" he yelled, at the same time banging hard with one fist on the door panels and shaking the handle viciously with his other hand.

The key to the truck was, in fact, protruding from the lock; the director turned it, the door swung open, and Verney in the cloak and hat of his role fell out. His colleagues gasped and stepped back on seeing—as they could not help thinking—a murderer dressed just as he had been when he had committed the crime.

"You're in a mess, Tom; don't say a word," said the director instantly.

"He's a very able young man," said Miss Phipps to herself. "He sees the thing immediately, with all its implications."

"What are you talking about?" said Verney. "I'm very sorry if I've held up the shot, but was it my fault I was locked in? Some ass locked me in. I just came in to have a last look at my nose, and some damn fool locked me in. Why on earth didn't somebody let me out? I've made noise enough, heaven knows."

"Where is your knife?" asked the director curtly.

"Here in my pocket," said Verney. He fumbled in the voluminous folds of his cloak and found a dagger. The director took it and bent it on its hinge; it was a trick knife, a prop. It was also, Miss Phipps observed, completely stainless. But that meant little.

"We had better search here, sir," said the police sergeant, appearing suddenly on the fringe of the group.

"What, for the knife? On Tyas Moor? There's a good deal of room for concealment," said the director ironically, glancing round at the wild landscape with its innumerable rocks, tufts, and hollows.

"It must be done, sir. We will begin with the trucks. An ambulance is on its way—we've summoned it by radio. Do I take it that you are all to have a meal at The Fleece in Tyas Foot?"

"That was the plan."

"It will be well to keep to it. If you will all go down there now, a police officer will accompany you and an Inspector will meet you there. We shall require a list of everybody present."

"But what's wrong? What's happened?" said the bewildered Verney, gazing anxiously from face to face.

"Somebody dressed exactly like you stabbed poor Anstruther," said the director with cool concision.

"What do you mean?" shrieked Verney. "What?"

In the middle of this anguished cry he became suddenly and violently sick.

"We'll see it now," repeated the director firmly, and the sergeant, bundling them all into the appropriate truck, acquiesced.

It was an awful thought, reflected Miss Phipps, squeezed in the rear of the pale and silent crowd, that in a few moments they would see on the screen the actual committing of a real murder.

The tension was almost unbearable as the screen showed Delia bounding happily to the rock, seating herself with an apparent youthful awkwardness which was really full of grace—"How do they do it?" marveled Miss Phipps—and Roger following with a conceited air, too well dressed and all too pleased with himself, as the part required.

"Everyone very quiet and still, please," said the director at this point.

There was a policeman at the truck door, observed Miss Phipps—a real one, she thought. Perhaps in a moment the murderer among them would try to escape and be arrested.

Then the crucial moment was at hand. On the screen the cloaked figure, hat well down over brows, sprang round the knoll, and shrilling, "Drop dead!" plunged the knife into Roger's chest. The white-boots shrieked and swayed; somebody behind Miss Phipps fell heavily against her.

"It's no use. There isn't a glimpse of the figure or the face, and the voice is artificially high, hopelessly affected and unrecognizable. It will be no help towards discovery," said the director, disappointed.

"That's as may be," said the sergeant, portentous. "Now, all to the Fleece, please. If anyone should attempt to run away, it would be most unwise."

"It would be a clear proof of guilt, he means," reflected Miss Phipps.

"You'd better come with me in the police car, sir," said the sergeant politely to Verney.

"Sergeant," said Verney, who still looked green, meekly climbing into the car. "I swear to you that I was locked into the dressing-room truck during this—this entire incident."

"I'm sure I hope it may prove so, sir," replied the sergeant.

Surveying those present as they sat round a large table in The Fleece inn and pretended to eat, Miss Phipps reproached herself for having made no earlier effort to know them as persons. Now she observed their age and sex, their appearance, their preferences. One of the pseudo-policemen sat next to Delia; it was the golden-haired young man who had proffered the artificial grass; Delia as cold and pale as marble leaned aside and made no response to his solicitous attentions.

Another actor-policeman sat very close to one of the white-boots. A young male dogsbody followed every movement of the director with anxious eyes; one of the camera crew who usually climbed about and held the microphone in odd positions sat in a corner beside the boy who had wielded the clapper-board.

The make-up girl received the wailing confidences of Verney who, now that he had shed his false nose, looked like a very pleasant inexperienced lad. From the other side of the table one of the secretaries gazed at him with pity and, Miss Phipps thought, love. Their hair and eyes and ears, their complexions, speech, and clothes, the way they held their knives and forks and broke their bread and raised their glasses, all became intensely interesting to her; for some revealing clue might indicate who had stabbed the unfortunate Anstruther, and why.

Just as the meal was drawing to its dismal close, the sergeant ushered a police Inspector into the room. A large, solid, fresh-complexioned man, he allowed his gaze to wander slowly round the table, missing very little in Miss Phipp's opinion. He cleared his throat. Everyone gazed at him with breathless attention.

"I am sorry to have to tell you," he said, each word ponderous and slow, "that Mr. Anstruther died on the way to the hospital."

The company moaned.

"Miss Phipps, please," said the Inspector sharply, in a totally different tone—even his eyes seemed to have sharpened as they picked her out. "This way, please."

Miss Phipps followed him meekly into a side room.

"Now, Miss Phipps," said the Inspector, reverting to his milder tone, "your evidence will be of great value, of course. We are aware that you are a trained observer and have assisted the police on various previous occasions."

"I don't think I can be of much help this time," began Miss Phipps, "because, you see—"

"You stood a little apart from the group during the filming. Others were engaged with their own job, but you were watching the action. Is not that the case?"

"Yes, but—"

"Anyone who was in your view in his own person during the stabbing obviously could not have done the stabbing."

"True," Miss Phipps agreed.

"We have a list of names. If you will just go through these names with us—"

"But I don't know their names, I know only their functions. I don't know them as *persons*. That is my difficulty here."

The Inspector sighed. "We will ask each member of the group to come in and check their names and addresses with our list.

When each has left, if he or she was in your sight *as himself* at the relevant moment, just say, 'Yes.' It could be a he or a she, could it not?"

"Possibly. The cloak covered the entire figure. But the voice, though shrill—obviously disguised—was male, I thought."

"That was Mrs. Dobson's impression too."

"Mrs. Dobson?"

"She was playing the part of Delia."

"Ah," said Miss Phipps thoughtfully.

"Ask them to come in one at a time, Sergeant. Your careful attention, please, Miss Phipps."

This exercise, carried out with due care, certainly diminished the number of suspects. The director, the camera crew, the white-boots, the clapper-wielder, and some of the dogsbodies, had all been in Miss Phipps's direct view in their own persons, without costume. The only figures out of Miss Phipps's view proved to be the wretched Verney and the group of extras in police uniforms clustered round the coach.

"The policemen, so-called, would surely have seen if one of their number slipped away," said the Inspector.

"You don't understand actors," said Miss Phipps. "Their eyes would be glued to the action being filmed."

"But Verney had the *right* to be at the rock."

"Verney was locked in the dressing room," said Miss Phipps.

"So he says. But one can fake these things. Stick the key in the lock on the outside, and hold the door handle fast from within."

"Verney didn't do it."

"Miss Phipps," said the Inspector, suddenly turning harsh and cold, "my sergeant has talked to these people. He is of the opinion, and I share it, that we have two probable suspects. One has motive, the other opportunity with, I agree, a much less certain motive. Verney had the opportunity—the cloak, the hat, the scene—"

"Not the right kind of knife," said Miss Phipps.

"Cakes have been cut," said the Inspector drily.

"True. But—"

"Or the property knife might have slipped and struck wrongly. I'm willing to believe it was an accident, and then Verney panicked. A confession would be the best course for him."

"Verney didn't do it."

"What leads you to that positive opinion, Miss Phipps?" said the Inspector with asperity.

"Who is your other suspect?"

"Mrs. Dobson's husband, who is playing an extra today—a policeman, I understand," said the Inspector. "He has some previous evidence of tantrums."

"Which one is he?"

"He has very yellow hair."

"Ah, the lad who brought the artificial grass for his wife's comfort," nodded Miss Phipps. "Well, there you have the murderer, I'm afraid. Poor young man."

"But he had so much less opportunity than Verney."

"Jealousy and all that. Cruel as the grave," continued Miss Phipps. "Roger—the dead man—was lively and handsome. The husband is—er—rather a wet blanket."

"Verney might have been jealous too, we understand," said the Inspector, very grim.

"Oh, really? I hadn't thought so, but I agree I haven't had much chance to judge. Delia is certainly very beautiful."

"I don't see it myself. A minx, I expect. The relevant point is that young Anstruther—Roger was well known to be a lady's man."

"Dear, dear! Well, he's met rather more than his deserts."

"From Verney."

"No. From Dobson."

"Your persistence is somewhat irritating, Miss Phipps. Verney had all the props, and the scene, at his disposal."

"There would be a duplicate cloak and hat about. Everything is carried in duplicate by this company, even fake blood. No, it wasn't Verney. I knew it was not Verney on the set, during the murder."

"Tell me why!" thundered the Inspector, his patience exhausted.

"I talked to Verney yesterday. He is a very serious young man, entirely dedicated to his profession, who believes in knowing his lines and uttering them as written. Dobson was an extra without lines—he would not have seen the script, he would not have known the murderer's lines. Verney assured me he would speak the murder-scene lines exactly as I had written them."

"And he did not do so?"

"Do you imagine I wrote a line like *Drop dead* in a serious murder scene?" said Miss Phipps, outraged. "I may have faults as a writer—but I am not as corny as that, I assure you. *Drop dead*, indeed!"

"I beg your pardon, I'm sure," said the Inspector. "But do you remember what you have written so well that you know on the instant when some of your words have been changed?"

"My dear man, of course!" said Miss Phipps, astonished.

MISS PHIPPS EXERCISES
HER METIER

A ll of a sudden Miss Marian Phipps felt lonely.
This was rather strange, for up to that moment she had
been enjoying the peace of this remote Shetland isle. After
the repeated discussions, the divergent human wishes, and the
frequent telephonings of the morning, the present silence—the
sheer absence of human voices—was restful in the extreme. The
island was small, but large enough to offer considerable grassy
slopes, and over the steepest of these her four companions on the
excursion were now climbing rapidly.

The dark cliffs rose to fine and jagged heights; the northern sea
was a rich dark blue with white surf fringes; the sun shone; the sea
birds—gulls, gannets, oyster-catchers, shags, terns, puffins, what-
have-you (Miss Phipps was not too well up in birds)—clamored
a good deal, to be sure, as they swooped about the sky; but their
various modes of flight were beautiful to watch, and their resonant
tones were a pleasant change from the motor horns and airplane
engines which formed her usual sound track.

The rest of the party had wanted to see the remains of the old
Viking settlement for which they had indeed come to the island, but
these lay on the far side of the steep hill. Miss Phipps, surveying its
gradient, and perhaps, in spite of her real affection for them, a little
tired of Inspector Tarrant and his wife after a fortnight's holiday
together—and certainly tired of Professor Morison and *his* wife after
a mere few hours—decided to remain idly in the vicinity of the tiny
harbor and landing stage. A neighboring bay, gained by climbing a
much slighter slope, was as far as Miss Phipps was prepared to walk.

If she felt a little less than her usual warmth toward the Tarrants
this afternoon it was not, she admitted at once, their fault but
just part of the usual exasperation of things in general, which so
often refused to fit, to go right. Today was the last one of their
stay in Shetland, and though they had seen several fine Viking
remains, everyone at their hotel in the main port had assured them

that those on Fersa were the finest, grimmest, most complete in existence. But to reach Fersa one had to proceed to a village on the mainland coast and there rent a boat. "Just telephone the village post office," urged their hotel acquaintances. "They keep a motor vessel for hire."

They telephoned. In fact, they seemed to spend the whole morning at the telephone. Sometimes Inspector Tarrant telephoned, sometimes his wife Mary did, sometimes Miss Phipps. All without result. At first a young man's voice had replied, saying crossly that the sea was too high, and besides, he hadn't the time. Then the wind calmed a little, so they telephoned again. This time a young woman's voice replied. Her voice had sobs in it, and cried out that she couldn't "fash" with them now.

After an hour's wait they telephoned again—and then again. The receiver was lifted and replaced, only a kind of moan being heard in the brief interim. Miss Phipps urged the Tarrants to give up Fersa and decide on some other excursion. Although disappointed as to Vikings, the Tarrants would probably have accepted her advice if it had not been for the Morisons, who now appeared to be seized by Fersa and telephone.

Professor Morison was one of those long, concave, balding academics devoted to abstruse subjects; he had a sallow complexion and sad brown eyes—the type whom Miss Phipps respected but regarded as supremely dreary. His wife, short, plump, fair-haired, bossy, appeared softhearted, but in defense of her husband she took on the consistency of marble. When the Tarrant party left the hotel to accompany some fellow guests to the ship about to leave the port harbor for Scotland, Mrs. Morison was again at the telephone in the hall.

"Her husband's away—her husband's out with the boat," she reported over her shoulder to the Professor. When the Tarrant party returned for lunch she was still telephoning.

Meanwhile, Miss Phipps had had a poignant experience. Indeed it was to the poignancy of this experience that she attributed her present sudden attack of loneliness; the usual well-adjusted balance of her feelings had been upset, leaving her open to alarms.

(For was she, in fact, feeling "lonely" now, or was she, in reality, for some inexplicable cause merely feeling nervous? She was uncertain.)

The poignant experience was simply the sight of a face peering out from the lower deck of the ship bound for Scotland. A young man's face, dark and handsome, but fixed with such a look of agony that Miss Phipps hoped never to see the like again. As Miss Phipps was a novelist, suitable explanations of other people's feelings were naturally apt to rush into her mind.

"Poor lad!" she thought with genuine pity. "Going away from home for the first time, I expect. The heart beholds the islands. A difficult place to leave. Mountains and sea. Poor boy."

On entering the lobby of the hotel she found Mrs. Morison again at the end of the telephone cord, and addressing her husband.

"She says her father-in-law will take us," she cried in triumph. With a sudden change of tone she added, "It'll cost enough."

"Er-hrrumph," said Professor Morison, concaving (Miss Phipps thought) almost more than before.

"Shall we go, James?" pressed Mrs. Morison.

"Er-hrrumph."

"Would you allow our party of three to join you?" said Miss Phipps, springing cheerfully into the breach. "That would lessen the—"

"Er-hrrumph!" said Professor Morison, straightening a little, hopefully.

"Mrs. Morison looked eager but still doubtful.

"We have a hired car at our disposal," Miss Phipps added as bait. Mrs. Morison beamed.

"A happy suggestion," she said. "I'm *sure* my husband will approve."

While she clinched the arrangement on the telephone, Miss Phipps flew off to tell the Tarrants of her achievement. It was not well received.

"Fancy spending an afternoon with that old stick!" growled the Inspector.

"Er-hrrumph!" said Mary peevishly.

"Very well, tell them you've changed your mind and don't want to go," said Miss Phipps, vexed.

"Of course we'll go," said Inspector Tarrant with decision.

"Er-hrrumph," said Mary in a kinder tone.

After lunch they drove down to the village, which was almost too tiny to be called a village, consisting chiefly of a post office, above which a home-painted board announced MACKAY. Near a tiny stone landing stage, just across the road from this building, tossed a small boat with an outboard motor, the boat attached to a red buoy. It tossed a good deal; looking out to sea Miss Phipps observed with interest that the waves were also tossing a good deal and were topped by quite a few whitecaps.

Professor Morison, carrying a pair of binoculars, a camera, and a notebook, with two textbooks protruding from his pockets, walked to the end of the little jetty and began to examine such birds as flew into view. Bill Tarrant, looking a little more cheerful, followed him, and Mrs. Morison trotted after them on her fat little ankles. Mary and Miss Phipps entered the post office and began to choose picture postcards. Mary, hearing the approach of a distant car, tapped sharply with a coin on the counter.

A most beautiful creature entered. A young woman, not yet 20, Miss Phipps thought; of dazzlingly smooth and unblemished complexion, with pale golden hair twined and piled about her head in thick lustrous swaths. She wore a thin white dress, so short that if another inch were subtracted it would almost be a belt, and so tightly modeled as to show every line of her lovely body except an inch or two hinted at by a few tiny scraps of lace.

She turned her head and Miss Phipps started; her beauty was marred by a heavy bruise on one temple, imperfectly concealed by a good deal of crude makeup, and her large pale blue eyes were red from crying. A wedding ring, and an engagement ring with a single no doubt much-prized pearl, decked the hand with which she pointed out, competently enough, the various categories of postcards and their prices. Her accent had none of the island lilt that Miss Phipps liked so much, and it seemed tinged with Cockney.

"What's come into ye, Zelda?" boomed an angry voice.

The post office door was thrust open vehemently, sounding its little bell, and in strode a solid grizzled figure wearing one of the patterned knit garments native to the island.

"Hae ye no sense, woman? Why can't Eric take the boat across? Dragging me all this way from ma sheep."

"Eric isn't here, Mr. Mackay," said Zelda timidly.

"Whaur's Magnus then?"

"He left."

"Did they go off together, then? Whaur did they go?"

"I don't know," moaned Zelda, almost weeping.

"Women!" exclaimed Mackay. "Sons!"

"I thought you wouldn't want to miss the chance of a boatload of passengers."

"How many are ye, then?" barked Mackay, fixing Miss Phipps with an angry glare.

"Five."

"It'll cost ye two pun ten."

"Very well," said Miss Phipps shortly. "You'll give us enough time on the island to visit the broch?"

Mackay gave a prolonged growl in which might be distinguished the vowels composing an assenting "aye" or "yaas."

"Ye may nae like the sea," he said with what struck Miss Phipps as rather sinister enjoyment. "It's a wee high. Come awa' wi' ye, then."

As they followed Mackay senior out of the post office and down the little stone pier, Mary and Miss Phipps exchanged glances indicating their unfavorable impressions of the dour boatman. Mary's raised eyebrows brought also a familiar accusation against Miss Phipps.

"I'm irritated by the way you find *a story* in everything," Mary had said not once but several times to Miss Phipps. "It seems an insult to reality."

But Miss Phipps could not help it—it was by now an inveterate habit, and usually she replied cheerfully to these accusations; and this time, as Mary suspected, Miss Phipps had been swept irresistibly into her dearly loved profession. She had begun her imaginings the moment she set eyes on Zelda and the bruise on the girl's temple. The lad with the agonized face was Zelda's husband; they had quarreled; he had struck her, then in shame and fury had left the island. And now this fierce old Mackay had come to confirm her imaginings.

Oh, yes, reflected Miss Phipps, surveying the strong aquiline features, the solid body and crisp staying hair, his older face is strongly akin to the face of the anguished lad on the ship; Zelda had said on the telephone that her father-in-law would ferry the party across to Fersa; the anguished lad is therefore this man's son and this girl's husband.

"Why will people make each other so unhappy?" murmured Miss Phipps. Eric, a good Norse name. As for Magnus, she could not fit him in; perhaps only a minor character in her burgeoning plot.

The Tarrants and Mrs. Morison stood the rough sea well; Miss Phipps enjoyed it, tossing her white curls to the breeze; the Professor turned a curious pea-green and was watched anxiously by his wife, but he yielded no further to queasiness. They landed on the island in a tiny bay, arranged a time for re-embarkation, and then the two married couples strode vigorously up the long green slope. Mr. Mackay vanished round a cliff in his chugging boat, and Miss Phipps wandered about.

It was then that Miss Phipps began to feel lonely. After all, she was apparently left by herself on a small island in the far North Sea, surrounded by a far from calm ocean. Nothing human was visible. The remains of an old cottage—empty windows, broken chimney, vacant doorway—served only to make the absence of life more obvious. The birds soared by uncaring—almost, one might think, contemptuous. Even a sheep's company would have been acceptable. But there was no sheep.

She could no longer hear the chugging of Mr. Mackay's engine. Suppose they had all gone off and left her! It was an uneasy thought. Yes, she did feel uneasy. "I'll go back to the landing stage," thought Miss Phipps. She turned; and bobbing in the waters of the bay beneath her feet she saw a gray head.

"It's a seal!" exclaimed Miss Phipps, delighted. For though on Shetland they had seen the towering brochs (like huge buckets turned upside down), eider ducks, underground funeral chambers, Vikings' descendants (at a gala) agreeably rigged out as Vikings, Shetland ponies with correct shortage of height and length of mane and tail, sheep with half their fleece hanging off their backs, jumpers of many patterns knitted from this silky wool, lochs, mountains, peat hags, seas in every mood, fishing fleets—indeed, almost everything they had expected and hoped to see in Shetland—their view of seals had been singularly scanty. To return to England without having seen some of these massive northern sea mammals would, Miss Phipps believed, diminish their prestige and credibility as Shetland tourists.

"A seal!" she repeated with delight. "I wonder if it lives in the rocks of this bay? Where do seals have their lairs, if any?"

Scanning the rocks which edged the little bay, all thought was suddenly struck from her mind. For beside a low seaweed-covered ledge of rock lay Mr. Mackay's boat, its painter wound round a protruding buttress, and on the ledge knelt Mr. Mackay himself, and he was actually—yes, actually—wringing his hands and bowing back and forth as if in uncontrollable sorrow.

Miss Phipps stared—at first amazed, then in horror. For what was it, lying amid the seaweed, urgently lapped by long waves, over which Mr. Mackay showed so much grief? He raised his face to the sky; tears coursed down his leathery cheeks. Wasn't the object over which he grieved the outstretched corpse of a young man in fisherman's jersey, a young man with dark curly hair, the image of the young man with the anguished face on the boat, and sufficiently like Mackay senior to confirm the relationship?

"Brothers!" she exclaimed. "It must be Magnus!"

Yes, now the story was complete—in Miss Phipps's bubbling mind. The dead boy was the younger brother; he had been paying attention to the older son's beautiful wife; the older son had caught him at it, taken him off in the boat to Fersa, tipped his body over a cliff, expecting the tides to carry off the corpse; but a hand or foot had caught in a niche of the rock and the body still lay there awaiting discovery.

But heavens, what was old Mackay doing now? He pulled it a foot, released it, then heaving the body to its side, pushed it into the waters of the bay. It rolled, paused, drifted, was sucked below a nose of rock, was freed by a stronger wave, then edged its way slowly toward the open sea.

Mackay looked up; Miss Phipps quickly hid behind a rock. A pebble shot from beneath her foot. She hoped he had not heard it or seen her; but she could not feel comfortably sure, for he stood still and gazed round the bay, even shading his eyes with his hand to give himself clearer vision.

There were only two possible courses of action, thought Miss Phipps: go down and confront him, or slip away unseen. With immense relief she perceived that the cliffs were too precipitous here for an elderly lady to descend with reasonable safety, not to mention ease. For a moment which seemed an hour, Mackay gazed and Miss Phipps crouched, peering sideways round her concealing rock.

Then at last the old man gave up his search, stepped down into his boat, released the painter and chugged away.

The moment he was out of sight beyond the cliff Miss Phipps flew. She climbed up the rocks behind her with no care for knees or hands, rushed up the green slope, ran down the rough path, and was sitting on a grassy knoll with her hands clasped round her knees, breathing hard but gazing serenely out to sea when Mackay in his boat came round the nose of the cliff and approached the rocks. Miss Phipps gave him a friendly wave.

"Have ye seen all the isle ye fancy?"

Miss Phipps found this inquiry a trifle sinister. Was he trying to discover if she had visited the bay which held the body?

"Enough," she replied in an off-hand but, she hoped, reassuring tone.

Mackay gave one of those northern snorts whose meaning can only be discovered by its context. He climbed out of his boat, tied it up to the iron ring provided for the purpose, and approached her.

He suspects me; I must admit, reflected Miss Phipps, that I'm afraid.

She looked with longing at the massive hillside beyond which her companions were presumably still engrossed in Viking remains.

"Wad it please ye to come round in the boat wi' me to fetch the others awa'?" suggested Mackay, obviously noting the direction of her glance.

Not on your life, thought Miss Phipps. There was a gleam in his eye which she found most disturbing. If she went out alone in the boat with him, she was sure there would be another body lost off this island. But how to put him off?

"Is there a landing stage there?" she said aloud, with an obvious note of doubt.

"There's a slab of concrete amid the rocks."

"We should probably miss them, wouldn't we?"

"We could always turn back."

"We could," began Miss Phipps, "but is it wise to take the risk of missing them?"

Mackay gave another island snort and extended his hand. Miss Phipps—unhappily, but not able to think of further delaying tactics—took it and rose. She gave a last despairing glance toward the hillside, and there, oh, joy, came her rescuers. Just over the brow appeared Professor Morison and Inspector Tarrant.

"There they are!" she exclaimed gratefully. "Bill! Professor Morison! Cooee!"

Deep in conversation they took not the slightest notice of her appeals. She waved, she cried out, she almost screamed, but Inspector Tarrant remained bent toward the Professor, who continually talked and pointed. Obviously he was deep in his favorite subject of ornithology.

"These birdwatchers," said Miss Phipps with irritation.

"Aweel, you can get in the boat and sit," urged Mackay.

"I'll wait for them here," said Miss Phipps, reminding herself how many a slip there could be between boat and rock. That iron ring, too—a nasty thing to strike one's head against. She withdrew her hand. "I'll wait for them here," she repeated.

"As ye please," said Mackay.

He withdrew to his boat, but with true Norse economy did not start the engine.

At long, long last the Viking-fans reached Miss Phipps. Professor Morison, his sad eyes beaming, was now talking about the varying coloration of puffins.

"You might have acknowledged my greetings," snapped Miss Phipps, peevish.

"I'm sorry, but we didn't hear you," said Bill Tarrant mildly.

After a further long wait Mary and Mrs. Morison arrived talking about fashions. They all got into the boat without incident, Miss Phipps taking care to descend with, and sit between, her two female companions.

The sea was rougher than before. Professor Morison's shade of green was now a darkling olive. Waves slapped overboard, and Miss Phipps, normally a lover of stormy seas, began to wish that they were safely ashore—really this tossing gave too many opportunities for an "accident." Mackay was capable of drowning the whole lot of them to save his son, she reflected.

"Hae ye bairns?" inquired Mackay suddenly.

It seemed the Morisons had none; the Tarrants admitted their two.

"And you?" said Bill politely.

"I have two sons, Eric and Magnus," said Mackay, glancing at Miss Phipps. "But they're foot-loose. Shetland's too small for them. They're both intending to be awa' to London."

"What will they do there?" asked Professor Morison. "No mountains, no sea, no birds."

"Zelda will like it. Eric's wife. Her at the post office. She's London-born," said Mackay, with a certain bitterness. "She came to the island on a holiday cruise."

"Oh, look, there's a seal" cried Mary Tarrant enthusiastically.

Glancing up, Miss Phipps found Mackay's eyes fixed fiercely on her. Of course—there was a seal at the entrance of the murder bay, she thought; if he learns I saw it he'll think I saw other things in that bay too. All this passed through her mind in a flash. As if she had never seen a seal in her life and would not recognize a seal if she saw one, she cried out cheerfully, "Where?"—and conscientiously scanned the horizon.

It was a good lie—accepted, Miss Phipps noted with great relief, where acceptance was most needed.

Two mornings later, with Scottish soil safely beneath their feet and Shetland lying far behind them in the northern waves, Miss Phipps began to argue with her conscience as to whether she should tell Inspector Tarrant of her Fersa adventure. It seemed, on the one hand, her duty as a citizen to do so. But on the other hand, she thought of old broken-hearted Mackay, of that silly lovely Zelda, of the anguished Eric . . .

"They will have enough misery as it is," she murmured, "and it won't do Magnus any good."

After a few moments she smiled. "Besides, I don't *know* any-thing—I don't *really* know. After all, it was only an exercise of my métier!"

It was one of the rare occasions on which Miss Phipps the professional novelist triumphed over Miss Phipps the amateur criminologist.

MISS PHIPPS ON THE TELEPHONE

The telephone rang.

Miss Phipps, dragged up from the cosy depths of her first sleep, mumbled, rolled over, and took up the phone from the table beside her bed. The time, she noted from the illuminated electric clock, was three minutes past midnight.

"Tettenham three four one eight," Miss Phipps said crossly.

"*Tettenham* three four one eight?" queried a voice.

"Yes," said Miss Phipps, noting that the voice was young, girlish, not very well educated, with a definitely northern intonation. She corrected herself and gave the new exchange, formerly known as Tettenham.

"Are you Miss Phipps?"

"Yes."

"Miss Marian Phipps?"

"Yes."

In anguish Miss Phipps ran rapidly over in her mind all her friends and relations and their present whereabouts. There was her niece with her family, there was Inspector Tarrant with his family. Which of them had had an accident? Which were near enough to London to warrant the police calling her rather than a relative? Which? Why? Where?

"Have you a brother called Randall Harvey?" continued the voice.

"No!" said Miss Phipps explosively, remembering her well-loved brother who had perished in the Normandy landing.

"No?" said the voice incredulously. "Are you sure?"

"Absolutely sure."

"Or a half brother?"

"No!"

"Perhaps your housekeeper has a brother of that name?"

"I have no housekeeper."

"Oh. Well." There was a pause in which the voice could be heard calling briskly, "Mr. Harvey! Mr. Harvey!" Then there was a

278

pause in which nothing could be heard. Finally the voice resumed. "There's been some mistake," it said on a note of disappointment. "Good night. Sorry to have troubled you."

"Well, good night," said Miss Phipps, taken aback.

She replaced the telephone with an angry clash, and rolling over, buried her head in the pillow and tried to fall asleep again.

But she could not. It was not so much a matter of sleep interrupted as of wounded pride. Miss Phipps was a novelist and a writer of detective stories. She often began a story by imagining some mysterious situation, then thinking up circumstances which would explain it. But try as she would, she could not explain that telephone call.

It was a local call, since the girl had not begun with the 01 which nowadays precluded all London calls from a distance. The girl was northern, probably Yorkshire, so that she may have been somebody connected with Miss Phipps's niece, who lived in that county. But she seemed to think some Mr. Harvey had known Miss Phipps and claimed to be her brother.

Miss Phipps, as a woman living alone with her name in the telephone directory, was not unfamiliar with calls from young men who wanted to "Come round and have a good time," promising to be her friend if she would let them. All such callers she terrified out of their wits assuming a booming schoolmistressy Oxford-English voice, addressing them as "young man," reminding them of their mothers, and threatening to inform the police. But young men of that sort, in that kind of situation, did not employ a young girl to do their telephoning for them. Moreover—and this puzzled Miss Phipps—the girl had sounded genuinely disappointed. She seemed really sorry that Miss Phipps had no brother named Randall. Or was she sorry for some other reason?

A mistaken identity, that's all it was, Miss Phipps told herself. Randall Harvey wanted another Miss Marian Phipps, of course. He was a visitor from Yorkshire who had a friend in London who had a sister named Marian Phipps who lived in Tettenham. Miss Phipps sat up crossly, put on the light, and took up the telephone directory. There was no other Marian Phipps in the Tettenham section. In fact, there were no other Phippses there at all.

Miss Phipps gave a loud angry snort. From under the pillow she drew the notebook and pencil she put there every night. She found her reading glasses and put them on. Sighing, she took up her pencil and wrote down carefully the exact time of the call and every word of the conversation.

At ten o'clock the next morning, as Miss Phipps was sitting at her desk struggling with a plot which declined to grow, a ring sounded at the door of her flat. Exclaiming irritably at the interruption, she bounced to the door and flung it open.

A young man stood there. He was in his twenties, Miss Phipps judged, personable, even handsome, dark, with hair and sideburns longish, but not too long to be acceptable to Miss Phipps's old-fashioned taste. His eyes were brown and sparkling, his suit, shirt, tie, and shoes almost up to advertisement standards. Miss Phipps looked at him with interest but coldly, suspecting a salesman.

"Good morning," he said.

Miss Phipps remained markedly silent.

"I came to apologize for that stupid telephone call last night," he went on.

Miss Phipps, unable to resist an expression of genuine human feeling, thawed.

"What was it all *about*?" she asked.

"Well—" began the young man.

His pause and perplexed eyebrows skillfully suggested that the tale was too long to be told from a threshold.

"Well, come in," said Miss Phipps, still rather cross. "Sit down and tell me all. But I warn you," she added grimly, "the story had better be good."

The young man, seating himself, cleared his throat.

He's going to lie to me, reflected the experienced Miss Phipps.

"We wanted to find out if you were in. So my sister—"

"Now listen to me," said Miss Phipps kindly. "The young lady was probably not your sister, and there was no need to invent Mr. Randall Harvey in order to find out whether or not I was in."

"Well, my wife then."

"That's better. Is she really your wife, eh?"

"Yes!" shouted the young man. "What do you take me for?"

"Keep your cool," advised Miss Phipps. "Why did you invent Mr. Randall Harvey?"

"I didn't invent him," said the young man. "We landed in France together on D-Day."

"Now, come, young man!" Miss Phipps said with some anger. "You're far too young for that. On D-Day you would be how old? Let's say, three?"

"My father and Mr. Harvey—" began the young man.

"Your father! Well, at least your chronology is improving."

"As a matter of fact—"

"That phrase usually precedes a lie, my dear boy."

"You're too clever for me, and *that's* a fact," admitted the young man, starting to rise.

"Why not tell me the truth?" suggested Miss Phipps mildly. "I am quite curious to know why you invented a Mr. Randall Harvey."

"I didn't invent him. He's all too real. He cheated me out of a sum of money, then said his sister would pay."

"But my name is not Harvey."

"He said you were a best-selling novelist who wrote under a pseudonym."

"Ha!"

"I saw paperbacks by you on the station bookstall."

"And so?"

"He had a northern accent and I saw a picture of a mill chimney on one of your book jackets, so it seemed a good guess you were from the north."

"Better and better."

"I have heard," faltered the young man, suddenly turning scarlet, "that you could write a check for ten thousand pounds and never feel it."

"Oh, my dear boy," said Miss Phipps sadly. "Very few people can write a check for ten thousand pounds and not feel it. Those who can are usually not aging novelists. How were you proposing to make me write this check?"

"Oh, I didn't have any such grand aspirations. I just hoped—for a little help."

"Now at last you're talking some sense."

"You sounded kind on the telephone," said the lad hopefully.

"How much do you want, and why?"

"My wife and I are actors in a touring group," began the young man. "And you see—"

"Don't tell me the manager went bankrupt and there was no salary for you?"

"Why shouldn't I tell you that?" said the young man on a note of pique.

"Because it's not *with it*, my dear boy—it's out of date. That sort of thing doesn't happen nowadays. You have a trade union, Equity, you know; you can appeal to them for help."

"Unfortunately it isn't an Equity matter. This fellow Harvey is—was—a friend of mine. He's been stealing money from people's coat pockets; somebody suspected and threatened to bring a court action if he didn't pay it all back. Of course, if he once got hauled up by the police his career would be done for—and he's quite a good actor, you know. That's the pity of it. Yes, really a very promising actor. So I lent him the money on his assurance he'd pay me back, but he didn't, and now we haven't the money to pay our hotel bill."

"Where is this hotel?"

"In Yorkshire."

"What are you doing in London, then?"

"We came last night after the show." (After the show, mused Miss Phipps, reflecting sadly on the distance from Yorkshire, the probable curtain time of the show, and the hour of the telephone call.) "To see if we could touch my wife's father. He's not a bad old boy, and the sum isn't very large. But he's away—"

"On holiday?"

"In New York on business."

"Do you know," said Miss Phipps with some solemnity, "I'm rather surprised that when you found out I was alone—for that was really the object of the Harvey ploy, wasn't it?"

"Well, y-yes."

"I thought so. I'm rather surprised," repeated Miss Phipps, "that you didn't try a spot of burglary."

"Oh, I wanted to," confessed the young man with a paradoxical air of virtue, "but Celeste was afraid you might get hurt. She's having a baby, you know."

"I'm glad Celeste has so much sense. And so you thought you'd come round this morning and try a sob story on a silly old spinster-novelist living alone."

"I don't understand you, Miss Phipps," said the young man haughtily, springing to his feet.

"By the way, what is your name?"

"Mark."

"Mark what?"

"You can't expect me to tell you that," said the young man.

"No. I don't expect so. Ah, there you are, Harrison," said Miss Phipps cheerfully, as the door opened and a large solid man in a doorman's uniform filled the gap. She now remembered with gratitude Inspector Tarrant's insistence on the installation of an emergency summoning bell from her flat to the front entrance.

"You rang, Madam."

"Yes. Just see Mr. Mark out, will you? *Off* the premises, please."

"Is he annoying you? Shall I ring for the police, Miss Phipps?"

"No. I don't wish to prefer charges," said Miss Phipps.

With some care Mark suppressed a sigh of relief.

"You, Mark, are a confidence trickster," Miss Phipps told him. "I don't recall what the modern phrase is—con man, is it?—but I'm sure you understand what I mean. I don't believe a single word of anything you've told me. Would a five-pound note be any use to you?"

"No!" Mark burst out in a fury.

"I thought not. Your suit is too expensive. To conclude, if there is a choice for me between tricking and being tricked, I prefer to be tricked. I prefer being the lamb to the tiger."

"You can keep it. It's a silly choice."

"Not in the long run, young man. Next time things won't go so well for you. I seriously suggest that you turn to honest work."

"What sort of honest work is open to me, do you think?" cried Mark with bitter resentment.

"Why not try writing for the magazines?" suggested Miss Phipps, handing him a copy of *Ellery Queen's Mystery Magazine*. "You have a genuine gift for story-telling. But my dear Mark, you must get your details right. Verisimilitude matters, you know—"

"Thanks for the advice," said the young man sarcastically.

"And I also suggest that you get married."

Mark snorted and withdrew, clutching, Miss Phipps noted with satisfaction, the magazine.

A CHECKLIST OF THE MISS PHIPPS STORIES

Plese note that stories that appear in this volume are marked with an asterisk. The second through the sixth stories originally appeared in a British magazine which has not yet been identified.

*"Author in Search of a Character." *Woman's Home Companion*, July 1937, as "The Missing Character"; reprinted *Ellery Queen's Mystery Magazine* [hereafter, EQMM], December 1952.

"The Tuesday and Friday Thefts." First publication unknown; reprinted EQMM, July 1954.

*"The Crooked Figures." First publication unknown; reprinted EQMM, October 1954.

*"The Spirit of the Place." First publication unknown; reprinted EQMM, December 1954.

*"The Significant Letter." First publication unknown; reprinted EQMM, February 1955.

*"The Incongruous Action." First publication unknown; reprinted EQMM, August 1955.

*"Chain of Witnesses." EQMM, May 1954.

*"Telegram for Miss Phipps." EQMM, June 1956.

*"Miss Phipps Goes to School." EQMM, November 1957.

*"A Midsummer Night's Crime." EQMM, January 1961.

*"Miss Phipps Improvises." EQMM, October 1961.

*"Message in a Bottle." EQMM, May 1962.

*"Miss Phipps Discovers America." EQMM, May 1963.

"Miss Phipps Jousts with the Press." EQMM, December 1963.

"Miss Phipps in the Hospital." EQMM, July 1964.

"Miss Phipps Considers the Cat." The Saint, April 1965.

"Miss Phipps and the Invisible Murderer." EQMM, November 1966.

*"Miss Phipps Goes to the Hairdresser." EQMM, December 1967.

*"Miss Phipps and the Nest of Illusion." EQMM, August 1969.
*"Miss Phipps Exercises Her Metier." EQMM, February 1971.
"Miss Phipps Is Too Modest." EQMM, December 1971.
*"Miss Phipps on the Telephone." EQMM, July 1973.
"Miss Phipps and the Siamese Cat." EQMM, November 1973.
"Miss Phipps Meets a Dog." EQMM, October 1974.

Chain of Witnesses

Chain of Witnesses and Other Cases for Miss Phipps by Phyllis Bentley, edited by Marvin Lachman, is set in Palatino and printed on 60 pound Natural acid-free paper. The book was typeset by White Lotus Infotech. The cover is by Gail Cross. *Chain of Witnsseses* was published in January 2015 by Crippen & Landru Publishers, Norfolk, Virginia.

CRIPPEN & LANDRU, PUBLISHERS
P. O. Box 9315
Norfolk, VA 23505
Web: www.crippenlandru.com
E-mail: info@crippenlandru.com

Since 1994, Crippen & Landru has published more than 100 first editions of short-story collections by important detective and mystery writers.

☞This is the best edited, most attractively packaged line of mystery books introduced in this decade. The books are equally valuable to collectors and readers. [*Mystery Scene Magazine*]

☞The specialty publisher with the most star-studded list is Crippen & Landru, which has produced short story collections by some of the biggest names in contemporary crime fiction. [*Ellery Queen's Mystery Magazine*]

☞God Bless Crippen & Landru. [*The Strand Magazine*]

☞A monument in the making is appearing year by year from Crippen & Landru, a small press devoted exclusively to publishing the criminous short story. [*Alfred Hitchcock's Mystery Magazine*]

See our website for a complete list of all our titles!